Dark Magic Series Book I

The Butcher and the Bard

J. E. Harter

This is a work of fiction. All of the characters, organizations, and events portrayed in this novel are either products of the author's imagination or are used fictitiously. Any resemblance to actual events, locales, or persons, living or dead, is coincidental.

Copyright © 2023 by J. E. Harter

All rights reserved.

No portion of this book may be reproduced in any form or by any electronic or mechanical means, including information storage and retrieval systems, without written permission from the author, except for the use of brief quotations in a book review, as permitted by U.S. copyright law.

Cover Artwork: Miblart

Editing: Erin Young

Map Design: Alec McK

Paperback ISBN: 979-8-9886106-0-1

Hardcover ISBN: 979-8-9886106-1-8

AUTHOR'S NOTE

The book contains subject matter that might be difficult for some readers, including extreme fantasy violence, blood, gore, language, sexual content, panic attacks, flashbacks of rape (consent withdrawn), and references to sexual abuse.

CHAPTER 1

Marai

Like a black smudge in a sea of white, a dark cloaked figure chased a man through a winter wood.

The cold wind roared as the man hurtled through the dense pine trees, his assailant right at his heels. Snow streaked through his thinning hair, mixing with the clouds of steam huffing through his chapped lips. He was losing speed. The stranger moved swiftly; a looming wraith, closing in.

In the hazy dusk light, wearing only his cloak and simple dressing gown, the middle-aged man tripped over a root. He tumbled into the thick layer of snow. Upon lifting his head, he came face to face with the sharp tip of a sword.

"Please," he begged, hands shaking as he clasped them together in prayer. The bellow of the wind was the only sound besides his whimpering. Sweat froze on his temples and upper lip as he gazed at the ominous figure looming over him.

The assailant's entire face was hidden by a black scarf, and the hood of their cloak was pulled down so far the man couldn't see their eyes. In one tattered-gloved hand, they held a lightweight broad sword to the man's neck.

"It wasn't me. Tell Isif I didn't do it."

The stranger said nothing. They were used to pleas—marks always begged for their lives before the end. A pitiable sound.

The stranger pulled back their sword and took aim.

"No, no! I'll pay him back."

The blade whistled as it sliced through the air.

"*Lirr save me,*" the man cried.

Sharp metal cleaved the man's head from his neck, and his body keeled over. His head thudded into the snow; the trail of red stark against the pure white.

The mercenary slowly wiped their sword on the man's cloak.

Their work now complete, a calm emptiness took over them. A numbness that came after every death and never truly left.

The stranger pushed back the hood of their threadbare cloak.

The young woman took a deep breath of the winter air, cleansing away the darkness from within. Needles of ice pierced her lungs, filling up that emptiness. At least she could still feel *something*.

Another day, another kill: a thought that didn't bring her joy or satisfaction. She sheathed her sword and stared down at the body. Another nameless mark. Another addition to a tally so long it could have encircled the continent.

The next storm was rolling in, loud and dark like a stampede of wild horses.

Marai… Marai. The rough, wicked wind seemed to whisper her name; a word that hadn't been uttered in years. Since her work was done in the shadows, all those involved were as nameless and shifty as she was.

She bent and searched the man's cloak. He had little on him, save a few coins. Marai pocketed the money—the man wouldn't need coin in the Underworld. Every cent she earned during the winter kept her one tiny step further from starvation.

The town of Gainesbury was nearby, but Marai hesitated. Gainesbury was not a stop she had intended to make. The town was surrounded by dense forests of pine and spruce, and sat on one of the highest peaks of the White Ridge Mountains. They were called "White" due to the snow, but the peaks were obsidian rock. The ridge was difficult to travel—steep inclines, rocky terrain, and paths that crossed the peaks with nothing beside them but a precipitous drop to nothing below. Behind Gainesbury, a few leagues away, were the Cliffs of Unmyn, which dropped down into a rough, frigid sea.

However, Marai had no choice. There was no other shelter nearby, and her stomach rumbled ferociously. She sighed through her nose. Despite her recent earnings, she had little money to spend, and the few coins in her pocket jingled forlornly. Marai tried to remain anonymous, performing low-paying work to avoid detection. It was the only way she would survive in a world that hated her kind.

Resigning herself to spending coin, Marai drew up her hood and scarf, and walked to the town of Gainesbury. Nearly frozen to the bone, she passed through its weathered wooden gate.

Gainesbury was devoid of life. Not a soul could be seen. It wasn't abandoned, though; smoke puffed steadily out of every chimney within the petite thatched houses. Firelight danced in the windows, proof that life existed here, somehow. The townsfolk knew that one didn't venture out into a blizzard.

She pressed onwards to the center of town, leather boots crunching in the already solid snow. She arrived in the main square, which was merely a large stone pillar engraved with the town's name. Marai pulled the tattered black cloak tightly around herself as the swirling wind and snow intensified. She then spotted her destination: the solitary, dilapidated tavern.

A gust of wind swept through as Marai pushed open the doors, causing those inside the small dining room to turn and glare. An uneasy hush fell over the room. Seven burly men sat at tables, clothed in thick skins and fur, faces drawn and lined with fatigue.

That's why I dislike these mountains. Constant winter and limited daylight took all the joy from people.

Her gaze stalled on a younger man seated alone in a corner, watching Marai with keen interest, his goblet frozen at his lips. He didn't look like a typical Northerner. The people of Grelta were fair and tall, muscular, built for hard labor and surviving treacherous winters. His coloring was tanner, body leaner. Astye was a diverse continent; the man came from some country further South.

Marai hated all those eyes and hastily closed the heavy wooden door, taking a seat at a table in the darkest corner. Noise resumed amongst the townsfolk and Marai's stiff spine relaxed. The bearded barkeeper gave her a wary look, but approached anyway. In small towns such as Gainesbury, people could not turn down a paying customer. It was especially rare for someone to pass through during the winter, when everything was scarce, including hope.

"Can I . . . get you anything?" he asked.

"Water and whatever warm meal you have," came her quiet, gruff voice from underneath all the layers. Marai's clothing, posture, and attitude alerted those in the tavern that this wasn't someone to approach.

The barman quickly dropped a wooden cup of water in front of her and retreated to the kitchens. Marai pulled down the scarf covering the lower half of her pale face, enough to take a sip. She kept her hood drawn, sensing the men's eyes boring into her back. There was always a heightened chance of being discovered if she lingered someplace too long.

Snow and ice thrashed around outside. Despite the chatter indoors, Marai heard the wind howling, windows rattling, as the snow blanketed her route out. She hated the cold. She'd always craved warmth and sun in places like the Southern coast.

Surprisingly, there was entertainment at the tavern that evening. Marai didn't turn to look when the musician took to the stage, but she heard the man introduce himself.

"Good evening," he said enthusiastically and received no response from his audience. His voice was young, light. He cleared his throat, a nervous sound. "My name is Ard the Bard. I'm thrilled to play for you today."

Ard the Bard?

Marai nearly choked on her water. Clearly, the villagers also thought his name was rather pathetic because they made no sound. The barkeep's frown deepened as he poured a few drinks.

"Right . . . then I'll get to it. I'm sure you all know this one," Ard the Bard said with a tremor to his voice. He strummed a few notes on his lute, and began to sing "The Girl of Veilheim." This was indeed a popular song and most folk around the Continent of Astye knew it. It spoke of the love the songwriter had for a beautiful young woman, who was coincidentally betrothed to five men at once. However, the song was old, having been written at least four decades prior. The original composer had been deceased for some time.

Ard possessed decent skill with the lute and his voice was quite melodic, but every song he played was written by another, more talented bard. A cover of someone else's success. All of his songs were in every musician's repertoire. There was nothing special about him. The villagers didn't exactly boo and hiss, but they hardly clapped at the end of each song. There was a smattering of applause after his earlier pieces, but halfway through, the villagers stopped entirely and began talking over him. She could hear the bard's confidence draining, wavering the further along into his performance he went.

Stew and rustic grain bread were deposited in front of Marai by a frumpy woman, most likely the barman's wife. She gave the mercenary a quick glance of disdain. Marai wasn't offended, nor was she picky; the thick, bone-broth stew was warm and had both venison and root vegetables. By most tavern standards, the food was more than satisfactory. She had wandered across much of Astye and had experienced her fair share of horrible food. Marai couldn't remember the last time she'd had a warm, hearty meal.

She ate slowly, savoring the warmth, blowing on the hot stew, but never once dropping her guard.

They don't know what you are. They aren't a threat. But Marai had never been comfortable amongst others. The weight of the sword and dagger at her hip eased some of those nerves.

She kept her ears open while she ate. This type of small town didn't get much in terms of interesting happenings, and what they knew of the outside world was little more than rumor, but occasionally a bit of important news snuck in.

"Did you hear—the King of Tacorn married again," one of the burly men said to his table of companions. They all had pints of ale in front of them, which they drank from steadily.

"What is that, his third wife?"

"Fourth."

The three men shook their heads. "Runs through 'em quick, doesn't he? Didn't his other wives all die?"

Marai had heard of the match between the Princess of Varana and King Rayghast of Tacorn. There were nine powerful kingdoms on the Continent of Astye. Grelta in the North was the most expansive. Tacorn was in the middle, the Empire of Varana in the East. The union between Rayghast and the princess had bolstered Tacorn's already plentiful coffers and armies.

"I heard Tacorn soldiers have been spotted on the border."

"*Our* border? Why?"

"Roughed up a few young fellows near the capital. Apparently they're looking for something. Or someone."

Looking for something? This was certainly new information to Marai. She'd noticed an increase of Tacornian soldiers in towns and cities further east when she'd passed through Varana a few months prior. Tacorn soldiers, like their king, were known for their brutality.

Ard the Bard continued his musical set. No one was paying any attention to him anymore. At another table, Marai's ears perked up at a different conversation.

"No, she truly bedded a vampire."

A skeptical laugh. "You jest! That's a fiction."

"I assure you, that's what Belme told me, and her cousin lives in Lirrstrass. It's apparently all the gossip there."

Someone slammed down their cup on the table. "You're telling me, *our* Queen Nieve of Grelta consciously let a vampire into her bed? Was she coerced? Threatened?"

"Don't know, but its name was Nosfis or Nosfilious."

"Abominations, the whole lot of them," a man said. "I wouldn't let one of them near my bed, if it were me."

"At least it wasn't a faerie. Damn magical creatures . . . I'm glad they're all dead."

Marai stiffened.

"How is Queen Nieve alive? I thought vampires kill their victims?"

"Our noble King must not be very satisfying then, eh?" More laughter from the table.

Marai finished her meal, her stomach full for the first time in days, and pulled up her scarf. The barman removed the empty bowl and cup from her place swiftly, eager for her to be on her way. Marai left two precious coins on the table.

One glance out the window to the howling, frosty gale, and Marai's hopes of leaving sunk. Thick white snow had completely covered the glass, and it was impossible to see the village through the blizzard.

I shouldn't stay. She didn't want to risk discovery, but she'd die of hypothermia or frostbite if she tried to sleep in the forest, as she preferred. In this powerful storm, when visibility was limited, she might even step off the edge of a cliff.

Marai let out a resigned huff and turned to get a glimpse of Ard the Lousy Bard.

It was the young man from the corner table. He was probably not much older than twenty and two. Tall, in a lean body, with wavy chestnut hair that fell into his eyes. His tunic, trousers, and vest were a little shabby and plain, and had none of the flair one might expect from a bard. Marai could see his displeasure at the lack of enthusiasm for his performance. His eyes scanned the crowd, mouth struggling to make a smile.

Lirr, take pity on him and end his misery.

Marai couldn't imagine the goddess would approve of Ard's lackluster presentation. She imagined Lirr shaking her head. Although, Lirr *had* blessed the young bard with adequate skill; he wasn't reaching his true potential.

The bard finished his set of songs. No one clapped, and he came to a nearby table, disheartened. He placed his lute on an empty chair next to him, a seat away from Marai. A little too close for her taste. She tensed as he sat.

"An ale, if you would?" he asked the barman, who gave him a frown of annoyance. He was clearly not pleased with the bard's performance, but brought him an ale just the same. He then held out his hand. "But I'm the bard. Musicians usually get free drinks when they perform."

"Aye, you would if you sang anything we haven't heard a thousand times before," said the barkeep. Ard reluctantly handed over a coin and drank a sip from the stein. Marai caught a flash of a dark brown birthmark on his left wrist. A strange shape—at first it looked like a splash of mud, but as Marai stared, it reminded her of a sunburst, with wavering rays extending from a circular center.

"The ale isn't even that good," he said under his breath.

Marai let out a quiet snort. The sound unintentionally caught his attention.

Ard brazenly turned to her. "Did you think my performance was that bad?"

Marai didn't move. People so rarely spoke to her. At first, she wondered if she should reply, but Ard waited patiently, his face expectant.

"You played well. Your voice is good. But you are a lousy bard," she said, getting to her feet.

The bard's mouth fell open. "Lousy bard? I beg your pardon, but it takes many years and much skill to learn all those songs. What would you know of music? Who are you to judge anyone's talent? Are you some sort of mysterious master of music? You, in your cloak and hood?"

If she'd known he would unleash such a barrage of words, she would have ignored him, but it'd been a while since she'd conversed with another person, and Marai found herself responding.

"I've been to a number of taverns in my life and heard some of the best musicians in The Nine Kingdoms. You, in comparison to them, are nothing."

Ard scoffed, leaning back in his chair. "I think *you* are equally as unwelcome here as I am. Maybe more so. At least I bathe."

It was unusual for people to initiate speech with Marai, but to be confronted and *challenged* by someone in this manner was entirely new.

Ard was unperturbed by her appearance and harsh manner, so she shifted her cloak, revealing the long blade at her side. A warning. Ard's eyes snapped to her sword and widened.

Marai ventured back to the door. She'd spotted a stable on her way in, a decent place to spend the night. Marai yanked open the tavern door and stepped out into the howling blizzard. Fighting through wind and snow, she ducked inside the stable. It was quite drafty and smelled of manure and musty hay, but it was better than sleeping outdoors. And it was free. It'd been months since she'd slept in an actual bed. A horse gave a soft whinny as she curled up on a pile of hay, hand on the hilt of her sword, and closed her eyes.

Ravenous lips were on hers. His tongue pried her lips apart and claimed her mouth. Like he owned it. Like it didn't belong to her anymore.

She tried to pull away. "Captain, please—"

Marai jolted awake. The stable came into focus around her. She was used to vivid dreams haunting her night after night. Working in the shadows, shame and death followed her everywhere; ghouls moaning in her ears. Reminding her that she would never be normal . . .

When the blue light of dawn seeped through the cracks in the boards, Marai awoke and brushed the hay from her clothing. It was deceptively dark outside, with the ground entirely covered in snow and the sun hidden behind opaque grey clouds. However, the storm was gone.

Marai adjusted the sword and dagger at her belt, then stepped into the powdery snow, over a foot deep. While her boots were thick, she could feel the cold soaking through them instantly. The snow came up to her knees, and not for the first time, Marai wished she had longer legs. No one had attempted yet to shovel a path, so Marai braced herself and set out on her way.

She'd not gone thirty arduous steps before she heard someone clattering after her.

"We're both heading out of town. Why not keep each other company for a few leagues to the next one?"

Marai whipped around as Ard rushed out from the tavern, belongings slung over his shoulder. What was this lousy bard up to? She turned her back on him and kept trudging.

The deep snow made her escape from Ard far more difficult. He was taller with strong legs, granting him easier movement. She could hear his grunts as he fought his way through the snow to her. "There may be bandits on the road. We can watch each other's backs."

"I don't need your company nor your help," Marai huffed, pushing faster through the snow.

"But you're a woman alone. Does that not concern you?"

"Not as much as your presence does," snapped Marai.

Ard barked out a laugh, as if she amused him. By the time she reached the main road, he was directly behind her. Marai turned left, and gallingly, the bard followed.

"Just as far as the next town. What do you say?"

Marai stopped and turned so quickly that the bard stumbled backwards to avoid bumping into her. Her hand went to her dagger. "*Why?*"

"Because I'm curious about you," said Ard, eyebrow arched. "A woman traveling alone? With a sword? Disguised? Makes me wonder what you're running from."

"I run from nothing."

Lies, a little voice in her head taunted. She wanted to rip the voice to shreds.

Ard squirmed about, ducking, trying to get a glimpse under her hood and scarf.

"It certainly looks that way from an outsider's perspective." He was loud, and outlandishly bright, and annoying. His lips tilted up into a cocky smile, and brown eyes danced mischievously.

Marai had no more patience for him. She unsheathed her dagger and put it to his unshaven throat in the span of a breath.

"You will not follow me," she snarled. "If you do, I'll slit your throat without hesitation." Up close, she noticed his eyes had flecks of gold in them, and he sported a strong, angled jaw and chin. Useless things perhaps to notice, but Marai had been trained to be observant of such small details. It made her a better mercenary. A more adept killer.

For a moment, Ard's eyes widened, but then narrowed as his mouth fell into a knowing smirk. "I know who you are."

Marai was glad her face was covered, because now it was *her* turn to be surprised. She quickly sheathed the dagger and turned back to the road. Ard followed once again, undaunted by her threat.

"You're the Lady Butcher."

Marai bristled at the name.

"Hah! I knew it. How extraordinary that I should run into *you* here in this crummy little town."

He stepped in front of her path. Contrary to everyone else she'd ever met, Ard appeared positively elated to be in her presence.

"If I'm the Lady Butcher then why are you following me?" Marai asked. "Isn't she a murderer? A criminal?"

"Yes, but only if paid to do so," Ard said with his playful smile. "I don't think you kill for pleasure."

Flustered, Marai shifted on her feet. "You know nothing about me."

The name Lady Butcher was feared by those who worked in the shadows. Which posed the question . . . how did this lousy bard know of her existence?

Marai didn't trust him and his effortless smile. Ard had no visible weapon; he'd be easy to incapacitate should he try anything. Her hand went to her sword this time.

"What do you want? To fight me? Capture me?" It wouldn't be the first time.

"No, no, no, I'm not stupid enough to try that," Ard said with a laugh, but his gold-flecked eyes drifted to her sword. Marai noticed a flicker of unease in his face. "I want to hire you."

Marai stopped. "Don't be ridiculous."

"I'm deadly serious." And he was. His face had lost its brightness. There was something akin to worry there now in his furrowed brow.

"You, a penniless, lousy bard, want to *hire* me?"

"Yes, I believe you are exactly the person to help me," he said. "I must get across the Red Lands safely and to the Southern ports. I intend to catch a ship in Cleaving Tides off this continent. My passage has already been arranged in advance. The ship sets sail in sixty days."

The Red Lands. Marai's face twisted cynically as she thought of the areas surrounding the neighboring, warring kingdoms of Tacorn and Nevandia. The Middle Kingdoms was its more formal name.

"You can get yourself across the Red Lands. You need no one's help to do so," Marai said sharply.

"Then you haven't heard what *I've* heard recently. The war is escalating. Anyone passing through the Middle Kingdoms could at any moment be caught up in a skirmish or full-blown attack," Ard continued, words tumbling from his mouth. "Tacorn soldiers accost travelers on the road, pillaging, injuring, or capturing anyone they claim is from the other side. It's not a safe place."

"Go around it," Marai said. She had no interest in stepping foot in the Red Lands. Tacorn and Nevandia's valleys and forests were stained with blood, hence the nickname. It was far too dangerous to get caught up in that nightmarish war, especially for someone like her.

Not only that, she was avoiding the Southern port city of Cleaving Tides. She'd made a powerful enemy there four years prior, and hadn't been back since.

This wasn't how normal commissions worked. Ard talked far too much and was too casual with her. Was he a threat? Her fingers hadn't left the handle of her sword. The only real way to get rid of him was to kill him, but he wasn't a mark, and she had sworn never to harm innocents, no matter how annoying they were.

"My answer is no." She started out again.

"*Please,*" Ard called. The desperation in his tone made her turn back around. Ard's gaze flit nervously to the woods around them. "I am . . . being hunted . . . by some disagreeable people. I'd pay you well to ensure safe crossing."

Curious, but not worth the trouble.

"I'm not a guard or a knight. I'm hired to warn, wound, or kill. That's all."

"Well, if someone attacks me, you can do one or all three of those things." Ard stared at her in anticipation. "I just need to make it to Cleaving Tides, and then I will be free to sail to Andara."

"Andara?" Marai spat out the word with a laugh. "No one sails to Andara. There's nothing there."

"Not true. I met a sea captain who's been there. He wasn't allowed past the port, but he swore there was a thriving town and civilization. People who've traveled there haven't ever returned, which either means they're very happy in their new life, or they died along the journey." He said this with a shrug. "Some people even think that's where all the fae fled to during the massacres. That it's a land of acceptance. For me, though, Andara is freedom."

Marai's body grew colder, and it had nothing to do with the freezing temperatures.

Could what Ard said be possible? Were there really faeries on Andara? Had they been welcomed by the mysterious Andaran people? A seed of cynical hope blossomed in her chest.

Marai's mouth twisted with confliction. This wasn't the commission she wanted to take. Not only was crossing through the Red Lands a foolish decision, she had no desire to travel *with* the bard. The journey to the Southern coast would take two months, and Marai didn't think she had the fortitude to withstand his irksome presence for a minute more, never mind several weeks.

She was used to sketchy details and working with seedy folk, but this bard was unlike her usual employers. She didn't *travel* with them. She didn't spend time in their company for more than a few moments. There was definitely something suspicious about the bard, something he was hiding. It was written all over his concerned face. To flee all the way to Andara...

He reached into his pack and pulled out a sack of clinking coins. "All of this now for getting me to the ship, and more when we arrive. I'll even book you passage on the ship to Andara if you're up for an adventure."

Marai studied the large tan sack. It *was* enticing—with that amount of money she could eat for weeks. And Andara... a place so far away no one could ever find her, where she may not have to hide anymore. Who was this bard running from? Where did he get all that money?

"Who's after you?" she asked.

His earlier swagger returned. He wagged his finger, smirking. Evasive. "Do you accept?"

Marai hesitated. She had no idea when her next job would come. How much longer could she stay hidden? Eventually, someone would discover her. Perhaps it was time to try somewhere new.

Maybe there is *a better life out there...*

Groaning internally, she reached out her gloved hand.

At first, Ard stared at it, looking unsure of what to do. He eventually dropped the sack of change into her open palm. Marai pulled at the cinched opening of the bag to check its contents, plucked out several gold coins, and examined them. *Real.* She tucked the bag into her own pack and turned up the road.

"I cannot believe I found *the* Lady Butcher." He chuckled loudly. "Lirr is smiling down upon me."

Marai froze and turned back to him.

"I have rules about how this will work. One, speak quieter. You draw too much attention and you are annoying me. Two, I am in charge. Yes, you paid me, but if you want to get to Andara alive, you'll do as I say. Three, I'm not your friend. I'm not a confidant. You will ask me nothing, and I will ask you nothing. Is this understood?"

Ard nodded slowly, eyes wide.

"And four, you'll tell me another name, whether real or made up, because Ard the Bard is idiotic and clumsily fabricated," Marai continued haughtily with a dismissive wave.

Ard crossed his arms, grinning again. Two matching dimples appeared on his cheeks, and Marai grimaced at the sight. "You just said you'd ask me nothing."

"I'll not spend the next several weeks traveling with someone whose name rhymes with his profession," she said, unnerved by the sincerity of his smile. "And it's not a request."

Ard actually laughed at that; a joyous, light sound that seemed strange to hear in a desolate, dim place like Gainesbury. Marai swore she saw the sun peek through the clouds a bit, as if his laughter made it want to shine.

"Fine. My name is Ruenen. But I'd appreciate it if you kept that between us, please," he said, smile fading. A tightness appeared in his jaw. He hadn't wanted to give away that secret. Now Marai had something on him, something she could wield to her advantage if necessary.

Ruenen. That was a Middle Kingdom type of name, in the Red Lands, the place he seemed so eager to avoid. He hadn't taken a pause to think. Marai guessed it truthfully was his name.

As for not addressing him as such, Marai had no qualms with that. She didn't want to be on a first-name basis anyways. The less they knew about each other, the safer they both would be. Marai trusted no one, *especially* charming young men.

"To Andara, then," she said.

CHAPTER 2
Ruenen

Ruenen was honestly surprised the Lady Butcher hadn't taken that sword and gutted him. He knew he tread a fine line with the mercenary. Her fingers hadn't left the hilt of her sword, a constant reminder of whose presence he was in. He'd impressed himself with his own plucky words, shocked at the lengths he realized he'd go in order to get away from this gods-forsaken land. To finally feel safe. To start over somewhere new.

Now he was in the company of a notorious killer. He'd been desperate enough to try the journey through the Red Lands on his own, then his luck turned when he saw the Butcher at the tavern. He'd been traveling through Grelta for several months, trying to avoid the Middle Kingdoms at all costs.

Ruenen had watched the cloaked stranger stalk in as a hush fell over the room. Even the fire in its hearth seemed to shrink back, its flames retreating from the darkness she brought with her. He kept his eyes locked on this traveler, watched how she never revealed her face, avoided conversation. He guessed what she was then. Their verbal exchange that night had affirmed it. When the Butcher went outside to the stables, Ruenen decided to hire her.

She was perhaps his only chance at survival. It was still a risky trip, despite having her in his employment. If they were successful, he'd be on a boat far away in a few weeks' time. If they didn't make it . . . Ruenen shuddered at the thought.

For the past several hours, he'd been following a short distance behind, watching her threadbare black cape billow in the winter wind. She was darkness incarnate, so out of place in the crystal white forest they'd been traversing.

Ruenen had imagined someone with the name Lady Butcher to be much larger and intimidating. Her cloak was tattered and dirty, boots worn. In fact, she seemed almost . . . insignificant. Perhaps that was what made her so successful—she was unsuspecting. No one would ever guess to look at her that *she* was the Lady Butcher. From the stories he'd heard, he expected to hear a more seasoned voice from beneath that scarf. Her voice, while gruff, was youthful. Sarcastic.

They walked in silence along the pure white road. The only sounds were the stiff crunch of the calf-deep snow beneath their feet and melodious chirping of birds. There was beauty in this forest; tree limbs covered in white, like frosted cream on a cake. Hoarfrost glittered in the sunlight like millions of tiny jewels. They came across no one else. Animals began to peek their heads out of their dens, sniffing the frigid air, wondering where to get their next morsel of food. The fresh pine smelled clean and clear. Ruenen could appreciate the simplicity of the world around him. Its stillness. Its peacefulness.

But he'd never been one for peace and quiet . . .

"Will we be stopping at the next inn overnight?" he finally decided to ask. The Butcher didn't respond.

A few more steps. "It's rather cold out."

"Do you have unlimited funds?" came her dry response.

"No. I gave you all the money I have."

"Then we'll sleep outside."

"We could find a barn, or beg for shelter at a stranger's door," Ruenen mused.

"We're a few days from the next town."

"We'll freeze to death out here if we sleep."

"That's why we should keep moving as long as possible."

There seemed to be no persuading her. Although, sharing any indoor sleeping space with the Lady Butcher was less than ideal to Ruenen. If she was frosty to him now, he didn't want to think about what she might be like in privacy, in a confined, intimate setting. The mere thought of it made him grimace.

Which got Ruenen thinking . . . what *did* she look like underneath her disguise? Was the reason she wore the scarf and hood at all times because she was afraid of people recognizing her? To preserve her autonomy? Ruenen had heard tales that she had a hideous deformity, a scar or burn across her face, a missing eye, or something gruesome. Maybe she was simply far too frightening to look upon and that was why she became a fighter-for-hire in the first place.

Ruenen was tempted to ask her, but those rules rang out in his head: *do not ask questions.* In fact, the lack of conversation made him all the more tempted to ask her a great many things. To do something more than drudgingly walk. Someone once told him he was a boy with a thousand questions. Silence was a catalyst for a talkative mind. Ruenen much preferred the din of a full tavern or busy city street to the desolate stillness of a winter wood in the mountains. His tongue itched. His lips twitched. He swallowed, gulping down the questions he wanted to ask.

After numerous more soundless hours, the Lady Butcher turned into the frozen forest. Several paces in, she chose a clearing in the woods where the massive evergreen trees were thick, but the snow on the ground was thinnest. The needle-laden canopy above had shielded this spot from significant snowfall. The Butcher took off her pack. Displeased, he too shed his pack and dug inside for his blankets. They weren't going to keep him very warm. The Butcher had only two frayed blankets.

Guess I don't need to worry about the Red Lands, since we're both going to die out here overnight...

Ruenen thought enviously of the warmth he could be enjoying at an inn somewhere.

Metal skated across metal as the Butcher unsheathed her sword. She crossed to a small downed tree. With several impressive swings, she cut off its dead branches.

She'll dull her blade doing that. But he caught a glimpse of the sword in the moonlight and saw it didn't have a single chip or rolled edge. Foreign, archaic symbols were etched into the glimmering blade.

Ruenen watched her methodically clear their campsite of as much snow as possible with her feet. Ruenen figured he'd better do more than stand there stupidly, so he followed her lead. She then laid several branches in a row onto the ground, making a rectangle, and then placed her blankets on top. He mimicked her. He wasn't sure if she noticed or not. She didn't seem too interested in what he was doing.

The Butcher then arranged the remaining branches and sticks into a nice pile in the center of their camp. She knelt down, her back to Ruenen, and when she stood again, there was a roaring fire.

That was quick... he observed, wondering how in the Unholy Underworld she'd managed to light the fire in a matter of seconds. He didn't see any flint or steel in her gloved hands...

She then pulled cloth-wrapped bread and hard cheese from her pack. Ruenen did the same. She turned away from him, lowering her scarf to eat. He caught a glimpse of her pale chin.

An owl hooted nearby, a deep, pure tone. By now, the sun was fully set and the snow was far too deep for hunting. They settled for their stale bread, cheese, and more silence. After his substandard dinner, Ruenen tried to sleep. Neither of them had bothered to remove their shoes or gloves. Ruenen's wool hat and the Butcher's hood remained on. It only hit him then how exhausted he was. His feet and legs throbbed from their quick pace through heavy snow. The cold was far too biting, and it was impossible to get comfortable enough to drift off. Ruenen shifted his bed as close to the flames as possible without burning himself. It did warm him a little. He pulled his blankets over his head, but before the fabric covered his eyes, he saw that the Butcher sat immobile upon her makeshift mattress. She was more used to these unfavorable conditions than he was.

Her gloved fingers wrapped tightly around the hilt of her sword. Would she stay awake all night?

A sudden warmth spread over him, settling around Ruenen like another blanket, and his mind emptied. His appendages and nose thawed. It wasn't exactly cozy, but shifting closer to the campfire had actually helped. Perhaps he *would* survive this night . . .

Ruenen awoke to the sound of movement. He pulled the blankets off his head. The sun wasn't up yet, but the indigo light of early dawn reflected off the crisp whiteness of the snow, making it appear brighter than it was. The Lady Butcher was already awake, collecting her belongings and putting them away in her pack. Ruenen sat up, disheveled, as the cold seeped back into his body. He grabbed his pack, stuffed his blankets inside, and then reached for his lute.

But the Butcher already had it in her hands.

"Be careful with that," he said.

"This is a silly thing to travel with. It encumbers your movements and slows you down. Unnecessary."

"To me, it's necessary," Ruenen said and held out his hand. The Butcher slowly returned the lute to him. "It's the only thing I own that has any value."

He had the clothes on his back, another shirt in his bag, blankets, and the lute. He didn't know what he would do without it, without the ability to make music. Ruenen had lost many things in his life, but he'd risk almost anything to ensure the instrument never left his hands. So much music had been played on its sixteen strings, even before his own. The wooden instrument held memories, stories. His fingers often itched to strum against its courses.

They started out again before the sun was fully up. None of the snow on the road had thawed; it would be another lengthy, cold day of traveling. Ruenen wished he had money at least for a horse. His feet and legs were numb once again, and he couldn't feel his fingers. He wouldn't have been surprised if his legs had fallen off because he wouldn't have felt a thing. His nose didn't stop running and he spent most of his time sniffling.

Other than a few briefly uttered sentences, they didn't speak again. His mouth wanted to form words, but he kept silent. *No talking. No questions.* He didn't want to further tempt the limits of her patience. If the stories he heard were true, the Butcher wasn't someone he wished to cross.

He'd heard tales of her in taverns and city streets. It wasn't just people in the shadows who knew about her—whispers circulated amongst ordinary people, too.

"I hear her sword can move faster than the eye," Ruenen once overheard someone say.

"She eats the flesh from the bones of her victims, so don't you be naughty or I'll set the Lady Butcher upon you," a mother scolded to her young son.

Folk in arguments or disagreements threatened to hire her. "Give me my money, or I'll hire the Butcher. She never misses her mark."

"So much blood! Limbs and heads severed."

Ruenen didn't truly believe those sensationalized horror stories, but he did know that the Lady Butcher never lost a fight, and she didn't often let others see her work. The Butcher was a lethal ghost, a cruel phantom. She'd become a type of myth or legend. Whether everyday people truly believed she existed was inconsequential. Her name floated from town to town on the gust of the wind, like that tattered cloak. She was a master in the art of murder.

The next day, the trees cleared in the timberline. The inclined path narrowed and the terrain became more rugged. How the Butcher knew which paths to take, Ruenen didn't know. He'd only seen her with a map in her hand a few times. She must've traveled these mountains before, knew them well.

They neared the summit; the village of Gainesbury was now far below them on the mountain. From his high vantage point, Ruenen could see the vastness of the Northern realm. Black mountains hid by snow, smoke-like mist clung to the peaks. A dark, endless sea. Forests of thick evergreens. It was a beautiful, immense, and lonely territory.

Ruenen's muscles burned. His calves began to seize. He couldn't catch his breath; each inhale felt shallow and labored in the high altitude. His pack and lute felt heavier and heavier with every step. Despite the fierce cold, he was sweating, which only made him colder. The tips of his eyelashes froze.

A bonfire caught his attention.

It was a little ways up the path. Several figures danced around it, chanting.

As he approached, he saw the old, dilapidated temple. The building was small and weathered, its black stone beaten and discolored from years of harsh ice and cold. Its pillars were chipped and cracked; large chunks were missing. Out here, alone on this mountain top, the temple seemed more sacred due to its proximity to the heavens and the gods. The thick grey clouds parted to allow for rich rays of sunlight to peek through, blessing the little temple.

The dancers were priestesses, twirling and swaying, cheering and singing the ancient language of the gods. Their heads and bodies were shrouded in robes of rich orange, the color of fertility, honoring the goddess Lirr.

The priestesses continued their dance, all bundled up in heavy furs atop their robes, unaware of the people passing by. They carried small woven baskets, and tossed minute objects into the fire. The flames burst in magnificent blues, greens, and pinks. Magic, but Ruenen knew it wasn't. The glowing colors were merely minerals, the natural reaction of rocks and salts meeting fire. Magic was forbidden in all Nine Kingdoms. The creatures that used magic had been killed.

The Lady Butcher didn't stop, yet Ruenen couldn't help but halt and stare. Every nerve in his body trembled as he watched the carefree, peaceful existence of the priestesses. Temples and monasteries always had that effect on him. A reverence, not for the gods they worshiped, but for the space inside, the monks and priestesses who so diligently lived their lives with honor and simplicity.

A tremendous sorrow sluiced through him. Staring at that temple, Ruenen couldn't get his feet to move. Emotions that he tried to suppress came bubbling to the surface.

It was Gelanon, the holiest day in the entire calendar year. People everywhere across Astye would be celebrating; tossing minerals into their own bonfires, hoping the gods would see the colors from the skies and bless them. Tomorrow, Ruenen knew there'd be many weddings. Pious couples that hosted their nuptials the day after Gelanon believed that Lirr was more likely to sanctify the union.

Ruenen couldn't remember the last time he'd celebrated Gelanon. He hadn't worshiped the gods since he was a child, and had laid out no recent offerings before them. Real or not, they'd abandoned him.

He turned his back on the temple, and rejoined the Butcher.

They traveled on a decline down the mountain path. His hamstrings strained with every step. It'd been days since Gelanon, and not a glimmer of sunshine had shone since. Ruenen had to focus on his balance with his pack, and try not to fall forward and tumble downhill. This was not aided by his heavily congested head. It began as a painful sore throat, then spread to his nose, causing him to sneeze and wheeze. The cloth he used as a handkerchief was full of snot, but he had nothing else. At one point, he had a sneezing fit that scared away all the birds in the trees.

The Butcher turned around.

"What?" Ruenen asked, wiping his runny nose on the sleeve of his knee-length green jacket.

"You're very loud."

"I can't just *stop* sneezing," Ruenen growled at her. "Have I been whining or complaining? No. I've been bearing my discomfort in silence. As you requested."

"You're drawing attention to us. You never know what might be lurking in the woods." She turned back towards the path. "And I don't want to catch your illness."

With a big sniffle, Ruenen asked, "You don't like me, do you?"

She slowly faced him again. "Did you pay me to enjoy your company?"

Ruenen scoffed. "Of course not."

"It doesn't matter then whether I do or not. But I certainly don't enjoy your constant humming."

Ruenen hadn't noticed he'd been humming that loudly. The mindless walking actually gave him the head space needed to start creating music of his own. Ruenen had heeded the Butcher's advice. *Lousy bard.* The words had stung, but he had to admit . . . she had a point.

"I've been traveling with you for five days in silence, and I'm sick, and I want more than one-word answers," Ruenen said, flinging up his hands. "You're the only person I have to talk to. I want to have one moment of conversation. Is that so hard for you?"

The Lady Butcher studied him. He could sense her intense gaze on him from under that hood. Her hands dropped. Her fingers inched towards the hilt of her sword. For a moment, Ruenen thought she might use it against him. He'd never be able to stop her if she did.

"I don't understand why you care if people like you," she stated, hand resting on the hilt; a crutch she used to avoid being vulnerable.

Still focused on her sword in case he needed to jump out of its reach, Ruenen said in a calmer tone, "I'm a performer. I can't help but care."

"Other people aren't worth your time. Or mine." She removed her hand from the hilt. The Butcher turned on her heel. "As a mercenary, I can't afford the privilege of friendship."

"Well, *I* like you," Ruenen said, knowing those words would frazzle her. Indeed, she stiffened. "Or at the very least, find you interesting."

Ruenen thought he heard a snort of skepticism from the Butcher as she hastily stalked off down the path. She was a miserable companion, despite how intriguing she was. And she'd called *him* lousy! He heard a girlish sneeze from up ahead and the Butcher stopped dead in her tracks. He could almost hear her growling as she pulled out a handkerchief from her pocket. Ruenen couldn't help himself—he grinned from ear to ear.

They finally encountered a sign of life on the mountain. It was the village of Silkehaven, minutely larger than Gainesbury. The town was sprawling, open, not entirely uninviting, but that same winter bleakness of Gainesbury echoed here, as well. Two children and their mother passed by, baskets in hand. The woman spotted Ruenen and the Butcher, and quickly ushered her family inside a thatched cottage. The kids gaped at the dark cloaked stranger from the window. In her ominous attire, weapons strapped to her sides, the Butcher appeared as a child's nightmare, so out of place in the quaint town. Even stray mutts whined and darted out of the Butcher's path.

"We'll rest here for a few hours and restock," she said, unaffected by the unwelcoming reaction she'd received.

Ruenen's heart lifted joyfully. Civilization! Rest! Warmth!

They entered the local tavern and Ruenen immediately searched the room. He looked for black armor, for emblem pins of two crossed swords signifying Tacorn. Nothing. He was safe there, for the time being.

Relieved, Ruenen shed his winter clothing. He removed his hat and ran his fingers through his messy brown hair. There were more people in this tavern than in Gainesbury. The room was larger, too, with more tables and a longer bar. Despite its stone walls, it was bright and full of casual chatter, which stopped the moment the Butcher walked in the door. The warmth of the fire in the large hearth was a lover's embrace. Ruenen approached the barman, feeling reborn. Here was another chance to test his musical talents on a fresh crowd, but more importantly, get them some much needed dinner.

"Are you in need of entertainment? I'm a bard, and will play for food and drink for me and my companion here," he said, gesturing to the Butcher. She sat a seat away, hood and scarf on, death personified. At that moment, a hacking cough sputtered out of her. She didn't bother to hide her loud sniffle, puncturing the air of intimidation. The barman glanced at her, then back at Ruenen skeptically.

"We don't get many singers passing through here," he replied, drying out the inside of a goblet with a rag, "but I suppose it wouldn't hurt."

Ruenen stepped towards the stage, but someone grabbed his sleeve.

"What are you doing?" asked the Butcher. "We cannot linger here."

"I'll just do a short set," he said, wrenching free from her grasp. "Besides, we need the food."

"You're being hunted. Someone could recognize you."

"Here? Doubtful. We're still in Grelta."

"You hired me to protect you. I'm doing my job," she said, crossing her arms.

Ruenen took another step towards the stage, intent to ignore her, but then turned back. "I need to do this. I *need* to feel like I have a life other than hiding. That I have some semblance of control, that I can feed myself and survive. That's why I perform, even if it's a risk."

His desire for safety always conflicted with his passion for performing, for creating a name for himself. It was hard to be a bard on the run.

The Butcher didn't move to stop him again as he took to the stage grandly. Ruenen introduced himself again as Ard the Bard. The Lady Butcher, he noticed, turned her back on him at the bar.

"Good afternoon. I don't suppose any of you have heard the song 'The Girl of Veilheim?'"

When he finished his standard set of songs to another unenthused audience, he came to the Butcher's side and ate the meal of honeyed ham, roasted potatoes, and bread that had materialized during his show. It tasted glorious, and though it probably was no better than any other food, his empty stomach sang its praises. The Butcher, it seemed, had already eaten during the set.

"I don't understand why I'm treated as such a failure," he said to her, signaling to the room of patrons who'd ignored his entire set. "You said it yourself—I *am* skilled. And people love those songs."

"Yes, but a true bard will write their own music," the Butcher replied. He detected a hint of amusement in her tone. "You're a cheap imitation of the original. They want something new."

Cheap imitation? Ouch. She really knew how to gut a person.

"I've tried to write my own music, but it's harder than you think. I don't seem to have a head for lyrics," said Ruenen. "Every great story has been written about already: epic battles, kings and queens, love, heartbreak, and death. I have none of my own stories I wish to sing about."

His own story wasn't one he wished to share. It wasn't safe, at least, not yet. Maybe in Andara, when he could perform without worrying if he'd be recognized. When he no longer had to look over his shoulder. When the flash of a knife at someone's belt didn't send his heart into frenzied palpitations.

The Lady Butcher shrugged, uninterested. And Ruenen stared at her.

"I could write about *you*."

The Butcher froze. "No."

"Why not? You're *the* Lady Butcher. You must have hundreds of tales I could sing about," Ruenen said. It was the idea of the century. Her story in song could be magnificent, the greatest ever written. If only he could get her to agree . . .

She hissed at him to lower his voice. "I don't want my life put into song. I won't become someone's entertainment in a seedy pub."

"But think of what it could do for your business," posed Ruenen, raising his eyebrows. "The more people who know about you, the more infamous you'll become, and the more money you'll make. Couldn't hurt, could it?"

"Yes, it could," the Butcher said, her tone laced with dread. She rose fluidly to her feet. "Let's go."

Ruenen gulped down his remaining mead and grabbed his ham and bread; he'd eat the rest on the road.

That night by the campfire, Ruenen felt that unnatural warmth swaddle him again, as it had every night of their journey. It was enough to stop the shivering. The warmth was curious. Perhaps he was getting used to the climate.

His fingers thawed enough that he took out his lute and began to fiddle with a tune he had created. He had no lyrics yet. That was always the hardest part for him. But he knew what his subject would be about. Although the Butcher was adamant against a song, Ruenen knew it would be successful. Her story was unknown. It was the perfect piece for him to write.

He created a catchy tune that was epic, grand and boisterous. He hastily scratched down notes on the scrap of paper a hunk of bread had been wrapped in.

A mischievous delight spread through him. When he crossed the ocean to Andara, he'd perform the song everywhere, and the Butcher would be none the wiser. Once he was aboard the ship, there was nothing she could do to stop him.

However, there was nothing glorified about this journey, either. This was not an epic tale Ruenen might sing about.

It was walking. Endless, tiring hours of walking. In the bitter cold.

Bards often embellished their work, but even *if* he were to write about his time with the Lady Butcher . . . there was nothing to sing. No amount of adornment could cover up for tedium.

Ruenen was getting used to the monotony. To the strained silence between them. They'd been traveling together for over a week, and besides those few tense back and forth conversations, the Lady Butcher ignored him.

They happened upon another, larger town, farther down the mountain. The weather was fair that day, not quite as biting as it had been. There were more people around than he'd seen in weeks, and it made him feel less alone, watching them all go about their business.

Northerners were sturdy folk. Women participated in hard labor, which was rare across the continent. In the other eight kingdoms, it was frowned upon for women to work. Several countries forbid it entirely. This rare occurrence was probably due to the Northern Queen, Nieve. She was an unusual ruler, based on the gossip Ruenen had picked up in his travels. Despite being married to the King, it was well-known that Queen Nieve governed the realm and made the decisions. Her leadership empowered Northern women.

The Butcher made Ruenen stop at a few market stalls to resupply while she lingered in an alley, watching like a hawk. It was the first time he'd had space away from her. He looked around, searching for Tacorn soldiers in black armor. The only seemingly suspicious person was the Butcher in her alley. He breathed a sigh of relief, but his stomach gurgled, as empty as his pockets. He had no money to purchase the food he and the Butcher desperately needed.

Let's earn some.

Ruenen stepped up onto a wooden executioner's gibbet, which was blessedly empty, and pulled out his lute. He swallowed down the nerves as his eyes swept the crowd, searching once again for armor and weapons. After announcing himself, the crowded market hushed to listen. Activity stilled. He began his first song in his standard set, "The Girl of Veilheim."

His original song about the Butcher wasn't yet finished. The tune was fully complete, and he'd successfully written decent lyrics in the first verse and chorus. There was so much more he wanted to add, so much more to learn about her to put into the song. He needed more material.

Ruenen performed "The Girl of Veilheim," only this time, the crowd actually *booed* him. Someone threw food at him, which landed squarely in his face and had definitely been half eaten. He supposed he didn't look the part of a bard; he hadn't bathed in days, his hair was matted, clothes worn. It didn't matter how good he was. The audience judged him by appearance alone.

And he supposed it wasn't typical for musicians to perform on gibbets where men were hanged.

"Get off before we string *you* up," shouted a beast of a man, making those around him roar with laughter.

"Swinging from a rope is better entertainment than this!"

"Thank you for your kindness," Ruenen said through gritted teeth.

He jumped off the gibbet, storming around to its side, trying to avoid the heckling of the crowd. He wiped his sullied face off with a cloth.

Well, I suppose I did get us free food . . .

In a wave of frustration, Ruenen's hand tightened around the neck of his lute. He felt the urge to smash his precious instrument upon the gibbet's wooden posts. Music was the only thing he was good at. The only thing he truly knew, other than running away. If he couldn't be successful on this continent, he could only hope audiences elsewhere could appreciate his skill. People here were vicious.

The Lady Butcher emerged at his side. Everywhere she went seemed to darken. She sucked away the very life around her. The heckling and calling stopped. The crowd dispersed. Ruenen saw all the fearful glances from the citizens on the street as they moved away. The Butcher took a few brooding steps towards Ruenen, her cloak fanning out in the wind, before they were both surrounded by a group of five large men.

For a moment, Ruenen panicked. He no longer cared about his pitiful performance and hollow stomach. His mind went blank and feet turned to stone as he stared at the menacing faces of the men.

They'd come for him. They'd finally tracked him down. How had he entirely missed them in the crowd?

You're an idiot, Ruenen. You knew this could happen.

Fear, cold and sharp, stabbed him all over.

But the men unsheathed their swords and pointed directly at the Lady Butcher with threatening glowers. Not him. They didn't even *look* at him. He could've been invisible.

"We know who you are," one snarled at her. "Killed our friend Janko a year back."

"Saw you leaving his house the night he died. Recognized you by your cloak and scarf, I did," said another, edging his weapon closer to the Butcher. "I thought you'd been a ghost. Thought my eyes played a trick on me. But here you are . . . real."

Other villagers spotted what was happening and stepped out of the way. Whispers of fear and excitement echoed on the streets. The market began to empty. Mothers ushered their children down different streets or inside shops. White, wide-eyed faces peered out of windows.

"Time to pay for what you did," said a third hefty, bearded man, inching closer.

"We'll cut you limb from limb, like you did to Janko," declared the first.

If the Butcher was nervous, she didn't reveal it.

"We should take this out onto the road, away from civilians," she said, holding up a gloved hand to mute them.

"Bitch, we're doing this here and now," the first man continued, the angriest of the group.

The Butcher merely walked past them, unfazed. The first man swung as she passed, but she dodged, spinning around as elegantly as a dancer, making the man stagger and stumble from the missed strike. She kept on walking.

Flabbergasted, the men followed her to the road, yelling challenges, horrendous and derogatory words. Ruenen was appalled by their language, but also relieved that the men weren't there for *him*. And now a part of him was excited . . . he hadn't seen the Lady Butcher in action, and was curious to see those deadly, legendary skills.

Once back on the snow-dusted road, and safely away from the eyes and ears of the town, the Lady Butcher turned to face the gang of seedy men. She crossed her arms, a stance Ruenen was so used to seeing now, and cocked her head to the side. "Now . . . what was it you wished to discuss?"

Ruenen choked back a laugh. The Butcher was a curious woman, to be sure. Despite her moody silences and the fact that she clearly didn't care for *him*, Ruenen found himself appreciating her. She was . . . snarky. Did she have a sense of humor underneath all that snippiness?

The men didn't find her amusing.

"Enough stalling," shouted one.

The Lady Butcher unsheathed her blade in one long stroke. Ruenen had spent seven years as a blacksmith's apprentice, and noticed the men's swords were poorly made and rusted. Inelegantly crafted. Weak. Whereas the Butcher's sword was unnaturally pristine and graceful. Someone with tremendous skill had made that blade. Its silver filigree on the hilt was unlike anything Ruenen had seen before: intricate, entwining metal. The craftsman in him yearned for a closer look.

The men charged her, swords raised. The Butcher sliced through two of them in one strike.

Blood splattered across the ground, and the two men crumpled. Ruenen watched as the remaining three charged again. They swung and she ducked, twirling on her knees to strike two of them across the femoral arteries. She leapt to her feet and stabbed the fifth man through the gut, then turned and cut off the heads of the remaining injured men in one elegant move. The fight was finished in a few movements.

At first, Ruenen couldn't believe how swiftly the brutal assault had occurred. He'd never seen such skill with a blade before, such lightness in her movements. It all had been effortless. Watching her had been like watching an artist at work. A dance routine. A song of blood, and gore, and metal.

After the initial shock wore off and Ruenen surveyed the bloody carnage, he noticed another astounding thing before him.

The Lady Butcher's hood had fallen back and her scarf had dropped to her neck on her finishing stroke.

The young woman standing before Ruenen had white blonde hair that was pulled into one clumsy plait down her back. Both eyes were bright, luminescent violet, a color Ruenen had never seen before; irises swirling in whorls like smoke. Her skin was smooth, the color of fresh snow. Not a single scar or blemish. Her face was thin and severe, but only because she was forcing it to be so with her furrowed brow and narrowed eyes. Ruenen thought that if she softened, smiled . . . she might be beyond lovely.

In fact, Ruenen was left speechless. Gods, the Butcher, his brooding, menacing companion, was beautiful, in an eerie, unearthly way. Those eyes . . . yes, there was something *other* about her.

She wiped the blood from her sword using a cloth and sheathed it with a sigh. She dropped the stained cloth, the rag she'd been using as a hankie, on top of one of the mutilated corpses. The Butcher then looked up at Ruenen with those inhuman violet eyes. His heart actually skipped a beat. He must've looked brainless, standing there with his mouth gaping open, because she sighed again heavily in exasperation. She pulled her hood and scarf back on as they were before. Ruenen realized he was probably the first person in years who'd seen her face and not been murdered outright.

There's still time, he thought mockingly.

"Why bother?" Ruenen asked as she fiddled with her scarf, finally finding words. His tongue felt thick and useless in his mouth. "I've seen what you look like now. It's not a secret anymore."

"It's cold," she said in a clipped tone. Her body moved rigidly. Ruenen was willing to bet all the money he didn't have that she was upset he'd seen her true appearance. "And I don't want the rest of humanity to know my face. I have no choice but to put up with *you*."

Now that he'd seen her, Ruenen suddenly craved to look upon her face again. What was getting into him? He liked women, certainly, and had admired many beautiful faces in the past. He'd enjoyed the nighttime company of a few of them. But those women had been soft, feminine, typical. Nothing at all like the menace before him. Was it because of who she was—the mystery of the Lady Butcher revealed? Or was there something else about her that made his mind go blank? Some sort of sorcery in the way those eyes had blazed, boring into his own, lodging in his lungs to make breathing next to impossible.

"Nice work . . . with the men . . ." He pointed a hesitant finger to the bloody carcasses on the ground, but didn't look at them. He'd seen blood and death many times before, and while the sight didn't faze him, he didn't like it.

"People hunt me for sport or glory. To kill the Lady Butcher would be an impressive feat, indeed," she said with a bite. "Or they are similar to these men, out to avenge someone else's death. I've been the Butcher for four years. I've rarely had a moment's peace. It's not a life I'd recommend."

"I imagine that's quite exhausting," Ruenen said, thinking about his own hunters, and how much he loathed looking over his shoulder all the time. "At least no one has thrown food at your face." He smiled. "My offer still stands: you can come with me to Andara. Leave all this behind."

"Maybe."

A moment passed between them. A moment of understanding. A moment of, dare he say, connection.

Slowly, the Lady Butcher raised her hood again so only her eyes and forehead were visible. He lost all awareness of the world around him. Her vivid eyes searched his, as if she were sizing him up, trying to reach into his mind to learn what he would do with this valuable information. Because he now held a powerful secret in his hand. The Butcher knew his name, and he had seen her face. They both had leverage over the other.

Yet, there was something about those eyes that made him want to tell the Butcher everything. He had to hold his tongue, the urge to divulge his entire, grisly truth grew intensely difficult to restrain.

The one thought his brain had, before forcing his legs to walk onwards, was that this girl, this Lady Butcher, wasn't at all what she seemed.

CHAPTER 3
Marai

She'd been sloppy.

The way he'd looked at her . . . eyes wide, lips parted, so utterly still. It was as if the breath had been knocked from his lungs. As if he'd just discovered the world's biggest secret. Something life altering. As if she wasn't a person, but a wonder. That expression trailed her with every step she took ahead of him. No one had ever looked at her in that way.

Marai should've moved differently. In the rare occurrence when her disguise would fall, revealing her face, her marks would never have time to truly look before they were dead. Ruenen's reaction had unnerved Marai, and she didn't exactly know what to think. Or where to go from here. But from the moment their eyes had locked, she knew that something had shifted between them. Something she couldn't take back.

So they continued their downhill slog through slushy winter roads in silence. Ruenen started attempting more conversation between them, sensing the awkwardness. He was trying so hard to get her to speak.

"Glad we're getting further South," he said.

Or "gods, everything in Grelta looks the same."

Marai never responded to him. She didn't know what to say. It was unsettling, how much he wanted to interact with her. He had been chatty before he'd seen her face, but now . . .

She could tell it bothered him—her silence. He'd always huff when he wasn't answered. It was as if he was trying to catch her off guard so that she would reveal some deep, dark secret by accident. He wanted to *know* her, and it was maddening. There was no reason for him to know a shard about her, and she intended to keep it that way. Keep that wall up, a safe distance between them. Ruenen was merely a means to gain coin. Perhaps even an escape off this continent. She wouldn't open herself up to him and risk her safety.

But sometimes, those frozen rocks of self crack, and it's impossible to stem the leak.

Especially when a bear is involved.

Marai heard its growls first. Its plodding paws in the snow. Marai and Ruenen were farther down the mountain, but the road had led them near the cliffs. On one side was the forest, the other the sea. And between them, a long drop. She and Ruenen turned to their left as the animal prowled out of the forest, nose twitching at their scent. Northern bears were rare; pure white, including their eyes, blending perfectly with their environment.

"Don't move," Marai said, slowly reaching towards the sword at her hip.

The bears of the North were monstrous, even in the winter when food was scarce. Unlike other bears on Astye, Northern white bears never hibernated. They were always awake. Always hunting.

"Lirr save me," uttered Ruenen as he took in the sheer size of the creature. It reared up onto its hind legs.

The bear snarled in hunger, snorting, showing its teeth.

Marai stood her ground as Ruenen gaped beside her. She raised her arms and the sword, making herself as big as possible. If the bear hadn't been starving, it might have walked away then. Instead, it returned to all fours and stalked forward. Marai pushed Ruenen aside as the bear swung an enormous paw her way. She blocked with her sword, and the bear's claws met steel. It roared in frustration and swung again, shoving Marai backwards onto Ruenen's foot. He swore as the bear pressed them closer to the edge of the cliff.

Marai swung back and forth. The bear retreated a step, but refused to let its prey go.

On the next lunge, the bear went for Ruenen. It swiped and Ruenen dodged, but slammed into Marai. His stumble knocked the sword from her hand. She watched wide-eyed as her precious weapon careened over the cliff in slow-motion, and fell far down to the beach below.

Marai's stomach plummeted with it, but there was no time to do anything about her lost sword.

She took hold of her dagger, forcing her to inch closer to the beast. When the bear swung again, she stabbed it in the paw. The white beast roared, opening its mouth to reveal those large teeth. Marai plunged the dagger into the side of the bear, feeling warm blood seep through her clothes. The beast jolted backwards, limping, snarling. Marai roared and growled, waving her arms. The bear huffed, and then backed away in submission, bowing its mighty head. Slowly, it limped into the forest and became one with the snow, save for the trail of blood it left in its wake.

Ruenen let out a long whistle.

"That was terrifying," he said with an almost-laugh. Marai turned to him, temper flaring.

"*You clumsy bastard,*" she shouted, pointing the bloody dagger at his face. "Now we have to go all the way down there to get my sword."

"I'm sorry I knocked into you," Ruenen said. "It's not my fault that *a bear* was trying to eat me."

Marai growled as ferociously as the beast. She turned on her heel and stalked along the side of the cliff. That sword hadn't left her side in eight years. Its absence left her feeling naked. Vulnerable. Weak. Things she abhorred feeling.

"There's no way to get down there," Ruenen said. "Just leave it."

Marai scanned the ledges of the cliffs. "Have you ever heard of a mercenary without a sword?"

"Can't you buy a new one? And what are you looking for?"

"There are steps near here . . ."

Scanning, scanning . . . *ah, there!*

Carved into the very mountain itself were a set of steep stairs that dropped off onto the black pebble beach below. Nailed into the cliff wall were thick iron pegs, attached to an old, weathered rope traveling all the way down the steps. The rope was there for safety purposes for travelers to hold onto as they climbed. Most people didn't use the treacherous steps, but time was not on Marai's side. She couldn't be parted from her sword. That meant death for both her and Ruenen.

Marai came to the first stair.

The black rock was sleek, shining with ice. She glanced over the edge of the cliff . . . it was a long way to fall.

She took a deep, steadying breath, as the ball of Marai's foot touched the step. Testing. Her boot didn't slip, but she'd always been light on her feet. Ruenen, on the other hand, wasn't. He came sauntering over and his face turned a little green at the sight of the stairs.

"Are you sure there isn't an alternate trail down?"

"Not if we don't want to travel another week out of our way, further from our destination," Marai said to him icily. "We'll miss the boat."

"I'll wait for you up here then," he said, shoving his hands into his pockets.

"You're coming down this cliff because I'm not climbing all the way back up. Walk down or I throw you."

Ruenen narrowed his eyes. "Fine. Then you lead the way."

Marai put her full weight on the step and grabbed hold of the rope. Carefully, painfully slowly, she stepped onto the next. A rough, biting wind whipped her hood off, momentarily halting her. A strong gust like that could easily force her off the steps. Another step. At twelve steps down,

Ruenen finally began to follow. He touched the step with the toe of his boot and winced. He pulled his foot back and paced on the edge of the cliff. He bit his lip, sucked in a breath, then stepped. And again.

They moved slowly, clinging to the old rope, step after step, in silence and complete concentration. One wrong step, and it would be over.

There were hundreds of them. Marai's mind drifted after step one hundred and fifteen. She wondered if Andara could truly be the magical answer to all her troubles. What would life be like for her in that mysterious, faraway land? Would she be able to shed her cloak for good, and live without fear and shame? Freedom, Ruenen had said. An ember of curiosity burned within her at the thought.

A scraping and gasping sound knocked Marai from her thoughts. She twisted to see Ruenen clinging to the rope with both hands, one leg dangling over the edge. Marai shot him a look, which he returned in kind as he set his foot safely back on the step.

It took hours to reach the bottom. Marai mused that it was the longest stretch of silence Ruenen had been able to endure.

Once her feet touched down on the pebbled beach, winter wind ripped through her, straight through flesh and bone. Ruenen leapt off the final steps to her side and gazed out at the wild open sea. Giant white waves crashed violently against the mountains and rocks jutting out from shore. The riptide here was strong and could suck a strong swimmer under in seconds. The wind and waves howled and thundered like a summer storm, the sky grey without a trace of sunlight.

Across those treacherous waters was Andara and the promise of a new life.

Marai retraced her steps on the beach to where her sword must have fallen from above. Something glistened amidst the black pebbles. Marai dashed to its side and grabbed hold. She examined the sword from all angles—not a dent. Not a scratch. It was as pristine as the day it was made.

"That's a good sword," Ruenen said from her side. "Most wouldn't survive a fall such as that."

"It's not a normal sword," Marai replied, causing Ruenen's eyebrows to rise.

"What does that mean?"

"It was my father's sword." Her eyes raked over the intricate gold and silver filigree. The twisted metalwork covered the entire the hilt, from round pommel to cross-guard. Two deep fullers ran down the length of the blade on both sides. She admired the lightness of the metal and twirled it in her wrist. Dimtoir, it was called. Holding that blade felt like coming home. Not that she'd ever had one. Marai imagined that was how it felt. "Forged long ago by the best craftsman of the time."

"How long ago are we talking?" Ruenen asked. "A century? Or back to the old times, the days of magic?" His eyes scanned the writing on the blade. "What language is that?"

Marai sheathed Dimtoir, the weight comforting at her hip. She gave Ruenen another look, hoping it would silence him from further questions. No one spoke of those days. Or magic.

Ruenen gave her a cockeyed smile, eyes playful. "I understand. You have your sword. I have my lute." He looked up and down the beach, that smile fading. "Where do we go from here?"

Marai shook her head, letting the feral wind rush through her hair. "We can move along the beach. There's a temple at the end, if I recall. We can cut inland from there."

She started walking and Ruenen came to her side. His stomach gave a mighty howl, and he clutched it dramatically. "I'm starving. Why didn't you kill the bear? We could've eaten it."

Marai took a step to her left, putting more distance between them. "My sword was my first priority." She glanced at Ruenen. "I only kill when I must."

"Oh, so you're an assassin with *morals,* then?" he asked, his tone amused.

Marai glanced at him again. He grinned, light dancing in his brown eyes.

Marai's temper flared. "Would you rather I kill anything in sight? Women? Children? Defenseless animals?"

"Were you looking at the same bear I was? I wouldn't call him defenseless, Butcher. He tried to eat us."

Marai narrowed her eyes.

"Easy, Sassafras, I'm only teasing." Ruenen held up his hands defenselessly, eyes wide with innocence.

For a second, her lungs tightened at the sound of the nickname. "Don't call me that."

Her annoyance, of course, made a sly grin appear on Ruenen's lips. "Why? It's a much better name than the Lady Butcher."

"Alright, *Ard the Bard,"* she snapped back.

Ruenen chuckled. "I walked into that one."

Marai had been given nicknames before, but not for a long time. Perhaps it should have bothered her more. Instead, something about the interaction made her heart clench and burn.

She could hear Thora's voice, the *tsk* sound that always went along with a scolding. Thora was always trying to reign in Marai's temper.

Don't be such a storm cloud, Marai. Calm that fury in your heart, she'd say, her brown face drawn with worry. Storm cloud. It was an appropriate nickname. Marai was too wild, too volatile for the proper, steady force that was Thora, who was always trying to mother.

That night, they made camp on the beach. It was too dark to continue, so they built a fire from the few bushes that managed to grow close to the cliff wall. At least there was no snow on the beach; the sea had washed it all away, and whatever flakes still dared to fall, the cruel wind made sure to blow them far out to sea.

A cold spray of water slapped Marai's cheeks. These were not the warm beaches of Cleaving Tides. There was no sand, no seagulls, no *warmth*. Marai had once fallen in love with the ocean breeze and the taste of salt on her tongue. Her heart still yearned to be out there on the water, as a bird or a dolphin, to feel so free and not tied to the repulsive land called Astye. From being what she was. If she could only get far away from those judging eyes and viper tongues that lashed her with derogatory terms, she could create a new identity somewhere else. Maybe Andara was that place.

After another meager dinner, Marai lay on her back and gazed at the night sky. The morose clouds of the day had dissipated and revealed a stunning display of twinkling lights against the pitch-black background. An endless sea of stars. Marai picked out the constellations of the gods. There was Lirr's harvest basket and Laimoen's dagger. It was a soothing sight; it made Marai feel so small and invisible to stare up at something so vast. The moon was just a sliver, but she didn't miss its shining face. The stars were all the company Marai needed.

Ruenen pulled out his lute, as usual. Marai was aware of Ruenen's song, the one he'd been writing about her. She'd toyed with threatening to cut off one or two of his fingers. One night when she'd been particularly sick with that horrible cold, she'd considered crushing the lute upon a rock. Now, Marai merely rolled her eyes. As much as she loathed and feared this song, it was harmless unless it was performed. So Marai let him continue to pluck away at his lute, mumbling incoherent lyrics. Every once in a while she'd catch words like "behead" or "ravage." Even their bear friend now made an appearance. She supposed the song was to glorify her, but it felt shallow and empty.

Ruenen knew absolutely nothing about her, other than the surface. If he knew the truth, her long list of misdeeds . . . he'd stop writing immediately.

He did stop playing then. Marai turned her head and met his eyes, open, curious, watching her. She quickly looked away, unsure if his gaze was admiring or scrutinizing. It made her uncomfortable, as if an unwelcome worm wriggled around underneath her skin.

Still, she had to marvel as she stared up into the inky expanse of the night sky—after everything he'd seen her do . . . Ruenen wasn't ever afraid.

Hands. They held her down. They raked across her body. She fought, but the hands were as strong as iron. She flailed, screamed, tried to kick, but powerful legs pushed her thighs apart, hands inched lower on her exposed skin.

She couldn't breathe. Fear turned her blood to ice. She couldn't, *wouldn't* let those hands take what they wanted.

She felt them on her shoulders, shaking her. A distant voice urgently called to her.

"Butcher!"

A butcher, yes, that's what she was, but had been reduced to this powerless girl against those hands. Blue and green water dragons entwined up his arms . . .

"Wake up!"

Marai's eyelids snapped open as her fingers wrapped around the hilt of her dagger. She unsheathed it like a crack of lightning and pressed the edge to the throat of the man before her.

Ruenen's eyes were wide as he stared at the dagger, his skin pale in the darkness. He'd fallen onto his rear and remained deathly still as Marai came to her senses.

It was Ruenen. Just Ruenen. Just a dream.

"I'm sorry, I didn't mean to wake you, but you were—"

"Forget it," Marai grunted, sheathing her dagger.

"You sounded like you were in pain—"

"*Forget it.*"

Marai turned over onto her side, away from Ruenen. She heard the pebbles shifting, clacking, as Ruenen crawled back to his blankets.

She refused to acknowledge what had occurred last night. She hated how nightmares gripped her, sharp talons against her skin, left her feeling weak and senseless, exposed and raw. She equally hated the shifty glances Ruenen shot at her throughout the afternoon, as if she'd disintegrate into tears or collapse to her knees. Her temper was on a short leash all day, and Ruenen sensed not to say a word. They both pretended like nothing had happened.

The temple came into view at the edge of the beach. It was centuries old, and had been carved into the rocky cliff. Shrines, temples and monasteries were scattered all over the country. Many places of worship were from before humans ruled the continent. Back in the time of magic.

But Marai slowed her steps when she spotted the charred human skeleton leaning against an inner pillar. The last time she'd been in this area, the temple housed several dozen priestesses and monks. Marai had sat outside and listened to their solemn chanting from within.

Now, the building was silent and abandoned.

"What do you think happened?" Ruenen asked, stepping closer to the blackened bones near the colonnaded entrance. His voice was soft and face had gone pallid. Marai walked through the portico and saw what she suspected: tremendous fire damage. Charred beams and rafters littered the floor. More bones lay amongst the rubble, turning to ash and dust. Anything of value had already been ransacked.

Ruenen came to her side, gazing at the sad remains of this gentle commune of devout followers. As before, at the temple on the mountain,

Ruenen's expression seemed to shutter. He looked away, squeezing his eyes shut, as if an echo of the fire seared his eyeballs.

"Do you think this was intentional?" he asked, voice tight.

Marai shook her head. "I'm not sure. It could've been an accident."

Ruenen began to mumble under his breath in the ancient tongue of the gods; something that sounded like a prayer or a chant. A prayer for the dead.

Her jaw clenched, and Marai put her own invisible walls up. She refused to let Ruenen see how this death of the innocent affected her. She stalked back out of the temple and tried to shove the image of those bodies from her mind.

It was curious that Ruenen knew the ancient tongue . . . only monks, priestesses, and a few exceptionally learned people knew that language. It was used only for ceremony now; for holy holidays, weddings, and funerals. So how did *he* know it?

Once Ruenen joined her, he said nothing. They climbed up a small hill from the desolate beach into the forest.

Marai set a snare that evening. She caught a rather skinny rabbit, but it was a welcome meal, the first meat either of them had eaten in days.

"Bless Lirr for this rabbit," sighed Ruenen with his eyes closed and hands in prayer. Marai watched him. The prayer seemed genuine. She'd never seen him do this before, but the temple had shaken him . . . he was ashen and quiet. What connection, if any, did he have to the gods? Or to the priestesses who served them?

That temple had worshipped Lirr, the Goddess of Creation and All Living Things. She was also the Goddess of the Land, Fertility, and Birth. Farmers prayed to Lirr for good harvests and healthy livestock. Women hoping to conceive a child lay offerings at her altars. Celebrations and festivals in Lirr's honor were always prevalent in the early spring.

It was said that Lirr created the world. Continental Astye was home to the gods before they left the earth for their own city in the sky, Empyra.

Marai was not a believer in the gods, and she never prayed to them. She'd lost her faith long ago, if she ever truly had it to begin with. She knew their stories, in part because it was engrained into every child on this land. But she also liked stories.

The creation tale of the gods had always particularly interested Marai. Laimoen was Lirr's partner—the God of Destruction. War. Death. Lirr and Laimoen ensured balance in the world. All life must eventually end, and death must occur before rebirth. It was that equilibrium of darkness and light that had always intrigued Marai. She imagined she would've been Laimoen's creature; that Lirr created Marai as a shadow of her beloved partner. If one believed in that sort of thing. Marai always found it strange that a land such as Astye could believe so strongly in gods, ancient and mighty beings of strength and wisdom and magic, but at the same time, abhor magic, itself. Magic was, after all, in theory, created by the gods.

And as magic was abhorred by humans, so were all "magical folk."

Marai skinned the grey rabbit and set it on a spit. While she waited for it to cook, she watched her companion once again strumming at his lute. He was less rattled now, and his color had returned to normal. Ruenen had barely stopped working on his song. He practiced it again and again, memorizing the notes and chords.

"Why do you need assistance getting through the Red Lands?" she abruptly asked.

Ruenen looked up, surprised. "Well, doesn't everyone?"

Marai narrowed her eyes as she turned the spit. "Most people can get through unscathed, as long as they can provide adequate proof of identification and reasons for travel if a soldier crosses their path. I would wager that you have neither of those things."

"You already know I'm being hunted. Can't we keep it at that?" Ruenen said, looking back down at his lute.

"By whom? Tacorn? Nevandia?"

"Might be best to assume both. And why does it matter to you anyways? It's a dangerous place for me, and that's all you need to know. And I thought you said no personal questions," he said the last bit with a bite.

Marai stared at him blandly. "You've asked me a thousand questions since our journey started. I asked you one."

Ruenen avoided her eyes, staring at the rabbit dripping fat into the fire below. His shoulders caved in a little, a hollow look appearing in his eyes. A mask had slipped. This person sitting in his body was not the same man as before.

What had Ruenen done to upset both warring kingdoms of Tacorn and Nevandia? It had to be something substantial if he was this concerned and avoidant. Was he a spy? A traitor?

Nevandia and Tacorn hadn't always been enemies. Centuries ago, they'd been one immense kingdom, wealthy and powerful, the crown jewel of Astye. Something happened, Marai didn't know what, that caused the kingdoms to splinter. Outright war broke out forty years ago. Tacorn's vicious King Rayghast wanted to unite the kingdoms under one banner. He was known for his brutality and torture of prisoners. Rumor said that there was something *off* about Rayghast. He wasn't in his right mind . . .

Inevitably, the two kingdoms would once again merge, but Marai knew it would be a bloody slaughter for the Nevandians. Tacorn was far too powerful, and Rayghast was ruthless. Nevandia needed someone to raise the banner again, to inspire its people, but the Steward on the throne was simply a placeholder for someone else. Someone who didn't exist. The royal bloodline ended with King Vanguarden Avsharian. There was no one who would be coming to Nevandia's aid when that bloody day finally arrived.

Ruenen strummed on his lute a while longer until the rabbit was browned and roasted. They sat in silence as they picked the meat off its bones, savoring the feeling of a warm meal in their stomachs. The weather had warmed a bit. Not as many snowflakes fell now that they were at the bottom of the mountains.

Ruenen uttered a groan of pleasure. "When I become a successful bard in Andara, I'll eat quail and pheasant every day." He licked his fingers clean. "And duck sautéed in sage butter."

"You'll be a fat bard, then," Marai quipped back.

Ruenen ignored her. "I heard that Clancy Fairweather is treated like royalty wherever he goes."

"You're no Clancy Fairweather," Marai said, receiving a scathing look from Ruenen. "And he's a pompous blowhard. You don't want to be compared to him. He has a better name than you, though . . . Ard."

Ruenen stuck out his tongue and Marai found herself smirking. She stopped immediately, plastering her serious expression back on. Ruenen raised an eyebrow at her, but pretended he hadn't seen her crack a smile.

"Mark me, one day I *will* be as famous as Clancy Fairweather. When I'm far away from this continent. And you will eat your words, Butcher." Ruenen picked up his lute again and quickly strummed a few chords. "I didn't always want to be a bard, though. Didn't think I had much choice in my life up until recently."

Marai began to settle into her bedding for the night, bringing her blankets up to her chin. She assumed Ruenen would get the hint that it was now time to sleep.

"I haven't been practicing long, but I remember the day a true bard passed through my village. It was when I was a blacksmith's apprentice. I was fourteen. It wasn't as if I hadn't heard music before, but it was the first time I'd seen people gather to watch someone play. And I saw the way the musician engaged the crowd and how their eyes would brighten and smiles widen. The tales were more epic than if they were merely spoken. More alive. I realized then the power music can have on a story. I wanted to do that."

Ruenen sighed. "Alas, I've yet to see anyone as enthralled with *my* performances as the audience was with that bard. He gave me his old, spare lute. This one, right here." He lifted it into the fire light. The instrument was heavily scratched and weathered, well loved. "The only gift I've ever received. The bard told me to experiment with it, listen to its sounds, hear what notes go together and which ones don't. I learned the songs entirely by ear by myself. I was rather determined. I'm still learning the notes and chords by name. I know them mostly by sound."

Marai wasn't musical, herself. She never had much patience to learn an instrument, nor much purpose to do so. However, she could appreciate the difficulties of learning to play without any tutelage. Most musicians had instructors who guided them. Ruenen was entirely self-taught, and it was his passion for music that pushed him forward, even though he wasn't very good yet. She could respect that kind of devotion to a craft.

"So you didn't want to be a blacksmith?" she found herself asking as the fire popped and crackled.

Ruenen lay down in his blankets and stared at the evergreen canopy above. A sliver of silver moonlight shone through, illuminating their thicket. "Peasants like me . . . we often don't get to choose what path we lead. But music opened a whole new door for me."

How true his words were. So few on Astye had real choices. Marai understood that feeling of being trapped, as both a woman and an outlier of society.

"Haven't you ever wanted to be someone else?" Ruenen asked her quietly from across the fire.

Marai looked up at the beacon of moonlight, the darkness thick around them, but comforting to the shadows in her soul.

"All the time."

CHAPTER 4
Rayghast

1 *4 Years Ago*

King Rayghast of Tacorn stood in the corner of the dungeon cell below the fortress. It was always cold down there, no matter the temperature outside. It was always damp. The putrid smell of mold, dead animals, feces, and other rotting things never seemed to dissipate. The dungeon had an air of emptiness, even with every cell being full of prisoners. Their petrified screams echoed endlessly off the stone walls, sounding like phantoms from the Underworld. To many, the Tacorn dungeon was worse than nightmares and death.

He watched the guard repeatedly strike the Nevandian knight in the face. Each punch sent a sharp thrum of pleasure through Rayghast's bones. The knight's eyes were swollen shut; blood poured from his broken nose and mouth onto his gold chest plate. The guard would only stop at Rayghast's command, or if the knight revealed any valuable information regarding the Nevandian King. Neither seemed very likely. Vanguarden's golden knights were extremely loyal, despite his weak leadership. They'd rather risk death than turn traitor. It made them particularly entertaining prisoners.

Rayghast's advisor, Cronhold, appeared at the cell door. The old man wrung his hands and licked his lips in anxious anticipation.

"We captured a monk, Your Grace," he said as Rayghast came to the cell door. The advisor was stooped over, a round hunch on his back. White wiry hair spewed from his ears. He'd served on the council for years under Rayghast's father, King Hershen, and now served his son. Cronhold's eyes flickered over to where the guard was mercilessly beating the Nevandian knight. The aged git winced.

Rayghast said nothing. He never spoke unless there was good reason to. He'd sometimes go days without uttering a word. He stared at Cronhold until the ancient, white-haired man realized he needed to continue his explanation.

"Uh, the monastery loyal to Nevandia was raided, as requested, Sire. The one on the border. Everyone, uh, slaughtered, except this monk. He's younger and newer to the monastery. We believe we might be able to, uh, get valuable information from him, Your Grace."

Another strike and the knight barely grunted. He was losing consciousness; nothing useful would come from him now. No longer entertained, Rayghast pushed open the cell door and walked past Cronhold out of the prison. The old man hobbled after him at a slow pace. Up the cold, stone stairs into the main castle, their footsteps reverberated from wall to wall, ensconced candlelight their only guide.

Once on the main floor, the atmosphere did not improve by much. At least it no longer smelled of piss and death. The castle was old. Every room, every hall was drafty and dark. It was the original castle when Tacorn and Nevandia were one kingdom almost three centuries ago, but it had been built long before that by the ancient fae. When the two kingdoms had split, Nevandia built its own elegant, modern palace. An entire city had sprung up at its base—Kellesar. A city of lights and culture. This castle in Tacorn . . . it held a fearsome presence. It wasn't meant to be magnificent, like in a fantastical fable, but to be viewed as powerful, intimidating, and impenetrable. Its keep had never been breached.

Cronhold could barely keep up with Rayghast's stride as he skulked down the stone hallway, past lifeless chambers. It was not a place one lived. A person would merely sleep there and never truly feel welcome. Rayghast had lived in it his whole life. Every room held a memory of his father, a sharp reminder of what Rayghast waged war for.

Rayghast then led Cronhold into the only place of life: the great hall.

It was a large chamber made from dark grey stone, similar to the rest of the castle. Black banners with two crossed silver swords, the Tacorn emblem, hung from the walls. It was a mostly colorless room. The only splashes of color were the maroon rug on the floor, which matched the cushions on the chairs, including Rayghast's imposing silver and granite throne at the head of the room, raised onto a platform. The room was large enough to host magnificent balls. It had the potential to be quite exquisite, but the space had seen no celebrations or events since Rayghast's own birth. He wasn't one for crowds. Most people were a nuisance.

A long dark mahogany table had been placed in the center of the room. There, the rest of the council was dourly seated. Rayghast despised them. They droned on and on for hours. He avoided council meetings at all costs whenever he could. But this time, it was necessary.

At the end of the long table sat a young monk, barely old enough to grow a beard. He straightened up when Rayghast entered. His ginger-hewed robe was wrinkled and disheveled, but he appeared otherwise unharmed. The young monk had come willingly, then.

Rayghast never sat during council meetings. Instead, he prowled around the table; a vulture, passing the monk, who shriveled under his black-eyed gaze. The boy's shaven head glistened with sweat.

"Tell His Grace what you told us," said Boone, his greasy black hair pulled back tightly. He commanded the entire Tacorn army. Heqtur Boone was the newest council member, and by far the youngest. His predecessor had been executed by Rayghast after failing to win over Nevandia at the Battle of Pevear on the border of Tacornian territory. It'd been a stalemate;

neither side claimed victory, but that wasn't enough for Rayghast. He wanted total, utter defeat.

"When I became a monk and chose to serve the Divine Lirr, I learned that the monastery had taken in a boy." The monk's eyes shifted nervously from Rayghast to Boone. No one ever seemed to enjoy looking Rayghast in the face for long. "I was told nothing, other than the boy's name, which they said was Leander. It was obvious to me, though, that this was a false identity. The older monks guarded the boy with such ferocity, never speaking about his parentage and how he came to be at the monastery. Any questions I asked, they politely declined to answer.

"Over the few months I was there, I couldn't help but notice how Monk Amsco and Monk Nori shielded the boy whenever an outsider came to call. They'd hide him away in the wine cellar until visitors left. The boy was always quiet and subdued, not like normal children of his age. He often appeared as if the entire weight of the world were on his shoulders . . ."

The monk paused, voice trailing off as he watched Rayghast encircle the table for a second time.

"Keep going," Boone said with an impatient trill of his fingers on the table.

Startled, the monk continued. "One day, I was tending to the gardens. Monks Amsco and Nori were giving the boy his daily lessons. I snuck up behind a bush, to hear what they so secretly taught him. They spoke to Leander of Nevandia, its geography, of King Vanguarden, and the duties of a king. The monks were teaching the boy how to lead."

The council members met each other's eyes from across the table. They all sat a little taller, a little more alert now. Rayghast continued to prowl.

"And then I remembered . . . prior to becoming a monk, I lived in a small Nevandian village. King Vanguarden and Queen Larissa visited once; a parade through town. I remember being in awe of Queen Larissa's effortless magnificence, the way her dark hair glistened and her cheeks were so rosy and tan—"

"Is there a point to your story? We don't care about your pretty words or infatuation with the Queen," spat Boone and the monk jumped again.

"I . . . noticed, despite trying to cover it, Queen Larissa's stomach was swollen and round. She absent-mindedly placed her hand there, the way women with babies in their bellies do. The way my own mother had done whilst carrying my younger siblings. The Queen was unmistakably *with child*."

Rayghast stopped his pacing and stood directly next to the monk, who shrunk a little in his seat. The other council members shifted in their chairs, but remained silent.

"At the time, I thought nothing of it," the monk continued, avoiding Rayghast's gaze. "I assumed word would come to us of the birth of a new prince or princess. But it never did. If the child had died during birth, news would still have spread across the kingdom. It felt odd to me. But the Queen's face was burned into my brain that day, so when I saw the boy . . . he looked almost identical to her, except for the birthmark on his left wrist. His age aligned to that of the unborn child. It all made sense to me."

A ripple of murmurs traveled up and down the long table.

"Our spy was right, then," Boone said. A smug smile slid onto his lips.

"But there is, uh, no record of Queen Larissa ever having a child," Cronhold said with a wag of his decrepit finger. "Baseless rumors. How could Nevandia have kept the boy's birth secret for this many years?"

Rayghast couldn't fault the old man for his skepticism. He, too, wondered the same. No servant, no midwife, had blabbed?

"When your troops were seen riding towards the monastery, the first thing the monks did was send the boy away. Monk Nori entrusted him to a stranger and her small daughter. I heard Monk Nori tell the woman, who'd been a weary traveler seeking shelter, to accept the boy as her own. I admit that I got distracted when the soldiers burst through the door. I didn't see which way the woman went. That was the last I saw of Leander before . . ." The monk took a deep, stammering breath. "Before the soldiers . . . slaughtered everyone."

Rayghast turned his cool attention to Boone. He almost never needed to ask the questions; Boone could read his face in an instant. He wasn't an unintelligent man, despite his humble upbringing.

"The woman with her children got away, Sire," he said in quiet resignation. "I saw them off in the distance, but didn't think anything of it."

Rayghast's eyes bore into him. Boone quickly looked down at his lap, ashamed. A vein pulsed in Rayghast's neck as he stifled the potent desire to strike the commander.

"If your account is true and correct," began Wattling, a squat, hefty man who was in charge of the treasury, "then King Vanguarden has a secret child . . . an heir to the throne of Nevandia, whom he banished away to a monastery to keep safe from the eyes and ears of Tacorn. Even from his own people."

More murmurs.

"Vanguarden hoped he could keep the boy hidden until he was old enough to ascend to the throne and take his place," mused Cronhold darkly to the council.

Rayghast had had an irking suspicion all along. Vanguarden had been far too vocal about his desire for an heir, and lack thereof. There were whispers for years. It was often spoken about across Nevandia, conveniently in places where it would catch the attention of Tacorn spies. Now Rayghast had proof. The boy was a weakness for Vanguarden Avsharian. An obvious target for assassination. If Rayghast had had confirmed news of the boy's birth, he would've disposed of him earlier.

Rayghast himself deigned not speak of his own lack of an heir. He wouldn't grant power to the supposed curse within his seed by speaking it out loud. Not after the traitorous blood in his veins sought to wreck him at every moment . . .

He pushed the thoughts aside like a curtain. Sent them back to the depths of his mind that he kept locked away.

"You were right to suspect the monastery of their false impartiality, Your Grace," oozed Boone, reaching out a hand, attempting flattery to make up for his failure. "So much for the Divine Wisdom of Lirr."

Rayghast ignored him.

All religious temples, monasteries, and sects were supposed to remain neutral. They didn't answer to any king or queen, only to the power of the gods. The monastery in question had broken this trust and had chosen a side by sheltering the child. It was good that Boone destroyed it.

Now Rayghast knew: King Vanguarden and Queen Larissa *did* have a son, the rightful heir to their throne. That blood line would survive, even if Rayghast managed to overthrow Vanguarden. Rayghast could not lay claim to the Nevandian throne, merge the kingdoms, as long as that boy existed.

The council's apprehensive eyes were all on Rayghast, including the quivering monk, who seemed to have realized that his usefulness had come to an end. Rayghast gestured to the guards at the door. In one synchronized movement, they had the monk out of his chair and dragged from the hall, screaming.

"I told you everything. Please, let me live!"

The heavy oak doors shut behind them. Rayghast could hear the monk's pleas distantly in the hallway.

The child would be around eight in age, the spitting image of his mother Queen Larissa. The peasant woman who'd smuggled him out of the monastery had many days' head start. However, Rayghast was confident that she wouldn't be hard to find, nor clever enough to avoid detection for long. He turned to Boone, who seemed anxious to please his King and redeem himself for his failure at not having captured the boy at the monastery.

"Find the child and bring him to me alive," Rayghast said in his empty, cold voice. "I alone will spill royal Nevandian blood. That is for no one else. Execute anyone who may be protecting him."

"Yes, Sire," Boone said with a long, low bow. "The boy will be yours within the month."

Rayghast held up a hand as Boone turned to leave. "Your report of the faerie lands in the North."

Boone's face brightened, a sinister glint in his dark eyes. "I have good news, Your Grace. The final faerie camps have been destroyed. We rounded up the remaining stragglers—a group of their warriors. Their magic was weak, though, through years of diluting their blood with humans. They could barely draw a flame, and were easily put down. Weak, disgusting creatures."

"So it's done, then?" Cronhold asked, his eyes wide with hope.

Boone's smile slid on like oil. "I'm pleased to say it is."

Cronhold let out a sigh. "At last, magic and its villainy has been stripped from this continent."

"The one good thing Vanguarden's father did," sniggered Wattling to the councilman to his left, "was to eliminate those faerie monsters."

Rayghast felt a stillness come over him at those words. Monsters, true. Magical, deadly monsters. He met Boone's cold eyes and nodded his approval. Boone promptly exited the council chamber, and jammed his black helmet onto his head. Other men of the council followed him out, whispering amongst each other. Cronhold lingered, shifting his weight from foot to foot, wringing his hands again.

"Your Grace," he said, "there is still the matter of King Vanguarden and Queen Larissa... if you find the boy, Vanguarden is still on the throne—"

"Once the boy is dead, Vanguarden will come challenge me, himself."

Rayghast never showed emotion. He would not let that weakness consume him. He was physically human, but had striven to become something stronger. Something without weakness. To rule ruthlessly, one needed to sacrifice anything and everything.

"People who love are simple. Once his son is dead, he'll have already lost."

CHAPTER 5
Marai

Two days later found them on a widening dirt road. A chilly wind rustled the branches above, but it wasn't as biting now that they were further down the mountain. The trees grew more diverse, deciduous than coniferous, although they were currently bare. A red, hazy mist settled around them from the low sun trickling through the branches.

As they continued towards the center of the continent, the roads grew less wild and more heavily trafficked.

There were other travelers on the road with them. Most were merchants or farmers with wagons of goods, or tradesmen passing to and from villages looking for work. They nodded their heads in timid greetings to Marai and Ruenen as they passed, staying on the opposite side. Ruenen avoided eye contact as much as Marai did. He seemed jumpier now that there were more people. He walked closer to her, quickened his pace, and popped up the collar of his coat to hide himself. But that didn't stop him from murmuring polite greetings to people as he passed.

Out on the road, one saw all manner of folk.

A dozen thieves burst out from their camouflage in the woods. Their cold, ragged breath puffed out like dragon smoke. They circled Marai and Ruenen, holding up their weapons, sporting missing teeth, matted hair, and ripped clothing.

"Halt!" one dark-skinned man said as the other thieves brandished their weapons at Marai and Ruenen. "Give us your coin, and we'll let you pass through unharmed."

"Does it look like we have anything to steal?" Ruenen growled, hands reluctantly up in the air. Marai didn't move. This was yet another delay they couldn't afford.

"You've a couple of nice-lookin' weapons," said a toothless man, eyeing Marai's sword and knives. "And that lute might fetch a fair penny."

Ruenen gaped. "My lute?"

Marai almost laughed—that banged up lute was worth nothing to anyone except Ruenen.

"Sonny, hand it over, and no one gets hurt," the man continued, stepping closer with his knife. "Although, I wouldn't mind a quick romp with your lady friend." His dark, hungry eyes grazed Marai's mostly covered face, scanned her body, a sick sneer growing on his lips. Despite her loose-fitting garments, Marai saw the man's imagination at work, peeling her clothing off piece by piece. Nothing sickened her more than a man sexualizing a woman for his own gratification.

His hands will never touch me.

"Empty your pockets," said a short man, raising his pickaxe threateningly towards Marai's throat. He wasn't much taller than her. "Don't want your woman to lose her head now, do you?"

The thief came no closer.

He was blasted off his feet and fell onto his back in the dirt.

Marai had merely moved a hand, yet the bandit had been hit with the force of a massive punch to the gut. She hadn't even touched him. Now she had space to unsheathe her sword. Swiftly, she severed the outstretched arm of the dark-eyed man. Marai felt instant satisfaction as he screamed.

The other bandits swarmed around them in chaos; a colony of filthy cockroaches. But Marai was faster and far more skilled than any of them. Their movements were clumsy, untrained, and slow. They didn't know how to work together or communicate. Against Marai, they were outnumbered.

Ruenen did nothing but stand there as she whirled around him, blocking and protecting him from the thieves. It was her hired duty, but a prickle of annoyance ignited in her.

"*Behind you,*" Ruenen shouted and Marai turned to see two men launch themselves at her.

Warmth spread through her palm and fingers as she pulled from within. She aimed once again at the two men; a wave of wind had them sailing into the air. This trick received an awed grunt from Ruenen. Soon, none of the bandits were left, their bodies crumpled in the dirt. The road to the Red Lands was silent and clear once again.

Marai cleaned off her sword on the shirt of a dead man. She grabbed a sword from the ground and shoved the hilt into Ruenen's chest. It wasn't a great weapon, but it was certainly the best of the bunch, and better than none at all.

"Perhaps next time you can help," she said, jerking her chin towards the bodies scattered across the road. Ruenen just held the sword limply and stared at her.

"That was *magic*," he said. Marai ignored him as she searched the thieves' pockets. She collected some coins, jewelry, and pieces of dried meat. "That thing you did with your hand. At first I thought it was a trick of the light, but I saw it clearly the second time. You can do *magic*."

Marai stood from her crouch and flashed her violet eyes at him. "Is that a problem?" Her hand went to her sword.

Ruenen shook his head slowly. "You're fae, aren't you?"

Her jaw clenched, teeth ground together. She broke her gaze with Ruenen, and stalked down the road once again before anyone came across the slaughter.

Ruenen rushed forward at her heels. Despite outward appearances and his aggravating personality, Ruenen wasn't stupid. He'd seen things. Marai didn't know how much of the continent he had traveled prior to their meeting in Gainesbury, but it was impossible not to pick up knowledge along the way. She'd spent much of her life trying to hide her true identity from humans, and sometimes slip-ups happened. But this was bigger than a mere simple mistake. She'd gone and shown Ruenen her face *and* her magic.

Normally, she'd kill the mark who saw her, but Ruenen wasn't a mark, and she didn't know what to do with him now. Her hand continued to rest on Dimtoir's hilt, just in case.

"Faeries are the only folk who can use magic," Ruenen continued, speaking more to himself than to her.

Anger rose within Marai's body like a volcano. A tinny ringing began in her ears.

Thora's maternal voice rushed into her head. *"Calm that fury in your heart."*

Marai envisioned Thora's elegant, pointed ears, her sharp features, unnatural ginger eyes. Saw her trying to be a parent when she was but a child, herself.

Breathe... breathe...

Ruenen wasn't wrong—faeries were the only true magical folk that Marai was aware of in The Nine Kingdoms. Werewolves and vampires had been lumped into the same category of magical creatures, despite having no true magic of their own. All of them, though, were deemed dangerous, untrustworthy, by mankind.

The fae had been stubborn. This was once their land. Centuries ago, they had once ruled over mankind. Now humans had control, and the fae had refused to leave. Stubborn. Foolish.

Ruenen jumped in front of Marai to stop her pace. "The last of the fae were killed years ago, when I was a child."

Marai shoved him out of her way and kept walking. He wouldn't give up. Everything with Ruenen was a barrage of questions. She didn't know how to avoid this conversation, but everything inside Marai was beginning to boil. She could feel the heat in her neck, pulse quickening, muscles clenching. White, hot anger pressed against her chest.

"That's how you've been lighting the fire every night, and how you've kept us warm. There's no point in trying to hide it now. I know! I *saw it* with my *own eyes*," Ruenen shouted after her.

Marai whirled around and Ruenen was right behind her. He didn't back away. He looked at her with a challenge on his face, his stance strong and sure. Marai craned her neck and looked up at him fiercely.

"Yes, the fae were massacred years ago. Brutally, savagely murdered by none other than Nevandia's exalted Kings Talen and Vanguarden leading the charge. And bonny King Rayghast from Tacorn made certain to finish the job."

Ruenen blinked, his strong stance melting. He took a step back.

"I've heard that before . . ." Ruenen uttered, his expression shifting into one of discomfort, mortification.

"Did you also hear then that the kings, like so many, were scared of faeries and their magic? Prejudice of something they could not understand or possess. They thought we kidnap human babies, steal, and use our magic to kill innocents." Marai's eyes were narrow slits as she glared at Ruenen. "Lies and ignorance."

"That's horrible." Ruenen's face darkened. "Everyone, human or not, has the ability to be cruel. Astye would be a much better place if people shoved aside their prejudice and fear in favor of kindness."

Marai's anger cooled at the softness of his voice, the shimmer in his eyes, the way he angled his ear towards her as if asking to hear more.

"Most fae were people of nature. They wanted peace," she said. "They wanted to be left alone to grow crops, have families, use magic for simple pleasures. King Rayghast had them all slaughtered, with the help of the other six kingdoms. They banded together to obliterate an *entire race* of people."

Marai remembered the screams. The fire. The sound of swords meeting flesh. The black-armored Tacorn soldiers. The panicked sweat of her father as he carried her away.

"How did you survive?"

Marai looked out into the woods, the final rays of burnished light fading amongst the bare trees. "My father was fae. My mother was human."

Her father's gentle, angular face, his pointed ears. Those beautiful wings painted like stained-glass. Marai had clung to him, and he had clung to her mother's hand, dragging her behind him. Tiny Marai had opened her eyes to catch a glimpse of her mother, curly blonde hair streaming behind her, gasping in fear and exhaustion. Her mother had been branded a traitor, a sympathizer, for marrying a man of the fae. Her own parents had disinherited her. There was no mercy in store for her from Rayghast's soldiers. There'd be none for Marai, even as a child.

"Are you . . . the last?" asked Ruenen, his voice softer still, cutting through the memories. Marai noticed the hint of tenderness.

She thought of Thora's image again. And now Keshel's face graced her mind, as well. Raife and the others . . . if they lived.

Marai considered Ruenen.

"There were more like me. I don't know if they're still alive; it's been a while since I left. We were all young, part-fae children. Fully-fledged faerie children had wings. They were easier to spot, harder to hide. None of them survived the massacre. We, the part-fae, grew up as orphans in a world that would've slit our throats the moment they discovered us. Some of us looked more faerie-like than others. I, thankfully, was born with mostly human characteristics."

Except for her eyes. Marai's violet eyes and magic were the only true tell-tale signs of her parentage. Her father had had violet eyes.

She remembered that night vividly, but little else before then. She'd been three when her parents had stopped running near the edge of the forest. Her father had shoved a heavy blade into Marai's tiny hands. His own sword, the only thing of his left in the world. At the time, Marai could barely hold onto Dimtoir's hilt. Her parents gave her to an older part-fae boy with long dark hair. Keshel. Her father had told Keshel to take her into hiding. She cried goodbye to her parents, screaming in Keshel's thin arms, as she watched her mother blow her a devastated kiss. Her father and those dazzling water-color wings wrapped his arm around her mother and forced her to keep running in the opposite direction.

Marai never knew what became of them, but she could only guess their ending came in the same brutal manner as the others. Keshel took her to a hovel in a tree, into an underground tunnel. There, amongst twenty or so other orphaned faerie children, Marai lived for a year as the rest of her people, parents, and friends were hunted down.

"Is that why you became a fighter-for-hire . . . because you couldn't have a normal life?" Ruenen worried his bottom lip.

"There will never be a happy ending for me or my kind," Marai said in bitterness. "Over the years, the number of part-fae dwindled further. Those who left and tried to live as humans were eventually discovered and executed. The rest of us gave up on the hope of feeling safe. I'd rather be out here with a sword in my hand than hiding in fear. Resigned. Cowering."

She hated being fae. She despised her magic. She hated all of it—a constant reminder of what she'd lost, and the life she could never have.

Ruenen went quiet.

"So what will you do with this valuable information, bard?" she asked, clenching the handle of her sword.

"Nothing," he said, noticing her hand. "Who would I have to tell?"

Marai plowed forward on the trail. She didn't look back to see if he was following, but she heard his slow, steady footsteps on the dirt.

Marai should've held her temper. She cursed inwardly at herself for revealing so much. She could have ignored him. He would've eventually given up his questioning, grown tired of it. But then he would have assumed, let his imagination run wild, created Marai's life story without an ounce of truth to it. If he was going to write a song about her, it might as well be accurate.

When Ruenen had looked at her with that open expression, she couldn't seem to stop herself from speaking. He'd regarded her, not with pity, but as if he'd felt her heartbreak. As if he'd known it himself. Marai had never been so forthcoming in her entire life. Perhaps it was for the memory of her parents and the other lost faerie souls that she'd told him. To give their deaths purpose. Weight.

What does he think about me now?

She glanced backwards once to find him staring at his feet, lost in thought.

Was it all an act? Was Ruenen disgusted? Most people on Astye despised the mere mention of fae. They were scared of people like Marai. Humans considered her a monster, no better than a bloodthirsty werewolf or vampire. Had he feigned sympathy so he could kill her in the middle of the night? Or hand her over to an angry mob in the next town for coin? That was what anyone else would do.

The light disappeared and Marai pulled off the road to make camp. She would've stopped earlier, but the walking helped calm her. As per usual, she and Ruenen set about their normal duties of finding firewood and laying out their blankets. They didn't speak; this routine had become so normal for them that they no longer had to divvy up duties.

Marai settled on a log and let her hand hover over the firewood. Ruenen stared at her hand, waiting for the inevitable magical flame. She obliged, watching his face the entire time. The accursed magic coursed down her arm and out through the tips of her fingers, igniting the dry wood. Ruenen's dark eyes widened in the firelight, but otherwise, he showed no signs of fear or revulsion.

"I know what it's like," he finally said, his voice a gentle flutter of a wing. "What it's like to be hunted for no fault but the blood in your veins."

Marai blinked at him, and that anxiety inside her stomach unknotted. Perhaps no blade would be at her throat tonight after all...

"Yes, well, let's hope neither of us gets captured by King Rayghast as we cross into the Red Lands," she said offhandedly. "He'll show me no mercy."

Ruenen paled as Marai watched his body stiffen. She couldn't blame his reaction to the mention of the King of Tacorn's name.

Rayghast was a terrifying ruler. His name was feared across the continent, and no one doubted that he'd soon overtake Nevandia. He was obsessed with not only surpassing his father King Hershen's legacy, but also Vanguarden of Nevandia. He pushed himself mentally and physically in order to become the fiercest opponent on the battlefield. It was said he had no fear. He'd charge into battle bare-chested, black charcoal and paint striped across his face, bald head, and body. Rayghast led his kingdom with an iron fist and more questionable morals than his father had.

Ruenen quickly grabbed his lute and began to strum, mumbling the same song under his breath that he'd been working on for days. Marai watched as his face contorted when he'd play a chord he didn't approve of. She could almost see him mentally scratch out a lyric by shaking his head.

"Is it finished?" she asked. A chill slithered down her spine—would Ruenen add new verses to his song about the truths he'd just discovered?

"Ah, no... almost," he said slowly, glancing from her to the fire. The clenching in Marai's stomach returned.

"Play me the song," she found herself saying. Ruenen looked up, quite taken aback by the statement.

"You want to hear my song?" he asked skeptically, almost fearfully. He wasn't afraid of her magic, but he was afraid of her hearing his music?

"Well, the song's about me, isn't it?" Marai pulled out a slice of dried meat from her bag. "I believe I have a right to hear it." She bit off a piece and chewed the bland, leathery jerky, waiting.

Ruenen took a deep, bracing breath. His brow furrowed. He then cleared his throat, those nimble fingers hesitating over the strings of his lute. He strummed a chord and began to sing.

We met in the town of Gainesbury.
Dark cloak and the shadows, she wore.
A phantom in black, full of fury.
At first I was scared, then I had to know more.

The thieves on the road were four dozen,
Swarmed us with swords and with knives.
Blade to my throat, I prayed like my cousin,
Please spare me, I have nothing to hide.

Without a word, she unsheathed her sword,
And cut down a villain before me.
Graceful and brutal, I strum this chord
But her face, will you never see.

The Lady Butcher–your dark demise,
Hire her, and she will take her prize.
The Lady Butcher–your greatest fear,
She'll kill you or save you, but only if she is near.

As she listened to the rest of the lyrics, Marai noticed several things.

The first being that Ruenen was definitely making their journey thus far sound more epic than it was. He exaggerated the number of attackers in the fights on the road. He also made it seem as if they'd been in more serious peril than they ever were. The bear was a highlight. He perfectly described its ferocity, a rabid beast, driven by nothing but hunger and blood. Unsurprisingly, he sang little about the endless, tedious hours of walking. However, Marai had to concede that the story he weaved worked well.

The second thing she noticed was that his voice grew in confidence as he sang. The songs she'd heard him play before didn't entirely suit his voice, but this one did. It was in the right key for him. His voice echoed throughout the trees, weaving through the bare branches. Ruenen's tone was clear and strong, almost effortless. Soulful. His playing grew more fervent by the end, and Marai appreciated the quick, flourishing riffs he added in the final chorus.

The last, and most surprising thing she noticed, was that she didn't mind the way he depicted her. The imagery in his lyrics made her sound like a brutal, exotic phantom, and yet also somehow heroic. Not at all the monster she had come to recognize in the mirror. He described how he came to employ her as the Lady Butcher, how he never saw her face, except for her amethyst eyes, a small white lie. How she had fought off small armies and protected him from certain death. It was all a grandiose, gallant, false story.

And he didn't mention magic at all.

It was strange . . . Marai didn't *dislike* it. In fact, if she was being impartial, she thought it was well written and might actually be a success.

But the song was about *her*. Even with all the lies and embellishments, it still revealed too much. Ruenen couldn't play the song in taverns and spread the word about the Lady Butcher. At least, not on this continent. Marai's entire livelihood depended on working in the shadows. Her survival depended on most people not knowing what she was. If anyone else discovered she was fae, she would be killed. Ruenen's acceptance of her parentage was rare. She was shockingly grateful for that, but no one else could ever know.

When Ruenen strummed his final chord, he looked up at her expectantly. His brown eyes brightened, twinkling in the firelight with a child-like buoyancy.

Marai sighed and looked away into the darkness. "It's good."

"It is?" Ruenen repeated, half pleased, half stunned. "You don't think it's too long?"

"No, a good story song should be long," Marai said, not meeting his eyes. "But you cannot play it."

"I don't mention you being fae at all. I didn't mention the magic. I tried not to give away too much."

"It doesn't matter, because once you start performing this song, people will start to watch for me. And then people will realize who and what I am. I'll never be able to operate in the shadows again."

"Is that really the worst thing?" pondered Ruenen, finally garnering Marai's gaze. "Come with me to Andara. You can start over there. Be anyone you want. Get a different kind of work, one where you don't have to be a mercenary. You can do something honorable."

"Honorable? You sound like a monk. What else am I suited for?"

"I'm not sure." Ruenen shrugged. "Maybe in Andara, you won't have to fight anymore. Perhaps there is a simple life out there waiting for you, with a home and a family."

Marai actually laughed out loud. A simple life? A family? That was a vision she dared not fantasize about. It seemed a fairytale.

"Can you see me with a husband and children? Playing house in a small cottage? Cooking and cleaning every day, satisfied with a life of ennui."

Ruenen smiled in a roguish, playful way, those brown eyes twinkling. "No, I suppose not . . . but you may surprise yourself if you welcome other opportunities."

"That's impossible."

Ruenen shrugged again. "I think you should let me sing the song."

Marai rolled her eyes. "Get some sleep. We've lost valuable time. We'll need to cover more ground tomorrow."

She lay down in her blankets and closed her eyes. A minute later, she heard Ruenen set aside his lute and do the same. The lyrics to "The Lady

Butcher," sung in Ruenen's melodious voice, lingered in Marai's ears as she tried to sleep.

Dammit. Now it was stuck there.

"Think you could do that thing where you keep us warm?" Ruenen asked. She looked over at him, lying there beneath his blankets. He shivered, possibly for dramatic effect.

Reluctantly, Marai lifted a hand into the air. The magic coursed through her arm, out through the tips of her fingers. A simple magic. One that took no thought or effort at all. An invisible bubble formed around their campsite, encasing them in the heat of the fire.

Ruenen gave her a half-smile in thanks. Marai turned onto her side and closed her eyes again, taking in the crisp scent of the forest through level breaths.

"Can I stop calling you Butcher?" came the actually-now-decent bard's voice after a moment. "You wanted my real name because you hated calling me Ard. Well, I hate calling you nothing. You're more than nothing."

Marai's heart clenched at those words. Why those four simple words meant so much to her weary soul, she couldn't comprehend. She didn't move. She didn't open her eyes, pretending to be asleep. After a moment, Ruenen must have believed her, because he fell silent and she heard the sound of his deep, even breathing.

She couldn't tell him her name. Ruenen had already grown far too comfortable in her presence . . . acting like some sort of companion. She feared he was growing attached to her. He'd hired Marai to do a job. She intended to succeed; to let him and his song get on that boat to Andara and sail away, never to hear from him again. The sooner they made it to the South, the sooner she could ditch him. Then she could return to the shadows—a place where no one knew her story. Where no one knew her face. She could be a monster yet again.

She wished he wasn't making that plan so difficult . . . because now she wanted it. That life Ruenen spoke of. The promise of freedom that awaited her in Andara.

CHAPTER 6
Ruenen

Ruenen was drenched to the bone as the heavens poured bitter rain down upon them. The road became far too muddy and slippery, squelching beneath their boots. It was miserable weather to travel in. If possible, it was worse than the harsh, snowy weather further north. At least then he had been dry. Now, he could hardly see the road in front of him.

"I think we should stop at the next town," he called up to the Butcher, who was keeping her usual steady pace. She didn't seem bothered by the rain at all. Ruenen was convinced that she was purposefully trying to ignore external feelings ever since he'd discovered she was fae. It felt as if she was trying to prove herself unaffected and detached. The Lady Butcher was mercurial. It left Ruenen feeling quite conflicted about her, always wondering what she was thinking, what she had seen, and where she would go once they parted.

Would she come with him to Andara?

It hadn't bothered him. The magic. That she was fae. In fact, a pivotal understanding had clicked into place. Now he could comprehend why she'd become the Butcher. It was only natural for her to push him away, to stay so rigid, when all she'd known was hatred towards her kind. And it had been the fault of the very kingdoms they were walking towards. Nevandia had begun it, and Tacorn had ended it: the slaughter of her people. How much anger did she hold in her heart at those kingdoms? Was every step towards them painful?

Signs on the road said they were near the large town of Dwalingulf. Ruenen had been there before, after he'd left his blacksmithing apprenticeship. He remembered the exhaustion and hunger, being so full of fear that Ruenen had been paralyzed by it. At the time, he had been so afraid of being spotted that he'd hid in an alleyway and stolen scraps of food that someone had tossed out as garbage. Over time, that terror had loosened its grip, especially the further away he traveled from the Red Lands.

But now they were heading back there, and Ruenen felt that familiar sensation in his body, fingers scratching down his spine, that knew he was nearing danger with every step.

Ruenen caught up to the Lady Butcher. Her face was barely visible under her hood and scarf, loose strands of wet hair hung limp.

"I know you don't want to stop, but it's wretched out here. We're only a half league from Dwalingulf. We could stop, have something to eat, dry off, then start out again once the rain stops . . ."

The Butcher kept walking.

"You can't ignore me every time you disagree with me," he said. The only response was the squelching sound of her boots. Ruenen's frown twitched in irritation.

Time to pull rank.

He halted entirely. Ruenen planted his feet, as best he could, in the slippery mud. "You are under my employ. I demand that we stop in Dwalingulf."

She paused then and turned around, pushing her hood back enough so Ruenen could see her violet eyes. They glared at each other for a moment. Ruenen's whole body grew warmer under her severe gaze. His heartbeat quickened. He stopped feeling the soaking clothes on his skin; he didn't notice the rain anymore. He could, however, feel a pulse in the air around her, as if her magic, as well as her annoyance, were rising.

Ruenen was aware that the Butcher could walk away at any time. He could never match her sword skills to stop her. Not to mention those magical abilities he could scarcely comprehend.

But he wouldn't look away from her. He wouldn't let her win. He wasn't always the spineless fool he pretended to be.

Suddenly, she bowed stiffly at the waist, gesturing to the road behind her. "Lead the way, Master," she said with false courtesy.

Panic and confusion suddenly seized Ruenen. It wasn't that she had given into him. That was a small victory. It wasn't the sarcasm or the mocking way she'd said "master." It was the gesture. The bow. Why had she chosen to bow?

After a strange, tense moment, Ruenen forced his legs to move. He passed her slowly, body straight as a knife's edge. The Butcher's inhuman eyes watched him as she held her performative bow. Ruenen walked in front of her the final half league to Dwalingulf. He could feel her anger fixated on his back.

They walked through the gated entrance to the town. Neither of the guards gave them any notice as they passed; all soaking wet travelers looked the same, like drowned rats. The guards seemed miserable themselves, scowling underneath a small awning that did nothing to keep off the rain.

Dwalingulf was a large, prosperous logging town near the Northern capital of Lirrstrass. Many of the old, two-story stone buildings had been standing for over a century, which was rare on the continent. It was a relatively peaceful city that was highly trafficked on the main road. It was far enough away from the Red Lands that it had escaped much of the never-ending war, but easily connected to other cities and kingdoms. Despite the weather, there were many people about, shrouded in their own capes and hoods. No one looked twice at Ruenen and the Butcher. He felt a morsel of relief at this. If it'd been better weather, more eyes would've been peering, but no one wanted to linger outside for long.

Ruenen led the Butcher through the streets, searching. Then his ears pricked up at a sound—music and laughter. A tavern was nearby. Ruenen turned his head and saw the painted sign above the door: The Birch Tree Ale House. Through the windows he spotted warm fires and several musicians playing on a stage. He looked back at the Butcher. Her hood and scarf fully covered her face once more. She gestured grandly again with that slight bow, egging him on to enter. He didn't need to see her expression to know she was still mocking him, incensed at his earlier challenge. With a huff, he walked inside, and he heard her follow.

The busy tavern felt like heaven. There were dozens of tables and a long bar displaying more than just ale. They also served a rough local Northern drink made from barley and nettles. It tasted like piss—Ruenen had unfortunately drank it before. The inside stone walls had been covered with white lime wash, then painted with ochre floral designs in mustard yellow and brick red. Decorative curtains framed the windows.

The roaring fire immediately soothed Ruenen's wretched bones. He pulled off his cap and shook his mane of brown hair like a dog, accidentally spraying two ladies at a nearby table. They gave him a look of disgust and mortification. He shot them an apologetic grin.

He led the Butcher to a table in the farthest, darkest corner, knowing that would be her preference. He set down his pack and lute, and removed his drenched coat in relief. Ruenen always felt at ease in a tavern. The room smelled of a collection of ale, tobacco, sweat, strong perfume, cooking, and memories.

The Butcher sidled into the seat opposite him, noticeably uncomfortable, her back and arms unyielding. She didn't remove her drenched outer layers, but her eyes were visible again. He tried not to look; he knew the protest he'd find there.

Ruenen waved his hand at the barmaid, who was pretty and round-faced with a dark mole on her cheek. She wore a dress that showed off her ample cleavage.

"You lot look like you could use a warm meal," she said over the boisterous music. The barmaid flashed Ruenen a flirtatious smile as she took in his dripping hair. "And maybe a towel?"

"Don't trouble yourself," Ruenen said and put a hand to his chest. "Your beautiful smile is warming me, heart and soul."

The barmaid giggled and blushed. Ruenen grinned.

"What can I get for you?" she asked with a coy swish of her fair curly hair. It felt good to have a civilized conversation with a woman for a change.

"We'll both have an ale and something warm to eat. Meat if you have it. Bread would be good, too." Ruenen glanced to the Butcher. "Anything else you want to add?"

"No," the Butcher said, with all the charm of a rock.

The barmaid's eyes flickered to the cloaked figure and her smile faded. She nodded, now wary, and exited towards the kitchen. Ruenen glared back at the Butcher.

"Must you be so imposing?"

"Do you want that woman?" the Lady Butcher asked, her voice level.

"I might have had a chance, but you made her uncomfortable," he said with an exasperated huff. "Why do you care?"

"I don't care who you flirt with or bring to your bed. You wanted to stop here. I'm only here by *your* command, but I was under the impression you were in a hurry to board your boat." The Butcher leaned forward onto the table. Ruenen stopped himself from saying anything further. That's what she wanted. She wanted to rile him up. Well, he wasn't going to let her goad him any further. He sat back in his chair and crossed his arms, gazing about the room.

It was a lively atmosphere, and the three musicians playing on the stage were first-rate. One had a drum, another a fiddle, and the third a pipe. They played pieces Ruenen had heard before, but a few he hadn't. All their music was upbeat and kept the tavern patrons happy. His toes tapped along with the beat of the drum as he watched them prance about the stage with confidence and joy.

Those musicians were living *his* dream. Gods, how badly he wanted to be up on that stage with them, entertaining a crowd. But Ruenen was now so used to boos and hisses, he was nervous about performing again. He didn't think he could bear another shameful show.

After a few moments, the girl returned with their ales. She gave Ruenen another coy smile, but the Butcher moved her hand towards the mug of ale so quickly that it gave the barmaid a start. She backed away and left. Ruenen groaned. It'd been several months since he'd been with a woman, and his body ached for that physical connection. The feel of a woman's soft skin. The intimacy.

Looking at the Butcher's severe posture, he knew he wasn't going to fill that void here.

The musicians announced they were taking a brief break and exited the stage. They walked to a corner table near one of the fireplaces and sat down to drink.

"I'll be right back," he told the Butcher. She sniffed her ale, uninterested.

Ruenen stood and approached the musicians at their table. "I enjoyed your music. I'm a musician myself."

"Oh, aye? What do you play?" asked the red haired, female fiddler.

"Lute. And I sing, as well," Ruenen said nervously, but stood erect and held his chin up.

"None of us can carry a tune," laughed the ebony-skinned drummer. His accent was from somewhere Ruenen didn't recognize. Possibly from Ukra, a small nation off the continent. "Not usually a problem since our audiences know all the words most of the time."

"Have a seat, boy," said the oldest, the silver-haired piper, who slid over to make room for Ruenen. He joined the musicians, heart lifting in his chest. "So tell us—what sorts do you play?"

"Oh, I'm no one. I play wherever I can. Mostly known songs, but I've been working on my own tune, though. It's coming along . . ." Ruenen recounted his performances at various smalltime pubs and inns like Gainesbury. The musicians exchanged glances. They all knew how pathetically unprofessional Ruenen sounded. With every pitiable word he uttered, Ruenen's hope sunk deep into his stomach.

"This isn't a kind business, nor is it forgiving," said the drummer. "Took us years to get where we are today, and we're not popular."

"No royalty has asked for our presence in their halls, if you catch our drift," chuckled the merry fiddler. "You'll find your way, lad. Every musician does. Be patient. Keep tryin'. Just gotta get the right audience and the right time."

Ruenen gave her a weak smile.

The barman gestured to the musicians.

"Time's up, lads," said the fiddler, taking one last quick swig of her drink, and the musicians stood from the table, smiling at each other. Ruenen thanked them for their time and conversation.

"Would you care to join us?" asked the flutist and Ruenen's heart leapt.

"R-really?" he managed to stammer out.

The piper smiled. "Ken the song 'The Merry Widow?'"

"Yes, of course!" It was an old bawdy folk song that always brought the house down in taverns. Ruenen had heard it many times, but never performed it himself. He preferred less lewd lyrics, but he was not going to pass up a chance to perform with real musicians. "Give me one moment."

He dashed back to the Lady Butcher at the table. Their food had been delivered, and she was nearly finished with her plate. Ruenen grabbed his lute.

"They asked me to join them. On stage."

The hand holding the fork stilled. "Don't mess it up."

Ruenen shot her a look. "Thanks . . ."

As he turned, he heard a snort of laughter.

Ruenen rushed onto the stage. His palms were sweating, and as he looked out over the crowd, his chest tightened with nerves. No soldiers. It was safe.

Just breathe, he told himself.

"We've got a special guest with us tonight, folks," the flutist said, putting his pipe to his lips. Ruenen glanced back at him. He nodded the go-ahead.

Ruenen strummed the first chord of "The Merry Widow." His voice rang out clear as a bell.

The audience immediately hooted and hollered, recognizing the song. Their enthusiasm gave him confidence, and when the band behind him joined in, Ruenen suddenly lost all his fear. He sang and played in a way he never had before. He strolled across the stage, engaging audience members, meeting their eyes, emulating the famous performers, like that bard he'd seen long ago. The patrons sang joyfully along with him.

He'd never felt this good in all his life. He never wanted this feeling, this magical night to end. He wanted to bottle the feeling and drink from it day after day.

The song finished with an enthusiastic applause. The fiddler clapped Ruenen on the back and the flutist applauded him. Ruenen took a bow, soaking it all up. This was the moment. The turning point.

"That was terrific, mate. You got one o' your own you want to try?" asked the old piper. He backed away and let Ruenen take the stage alone.

One of his own . . .

Ruenen glanced over to the Lady Butcher in the corner. She stared at him like she knew what was coming. He *had* to do it. This was probably his only chance while he was still on Astye soil. This was the moment.

"This song's new. A tale you haven't heard before," he said and the crowd hushed in anticipation, leaning closer towards the stage. "'The Tale of the Lady Butcher.'"

There were murmurs amongst the audience. A few had no doubt heard of her. Ruenen began his song, and as he picked up steam, he bounded across the stage, telling the most incredible story. The audience ate up every single lyric. They ooooed and ahhhed at exactly the right places, laughed a few times. Ruenen had them all in the palm of his hand with every note he plucked. It was heady and intoxicating.

When he finished, the room roared to life. He had never heard such applause. Cheers and shouts of "encore" rang in his ears like a symphony. It was his opus. The three musicians applauded, giving him their congratulations, and asked him to stay on stage and finish out their set for the evening. Ruenen heartily accepted and played the rest of the show with them, singing well known songs, but "The Tale of the Lady Butcher" by far garnered the most applause. Ruenen was walking on air.

At the end of the night, Ruenen returned to his corner table. Everyone wanted to shake his hand. Everyone except for the Lady Butcher. He could hardly see her at the table; she'd sunk so low in her seat. He plopped himself down in the chair and ravenously ate his cold chicken. He didn't care—everything was suddenly glorious and wonderful, even stodgy mashed potatoes.

The Butcher said nothing to him about singing the song. No one in the room had made any connection to her and the pivotal figure in his song. In fact, everyone in the pub was so caught up in the music that they hadn't noticed the shadow in the corner. He knew he'd betrayed her in a way, but Ruenen had hoped she might appreciate his attempts to change her image. She'd said people viewed faeries as evil. Well, the Lady Butcher in his song was portrayed as a reluctant hero . . . possibly much closer to the real-live Butcher than even she believed.

The owner of the tavern approached him, grinning widely. "Excellent, excellent," he boomed in glee. "Been a while since we had such a crowd. That song of yours, the Butcher one . . . great piece. Would you come again tomorrow and play it?"

"You want me to sing it again?" blanched Ruenen.

"I bet you there'll be more people in here tomorrow once the word gets out about you."

"I would . . ." said Ruenen, but then he glanced back to the Lady Butcher. She was glaring icily at him, those violet eyes visible under her cloak. "I must be on my way. I have nowhere to stay tonight."

"Well, that can be easily arranged," the owner said and gestured to someone nearby. "Also, here's your earnings from the night. Only fair, since it's 'cause of you we had such a profitable evening. The other musicians already got their cut." The owner deposited three coins into Ruenen's hand; not a lot, but they were welcome since he and the Butcher were running through money quickly. Supplies were more expensive in the winter when things were scarce.

A bearded man in a knit cap approached and shook Ruenen's hand.

"This here's my brother. He owns the inn right next door," explained the barkeep.

"I got a vacant room for you. Only a coin," said the innkeeper.

"Well, I suppose it wouldn't hurt to stay the night . . . it's raining and I don't fancy sleeping in it."

A foot kicked him from under the table. Ruenen pretended not to feel the pain in his shin as the innkeeper beamed and called over the barmaid. She'd been wiping down a table nearby, but fluttered over to Ruenen with her seductive smile and swish of hair.

"My niece," the innkeeper said. "She'll show you to your room."

"Follow me, then," she said, fluttering her eyelids at him. Ruenen gulped as his hands began to sweat. He handed Marai the bag of coins, hoping to pay her back over time for the money she'd already spent on him. He and the Butcher gathered up their things. At the tavern door, the three musicians waited.

"I cannot thank you enough for your generosity," Ruenen said to them, shaking each of their hands in turn. He'd wiped off his sweaty palms beforehand on his pants. "You have no idea what tonight meant to me."

"You've got talent, lad," said the flutist with a twinkle in his grey eyes. "You need to trust yourself."

Ruenen bid them all goodnight and followed the barmaid outside to the building next door. It was similarly decorated and styled to the tavern. She took him up a flight of stairs, and down to the third room on the right side of the hallway. She then stood in the doorway expectantly.

"Here's your room. Is there anything else you need?" Ruenen felt a rush of heat course through his body as the barmaid looked him up and down. "Or we can go somewhere else . . ."

Her eyes traveled to an open linen closet a few doors down. She tilted her head up and puffed out her lips. He was about to answer, to reach out and perhaps stroke her cheek or a lock of her hair, when the Lady Butcher appeared, and pushed past them both.

"That will be all," she said gruffly, yanking Ruenen inside the room and slamming the door in the girl's face.

Ruenen rounded on her. "Must you be such an unrelenting barbarian?"

The Lady Butcher removed her cloak and scarf, tossing them on a nearby chair. He felt his mouth go dry as he took in her white-blonde hair, so long it was braided all the way down to her lower back. Her pale cheeks were tinted pink in anger. The Butcher speared Ruenen with a look that would have probably made anyone else cower. Her face was tight, eyes gleaming, lips reared back to reveal her teeth.

But Ruenen never recoiled from her.

"You've already made two grave errors here tonight. The first being the song you sang when I explicitly told you not to. The second being that you accepted this room, the coin, and the promise of playing again tomorrow," she scolded, her hair curling loose from its braid. Ruenen briefly thought she would've been beautiful in that moment, if she wasn't so horrifying. "We should be leaving here at once. Eventually, someone will make the connection between me and your song, and they will come after me."

"Don't be so dramatic—"

"Or you—we're getting closer to the Red Lands. You're being hunted. Someone could recognize you. My identity, *and your safety*, are at stake." She stared him down, still and cold as a winter's eve.

"You're right," Ruenen said, throwing up his hands. "I'm aware that I'm reckless, but we're still in Grelta. We haven't seen a single soldier in all the days we've been traveling. I thought that maybe it might be safe here. I assess every room I walk into. I have for years. I know you think I'm a fool, but there is a *purpose* to the way I act."

He clenched his jaw, swallowing the other words he wished to say. He was revealing too much. His mask had slipped. He'd dropped out of character. Could she sense it?

"We'll leave town as soon as I'm finished tomorrow," he said, putting the mask of the foolish bard back in place. "And isn't it nice that we get cheap lodging tonight? We don't have to sleep out in the rain."

The Lady Butcher closed her eyes and let out a frustrated breath. Perhaps she realized there was no point in arguing further. They were in a private room, it was comfortable, and Ruenen suspected that even she could appreciate its warmth and dryness. It was simple and common with a wooden bed big enough for three, two chairs around a small table, and a nightstand.

"You sleep on the floor, then," she snapped at him and threw a blanket and pillow from the bed his way. She quickly removed the weapons from her belt, as well as her leather gloves and thick sweater.

"I beg your pardon, but *I* am the reason we have this comfortable room in the first place." He threw the pillow back at her, which she dodged. "*You* sleep on the floor."

The Butcher threw the pillow once again, harder than before. Ruenen caught it and found himself grinning.

"Stop it," she said, her anger strangely replaced by something else. Her eyes flit to Ruenen's face and then away. Was it discomfort?

"Stop what?"

"Smiling at me that way."

Ruenen could only grin wider. His voice dipped to a husky tone. "Is it bothering you?"

"You look like you're going to attempt something sneaky," the Butcher said and awkwardly removed her long-sleeved black tunic, revealing a thin charcoal-gray undershirt. She didn't look over at him again as she continued to ready for bed.

Ruenen had never seen this much of her before. The Butcher was always entirely covered from head to toe. She seemed so much smaller without the menacing weapons and cloak. Her arms were thin, but Ruenen could see the lean muscle. The clothing she wore was designed to hide her true physical structure. Ruenen knew she would hate that his gaze lingered upon her, when she tried so hard to appear ominous. But she wasn't truly . . . there, standing before him, the Butcher looked like a normal girl. He stopped his eyes from remaining too long on the slight swell of her breasts beneath the undershirt.

Gods, it really *had* been a long time since he'd lain with a woman . . .

He cleared his throat to distract himself. "Have people never smiled in your presence before?"

"No," she said with a bite. "Most people consider me a monster."

Ruenen blinked. The young woman before him now looked nothing like a monster. She was no more than twenty. She hid it well, put up that cold, ruthless exterior, but Ruenen had more than once seen hurt flash across those eyes. He knew a thing or two about masks.

"Do *you* consider yourself a monster?"

"I'm a faerie and a murderer." She said it with such malice that Ruenen realized that maybe the Butcher didn't *want* to be fae.

"I'm sorry . . . that people can't look beyond their own fear and judge you before they know you . . ."

The words slipped out without thought. The Butcher didn't drop his gaze. She held it, latched onto it, and he could feel a tug from deep within himself. A tug that felt both unnatural and also as real as taking a breath.

"I'm not a hero," she said, her voice and face tight, perhaps thinking of the Butcher from Ruenen's song.

He sent her a playful smile, raised an eyebrow. "Neither am I."

She studied him, those eyes raking over every part of him, as if she deciding whether to stay mad, trying to decode his recklessness and humor. Her eyes flashed away eventually, and the room suddenly felt colder. She moved on to unlacing her boots. As she pulled them off, Ruenen heard the clink of something metal fall to the ground.

The Butcher quickly knelt down and plucked a small item up off the floor. She pocketed it instantly.

"What's that?" he asked as he removed his own boots, tattered green jacket, and vest.

"Nothing that concerns you," she retorted, but her icy demeanor was gone.

The Butcher was being secretive, but was already in a foul mood, so he didn't press it. His fingers hesitated on the hem of his shirt when he thought of his proximity to her. For an odd reason, he didn't feel comfortable being that physically revealing in front of her. He'd shared rooms many times before; it was common for inns across Astye to fit several strangers into one room, but there was something very *intimate* about sharing a room with the Butcher. Even though their distance apart was almost the same as how they slept each night in the woods . . . it felt different.

He eventually pulled the shirt over his head, exposing his bare back to the Butcher. He wasn't sure if she saw him or not, but he quickly wrapped himself up in the blanket on the burgundy rug in front of the fireplace hearth. It wasn't *un*comfortable, but he wished she'd given him the bed.

Or shared it with him. Gods, it's not as if he would touch her or anything . . .

Unless she wanted to. He could feel that ache, that need stir inside him, when he thought of stroking a finger down her smooth skin, those wild eyes latching onto his, the feel of her in his arms . . .

Ruenen flushed and blinked rapidly, trying to wipe away those thoughts. He took a few deep breaths.

What in the Unholy Underworld is wrong with me? He hoped his sudden, unexplainable mood shift wasn't noticeable. He chanced a glance in her direction.

The Butcher was cozily lying on her back beneath the sheets, eyes already closed. She looked almost peaceful, the usually serious lines on her face smooth and soft. Ruenen sometimes forgot that she was young. A sleeping princess in a storybook.

"Are you awake?" he asked her, unable to stop himself. Gods, he was acting like a needy adolescent.

The Butcher grunted in response.

"Tell me about magic."

"No."

"Why not?"

"Because discussing magic is unwise."

Damn. He wanted to know what the Butcher was capable of . . .

"Fine. Then tell me about your family."

The Butcher opened her eyes and stared at the ceiling. "Why do you want to know?"

"Because you lost them. I lost mine, too."

The Butcher turned onto her side, her hands rising to cradle her cheek against the pillow.

So young, so lovely, Ruenen found himself thinking.

"I told you. My father was fae. My sword belonged to him, and his father before that."

"And . . . ?"

Her eyes narrowed. "And . . . he was old."

Ruenen frowned. "You're bad at telling stories."

The Butcher shot him a Look. Ruenen smiled, which only made her roll her eyes. He had been gifted the uncanny ability to diffuse situations with charm, and he could tell that it was working on the Butcher.

"My father had lived two centuries before meeting my mother. He was supposed to live for centuries more. I only got him for three years." The Butcher stopped and stared at Ruenen. He rolled onto his side and leaned his chin on the knuckles of his left hand, getting comfortable. The Butcher sighed, recognizing his interest. "My mother was from a human village nearby. I was told it was love at first sight for him." She smirked slightly and shook her head. "I don't believe that's possible. Sounds like magic to me, but no magic can make two people fall in love."

"I thought faeries had mates, someone they're predestined to be with or something."

"Where did you hear that?"

"Oh, just in my travels . . ."

"Some fae found their mate, but it didn't happen often. I was told Lirr and Laimoen are mates. They created the fae with an intrinsic purpose to each seek their perfect match. One faerie's magic called to the other; a tug and a desperate need. I've never seen a mated pair before, but I've heard it was quite powerful when a faerie met its mate for the first time."

"Can a faerie and a human be mates?"

The Butcher raised an eyebrow and Ruenen blushed, cursing his impulsive mouth. "No, it's not something that occurs between different species. My parents weren't mates. But still, my mother gave up everything, her entire life with humans and her family, to be with my father. That was how much she loved him."

"What did her family think of her running off with a faerie male?"

"You're full of questions tonight," she said with a scowl. Ruenen shot her another wide grin. "She knew she'd be banished forever from her people. They were unforgiving. And my mother knew that one day they'd kill my father for stealing her."

Ruenen saw her shudder under the blankets. They had come, he knew. Those wretched humans had taken her parents from her.

"They were both kind. Quick to laugh, I remember. My father would sing songs of the fae, in our native language, me in his lap. My mother would sway along as she cooked, and sang, weaved and embroidered. The walls of our cottage were covered from floor to ceiling in vibrant tapestries." The Butcher took her braided hair in her fingers. "I look a lot like her. Every time I see my face . . . I see her looking right back. But a twisted version. Not pure or kind, like she was."

Perhaps that was yet another reason why the Butcher covered her face.

"I never knew my parents at all," Ruenen said with as much gentleness and sincerity as he could muster. "It's better that I never knew them . . . I never have to miss them."

Ruenen knew who his parents were, of course, from stories others had told him. But they were both long dead, and that fact never hurt him. Memories of them never plagued him. They were as good as strangers.

"On behalf of all humans everywhere, I'm sorry for what my people did to yours," said Ruenen.

"I don't blame you for it," the Butcher said, her lips twitching.

"I know, but I don't want you to think that all humans are horrible."

"I don't think that at all."

Ruenen saw the unusual openness on her face, and he had to ask her again. "Tell me your name. Please."

"Why do you care so much what my name is?" she asked, but it lacked her usual edge.

"We're sharing a room. We spend every moment together. I just . . ." Ruenen paused, unable to properly pinpoint exactly what he was thinking.

She made him feel a hurricane of things, most of which he didn't understand. Questions upon questions bounced around in his head. "I feel like while I don't know you, I *know* you. And it's strange to look at you and think 'Butcher' instead of your name, because 'Lady Butcher' isn't who you are, it's what you do. It's not all you are . . ."

He felt his face go red again and he quickly turned over to look up at the ceiling. The firelight's shadows and flames danced upon the wood. He could sense her hesitancy, a weight in the air. He'd been foolish to try to dig so deep.

And then came her voice, so soft and gentle he wasn't sure it was hers.

"Marai."

All the air left his lungs. His heart slowed.

Neither of them said a word after that. She turned over onto her other side, her back then facing him. All Ruenen could see was her pale blonde hair peeking out of the crisp white sheets.

Marai.

Ruenen felt a tingle all over his body. Her name had power in it. Perhaps it was her fae magic. Or maybe it was that she'd given him something willingly without a fight. It was as if her name had unlocked something inside him and all he could think about was her name, over and over, a siren calling. He fell asleep thinking of that name, and how badly he wanted to reach out and hold her hand.

Ruenen awoke, as usual, to the sound of the Butcher, *Marai,* moving. He opened an eye to see her sweeping her cloak around her shoulders and clasping it at the neck. She glanced at him, wordlessly.

"What time is it?" he grunted, sitting up. Ruenen stretched and yawned lazily.

"Mid-morning," Marai said, now lacing up her boot. She was all stiff again, as if last night's conversation hadn't happened. Ruenen had slept late and Marai hadn't woken him. He hadn't realized how tired he truly was. Days and days of walking would do that to a person.

Once they'd collected their belongings, Marai and Ruenen went back down to the tavern. The room was already packed to the brim with people. Ruenen's jaw dropped as the bar owner rushed over to him, grinning.

"They're all anxiously waiting to hear your famous song." The man was practically skipping.

Word had traveled fast in town. Every seat and table were taken. People stood at the back, craning their necks to get a glimpse of the stage. Ruenen could barely contain the pride he felt.

"Think you can play both now and this evening?" asked the barman, raising hopeful eyebrows.

"Uh . . ." Ruenen looked at Marai, whose face was once again covered. "I can only do the one, I'm afraid. We must be on our way after that."

The owner nodded, but his smile lost some of its joy as he returned behind the bar.

"This is a bad idea," Marai hissed. "I'll be waiting outside." She slipped through the open tavern door as if she hadn't been there at all, a ghost or mirage.

Ruenen felt more confident than the previous night, and took to the stage like he owned it. Now he was up there alone; the three other musicians had left, on to their next show. He started with a few well-known songs before he got to "The Tale of the Lady Butcher." As soon as he started playing, people began to applaud. A few must've returned to hear the song again. At the chorus, voices began to join in with him. The pretty barmaid sang along, bopping her head to the rhythm as she cleaned a table.

Finally, after years of trying, Ruenen could see a future for himself as a performer. He was *finally* being appreciated for the endless hours of work he'd put into his craft. He'd never felt so alive in all his life.

The door to the tavern burst open.

Nevandian soldiers in their golden armor swarmed the room like a hive of bees. People got to their feet, backing away, as the Nevandian soldiers marched in. The barmaid and owner immediately set themselves to work waiting on the soldiers. More patrons, no matter who, meant more money.

Ruenen stopped playing at once and found himself rooted to the spot. His legs wouldn't budge. He was frozen. Why were they here? They were still in Grelta, days away from Nevandian territory!

He felt a tug at his arm, making him jump.

"Come, out the back," whispered Marai, guiding him from the stage and out the back door during the commotion. There were more glistening gold soldiers in the streets, and Marai slithered from alley to alley, grasping Ruenen's wrist firmly.

He was in a haze of horror. For a moment, he thought he'd left his lute behind, but then stupidly saw it was slung over his shoulder. Marai had their other belongings slung on her back. They crept on tip toe, despite the sloppy sounds their feet made as they tread over mud and wet stone.

The entire town was flooded with Nevandian soldiers. Their armor was dirty and dented, as if they'd been on the road a long time. Some of them had gashes and cuts across their faces, a possible sign the troops had fought in a recent skirmish with Tacorn. They'd probably stopped in town to restock and rest, but that didn't mean the people of Dwalingulf trusted them. The other travelers and townspeople kept out of the army's way, hiding behind stalls, doors and windows.

The large stone wall and gate provided the only entrance and exit in Dwalingulf. Ruenen and Marai had to make it out before anyone questioned them. And Marai didn't exactly look unsuspicious.

Ruenen cursed under his breath. Marai had been right—they shouldn't have stayed. They should've left town last night and made camp in the woods off the road.

He pulled his hat lower over his face and popped up the collar of his jacket as Marai continued to guide him swiftly through the town, hiding behind crates and horses. They ducked behind a wagon full of hay.

"You, there," came a masculine voice. Ruenen and Marai froze, backs turned to the soldier in mid-stride. Ruenen didn't dare breathe or move. The footsteps neared.

Had he been recognized?

"Don't say a word," Marai whispered to him. She lowered her hood and spun around. Her lips parted into a dazzling smile. She batted her eyes at the soldier, and twirled a strand of hair in her finger. Even her stance shifted; she jutted her hip out to the side. "Can I help you, sir?"

Ruenen blinked. Marai was the perfect imitation of the flirtatious barmaid.

The soldier's footsteps stalled. "I'm searching for a healer. Can you point me in the right route?"

"I'm afraid I'm not from here, and don't know the town," said Marai, smiling. She acted as naturally as if she flirted with men all the time. "Are you injured?"

"A few of my men need care. We were chased all the way up here by a unit of Tacornian soldiers." The man's voice grew bitter. "Only just got away from them."

"I'm very sorry to hear that, sir," replied Marai.

Ruenen hadn't moved, but watched her from the corner of his eye. He'd been right earlier—Marai only made her facial features harsh because she was always wearing that mask of the Butcher. Currently, her face was bright and alive, pretty and soft. But in her eyes, Ruenen saw that sharpness, that edge that was always there. She could fool the soldier, but never him.

"I appreciate the assistance, miss," said the soldier, who stepped closer. "Perhaps you'd care to join me later at the tavern for a drink . . . unless you are otherwise engaged?"

Marai giggled. *Giggled!* Ruenen blanched.

"No, I'm sorry. My brother and I must be on our way. Best of luck to you."

"Be careful on the road," said the golden soldier. "That Tacornian unit is still out there. I'm sure those brutes wouldn't be gentle with a young lady."

Marai gave him another swift smile, then pulled up her hood and took Ruenen by the wrist again. The soldier walked away, and Marai crept back into the streets.

Ruenen and Marai dodged other travelers at the gate trying to leave, and found themselves back on the road. They needed to put hard distance between themselves and Dwalingulf. Ruenen's heart pounded against his ribcage as his eyes darted from tree to tree, expecting to see black-armored men leap out at any moment. Marai pulled Ruenen off the road and into the woods, but not so deep that they couldn't see the road.

Ruenen hadn't noticed Marai's hand had drifted from his wrist to his own hand. When had that happened? She saw him glance down at their conjoined hands, and she quickly let go, as if burned by his touch. The mask of the Butcher was now firmly back in place.

They walked for miles in silence.

The sick feeling in Ruenen's gut wouldn't leave. That had been far too close. He didn't know what would've happened if the Nevandian soldiers had stopped him for questioning. He wasn't certain he could've compellingly lied to them, and his obvious avoidance might have convinced them he was a Tacorn spy or something else sinister.

"I'm sorry," he said to Marai's back eventually. She walked in front of him again, taking the lead, asserting her control. "I should've listened to you."

"Yes, you should have," she said, but Ruenen was surprised to hear no anger to her tone.

She had done her duty. Marai had gotten him out of harm's way. While he had frozen, she'd remained calm and alert. He didn't know how to thank her.

"Next time you should remember and make better choices," she said softly.

He nodded. The back of his neck burned from embarrassment. He felt ashamed of his bravado. He'd been taken in by the excitement of admiration and celebrity. That wasn't him. It had been so easy to fall for the intoxicating adulation. What was worse, he was also humiliated by his fear, that inability to think or move when those soldiers appeared. He'd been paralyzed. He'd wanted to run, but couldn't. He hadn't felt that weak in a long while.

Thankfully, it didn't seem as if the soldiers were following them. Ruenen hoped that none of them had connected the bard on stage to anyone of importance. All he had to do was make it to the ocean. He was almost halfway there by now. A few more weeks and his feet would leave the soil of this gods-forsaken continent and never return. He'd finally be safe in Andara.

He'd never have to run away again.

CHAPTER 7
Marai

"We're running quite low on funds again," Marai announced one afternoon a few days later. They'd stopped to refill their water canisters at a cool stream further from the road. They'd had to backtrack closer to the Greltan capital city of Lirrstrass due to a blockade. A dam had apparently broken and flooded most of the roads. A setback, for certain, adding more days to the journey.

Marai held the now-light change purse Ruenen had given her at the start in Gainesbury. "If I'd known that I'd be paying for your food, as well, I wouldn't have accepted this commission."

Ruenen grinned at her sheepishly. "I gave you everything I had."

"If we're to make it to the Southern ports, we'll need more money," she said, and put the change back in her bag. Even with the amount Ruenen earned in Dwalingulf, it wouldn't be enough to last until they reached Cleaving Tides, nonetheless book passage for Marai on the ship to Andara.

"Should I perform for tips in the street?" Ruenen asked.

Marai scowled at him. *Does he ever learn?*

"We're not making that mistake again. No, we need to find a new commission."

Ruenen choked on his water. "*We?*"

"I've been paying for you, out of my own pocket, so the least you can do is help me." She didn't *want* to bring Ruenen further into her world, but she didn't have other options.

"Fine, but where are we going to find someone who needs to have someone . . . taken care of?" asked Ruenen, dropping his volume. Marai smirked.

"I know a place near here," was all she said before setting out. Ruenen followed her, feet crunching in the dirt. The weather was fairer here; winter was finally releasing its arctic fist. The Middle Kingdoms had milder winters than the North, anyways. It was probably still snowing up in the White Ridge Mountains. Marai was glad she could now be outdoors without worrying about frostbite.

The town where she was taking Ruenen wasn't labeled on any map. It was tucked away in the forest, a world unto itself. It had no formal name, but it went by many—the Nest, Vice, and the Den were just a few. Marai called it Iniquity. It was the place where people like her, those who resided and worked in the shadows, went to conduct their business and to live freely, without the constricting rules of a kingdom. She tried not to linger there for long.

Iniquity was a day's walk from their location at the stream. Marai had been there often and knew the slight clues that guided Iniquity's patrons, those who already knew of its existence: the hollowed-out tree, the murky pond, the black, dead gnarly bush. These things were unnoticeable to the normal eye, but each hint brought her directly to the doorstep of Iniquity.

The forest gave way to a shrouded village with ramshackle buildings. The trees overhead kept this place in constant shadow, even when the sun was high, like it was now. All the shops leaned precariously, as if a slight breeze might knock them over at any moment.

"Don't look at or speak to anyone," Marai said out of the corner of her mouth. She'd already covered herself with the cloak and scarf. Before arriving in town, she'd instructed Ruenen to pull his hat down as far as possible and pop up his jacket collar again. It hid portions of his face, but not enough.

The town purposefully gave off a "don't come here" vibe to ward off any unsuspecting travelers. No one cared about cleanliness in Iniquity. There was no street or path; everything was dirt and earth. Bones and garbage lined the walkways. The shop windows were all smudged, dirty, and no signs hung above their doors. However, there were no beggars in Iniquity. There was little charity in a place such as this; beggars had better success in larger, more common cities. Here, they were more likely to be eaten than fed.

She felt a yank of agitation in her stomach at the thought of bringing Ruenen to Iniquity. He seemed completely out of place, with his jaunty gate, sun-kissed skin and bright smile. His eyes widened as he took in the sights and sounds of Iniquity, nearly stumbling into a pile of dead rats. Marai heard a snigger from a window somewhere.

Ruenen grew paler as they passed an eyeless and noseless man eating something that looked like a human arm outside a butcher's shop. The door was wide open, and Marai caught a strong whiff of blood and decay from within. They were met by the stares of an old stooped crone, and two shady men smoking something quite pungent outside the apothecary.

"Is that a vampire?" Ruenen gulped as they walked past a pale, red-eyed man in a shin-length silk robe. A jade pendant hung from his tasseled sash. He flashed a set of fangs at Ruenen in a challenge before he bit into the neck of a young woman dressed in only a low-cut, sheer slip. She moaned with desire.

"I told you not to look at anyone," Marai scolded and grabbed Ruenen's arm to pull him closer. She didn't want him wandering off anywhere.

"Do you come here often?" whispered Ruenen, leaning towards her ear. He'd put on his most menacing glower, but it looked wrong on his face. He wasn't made for this type of darkness.

"Only when necessary," Marai said, "when I'm in need of quick coin. I can always get a commission here."

She'd been to Iniquity many times over the past four years. Whenever she was in the area, she'd stop by to collect a commission. Sometimes she was lucky and her mark would be local, allowing her to get a second or third commission in one visit. Other times, she was sent across Astye on journeys that would take weeks to complete. She'd then have to return to Iniquity to collect the other half of her payment.

"How come no one regulates this place? Doesn't the King of Grelta care that there's a whole town of criminals and vampires in his realm?"

Marai snorted under her breath. "Because it would sprout up again somewhere else. People like me . . . we always find ways to do our business. It's easier for the King to let this one town continue its dealings than for us to spread out across Grelta, infiltrating other villages."

"So no one here ever gets caught?"

"Not by the crown. Folk in the shadows circulate everywhere. No one is safe here."

The two brown-skinned men with smoking pipes sauntered past in deep discussion, their Western accents thick. "I heard he was cursed by a faerie."

"Good, the bastard had it coming. Rayghast's the worst of them all, invading Varana that way. Now he's sending troops into Grelta, stirring up trouble." The man took a long drag of his pipe, then blew out blue smoke. "What was the curse?"

"Not sure, but I bet that's why he's so hell-bent on taking over Nevandia," said the other, and they passed out of earshot.

"How are we going to get a commission?" Ruenen asked Marai, completely unaware of the conversation Marai had eavesdropped into. Her ears were used to picking up scraps of news wherever she was.

"They know who I am. If they want something from me, they'll come."

Marai quickly gazed over roughly-drawn sketches on wanted posters. They were displayed in windows so filthy, she couldn't see inside the buildings. None of the posters were right for the commission, as they all would take her to other locations on Astye. She was hoping to find something local and quick.

At the end of the street sat the artifacts dealer's establishment. In truth, it was one of the few places on the continent that still housed magical items and books. Marai had never stepped foot inside before. It always seemed so taboo. She'd thought about it many times, but never wanted to draw attention to herself. On that day, however, she found her pace slowing as she neared the door. She'd be leaving Astye soon for Andara. This might be her only chance . . .

Her feet stepped over the threshold and into the shop.

The slanted room was covered in floor-to-ceiling shelving. Books, papers, and objects filled in every shelf, every space within the cramped, dark shop. A layer of dust covered everything. A desk sat against the wall opposite the door where a middle-aged woman shuffled through papers. She looked up over her spectacles when Marai and Ruenen entered.

"Buying or selling?" she asked, a slick smile appearing on her soot-smudged face.

"What do you know about a bloodstone ring?" questioned Marai, curtly. At her side, Ruenen gave her a quizzical look.

The woman crossed her arms. "There are many bloodstone rings out there. They may be rare to find on the continent, but other countries, such as Casamere, mine them. Do you have a ring with you?"

"No."

The woman frowned. "Then there's nothing I can help you with."

"Do you know of any powerful bloodstone rings?" Marai pressed. The woman raised an eyebrow.

"Bloodstones are the gems of courage and strength. Many great warriors wear them on the battlefield. They are known to bring out the inner powers of its bearers," the woman said. "But a *truly* powerful bloodstone ring? There's only one I know that ever existed, and no one has seen it for centuries. I'm not sure what powers it possessed. It was a dark ring, cursed for a dark purpose."

A chill ran down Marai's spine. She tossed the woman a coin and stalked out of the building.

"What was that about?" asked Ruenen, walking closely by her side, his arm grazing hers, making her breath catch for a moment.

Marai led him to the center of the village—a stone with a twisted, chaotic symbol of a dagger etched into it, honoring the God of Destruction, Laimoen.

"Focus on the task at hand," she said in a hushed tone.

"You never ask anyone anything. You avoid places and people at all costs, yet you voluntarily entered that shop and asked about a ring. Why?" His tone was serious, challenging. Marai's stomach did a back-flip. In those rare moments when he stopped acting like a foolish bard and revealed the stronger version of himself, Marai couldn't help but feel a tiny thrill quicken her pulse.

"It has nothing at all to do with you," she said, shutting down his challenge. Ruenen scowled, but pressed her no further.

They stood at the stone for a while. Marai watched every person who passed from beneath her cloak, but none of them glanced her way. Not today.

After a long period of time, a man approached them. He was hunched, but moved swiftly, face covered by a white mask. A grey cloak billowed around him.

"The Lady Butcher?" he asked, although he knew the answer. She didn't look like other fighters-for-hire. As far as she knew, she was the only female in the industry. There was no mistaking her in Iniquity. Marai nodded. The eyes beneath the mask flickered over to Ruenen.

"And companion," Marai said. The eyes flicked back to her. A gloved hand reached out from under the cloak and handed Marai a folded piece of paper. Marai quickly read it and groaned internally.

Nosficio, the vampire. A regular here in Iniquity, but an unfortunate mark. Deadly.

She tore the paper into shreds and tossed them into the muddy puddle next to her. "In what manner?"

"Just a message." The masked man reached into his cloak once again and pulled out a pouch of coins. "Half now, and the remainder when the job's done."

Marai regarded the high quality of the man's cloak and boots. The paper had been thick, and the name had been scrawled in real ink. He was sent by someone with wealth. "I require double," said Marai, and the man flinched.

"Double?"

"As you can see, there are two of us," said Marai, and the eyes beneath the mask glanced at Ruenen again. Ruenen glared at the hunched man, straightening taller to tower over him. Marai's mouth twitched into a smirk. The masked man reached into his cloak and reluctantly pulled out another pouch of coins. He turned and walked away down the alley. Marai pocketed the money.

"Who's Nosficio?" Ruenen asked in her ear, his breath a warm breeze through the fabric of her cloak. The sensation infuriatingly heated Marai's cheeks.

Walls up, storm cloud.

"Our mark."

Marai knew who Nosficio was. He was the most notorious vampire in Iniquity, possibly in the entire Nine Kingdoms. He was known for draining the bodies of attractive young men and women, nobles and peasants, leaving them scattered across the land. He wasn't at all secretive like most vampires. She'd been in a tavern once right after he'd taken a victim in the city of Fensmuir. It had been a horrific sight to see the poor boy's mangled body, his skin grayish white from the lack of blood. Marai was inclined to do more than give the vampire a message . . .

Nosficio was old. Almost as old as records go back. Perhaps, even, one of the first vampires. People believed vampires were created by Laimoen, himself, pure death and chaos, creatures of darkness. Marai believed it. She'd never met a vampire who could control their bloodlust. She'd been commissioned to kill one once before. It hadn't been easy, and that vampire had been younger than Nosficio.

"What does he mean by 'a message?'" asked Ruenen.

"Our employer doesn't wish Nosficio to be killed. We're just supposed to harm him enough so he understands to be cautious from now on. Unless things go wrong, of course."

Then she'd have to kill the vampire and risk not receiving the second half of the payment.

Marai skulked to where the other vampire stood near the entrance path of Iniquity. He'd finished drinking from the young woman and was now licking his lips, counting coins in his palm. He wasn't Nosficio, but equally as dangerous.

"Where is Nosficio?" she asked him. The vampire handed the coins to the woman, and she returned inside the pleasure house. Ruenen shifted awkwardly as the vampire's eyes slid from Marai to his.

"Uh oh, is he finally getting punished for his wrongdoings?" asked the vampire, his long dark hair a shiny curtain of ebony. "Not sure you two are enough to stop him." Vampires were loners, but they did generally have an idea where others of their kind were. There were so few of them left on Astye, Marai assumed they were hyper-aware of each other. She also knew they didn't invade each other's territories, but Iniquity was free-game. "You're in luck. He's inside, doing what he does best."

The vampire disappeared in a flash of dark wind.

Marai stepped inside the building, Ruenen at her heels. The room smelled of sex and perfume. It was a heady scent that made Marai cringe, but Ruenen didn't seem to mind. His expression glazed over when he saw several people engaging in intimate acts in the middle of the room.

Nosficio wouldn't be out in the open. He would've secured a private room. He liked his notoriety, but he preferred to do his work in solitude.

Marai climbed the stairs, half-dragging Ruenen from the orgy. They crept down the hall, Marai putting her ear to every door. She heard flirtatious laughs, and the grunts of those in the thralls of consensual enjoyment. None were Nosficio. The screams inside would be from pain, not pleasure.

A door opened. Marai shoved Ruenen against the wall, placing her hands upon his chest. His eyes opened wide and his breath hitched. Slowly, he placed his hands on Marai's hips and pressed his forehead to hers, against the hood of her cloak.

His hands, though... Marai tried to relax, to not notice the feel of those hands on her waist, as two drunk whores and a man stumbled out of the room, giggling.

"All yours," said an olive-skinned prostitute as she passed Marai and Ruenen. None of them glanced their way.

Once the lovers were clumsily walking down the stairs, Marai jolted back from Ruenen. He stood against the wall, cheeks flushed with color. His eyes had darkened a little and his teeth bit his lower lip. A strange rush stirred through Marai when she saw those teeth. She turned away from him and kept prowling the hallway.

Walls up. Walls up.

A high-pitched scream ruptured the air. Marai ran to a door at the end of the hall and kicked it open.

Nosficio, in finely tailored silver and black, held a partially-clothed prostitute in his arms. Marai spied puncture marks on her neck, wrist, and left breast. She was pale and weak, but not dead yet. He hadn't fully drained her.

Marai unsheathed her sword as Ruenen barreled in behind her.

"The Lady Butcher," crooned Nosficio, his voice like lethal velvet, old and reserved. His crimson eyes took in the sight of her. "I knew we'd eventually meet. You're a legend, and so am I." His tongue stroked across his teeth as those ancient eyes met Ruenen's. "Who's the strapping gentleman with you?"

Marai didn't respond. She twirled her sword by the handle, stepping forward. Nosficio dropped the woman to the floor as he would a sack of grain. He straightened up, adjusting his tunic. His charcoal dreadlocks were long, longer than Marai's braid, and pulled back tightly by a ribbon. His skin wasn't as pale as other vampires, as if he was once from the darker-hued kingdoms in the South or West before he'd been turned.

"I admit that I've always wanted to meet you: a female assassin who's never missed her target. Are you here to kill me? Who sent you, I wonder? My list of enemies is longer than even yours," he said, showing off those long fangs in a sick grimace. He could have been considered handsome if his cheeks hadn't been so hollow, skin so grey it was almost blue, and red eyes blazing, full of danger. He eyed Marai like a prized pet, something he desperately wanted.

Nosficio moved so fast Marai barely had time to dodge those long, perilous nails of his. Talons, nearly. Vampires were stronger and faster once they'd fed, and were difficult to catch. Marai jumped and danced from his swipes, taking a swing of her own, which missed. Nosficio disappeared like a mirage, and then emerged behind Marai.

She turned in time to see Ruenen hurl a wooden chair at Nosficio's back. The vampire was within inches of Marai's neck and halted once the chair struck him, shattering to the floor. Marai took his moment of hesitation and swung with her blade. The vampire skittered away to her front, grabbing her throat with those spindly fingers. He pushed her against the wall.

"Tell that hunchback that I don't answer to the Queen of Grelta," he snarled, fangs flashing. Marai caught a whiff of blood on his breath.

So the rumors were true. Marai had heard in Gainesbury that Nosficio had an affair with Queen Nieve of the North.

Nosficio's grip on her throat tightened, cutting off Marai's airflow. He lifted her up from the floor against the wall, but Marai's knee slammed into his groin, and he dropped her with a yowl. He dodged her next swing, and the next, disappearing with unheard of speed. She tried to stop him with a pulse of magic, but he evaded that, too.

Once again, he had her pinned against the wall, teeth at her exposed neck ...

Then a stake jammed through his back.

Nosficio shrieked as he stared down at the bloody broken chair leg that now stuck out from his stomach. Marai glanced around the vampire to see Ruenen, face ferocious, eyes dark. The vampire collapsed. The injury wouldn't kill him; only a stake to the heart or decapitation could undo a vampire.

"Get the message?" Ruenen snapped down at the writhing vampire.

Shock rattled through Marai at Ruenen's fiery calmness, but she knew the chair leg wasn't enough. She quickly knelt next to Nosficio and pulled her knife from her boot. She stuck the blade in his mouth and yanked out one of his fangs. The vampire roared as blood gushed from his mouth.

"*Fuck you*," Nosficio hissed at Ruenen, who seemed appallingly unperturbed by the whole ordeal. He glared down at Nosficio as if he had done this a thousand times. Like he, too, had the callous heart of a mercenary.

Marai ripped the other fang from his mouth. Nosficio screamed and carried on for a moment more before he went still. His crimson eyes burned with fury at Marai and Ruenen, but he settled his breathing and glared at them. "Message received."

Marai tossed the two fangs onto his chest. They'd grow back eventually, but until then, the vampire couldn't feed. Served him right. Ruenen knelt next to the woman on the floor, fingers at her pulse.

"She's alive, but barely." He lifted her up into his arms. Marai's thoughts snagged on the strength of his arms, admiring the effortless way he'd lifted the woman. Marai and Ruenen moved to the doorway.

"You two make a formidable team," Nosficio said, sitting up with a wince. He yanked the bloody chair leg from his gut with a grunt and tossed it aside. Those ancient red eyes burned with curiosity at Marai. "Does the mortal know that your hands are as bloody as mine?" Marai stiffened. The vampire leered, showing off his bloody mouth. "Despite your complete desecration of my body . . . I can admire the work of someone as skilled as I am. I hope we meet again to continue this, Butcher. You are . . ." his nostrils flared, "intriguing."

Marai left the room. She skulked out of the whorehouse and into the street. Ruenen deposited the unconscious woman with the madam of the establishment, then silently came to Marai's side. The hunchback was there waiting for them at the stone. He said not a word as he passed over the remaining payment, and then disappeared with the mist in the alley, most likely on his way back to the Queen of Grelta. The Glacial Palace in Lirrstrass wasn't far away. Marai tucked the money away from the prying eyes of the duo of hooded figures nearby. She marched down the street with Ruenen, who hadn't dropped that fierce expression.

Once out of the limits of Iniquity, Ruenen finally let out a laugh. "Now, *that* is something I never want to do again. Remind me never to get on a vampire's bad side."

"I think you already are," Marai reminded him and removed her hood. Her pockets now jingled jovially with coin, and Marai also felt intense relief. Nosficio was far easier of a mark than she originally thought, and Ruenen managed to not get himself killed. In fact, he'd stayed calm and fought against Nosficio without fear. Perhaps the primordial vampire had gone easy on them . . . or it had something to do with who had *sent* Marai.

Queen Nieve of Grelta. She was the only woman Nosficio had ever failed to kill. Many said that the Queen of Grelta was a force, herself. Cunning and daring. A woman interested in . . . different experiences. Someone who wouldn't balk at sexual relations with a vampire. It was a story that piqued Marai's curiosity.

Whatever the reason, they now had plenty of coin to make it to the Southern coast and Andara.

"I don't care, by the way," Ruenen suddenly said, coming to Marai's side. His eyes had softened back to normal, glistening in the low afternoon sun. "What Nosficio said, about you . . . I'm aware of the things you've done, and I can imagine the rest. But you're not him, Marai. I can *see* you. You're not a monster."

Marai pursed her lips, her chest tightened. She was unsure how to react. Those words seemed small and simple, but they weaved through the garbage deep within her soul and glowed as threads of burning light. She wasn't like Nosficio . . . she didn't kill for pleasure. It had always been a means of survival. Even with her magic, she only used it when absolutely necessary to avoid detection. She'd be captured and killed if anyone discovered her lineage. But to hear from Ruenen that he saw her, underneath all the blood and gore . . . well, his words meant more than he realized.

A storm cloud, yes. A creature of rolling thunder and flashing lightning. But perhaps not a monster . . .

Marai let out her breath and met his gaze. "You were good in there," she told him and Ruenen beamed. His annoyingly endearing dimples on full display. "Come, let's get back to the road."

"That's the best compliment I've ever received," he mused.

Marai snorted.

CHAPTER 8
Ruenen

Who knew stabbing a vampire could feel so empowering?

Ruenen didn't often get chances to fight anyone, to be bold and daring. Usually, he was forced to shy away from confrontation, to blend in. Adrenaline had rushed through his veins as he watched the vampire pin Marai's small body to the wall. She'd struggled against his heightened strength and speed. Marai could have *died*. Ruenen had shoved aside his usual role of the lily-livered bard and donned a new mask. In truth, it hadn't felt like a mask at all. Pure fear for Marai and fury at Nosficio blinded him to anything but action. Even now, three days later, Ruenen still felt the lingering effects in his body. His fingers itched to relive his encounter with Nosficio the vampire, so naturally, he wrote a song about it. Ruenen entitled the piece "Taste of Death."

"Good name," Marai said, causing Ruenen to sit taller on his log. Compliments from her always brought heat to the back of his neck.

A shift hadn't only occurred within Ruenen. Marai now regarded him with more interest than before, shooting him side-eyed, curious glances as they walked onwards. The impressed look on her face when he'd thrust the chair leg through Nosficio's gut ... Ruenen had surprised her, and nothing ever shook the Lady Butcher. His chest swelled in the knowledge that *he* had.

Each night when they made camp, Ruenen pulled out his lute and strummed away, making up lyrics on the spot. Something about his performance in Dwalingulf and the events at Iniquity had released a flood gate of motivation for him. He wrote a song about their travels called "Road to the Red Lands" in the span of one night, but Ruenen never mentioned Marai. She didn't seem to mind his music anymore, or perhaps she'd given up. He often caught her ear angled towards him, listening in. There was yet another he was working on, a ballad which he hummed often during their walking.

"Sometimes a song hits you, so clearly, that it bursts out of your throat," he explained to Marai one night after making camp. "I can barely contain the music inside of me now."

They were only a day from The Pass, the main road that split down the center of the Middle Kingdoms. The next leg of the journey would be the most perilous. Ruenen's nerves grew with each curve in the road and wooden, arrowed signs pointing to the Red Lands. He focused his anxious energy on the strings of his lute. Marai's attention honed in on the bouncing of his knees.

"Why Andara?" she asked suddenly, stalling Ruenen's hand on the courses. Marai lanced him with the steady, intense gaze Ruenen had grown accustomed to. "You could catch a boat to Ukra or Listan from the Greltan ports, or even Casamere from Ehle. Why go all the way to Cleaving Tides to travel to a country people know very little about?"

Ruenen set aside his lute, aware that she was trying to distract him from his jitters. "That's the whole point. Andara's so far away and difficult to get to that no one will bother coming after me."

"Even though you know nothing about what awaits you when you get there?" pressed Marai, raising an eyebrow. "It could be a country of cannibals, or inhabited only by giant slugs."

He shot her a withering look. "I know *some* things, Sassafras. Sailors and tradesmen aren't allowed past the ports. Apparently, there's some kind of invisible wall preventing people from stepping further on land, but if you intend to stay on Andara, they'll let you through."

Marai's eyes widened. "An invisible wall? Do you mean a shield?"

Ruenen nodded once. "That's why people think faeries fled to Andara: evidence of magic."

He watched her face brighten with interest; the usual harshness completely gone. Marai even leaned closer to him. "Who told you all this? The captain of your ship?"

"He said he'd only been there once before a few years ago. While the captain couldn't see any magic, he said he could *feel* it in the air all around him. But it didn't seem threatening to him. He thought the shield served as protection from outsiders. The people he met there at the harbor were friendly enough."

"How did you meet this accomplished captain, anyways?" Marai's tone was casual, as if feigning interest, but Ruenen knew otherwise. This was the most she'd ever questioned him. The mysterious land of Andara had also trapped her within its alluring net.

"Two months ago, not long before I met you, I was at a tavern in Lirrstrass. I got to speaking with this captain who was doing business in town. I told him I had an interest in exploring abroad, and he said he'd been basically everywhere on charted maps. I asked him, 'what's the farthest place you've ever sailed to?' And he said 'Andara.'" Ruenen had wondered at the time how a man so young as the captain, in his late twenties, had already accomplished a feat most men twice his age wouldn't have dared. He'd been instantly impressed with the young captain, who had an air of adventure and intelligence mixed with his natural charisma. "He told me that the voyage nearly sunk his boat. The waters were so rough, storms so violent, that he almost turned back multiple times, but the captain said he enjoyed a challenge, so he pushed on.

"From the harbor, Andara looks like any other port you might find on Astye, but with far fewer boats. He said he recognized a ship from

Yehzig, Andara's closest trade ally. A dozen men monitored the port, but the captain said they didn't seem to have any weapons. A few of them, he noted, had really distinct, unnatural eyes that seemed to glow."

Marai's own pinned Ruenen in place as she leaned even further towards him slightly, gobbling up the story.

"The captain asked one of the dock workers what lay beyond the shield, and he replied 'secrets.' The captain swore he heard two workers whispering about a faerie queen."

Marai sat upright on her rock, whole body stiffening. "That's impossible."

"Why?"

"All fae royalty died a few centuries ago during the rebellions."

"Well, maybe some of them escaped to Andara. Or maybe there were fae already there to begin with. I don't know anything about faerie queens, but that seemed a fairly large secret to hide in Andara."

"Were you never told the stories of the ancient fae?" asked Marai.

"Lousy human bard, remember?" Ruenen quipped, pointing a finger at himself.

"My apologies, I forgot," Marai said, the traces of a smile brimming on her lips. "Long ago, when fae ruled this continent, they lived mostly in the North, East, and Middle Kingdoms, where forests and greenery were plentiful. In the old tales, Lirr created beings of both darkness and light, always striving for balance. She plucked a tooth from Laimoen's mouth and created vampires. From the sinew of his forearm—werewolves. Humans were birthed from a piece of Lirr's own heart. But the fae were said to have been created by Lirr as a mirror image of herself; powerful beings who were one with nature. She buried a bright kernel of her magic into the earth, and so faeries were born."

As a child, Ruenen had heard a very different creation myth. Humans believed magical folk were created by Lirr as punishment on the world. That she'd turned humans into creatures of darkness, chastising them for their wrongdoings. Vampires were eternally damned to drink nothing but blood. Werewolves transformed gruesomely at each full moon. The fae were always considered the most corrupt and twisted of all, because the dark magical gifts in their blood urged them to torture humans. Ruenen had never known what to believe as a boy, but now, hearing Marai's story, knowing her the way he did, he felt more inclined to believe the fae version. It was far more poetic, and less fire-and-brimstone than the human tale. Lirr was not a vengeful goddess. She was pure light and love.

Marai continued. "The ancient fae were masters of elemental magic, controlling land, air, water, *and* fire. The faerie queens were the most powerful, though. Something about female fertility attracted more magic, I was told. A gift from Lirr: the ability to create."

"And they all died during the rebellions?" asked Ruenen, awkwardly scratching at his neck. He knew that human slaves had risen up and vanquished the fae. The roots of prejudice towards faeries grew deep on the continent. It pained him to think that if Marai hadn't been so lucky, she might have been murdered like her parents.

"By the time I was born, the royal lines had been eradicated," Marai said. "Their power is all but gone, diminished by centuries of breeding with humans to survive. The original fae, those of pure blood, not even from royal birth, could live for hundreds of years. They all perished from old age or war years ago. My father was one of the few left of pure fae blood."

Ruenen bit his lower lip. He'd seen Marai call forth a wind and light a fire with a snap of her fingers. That simple magic had amazed him, but thinking of the ancient faerie queens and the goddess-like power that they'd commanded left Ruenen feeling a little queasy. If a faerie queen still lived on Andara, what sort of country would it be? Did she keep humans as slaves? Or did she cohabitate with them on Andara in peace? Was magic celebrated there? Judging by Marai's furrowed brow, she was wondering the same things.

"Based on that one conversation, you decided to go to Andara?" she asked.

"I asked the captain if he ever planned to go back, and he said he would for the right price. I was so desperate to leave that I offered what I could for passage, nearly all of my savings, and he accepted."

"Generous of him," Marai said wryly. "Why not sail out of Grelta? You were both there already, and it's a shorter distance to Andara."

"You've seen the Northern Sea. It's nearly impossible to get a ship close enough to land before it's thrown against the rocks and sunk. The captain's ship is docked in Cleaving Tides, along with his whole crew. He still had some business in Grelta, but said I should meet him there in a few weeks' time."

"How do you know he won't just take your money and abandon you?"

Ruenen smiled sheepishly. "I don't. He seemed like a good, honest man, with an audacious spirit. I talked to him for hours, and he even bought me a drink. I pray the ship will be there when we arrive. I must keep my optimism. I can't give in to doubt or fear. All I can do is hope, and rely on the kindness of strangers."

Marai scowled, and searched within her pack, yanking out her blankets. "For someone on the run, you're far too trusting."

"And reckless and cowardly," he reminded her, so used to her usual scoldings. Ruenen caught a glimpse of her smile as she lay down for bed amongst dead leaves and dry moss.

"No, not cowardly," she said, and drew the threadbare blankets over her head. Ruenen's heart lurched knowing that she'd seen through his mask. "Goodnight, Bard."

He smiled into the darkness, staring at her back and the shape of her petite form beneath the blankets. "Goodnight, Butcher."

CHAPTER 9
Marai

The Pass neared.

They'd purposefully avoided the other towns on the road since Iniquity, in case the Tacornian and Nevandian units were still out there. They hadn't spoken about Ruenen's reaction to the Nevandian soldiers back in Dwalingulf, but Marai had seen the way the color had drained from his face. She'd almost tasted the fear and sweat dripping off of him. And yet, he'd taken down a homicidal vampire without any hesitation, with nothing more than a chair. He'd appeared confident and fearless in that room. Ruenen was turning into quite the paradox.

It left Marai wondering—which side of Ruenen was real?

The travelers on the road lessened again, and those they did see were heavily armed and skittish. No one made eye contact, including Ruenen. People kept their heads bowed and moved swiftly. Some folk wore the black and red crossed-sword emblem of Tacorn pinned to their clothing, showing off their allegiance as an added protection.

Marai didn't need a sign to notice the shift in atmosphere. Everything, including the forest itself, seemed on heightened alert. On edge. A tension lingered in the air, on the face of every person they passed, and Ruenen absorbed it. He grew quieter with every step. He even stopped humming.

Marai and Ruenen had formally entered the Red Lands.

The northern borders of Tacorn and Nevandia were hilly, similar to Grelta, but the terrain was less wild, with a clearer, flatter road. Soldiers from both sides were known to patrol town to town, looking for someone to scrap with. The number of soldiers would only grow from here.

Another new concern in Marai's mind was Nosficio. Although they were merely the messengers, there was always a chance the vampire wanted revenge for what happened in Iniquity, but Nosficio's ire would more likely be aimed at the Queen of Grelta. Marai hoped Nieve was prepared. Normal people shouldn't cross a vampire, especially one as ancient and deadly as Nosficio.

Marai and Ruenen passed a set of three rickety stalls on the Nevandian side of the road. The merchants sold withered vegetables and tattered fabric. Color seemed to have been leached away on the Nevandian side. Everything was hued in subdued browns and grays, whereas on the Tacornian side, green was already budding in the trees. Marai could see the strain on the dirty faces of the Nevandian merchants and their bony children. Their shoulders were hunched and eyes darted about, flinching at the loudest sounds. Ruenen stared at them for a moment and quickly looked away, face pained.

There was something else Marai began to notice. A darkness, an eerie sensation followed her as soon as they'd entered the Middle Kingdoms. She felt it in the ground beneath her feet, in the air she breathed. Twice, she thought she saw a shadow in the trees; an inhuman shape, horns, claws, a strange growl and screech that didn't come from any animal she'd ever heard. Maybe she was imagining, but it left her uneasy.

Something was wrong with this land. It made her restless, even in sleep.

That first night in the Red Lands forest, Marai had one of her all-consuming nightmares. Hands, strong and persistent, demanding, pushing, tearing, pinning, taking. This time, the hands wore a bloodstone ring, its spots of red like blood on bed sheets. Then the dream shifted, and a new face appeared. She heard him, an echo, and her heart ached.

You have a power inside you, Marai, Keshel's steady voice told her.

Keshel, the boy who'd saved a trove of part-fae children. Merely a child, himself, burdened with raising others. He and Thora, father and mother, forced to become adults far before their time. Forced to deal with the feral, angry thing that was Marai. Obliged to listen to her spew words of vitriol, like a viper. She envisioned him always as he was the last time she'd seen him . . . the day she'd left.

He'd stood there, his inherent stillness, those angular dark eyes boring into her own. Keshel had never begged her to stay. He'd always hoped that her natural inclination to run and rebel would dim eventually. That the charge in her veins would fizzle out. But she had turned her back on him, on the others, without any feeling in her heart.

And now she was too far gone to ever return. How could she ever face her people again? Keshel could never learn how far she'd slipped.

That was how she woke up, that final glimpse of Keshel's disappointed face as she turned away from the cage that had held her. Her breath was ragged and mind whirling, unsure where she was. She caught Ruenen staring, his face tight with something. Worry? Marai wasn't sure, but he hadn't attempted to wake her since the last time, when she'd put a blade to his neck.

To Marai's chagrin, more torrential rain graced them, and they were forced to pass through the Tacornian town of Havenfiord. The town had grown in size since the last time Marai was there. It wasn't truly a surprise with more Nevandians fleeing to Tacorn daily due to the poor harvest and Rayghast's endless, violent assaults. More grey stone houses and buildings had sprouted up, and Marai spotted more being erected as she passed. Carpenters, masons, and blacksmiths were hard at work. Towns in the Red

Lands were often rebuilding houses that had been destroyed in brawls between the two kingdoms. There was plenty of opportunity in prospering Tacorn for tradesmen.

The town, despite the rain, bustled with people, all wearing their Tacorn emblem pins. These people looked healthier than the Nevandian merchants on the road. They were better dressed in less shabby clothing. Gods, many of them even smiled. Their coloring was similar to Ruenen's dark hair and eyes, tanned skin. Marai had to admit that he stood out less here than he had in the North. No one looked twice at Ruenen as he and Marai passed stalls full of fresh produce, meats, and cheeses.

"Keep a low profile," Marai said to Ruenen, who was already ducking his head, but there wasn't a soldier in sight.

"All hail King Rayghast," shouted a fanatical man on a street corner. People gathered around him, on hands and knees, in a show of exaltation. "He is blessed by the gods!"

"Hail the King," the worshippers shouted to the sky, swaying like reeds in the wind, puppets controlled by a higher power. "Hail Lirr!"

Perhaps it's true, Marai wondered. Tacorn had gone through a miraculous transformation once Rayghast ascended to the throne. Had the gods truly taken a side in the war?

Marai noticed the women in town kept their eyes low, always so docile, in a way that infuriated her. A man shoved his wife through the market, ordering her about. Marai's fingers curled around Dimtoir. Nothing would have delighted her more than cutting off the bastard's head. Women were often treated as lesser beings on Astye, but nowhere more so than in Tacorn, where Rayghast allowed men to treat their wives, daughters, and sisters like property, the way a farmer views his goats.

No, Lirr couldn't possibly support Rayghast's cruelty.

After careful inspection of the street, Marai and Ruenen passed through the market. People seemed more relaxed here than she'd seen on the road;

they purchased and sold their goods without fear. A man played the fiddle on the corner and several small boys danced at his feet.

"Are you her?" came a voice from behind them. Marai tore her eyes away from the husband and wife to see a gawking man with a rough, dark beard. Two more men stood behind him, watching Marai with wide-eyes. They all had tools slung in their belts. Tradesmen of some kind. "The Lady Butcher?"

Their mouths hung open as they took in her ominous appearance. Marai's hand tightened around her sword.

"I beg your pardon, gentlemen?" asked Ruenen, stepping in front of Marai protectively, but he smiled at the strangers.

"People are talking about her on the road. The Lady Butcher. Apparently, some bloke wrote a song about her," the tradesman explained.

Marai had to keep herself from audibly snarling like a wolf. *Dammit, Ruenen.*

"She's got the black cloak," one of the other men said, pointing an awed finger at Marai, but none of them seemed at all afraid of her. Clearly, Ruenen's song had indeed made her something of a legend.

"No, no! Not her," Ruenen stammered, waving a dismissive hand, grinning like a fool. "This is my sister. Harmless as a rose bud. She has the pox disease, though. She keeps her body covered at all times." The men gasped and staggered backwards. "She's only contagious if you touch one of her open sores."

Nearby Tacornians careened down the street as fast as a stampede. Ruenen howled in laughter.

"Let's get back on the road," growled Marai. A specter, she disappeared into the evening throng of townspeople, not waiting for Ruenen. She couldn't stand to look at him right then.

It was barely misting by the time she made it out of the town and to the road again. The woods eerily glistened in the grey after-rain fog, leaving behind a deep cedar and metallic smell from wet leaves and stone.

Marai leaned against a tree trunk, sharpening her knife on a stone until Ruenen appeared a few minutes later. He had popped up his collar and pulled his hat down, once again trying to blend in, no longer reckless.

"Where are we camping for the night?" he asked, eyes flickering to the knife in her hand.

Marai refused to say another word to him. She led him up the road a little, to give themselves distance from Havenfiord and those who may have recognized her. There was a thicket of trees with a decent clearing off the road on the Nevandian side. Marai and Ruenen set up camp there. She hovered her hand above the damp sticks they'd gathered for firewood. Heat coursed through her, from the pit of her stomach up to the tips of her fingers. The wood instantly dried and flames burst forth from her hands, illuminating their thicket. With the merry campfire burning, they wrapped themselves in their blankets and settled in for the night.

Marai heard the crack of twigs and crunch of leaves. Her eyes snapped open. It was dark out, early morning. Their fire had grown dim, but it was bright enough to attract the attention of others.

Was it the shadow creatures?

No, there were voices.

Marai bolted out of her blankets, grabbed her sword, and stood ready. Ruenen slept with a slight smile, as if he was imagining a pub owner handing him money. She kicked him lightly in the stomach. He gasped, awakening with a start.

"What was that for?" he shouted at her.

"*Shhh*," she hissed. Ruenen glared at her for a moment, rubbing his stomach, and then heard the sound of the men approaching loudly. Marai guessed there were at least a dozen or more heading directly to them. Ruenen stood, sword in hand, hair rumpled from sleep.

Finally, the men came into view. It was hard to see them at first; they all wore matte-black armor and helmets covering their heads. A few of them had long torches, but the sky remained cloudy from the rain so there was little moonlight to illuminate them. Marai didn't need to see more, however. She knew who they were.

Tacorn soldiers.

They didn't seem surprised to see Marai and Ruenen, which meant they'd spotted their campfire light from the road and had followed it. Ruenen's throat bobbed up and down as he swallowed. The men slowly surrounded their small encampment.

"Greetings," said the highest-ranking man there, taking off his helmet. He had a fresh cut across the side of his neck. "I hope we're not disturbing your slumber."

Neither Marai nor Ruenen said a word. The color had drained from Ruenen's face in the firelight. He stood stock-still, frozen on the spot, the sword limp in his hands.

"No Tacorn emblems, I see," the captain said, leering. "A few hours ago, we were ambushed by Nevandian soldiers on the road. Barely escaped with our lives. Lost some good men, as well as our horses."

As he spoke, other soldiers roughly seized Marai and Ruenen's packs. They dumped the contents out on the damp ground and scavenged up all the food and newly acquired coin. Marai counted seventeen soldiers in total. She supposed she could handle them on her own, but with Ruenen to worry about . . .

"Tacorn appreciates your generosity," the captain smugly said, wiping the blood from his cut with his gloved hand. His eyes focused on Marai, whose hood and scarf were off, face on full display. The soldier swaggered towards her with a sickening, lingering gaze. "We've been on the road a while. Been a few weeks since we've come across a girl as *fair* as you." The captain was being generous with that remark. She hadn't bathed in days, and her hair was as tangled as dead vines in a briar patch. The captain glanced nonchalantly to Ruenen. "You don't mind, do you? Just a taste. For me and my men. Then you can have her back."

A few soldiers encircled Ruenen and shoved him to the ground, holding him there. The captain took another step towards her.

"Drop the sword, sweetheart. Don't want to go making any fuss, now." His eyes shimmered with anticipation. "Women can't wield such heavy weapons, anyways." He reached out an eager arm.

Marai promptly cut it off.

The captain screamed. Blood spurt from his severed appendage.

For a moment, the other soldiers gaped. Marai rapidly began to whittle down their numbers, soldier by soldier, a wraith moving in the night. Seeing their fallen comrades, the soldiers came to their senses and began to fight back.

She used her magic to blow a couple of them off their feet so she could tackle fewer at a time. Already, six were incapacitated.

"*Stop*," shouted someone.

A soldier had Ruenen in a death grip, a knife to his neck. Ruenen looked beyond terrified as the sharp blade pressed against his windpipe. Marai didn't stop. She didn't slow down. The only way out was through these men. She did not have surrender in her. Her tactical mind shuffled through possible maneuvers—how to save Ruenen's life, as well as her own.

Perhaps there was no saving him at all. Was his life worth risking her own? She could let the soldiers kill him. It allowed for a distraction so she could either escape or finish them all off one-by-one. She could go to Andara on her own, and that damned song would never haunt her again. That foolish dimpled smile and his trusting words . . . it'd all stop before it grew into something deeper . . . something more difficult to control. Something she'd vowed to never happen.

But she wouldn't let him die. Not tonight. Both of them were walking out of this camp together.

Marai took the knife from her boot and threw it, hitting her target, the neck of the man holding Ruenen. The soldier let go. Blood gurgled from his throat and mouth.

Ruenen knelt down and took hold of his sword again.

Marai could hardly believe what happened next.

Ruenen sliced off the legs of his captor. He spun and stabbed upwards into the belly of another soldier nearby. In a flash, Ruenen was on his feet, cutting through soldiers as effortlessly as Marai. She didn't have time to watch this miraculous discovery, as there were a handful of men left. A couple of them ran off into the night; those fleeing cowards were now out of reach.

Marai and Ruenen worked individually, separating the soldiers into smaller, more manageable groups between themselves.

Her senses heightened. Her mind and ears were laser focused. All she could hear was the clang of metal. Grunts and yelps. The spurt of blood. Thumps as the last of the bodies hit the ground.

Ruenen swung again, turning as he went, unaware that the other soldiers were now all deceased. He was in a blind rage, the kind of focus battle-worn people exhibited. He swung, and Marai turned too, in time to block his attack.

Their swords clashed loudly.

They stood frozen in time, their bodies heaving with adrenaline.

This man, this stranger, she'd been traveling with . . . he wasn't *just* a bard. He wasn't a frightened novice. Ruenen was a skilled swordsman, and he'd killed before. His eyes were almost feral. It was the face he'd worn when staring down Nosficio.

Suddenly, Marai was furious.

She abruptly dropped from their stalemate. Ducking, she then used her magic, calling upon a swift wind, to blow Ruenen off his feet. He fell onto his back a yard away.

Marai ran over and put the tip of her blade to his throat. He plastered on his fearful expression again, arms raised, submitting. But his eyes never left hers as she stared down at him. They weren't the eyes of a frightened man. They were *challenging* her.

"You've been playing the helpless fool," she snarled. Her hair had come loose from its braid and the wind blew it uncontrollably around her. The breeze felt electric, pulsating with power and magic and her own fury.

"If you put that away, I'll tell you everything—" began Ruenen, and Marai pressed the tip of her sword lower, right over his heart. One push and the blade would pierce through his flesh and into the beating organ inside. One thrust and the liar would be dead. Ruenen's serious gaze never left her face, as if daring her to do it.

"*Who. Are. You?*"

CHAPTER 10
Rayghast

Nine Years Ago

The child had all but disappeared. For years they searched, years without word. There were rumors, yes, but no precise whereabouts. It was maddening. No one, it seemed, was competent, and Boone was beyond disappointing. Rayghast had hired dozens of spies to track the boy. The woman and her daughter, who had originally taken him from the monastery, had been found dead of some illness at a village in Ehle. There'd been no sign of the boy. According to the folk of the small community built under an overhanging cliff, the woman had lived there for the past two years and they'd never seen her with another child. Boone assessed that she'd rid herself of the boy long before.

"From what intelligence we've gathered, the boy has been passed from person to person," Boone told him one evening. Rayghast was in his bedchamber, a young servant woman on his bed. Someone, a vassal, had brought her to Rayghast, thinking she'd bring him pleasure. He procured his release from his own hand. He didn't need her; didn't even touch her, but the dark thing inside him found a twisted enjoyment from watching the woman cringe every time he looked at her. "We've spoken with some of these people, the ones who did not try to run from us. They claim they never knew who the boy was. They all had been told the same, look out for him and pass him on when the time was right. Stupid, really. Stupid, and yet . . . successful."

Rayghast grunted as he found release in his own hand, the woman's frightened face the image he held onto. He didn't crave physical touch, but every so often, that release was necessary. A primal need satiated for the time being. He stepped away and wiped himself off with a rag. Sweat beaded on his bald head.

Ilfe had died a week ago. His second wife. And like his previous, Queen Ilfe died with a child in her womb. Another in what Rayghast knew would be a string of queens, long enough to make a pearl necklace. Each of them healthy, but for reasons beyond anyone's control, their bodies could never complete the birthing cycle. And while the healers and midwives had assured him all was well, Rayghast knew it would never be for any of his wives. Ilfe had succumbed to a wasting disease in her third trimester, taking Rayghast's heir with her into the Underworld.

His heart didn't bleed for the loss. He married out of necessity. Formality. Duty. Ilfe had been but sixteen. A girl, taken from the world when she'd barely entered it, herself. Rayghast couldn't afford to let himself feel for her. He knew his queens would all end up the same, but duty was duty, and he didn't want anyone questioning his own seed's strength.

Until the moment the council found him another suitable bride, he was satisfied with his hand.

"We've lost track of his whereabouts," Boone said cautiously. "The last person we spoke to said he and his wife brought the boy East. He said they passed the child off to a silk merchant on the road. We have not yet tracked this man down, but the couple supposedly made the transaction near the Empire of Varana."

"So why are you here?" Rayghast asked in his distant, stern voice. Boone swallowed.

"Our spies are searching Varana as we speak, Your Grace. I thought you'd want to hear the latest update from me personally."

Rayghast surveyed Boone's oily hair, a few strands of silver prematurely streaked amongst the ebony. His tight mouth and jaw, the way his fingers clenched the helmet at his side. This position was running him ragged. Rayghast walked towards him and he could see Boone try hard not to flinch. Boone was smarter than his predecessors. Braver. He'd been relentless in his search, but the boy was cunning and hardly left a trail. Astye was a vast continent with many places to hide.

"Not just Varana. Check Syoto. Check Grelta, Henig, and the ports. Check everywhere. He may be hiding in plain sight."

"Yes, of course, Your Grace," Boone said. "How do we know he hasn't left these shores? He could have jumped aboard a ship anywhere. The boy would be about thirteen by now. He could handle a long journey across the sea."

Rayghast's fists clenched at his side. "That's why I suggested the ports." Boone gave him a curt nod. "Use whatever means necessary."

"I have every man on it." Boone said with a deep bow, aiming to exit.

"What of Vanguarden and Larissa?"

Boone met his icy stare, one of the few to truly ever look Rayghast in the eye, but never for long. "They are weakening daily, Sire. By some strange occurrence, their lands continue to rot and decay. Nothing grows there anymore. Vanguarden himself is a formidable foe on the battlefield. He may not have his father's intelligence and fortitude, but Vanguarden will not run in fear. He will not give up, even as his country suffers. Morale is low, my spies have said. He's at odds with everyone in his council."

King Vanguarden, Talen's foolish heir. He was much like his father in every aspect except where it mattered most. A great swordsman, but not a great ruler. He'd let his country slip, the harvests fail, his people begin to starve. Lands that had once flourished with vibrancy, pride, and coin were becoming barren. Tacorn continued to grow and prosper, its fields flourishing with crops and livestock, more than the country had ever had. As if it was pilfering the very life from Nevandian lands.

Vanguarden cared more for victorious war and infamy than for the prosperity of his subjects. The people of Tacorn believed that Lirr had removed her blessing from Nevandian lands. People whispered it was because Vanguarden disregarded the goddess, that he thought himself more important than the gods. Vanguarden was exquisitely handsome. He spent too much time posing for portraits with his beautiful Queen Larissa than actually leading. He was a superficial king. A ghostly copy trying to uphold Talen's legacy.

The King's arrogance would be a most formidable weapon in Rayghast's arsenal.

"I am sorry to hear about the loss of Queen Ilfe," Boone said, his tone earnest. Rayghast's blackened fingers twitched in acknowledgement. "And the child. Such a terrible, terrible thing. My deepest sympathies, Your Grace. I'm sorry I wasn't here for the funeral."

Rayghast said nothing. He merely pulled on a pair of trousers.

"Our spies say that Queen Larissa's sister in Nevandia perished from the same wasting illness," continued Boone as Rayghast put his arms through a silk robe. "It seems to be affecting those with feeble constitutions: pregnant women, babies, and the elderly."

"Women are weak," Rayghast said. He would never let himself be taken by illness, or anything other than a blade on the battlefield. Neither of his wives had been strong enough to fight the curse. That faerie swine had cursed his bloodline to ensure he would be the last. He would have cut off her head sooner if he'd known she had that kind of power.

By Lirr's Bones, the faeries had all been disposed of by Rayghast, himself. The last surviving one on Tacorn lands was the oldest fae he'd ever seen, wrinkled and covered in tattoos, colorful wings fading with age. She had pointed her gnarly finger at Rayghast as he pressed his blade to her throat.

"Your line ends here," she had crowed into the darkness of the summer night in that Tacorn wood. Rayghast had demolished the fae camp where she'd lived; faerie blood was smeared across his bare chest and arms. "You will never sire an heir. All women who carry your seed shall perish. You will have power, but it will be fleeting. Someone else will take it from you after your death."

He'd cut off her head then. Watched it tumble away, her hair a mass of tangles, brambles and leaves caught in the strands. Rayghast ripped the wings from her back and had them hung on the fortress walls at Dul Tanen. Rows of once-colorful wings still decorated the castle library and hallways. His war trophies.

The wicked crone's curse was why he needed to finish the fight with Nevandia. He needed to end this so he could move on to the rest of his great conquest.

"Strike the Queen," Rayghast said to Boone, whose eyes narrowed in confusion. "Put your spies around her. Remove Larissa from this world, however you wish. Then Vanguarden will come crawling to me."

"It will be done, Your Grace."

"Bring me the boy," Rayghast ordered, sharply tying the belt of his robe. "The next time you return, you'll convey promising news or I'll see you hanging from the gibbet."

Boone nodded in terse understanding, swallowed, and left the room. Rayghast turned back to the servant, who had stayed silently on the bed, watching with wide eyes. With a mere look, the woman leapt from the bed and dashed out of the room, clutching her hand to her heart. Rayghast slammed the chamber door.

He paced back and forth across the rug before the fireplace, hands latched behind his back. Black smoke clouded his brain. So many moving pieces. He was waiting on word from Varana, if his spies were successful in infiltrating the castle. Nevandia was the first jewel in Rayghast's crown. Alliances would be formed, and then crumble as Rayghast seized more and more. The combined strength of Tacorn and Nevandian forces could overwhelm a broken Varana.

But despite all his scheming, all his great plans, one missing piece remained.

Vanguarden's whelp, born from his beloved Queen Larissa, must've been smart, brave to have run all these years. The true son of a king. Those monks had trained him well. But eventually, death would catch up to him, son of Nevandia. Death would be there with a blade at his chest, and Rayghast would have him then.

And Nevandia would fall.

CHAPTER 11
Marai

"Who are you?" she repeated when Ruenen didn't respond. He opened his mouth, then closed it, opened it again. Marai pressed the tip of her sword a little further, only slightly piercing the skin.

"*Alright,*" he yelped, scooting his bottom backwards an inch so that the tip was no longer touching him. His chestnut hair fell in front of his face and he tried to blow it out of his eyes with a quick puff. In the fading firelight, Marai spotted flecks of blood on his cheeks and forehead. "You're not going to believe me, though."

"Why *should* I believe you?"

Ruenen's eyes never left hers. She could almost see the inner workings of his brain, his calculations, his thoughts, as he struggled to find the words.

Anger sparked in her veins. A charge traveled up and down her spine.

"I've trusted you with my own secrets, and you've been lying to me this whole time," she said.

This was why she never grew close to people. This was why she lived a solitary life. Because betrayals hurt too deeply. Because people always let you down. Because it is easier to feel nothing than to feel such anger and disappointment.

But still, Marai listened. She wanted to hear answers from his lips. The truth.

"I'm . . . I'm not a bard. Well, I'm *trying* to be one, but that's not who I've been," stammered Ruenen, but no fear showed in his eyes. That challenge there, yet again. "I was an apprentice to a blacksmith for several years in Chiojan—I told you that. It wasn't a lie. From the time I was ten to seventeen, I learned not only how to make weapons, but how to use them. Tomas Chongan was my master, an excellent craftsman and a good man. He took care of me when no one else would."

Marai watched hurt flash across his face. Ruenen disappeared for a moment, lost in thought somewhere. His eyes held a distant look. Then he returned his gaze to Marai and continued on.

"Every time someone came to the forge requesting a sword, I asked them to teach me something. A couple of the swordsmen could even rival you, I bet." Ruenen shot her a hasty smile Marai did not return. "I *needed* to know how to wield a blade in order to survive, despite feeling quite safe with Chongan. The safest I've ever felt."

"Safe from *what*?" pressed Marai. She hadn't moved, not a single muscle. She saw no deceit in Ruenen's face.

He issued another puff of air to remove his hair from his eyes. "If you let me finish speaking, you'll know more in a moment."

"Why hire me at all when you can clearly protect yourself?"

A crease formed between Ruenen's brows. "Because I needed to appear unsuspecting, to hide in plain sight. Having a fighter-for-hire around would tell people that I was weak. No one would look twice at me, performing as a shabby bard." He flicked a hand at her. "Let's not forget that you're full of secrets, too."

Marai glared at him. "This is not about me. Finish your story."

She lowered her sword. Relief washed across Ruenen's face, his body relaxed, yet he did not move from the muddy ground. Marai hovered over him threateningly, waiting for the truth, waiting for the tight, compressed feeling in her chest to ease.

"The summer I was seventeen, Chiojan was attacked by Tacorn soldiers. They ravaged the city. They came to my master's shop and destroyed it, murdering him without care or respect. A great artist, a craftsman, wiped from the earth without a second thought. They slaughtered his family: a wife and three children. I could do nothing but watch. I didn't try to stop the soldiers, I was . . . petrified."

Ruenen shivered, his face haunted by the death he'd seen. Marai knew that expression. She'd seen it in her own reflection from time to time. Death left a mark, an internal scar, that was impossible to fake.

"The death count in the city was astronomical—buildings burned, bodies lining the streets surrounded by pools of blood. It was a horrific warning. A warning to everyone, including Emperor Suli of Varana, not to harbor what Rayghast viewed as his rightful property."

Marai had visited Chiojan in the Eastern Empire of Varana two years after the massacre. It was still recovering from the destruction, even then. Most thought the carnage had been a message sent to the powerful, prosperous country of Varana. A message that Rayghast was a king to be feared. Emperor Suli hadn't retaliated. The two kingdoms had settled their differences with a trade deal and payment for damages. All that loss of life whittled down to politics.

She couldn't blame Ruenen for not raising his sword against those soldiers. She couldn't fault his fear. He'd been but seventeen. No seventeen-year-old human would've had the courage to stand up to an army that thrived on violence.

"But the soldiers didn't come to wreak havoc on the city. It could have been any city, any town on the continent. It wasn't about the message of power. That wasn't why they were there. Not at all. They were looking for *me*." Ruenen finally looked away, face tight with pain and shame.

"Are *you* really so special?"

"I'm not, but King Rayghast thinks I am."

"Why was your life worth more than the lives of the hundreds of dead?"

Ruenen's eyes blazed. "Rayghast is hell-bent on finding me, because he can't overthrow Nevandia while I live . . . because I am their lost prince."

Marai let the words ring in her ears a moment. It sounded similar to a story in one of Ruenen's fantastical folk songs. It couldn't possibly be true.

"There is no lost prince of Nevandia," she said after a long moment. "There have been rumors for years, but that's all they are—rumors, speculation."

"I can assure you that they're not mere rumors," Ruenen said bitterly. The feeling returned to Marai's legs, and she began to pace.

"King Vanguarden sired no heir."

"No *known* heir, but he had a son."

"Queen Larissa was never pronounced with-child."

"Nor would she have been, if they weren't scared for their lives. Rayghast was conquering more Nevandian territory every year, his army so strong and vicious that Nevandian forces crumbled against them. Vanguarden and Larissa wanted to keep their child a secret, to raise him in safety so that even if they perished, Nevandia still had a chance."

Now that he mentioned it, Ruenen did look remarkably like Queen Larissa. Marai had seen paintings of the Queen before in the Nine Kingdoms Library in Syoto. He had her eyes and brown hair, the straightness of her nose. Larissa was renowned across Astye; women everywhere tried to mimic her style, and Marai had heard many men wanted to marry her before she became betrothed to Vanguarden.

"Only those in Vanguarden's inner circle knew that Queen Larissa was expecting."

Marai halted her pacing. "Even *if* Larissa had been pregnant, who's to say that she didn't lay with another man? The 'lost prince' might be a bastard."

Ruenen flinched. "You don't think the thought hadn't occurred to me? I've been told by many of Vanguarden and Larissa's intense love for each other. Their love was eternal, or so the stories say. I don't believe either of them would have ever lain with another." His jaw tightened.

"How did they hide their child?"

"They knew they were in danger. They knew it was only a matter of time before Rayghast took the kingdom, so they hid their infant son in a monastery on the outskirts of Nevandian borders, so he'd stay safe until he came of age," said Ruenen, speaking quickly now, as if he'd been keeping this secret for years and couldn't hold it in any longer. "But Rayghast had heard the rumors, too. Because of this, I was passed from person to person. I survived due to the kindness of strangers. That's how I landed in Chiojan with Master Chongan. I owed him my *life*. But everywhere I went, destruction followed. First the monastery, then Chiojan. I haven't been found yet because Rayghast is looking for a prince, not an impoverished bard."

Prince . . . Ruenen was a prince. Not some lousy bard. Not a penniless vagrant. But the heir to the throne of Nevandia.

The heart in Marai's chest beat furiously.

"When Rayghast killed my father on the battlefield nine years ago, he knew the line had not ended. Rayghast understood that the only hope of truly gaining control of Nevandia lay with the lost prince. Because once he killed me, he could finally become the almighty ruler of the Middle Kingdoms."

Ruenen raked his hands through his hair, a revolted look on his face, sorrow in his eyes as his gaze met Marai's. There was no deception there at all.

"Then your name is . . ."

"Ruenen Avsharian," he stated. The words rattled Marai's bones. Even the trees seemed to slant closer to hear Ruenen's confession; Marai could almost hear the forest breathing. "That's why I have to leave these shores, Marai. Why I have to brave the treacherous journey to Andara. Rayghast will never stop hunting me."

The air felt heavy. A light mist clung to Marai's skin like a blanket, the metallic smell of blood wafted in the air around their camp. Little time had passed since fighting the soldiers, but Marai felt like it had been hours. In a matter of moments, her world had been upended. In fact, the entire fate of Nevandia undoubtedly rested in the hands of the person before her.

"If this is true, do you not think he would just send soldiers to follow you across the ocean?" she asked. "Rayghast would never let you go."

"It might buy me a few more years . . ."

Marai heard the resignation in his voice, the hint of sorrow there once again. She stopped pacing and turned to face Ruenen.

"Why don't you take up the throne, then? You could be commanding an army now, fighting Rayghast, not running from him. Your people would raise the banner for you."

"I'm not a king," Ruenen said with a disgusted laugh. He finally got to his feet and wiped his muddy hands on his pants. "I may have royal blood, but I'm *not* a ruler. I've lived a poor man's life, trying to survive one day to the next, to not starve or be killed. I've never seen the capital city of Kellesar. I don't know how to command an army. I don't understand anything about the politics of running a country." He gestured to Marai. "*You* know me. Do you think I could possibly be in charge of a kingdom?"

Looking at him then, covered in mud and blood, hair a mess, several days stubble on his face, Marai felt mirthful laughter boil up inside her, but she didn't break a smile. However, she'd seen him fight off those Tacornian soldiers with tremendous skill, and earlier incapacitate Nosficio with merely a chair. His back had been straight, erect, focused and determined. He'd looked like a king then.

Marai squared her shoulders. "You'd rather forsake your people, your destiny, and give it all over to Rayghast because you don't fit the typical image of a king?"

Ruenen's face was always an open book, so it was no surprise that he cringed and avoided her eyes, that look of shame and guilt unmistakable.

"I wouldn't know what to do. I couldn't make decisions. I may know swordsmanship, but I know as much as a common man on how to manage a kingdom and win an endless war."

"Ruen, you would have advisors—"

"*Marai, I am not a king,*" Ruenen shouted, throwing up his hands. "I will never be King. Of anything. *You* would make a better ruler than me. I just want to play my music and run as far from here as possible."

There was something about the way he stood: so defeated and lost, shoulders slumped over and arms wrapped around himself. She could see it then, the way the constant fear and running, losing every person who had ever helped him . . . she could see the toll it had taken on him. He pretended to be carefree and confident, but it was all a performance, the same character he portrayed on stage. This hollowness he now displayed was the true heart of Ruenen.

She knew who that person was. Marai had often felt it within herself.

"Is that why you were so frightened of the Nevandian soldiers in Dwalingulf? Because you were afraid they'd recognize you and take you back to Nevandia?" Her tone was gentle and wary. "If I were you, I'd go home to Nevandia and take up the throne. Speaking as someone who has witnessed the downfall of her people . . ."

Ruenen looked away, afraid to meet her eyes. He said nothing more. Neither did Marai.

The dark of night was fading into the dull grey of morning. Marai wiped off her sword and sheathed it. The mist was clearing up, now a gentle kiss across her exposed skin. It refreshed and calmed her. There'd be no more sleep. The Tacorn soldiers who escaped would return to gather their dead, most likely with reinforcements. The longer Marai and Ruenen stayed there, the more at risk they were. Whether she accepted his tale or not, Ruenen had employed Marai to get him to the ocean. She'd do as she was commissioned to do.

"You should've paid me triple for this," she said, unable to keep the slight smirk from her mouth.

Ruenen's face softened. "Can you blame me for not telling you when we first met?"

"No."

"You wouldn't have believed me."

"I barely believe you now."

Ruenen chuckled, low and short, but a flicker of his usual life came back to his face. It was a relief . . . that he hadn't always had a mask on. That there were things he'd shown her from the start . . . his smile. That had always been real.

"I could go sell you out to Tacorn. I wouldn't have to work for a whole year."

Ruenen stilled. "Another reason why I didn't tell you my identity."

Marai knelt next to each soldier, emptying their pockets of the coin they had stolen. She bent over to remove her knife from the neck of a soldier. Ruenen let out a small breath and bent down to pick up a better, sturdier blade from the deceased captain.

"You called me Ruen."

Marai looked up, meeting his eyes. They had warmed slightly, the hollowness in them gone again. Marai felt a little heat creep up her neck and into her cheeks. The name had just jumped out of her. She hadn't thought as she'd said it. Hadn't realized she'd uttered it.

"No one has called me by my real name in decades, since I was at the monastery, and only in private by Monks Amsco and Nori. The rest of the time, I was Leander. And to Master Chongan I was Hiro," Ruenen said, sheathing his new sword into the loop of his belt. "No one has ever given me a nickname before." He smiled again. "I don't mind it."

That heat seared on her face and Marai quickly looked away, hoping Ruenen hadn't noticed. "Why *did* you tell me your real name, anyways? Since you were running . . ."

Ruenen closed the distance between them in a few steps. He didn't touch Marai, but she could see how his fingers considered reaching for her arm. She looked up into those pretty, brown, fawn-like eyes, and could have sworn she felt her breath catch for an instant.

"Because from the first moment I met you, I wanted to trust you," he breathed. There was no lie in his face. No deception in his voice. That open-book expression was clear and searching. "I don't know why. I couldn't see your face because of that stupid scarf and hood." He smiled again. "But I knew I could place my trust in you because you were running from something, too. The money was an added incentive."

His mouth widened into a grin, and Marai felt a wall come down inside her. Just one wall, not all of them. But he'd slowly been chipping away for weeks and she hadn't noticed until then. She tried not to let the significance of that matter to her. So much of her life had been *walls up, shields up,* and there Ruenen had gone and lowered her defenses in three weeks.

"I'm sorry I hid this from you. I never wanted to deceive you in any way. And I promise, for as long as we're together, I'll not lie to you again." Ruenen stepped one inch closer. Marai didn't back away, not as she stared up into that hopeful face. She'd forgotten how much taller he was than her . . .

"I believe you, Ruen," she said and meant it. Ruenen practically collapsed with relief, his eyes shimmering with gratitude and something else Marai pretended not to see.

She busied herself with gathering the scattered supplies. Ruenen smothered the remaining embers of their fire by kicking in dirt. They couldn't be seen on the road from now on. Their cover had been blown. Marai hadn't used much magic, but it was possible that the soldiers who got away saw her. She only hoped they wouldn't associate her with any kind of magical being.

Marai led the way further into the woods. She knew the Nydian River was close. They could follow that straight through the Red Lands and remain as undetected as possible.

Marai frowned, however, once her back was turned.

Prince ...

Her commission was far more wrought with complications than she could have ever imagined.

She now had to keep the lost Nevandian prince safe.

CHAPTER 12
Ruenen

*R*uen.

It had just slipped out. He knew she hadn't meant to say it, but it was actually kind of . . . sweet. The pink on her cheeks when he'd mentioned the nickname. In the weeks he'd known her, he'd never seen Marai look so human with her wide eyes and softened expression. She'd be mortified if she knew her blush had been so apparent. He'd have another blade to his throat in an instant. As he walked closely behind her, he smiled, closing his eyes, remembering that image, how it warmed his chest, filled him with something good, something light . . .

Before he tripped on a stick and fell right into her, pushing Marai forward by accident.

She whirled around, her hand on her sword's hilt, then rolled her eyes. Ruenen shrugged in the form of an apology.

That trace of rosy vulnerability was now gone from Marai's face. She was back to impenetrable stone.

So feisty, he thought and smirked. Marai narrowed her violet eyes, and then returned to walking.

Ruenen had meant to keep his past a secret. He'd never meant to tell her anything, but it had felt so freeing to finally say it all. He'd kept that secret locked up inside his entire life. Ruenen hadn't expected Marai to believe him. He assumed she was going to dice him up right there next to the fallen Tacorn soldiers.

But she hadn't. Marai believed him.

Of course, that left Ruenen with more questions. The Lady Butcher always kept him guessing, always played the long game. Like her life depended on it, and Ruenen supposed it did.

Now he had no more secrets from her. There was nothing for him to hide, and he'd never felt so utterly *known* by another person. Those who knew him before, Monks Amsco and Nori, Master Chongan and his family ... they were all dead. Because of him. And Ruenen didn't want to imagine how many of those kind, selfless strangers had been tracked down over the years for helping him as a child.

As he stared at the back of her long hair, those tense shoulders ... would Marai be taken from him, too? She hadn't given him a firm decision on whether or not she'd go with him to Andara. If they made it to the ocean, and Marai decided to stay in Astye, would Rayghast come for her? Eventually the King of Tacorn would find out she aided him. Could Ruenen sail away, knowing that he'd left Marai to be captured?

Dread curled in the pit of his stomach. The thought of Marai in that villain's hands made Ruenen's blood run cold, his anger sear like a forged blade, and fingers curl into fists.

Was she thinking the same thing now? Regretting her decision to take his commission? Marai wasn't foolish, she knew the target on her back. For all he knew, the Butcher may have been cursing him under her breath. And yet ...

Ruen.

He found himself smiling again.

It felt like spring. The sun shone in a way that Ruenen hadn't felt for months, heralding in a time of growth and warmth. Though the trees remained barren, those temperate rays cast down upon his face, warm and smooth as syrup. He took off his wool cap and jacket, and tucked them into his pack.

"How does your magic work?" he asked Marai in a blasé way that he hoped would catch her off-guard.

"You asked me before, and I didn't answer you then," she replied and lowered her hood, basking in the sunlight, too.

"I was hoping you'd be in a more generous mood."

Marai glanced back at him. "I don't want to use magic."

Not the answer he expected. "Because you're afraid of being discovered?"

"Yes, but also because . . . magic has only ever brought me pain and suffering."

"I'd have thought it'd be fun to use . . ."

"I never properly trained. I've spent my whole life shoving the magic down, so much so that now I don't know how to do much with it," she explained. "And I tire quickly. It drains me physically when I use it several times in a day."

"Fae magic is elemental, right? You can light a fire and call forth a wind."

Marai gracefully leapt over a large, downed tree trunk in their path. "Faeries have always been more connected to nature. Lirr created us that way. Some of us have affinities for certain elements. I cannot control or create water or earth—never been able to. But there is magic in every growing, living thing. If I concentrate, I can feel it all around me, like a soft, warm flutter against my consciousness. I can *feel* the water, even if I cannot grasp its power."

"What does it feel like when you *do* use it?" Ruenen's long legs stepped over the tree and came to her side.

Marai narrowed her eyes, thinking, as if she'd never thought about it before. "Magic comes from within, like raising a bucket of water up from a well . . . pulling hard on that rope until the bucket comes to the surface. It feels kind of . . . effervescent as it travels through my body. But the well only goes so deep. No faerie has limitless power. I'm only half-fae, barely trained, and I've avoided digging too deep into my magic. I'm nowhere near as powerful as the ancient fae."

Ruenen came to her side. "You shouldn't be ashamed of your heritage. Of your blood. You are who you are—embrace it."

The corners of her mouth twitched. "Says the prince running from his crown," she stated sardonically.

Ruenen scowled. "I'm merely saying, *Sassafras*, that you've been given this gift of magic . . . you should use it."

Marai paused suddenly, tilting her head like a bird, listening. Sensing.

"This way," she said, ignoring his previous comment. That was the end of that conversation. Ruenen sighed.

Marai brought them through the trees to a riverbank. Those half-fae genes and the magic she hated allowed her to sense the water. There was no way Ruenen heard the sound of that river from where they'd been standing moments ago.

Ruenen knew this river. It was the Nydian, and it traveled from the Northeast through the Middle Kingdoms, and dumped out in the Baurean Sea. The current was slow and lazy in this section of the Middle Kingdoms. Ruenen heard it babbling and lapping onto the shore. He'd always found the sound of water to be a music of its own—dulcet and yet sonorous. Nature always created the best symphonies.

Marai set down her pack in the moss and Ruenen swore he saw a grin on her lips.

"I'd like to spar with you," she said, and Ruenen froze in the middle of putting down his lute.

"Why . . . ?"

Marai stood, grabbing her sword. "You have skill with a blade. I want to see how much."

She was going to make him pay for lying to her. Gods, help him. Ruenen tossed his head, getting his hair out of his face, and then reached for his new Tacorn sword.

"I'm not . . . incredible, or anything," he said, nerves building as she stalked around him, violet eyes focused on her prey. Marai's sword twirled in her grasp, as if she wasn't holding a deadly weapon at all. He'd seen her kill before, but now that lethal focus was on *him*. He winced in anticipation.

And then she launched herself at him.

He barely had time to bring his sword up to block. She was lightning quick and had more strength than she let on. Ruenen may have been physically stronger, but it didn't matter because she was swift and precise, so light on her feet. He'd seen her use these techniques on others before, but never had he been on the receiving end of the tirades. He parried, blocked, did all he could to stop her blade from slicing through him. Ruenen was certain she was holding back. He would have been dead ten times over if Marai had really been trying.

But he didn't stop. He met her blade strike for strike, their swords clanging together. Ruenen had been so busy watching her sword that he hadn't noticed her face, but he managed to spare one glance.

Marai was trying hard not to smile. He could see the upturned corners of her mouth, the crinkles around her eyes. Hr couldn't help himself as he grinned from ear to ear. Suddenly, the sparring became easier. He relaxed, enjoying the movements and sounds, the heft of his sword, and the jolt that went through his arms every time their blades connected. It'd been a long time since he'd truly sparred with anyone, wielding a weapon not to protect himself, but for fun.

After a round of intense back and forth, Marai dropped her sword, her chest lifting up and down as she breathed. Ruenen lowered his sword, unsure what the next phase of her trick would be, but Marai merely sheathed her blade and sat on a log. She took a long sip from her canteen.

"You're very good," she said, tossing that compliment out there like it meant nothing. She never gave compliments. He knew it *did* mean something, to both of them. He sat with her on the log and wiped the sweat from his brow. "But you're too heavy on your feet. It doesn't allow you to pivot easily. Stay up on the balls of your feet."

"I appreciate the words of wisdom," he said with a wink. Marai lifted an eyebrow, then shook her head, trying to chase away the urge to retort something snide. "Not quite as good as you yet."

"You never will be."

Ruenen made a face. "Why not?"

"Because you're human. You don't have fae reflexes or agility."

He crossed his arms. "Well, that's a very defeatist attitude." Marai snorted. "Where did you learn?"

So quickly, her face shuttered. She looked down at the ground, all the ease and connection they'd built was broken.

"I'm sorry," Ruenen blurted, "I've always asked too many questions."

Marai glanced back at him. "You are rather nosy today."

He chuckled, the tension dissipating. "What can I say? You're the queen of mystery."

The intensity of her gaze fueled the flames building in his core. And then it was there—a swelling sensation in his chest. An overwhelming, all-encompassing sensation, as if he were falling from the edge of the Northern cliffs; falling and falling, the ground never coming to meet him.

Marai seemed to feel the shift in him, too. Her back straightened and Ruenen heard the sharp intake of her breath. She leapt to her feet, avoiding his eyes.

But she said to him over her shoulder, "pirates taught me."

Well, he certainly hadn't been expecting *that*.

"Before I became the Lady Butcher, I spent time on a pirate ship. The captain and crew taught me how to wield a sword. As well as other things . . ."

Ruenen opened his mouth to ask twenty questions, but Marai was already shucking off her boots, her cloak, her leather gloves. She stood at the river's edge and looked back over her shoulder at him. A sun beam graced the top of her head, surrounding her in golden radiance. Ruenen must've been gaping, because her face hardened. Her eyes didn't, though; they danced in amusement.

"Turn away," she commanded, and Ruenen, unsure of how to respond, turned around on the log. His whole body stiffened. "You can bathe once I'm done." He heard the rustling of clothes and the hesitant steps into the water.

He heard Marai elicit a shiver as a small splash indicated she'd walked into the river. The sound of that shiver sent his own skin prickling with goose bumps.

Turn around, his immature mind suggested.

Marai would behead him if he turned around, but did she realize how unbelievably hard it would be to avoid imagining that delicate, smooth skin exposed, wet hair unbound . . . how much he wanted to be in that water with her, how badly he wanted to touch her . . . Was she doing this on purpose? Toying with him? Or maybe he was reading too much into her actions.

Oh gods. Ruenen felt the heat radiating from him, all his muscles going taut. His imagination had been too good as he heard her splish-splashing in the river. Could she *see* his reaction? He leapt to his feet and walked a few steps away from the river.

He'd given her all his secrets and closed the bridge between them. She'd then given him a gods-damned nickname. That had been the moment when something fundamental shifted between them, a different type of magic, and Ruenen knew it. He'd felt it in his heart then. At least for him. He didn't think it was possible to ever view Marai as the Lady Butcher again. She was so much more than that.

Ruenen tried to breathe, clear his mind, steady his body so she couldn't tell the inappropriate things he'd been thinking about. It was harder than he thought...

Something else was harder, too.

Damn! Ruenen ran a hand through his hair and bit his finger, thinking the pain might take his mind off it. Thank the gods his tunic came to his thighs.

"Done yet?" he called, trying to make his voice sound nonchalant.

"Almost," Marai said and he could hear the mischievousness in her tone. She absolutely knew. Had she wanted him to react this way? Was she flirting with him or was he simply overcome by his own wants? Gods, he could know her a thousand years and never understand her.

He heard the splashing and her squishy steps in the mud, a rustle of clothes, and then after a long moment, there was a tap on his upper arm.

"You can turn around now, Ruen," Marai said. He looked over his shoulder.

Her loose hair was dripping wet on a different, dry tunic, her lips a little blue from the cold river, skin pale as death, but she was cleaner than Ruenen had ever seen her. She didn't look nearly as intimidating like this... just a girl, pale and lithe, coming out of the water like a mythical mermaid.

She plastered that usual steely expression on, but her eyes sparkled. With curiosity? Ruenen didn't know, but he hoped that she might feel the same. Marai returned to her cloak and wrapped it around herself as she sat on a log. Her wet clothes were draped across a tree branch to dry out.

"All yours," she said with a jerk of her head towards the water.

Ruenen rigidly walked to the edge of the river, avoiding her gaze, cursing himself for letting her get to him in that way. The cold water would do him good in this moment, calm the heat coursing through his veins. He took off his boots, his vest, and started lifting his shirt, when he noticed she was watching him.

"Do I not get the same privacy as you?" he asked her, raising an eyebrow. Marai caught herself staring, eyes widening. He felt a shudder like butter on toast melt down his back as she twisted away on her log.

What was going on? Marai seemed caught up in the confusion, as well, like she knew they'd crossed a threshold.

He yanked his shirt and pants from his body and gave them a whiff. They smelled ghastly, and were covered in layers of blood and dirt. He brought them with him into the river and nearly froze to death. This was some type of torture. How had Marai managed to stay in it as long as she had?

He walked further in until the river reached his stomach, then ducked under the surface, feeling the water like tiny daggers across his skin, and came back up, sputtering. He shook his hair from his eyes and saw Marai sitting on her log, striking face perched in her palm. Most of her body was turned away.

"*Marai,*" he shouted with a wave, bringing her attention to him. He wanted to see her reaction. He wanted to tease her, to *flirt* with her as he did with other women. He didn't have anything left to hide.

Marai swiveled around. Her hand had snapped to her dagger at her belt. Ruenen grinned as he saw recognition in her face that he wasn't in trouble. His skin warmed again as those amethyst eyes glanced down at his exposed chest. Ruenen was not the most muscular of men; he was lean and toned and strong. He felt his own cheeks redden as he watched color bloom on her face, as well. But she shot him a withering look and turned back around, face red. Ruenen's spirits sunk a little . . .

He didn't think he could stand the cold a moment longer. He turned his back to her and quickly washed himself and his clothes before he died of hypothermia. He walked closer to the shore and frowned at his wet clothing. He didn't have another set, so he was forced to put on his drenched ones. Ruenen's whole body shook as the icy, wet clothes clung to his frozen skin.

A snap of fingers, a strong gust of wind, and suddenly, his clothes were completely dry. He glanced over to Marai, sitting on her log, fingers in the air. Ruenen swore he smelled the magic. It was a strange scent, ether and crisp air, bubbles and smoke. *Effervescent,* she'd said. He took a deep breath, letting it fill his lungs, the magic residue almost tickling inside.

Ruenen couldn't help but smile. She hated using magic, but had done it to keep him dry.

Marai twirled around to face him, all business, blush vanished. The mask of the Butcher was back.

"We need to leave. We've been here longer than we should have."

"Can't we at least have food? I'm starving," Ruenen said, rubbing his stomach.

Marai thought for a moment. "Fine. We can go further up the river to catch a fish."

"Why can't we fish here?"

"We scared them all upstream when we bathed. We'll have better luck there."

Ruenen hesitated. He needed space from her to clear his mind. Only a little while, enough to calm down and be able to look at her again without blushing.

Marai scowled. "You don't want to go anywhere, do you?"

Ruenen placed a guilty expression on his face. "I'm horrid at fishing, I swear it. I'd be more of a hindrance than a help." He hoped she couldn't scent his lie.

Marai rolled her eyes and shook her head. "I'm a servant," she muttered, but she miraculously relented. "Don't stray from the camp." She looked back down at him like she had something more to say. Her mouth opened slightly; her eyes searched his face. Then Marai turned sharply and strode off along the riverbank.

What had she been going to say?

"I'll ask her when she gets back," Ruenen said aloud to himself.

While he waited, Ruenen pulled out his lute and strummed out the new song he'd been working on. He had all the slow, beautiful notes and chords figured out, but the lyrics were causing difficulties. Ruenen knew exactly what he wanted to say . . . but it was complicated to put those feelings into words. Because as soon as those words, those lyrics, were voiced, then he would be admitting far too much truth. He wasn't sure if he was ready to take that leap yet.

The thought of her flushed cheeks, and more lyrics burst from him in a glissando.

Whenever he got sucked into music, he'd lose track of time. Minutes blended together in harmony. Ruenen wasn't aware how much time had passed before he opened his eyes again, returning to the world around him. A rustling of leaves caught his attention. His stomach gurgled again loudly. It must have been late afternoon judging by the angle of the shadows caused by the sun. A few buttery-soft rays peaked through the canopy above. Marai had been gone a while.

Ruenen set his lute aside as the footsteps grew closer.

"Thank the gods, I'm starved," he called over his shoulder.

"You're going to have to wait a little longer, friend," came a male voice from behind him.

Ruenen leapt to his feet, taking in the sight of two dozen brawny, stern, black-armored Tacorn soldiers, all leering at him. He'd lingered too long. Ruenen had been so distracted by Marai and his music that he'd stopped worrying, stopped fearing.

And that was going to cost him.

"Can I do something for you, gentlemen?" he managed to stammer out, frozen where he stood by the log. The man who had spoken had a large black feather plume on his helmet, which was currently hooked under his arm. His black armor itself was far more embellished and cleaner than the other soldiers around him. A deep red cape fanned out behind him.

The soldiers slowly spread out around the campsite.

"Perhaps you can help us," said the general, feigning politeness. "We came across two of our men on the road. Said they'd had trouble at a campsite further in the woods last evening. They mentioned the use of *magic*. When we went to investigate, we discovered several of our good men dead at the scene. All of their pockets emptied."

Ruenen tried not to show any recognition, and stifled the nervous swallow. All he wanted to do was turn and run, but there was nowhere for him to go. Even if he managed to get past the soldiers, he couldn't outrun them all. He hoped his expression displayed surprise and innocence.

The commanding officer took a seat on the log opposite Ruenen. His salt and pepper hair was slicked back tightly, greased with an oily substance, marking his high standing and wealth. His cold dark eyes surveyed Ruenen casually.

"With your site here being about a few hours' walk, perhaps you heard or saw something?" he asked, spreading his legs on the log as he leaned forward, taking a commanding stance. This man oozed power and importance. The other soldiers barely moved at all.

Lie. Quick.

"Alas, gentlemen, I cannot help you. My lady and I have been here two days . . . enjoying some *relaxing* quality time by the river." He smirked, gesturing to Marai's clothes on the tree branch. "She's off getting us supper. I expect her to return shortly."

The commander looked from the clothes back to Ruenen, his face impassive. "So you were entirely unaware of the slaughter happening not far from you? I find it hard to believe that you heard nothing."

"We were both otherwise engaged at the time," Ruenen said, twisting his expression into one of mischievous pleasure. "My lady is rather . . . *vociferous* during certain activities. Neither of us could hear anything."

"All night?" pressed the general, eyebrows raised. Ruenen chuckled in a deep, raw tone he'd never used before. It felt unnatural, but he'd play any role if it meant he could escape.

"If you saw my exquisite lady, you'd understand," he crooned, putting his hands in his pockets. He was good at lying, but that didn't mean he liked saying such things. "Her breasts are rare things of beauty, and she has a sensuous, naughty mouth. She's indefatigable, if you know what I mean."

The words were as acidic as poison on his tongue.

"Shame you didn't hear anything. The criminals at large must be captured and held accountable by Tacorn. King Rayghast doesn't take kindly to thieves and mountebanks so close to his lands. Especially if they have magical abilities." The general's eyes flashed. "And the murder of even one Tacorn soldier is punishable by execution. We found fifteen dead."

Ruenen stiffly nodded as the commander leaned forward further.

"You look familiar," he drawled, eyes narrowing.

"Ah, perhaps you've seen one of my performances," Ruenen said. "I am a well-known traveling bard." He grandly waved at his lute. "I recently performed to a full house in Dwalingulf. Have you heard of my song about the Lady Butcher? People are raving about it."

He winked, trying to stand up as tall and confidently as possible, hoping they didn't see his legs shaking.

The commander's expression didn't change as he said, "play it for us."

Ruenen hesitantly picked up his lute and glanced around him. The dozen other soldiers had stepped in closer, tightening their circle around the camp. Even if he was close enough to grab his sword, he wasn't sure he could take on so many soldiers fully at attention, hands on their own hilts.

Do as they say. Keep playing the game. Buy time for Marai to return.

He played those opening notes of "The Lady Butcher," convincing himself that this was just another audience, another tavern. The soldiers stood at attention the entire time. Ruenen strummed and sang with all the heart he could muster, desperately trying to keep his voice from wavering, keeping those nerves at bay.

When he finished, the forest remained eerily quiet and still. No one moved. The general stared at him blankly. "You're very good. Catchy tune."

Ruenen bowed dramatically. "Your compliment honors me, Sir—"

"Boone," said the general, now getting to his feet. "Commander of the Tacorn army. What's your name, bard?"

"Ard," blurted Ruenen, watching Boone casually skulk towards him. As the commander neared, Ruenen could see the bluish tint under his eyes. His face was covered by days' worth of stubble. The man hadn't slept or rested in a while.

"Ard the Bard?" Boone repeated, no hint of emotion. "Shame that such a skilled musician has such a terrible name."

Ruenen scowled despite himself. "I've been told."

Boone stopped right in front of him, intense eyes raking over Ruenen's face. "That's not why you're familiar to me, though. You look strikingly like someone I knew long ago."

"Oh?"

"A certain queen."

Ruenen felt his whole body tense. He wasn't sure he could hide the fear now crushing him. He forced out a harsh laugh.

"A queen? I'm afraid I have never had the pleasure of knowing a queen. I'm assuming she was quite the looker if I resemble her."

Boone's eyes scrutinized him again. "She was. It was rumored she and her husband had a lost heir. I've been tracking him."

Lirr's Bones.

"Is that so?" Ruenen couldn't stop the swallow.

Boone glanced to his men behind Ruenen. "Check him."

Strong hands grabbed him. Ruenen fought and struggled, horror filled every vein and organ inside him, but those hands forced his own out in front of him, turning them over to reveal the underside of his wrists, and the dark sunburst permanently sketched onto his skin.

They knew about his mark.

Boone's eyes ignited with a cold, merciless flame. "Hello, Prince."

The soldiers yanked Ruenen's arms behind his back. He felt the ropes at his wrists as more began wrapping around his arms and torso.

After twenty-two years, Rayghast had finally found him. Ruenen shouldn't have been so reckless. He shouldn't have become distracted by Marai. How stupid to have come so far, been so close . . .

His thoughts turned to Marai. Pure panic rushed through Ruenen, blinding him, his ears ringing. He almost fainted at the thought of Marai's lifeless, bloody body. Gods, he hoped she lived and would run as far away from all this as she could.

Don't come after me, he sent out into the world like a prayer that hopefully she could hear. *They know about the magic.*

A piece of dirty cloth was forced between his teeth and tied behind his head. His shouts were muffled as the scratchy fibers of the fabric caused him to choke and nearly wretch.

Boone's eyes shimmered like two black beetles. In victory. "Let's pay a visit to the king, shall we?"

CHAPTER 13
Marai

She stood in the cool water, wooden spear in hand that she'd sharpened with her dagger. She'd taken off her boots, rolled up her pant legs to her knees, and waded out into the frigid water. Marai had spotted the pink, fleshy trout from the bank, but they were all swimming farther upstream than she had originally wanted to go. The call of her stomach had pressed her forwards into the water. And there she stood, still, waiting.

In a flash, she speared two fish that had breezed past her leg. Satisfied, she climbed out of the river and wrapped the fish up in a cloth. Her gaze landed on a bush nearby where small red berries had begun to grow, the first signs of spring. She gathered as many as would fit in her pockets, and tossed them into her mouth. With a delightful pop, the berries burst, their tart sweetness heightening all of her senses.

Prince . . . so hard to believe.

She understood why Ruenen had kept his secret. Rayghast would kill him if he was ever found. Marai knew what it meant to have a target on your back.

But that didn't explain what had happened with Ruenen back at the river.

Marai knew she'd left him confused. Gods, *she* felt confused now. She saw how flustered he'd gotten, the red in his cheeks and neck. He'd become riled up far too easily, and she had done nothing other than bathe.

She forced herself to stare at her rippling reflection in the water. Her white blonde hair draped over her shoulder, her face clean and bright... she had to wonder. Was Ruenen's reaction because of *her* or had it simply been so long since he'd been with someone that any woman would do?

She wasn't charming. She never batted her eyelashes, never gave a coy smile. Marai had never thought of herself as attractive. In her line of work, appearances didn't matter. In fact, it was essential no one knew what she looked like. She'd shut down that minimally feminine part of herself long ago in order to survive the callousness of the world. Women of Astye were not allowed to do what they wanted with their bodies, let alone their hearts and minds. As a mercenary, Marai was free from those expectations and customs. She had unchained herself from at least one shackle of the bonds that always held her.

At first, she'd wanted to test his sword skills to see how much he knew. Petty, yes, but entertaining. The part that truly bothered her was that his reaction had felt slightly... invigorating. Ruenen had been so agitated, so heated. It was bizarre to know that she had that kind of effect on him without trying.

There was power in that, surely. A strange, heady sort of power that Marai had never utilized before. One she didn't know she had.

It wasn't magic. That power was something else entirely.

She never explored or considered her own sexuality. The times she *had* been intimate with someone... well, she never wanted to think about that.

Marai growled at herself, for the stupidity of caring about something so meaningless.

What does it matter if Ruenen finds me attractive? It doesn't change anything at all.

Their relationship was strictly professional, and Marai had no patience for that type of girl, the type who cares what men think. She would *not* allow herself to become one of them again.

"With *that* scent, I'm very curious what you're thinking about," came a velveteen voice from the trees.

Marai whirled around to see a figure hooded in a mauve cloak. She held up the spear and shifted her position. The stranger stayed in the shade, a section of the trees that was darkest.

"Oh, put the spear down, Butcher, I'm not here to hurt you," said the figure and tilted up his chin so Marai could see the face underneath.

Nosficio.

She only tightened her stance.

"Remarkable," he said, "to see under the cloak. So young. So fair. I wonder what you taste like."

"Are you here for revenge?" she asked and Nosficio smiled, no fangs in sight. They hadn't grown back in yet. A small relief, but he was still faster and stronger than she was.

"I told you . . . you intrigue me." His blood-red eyes assessed her, up and down. "I tracked you from the Den. I wanted to learn more about you and that human companion of yours. From what I smelled of you when we met . . . you are not human."

Marai didn't lower her guard as she watched him pluck a bramble from his luxurious velvet cloak and flick it away.

"How can you be out here in the daytime?"

Nosficio cocked his head to the side. "As long as I'm covered, I can travel in daylight. Many vampires dare not risk it, but I don't fear the sun." He lifted a gloved hand into a beam of light. "It's good for us to be out in the day. Otherwise, we lose ourselves to the night, and what little humanity we still cling to."

Surprise ran through her. It must've shown on her face because Nosficio smiled wickedly at her again. "I'm not all the rumors you hear in the shadows, Butcher."

"What about Queen Nieve? Are those rumors true?" Marai asked. His jaw tightened and a muscle twitched in his neck at the mention of her name.

He crossed his arms, nonchalant. "The Queen of Grelta and I are . . . acquaintances."

"I heard you were more than that."

"Queen Nieve is unlike any woman I've ever met," he said, eyes flashing. Marai saw it, for just a moment: affection. But it was gone as he zeroed in on her again. "As are you, Butcher. I haven't smelled or tasted faerie blood in decades." She wasn't surprised that he knew. Vampires had incredible sense of smell. He sniffed the air and sighed. "Your blood smells like ether. A spark. Dangerous and wild."

He closed his eyes, as if savoring the taste of her scent on his tongue. The hair on Marai's arms rose.

"If you think I'll let you near me, you are mistaken."

Nosficio laughed, a deep, throaty sound. Arrogant. Playful. "No, as I said, I followed you out of curiosity. I've heard so much about the Lady Butcher. I've wanted to meet you for ages. I knew it was only a matter of time before Nieve sent a mercenary my way. What luck for me that it was *you*."

The light shifted, splaying more shadows across the bank. Nosficio stepped closer to Marai and she inched backwards, her boots squelching in the mud.

"I couldn't place your scent before. It's different from other fae. Last night confirmed it for me." Marai started. Nosficio had been there, watching from the darkness, as she and Ruenen dispatched the Tacornian soldiers. "Your skills are impressive. But it was your anger, when listening to your human prince, when I sensed the true depths of what you are."

Her body tensed. Would Nosficio use that knowledge against them? Would he go to Rayghast?

"I'm half-fae. There's nothing special about that."

Nosficio's eyes opened wider. "You don't know? You don't *feel* it?" His lips parted, his brow furrowed, not in aggression, but confusion, when Marai didn't respond. "The air changed around you. It felt . . . *charged*."

Keshel's words snuck into her ears, taunting her. *You have a power inside you, Marai.*

"I don't know what it is, but it felt unlike anything I've seen for hundreds of years. And even then, it's . . . different," said Nosficio. "The fae of old could do many incredible things. They could shake the earth with their powers, create doorways in the air, kill hundreds with merely the flick of a hand—"

"There's nothing special about me."

"You're wrong, Butcher. Your magic will awaken soon. It's practically clawing to get out." Nosficio's dangerous smile returned. "Watching you is exciting."

Marai stared at him dryly. "You can leave now."

"Is my presence bothering you?"

"Forgive me if I don't want to associate with a blood-thirsty vampire. I don't trust you."

Nosficio laughed again. "Oh, darling, there are creatures worse than me in these woods."

"What do you mean?"

"Haven't you noticed? Something is *wrong* with these lands . . ."

For the first time, Nosficio looked worried. He scanned the trees, a somberness settling across his features. Marai *had* noticed as soon as she entered the Middle Kingdoms, that eerie sensation, like dozens of eyes watching her. The lingering scent of pepper and sulfur on the wind. The strange pulse beneath the ground.

"It's been happening slowly for years now . . . every time I step foot in the Middle Kingdoms, I can feel it growing darker."

The shadows. The creatures. Marai barely took a breath as Nosficio stared at her.

"You've seen them, haven't you?" he asked.

"Do you know what they are?"

"No. I stay away from them. They aren't supposed to be here..." Again, the vampire's eyes examined his surroundings. "Someone is waking them up. Or creating them. I don't know, but their numbers keep rising."

Marai's brain was having a difficult time keeping up. She'd seen the strange shadows, herself. Nosficio wasn't lying. And she could feel it, too—something wasn't right. The land felt wrong, as the vampire had said.

"That's not why I'm here, though," Nosficio announced, breaking Marai's train of thought. "I wouldn't have made my presence known at all, had I not come to warn you."

Marai froze. "Warn me?"

"Your princeling is gone."

Dropping the spear, Marai turned and sprinted back towards the campsite. Behind her, Nosficio made no sound. She only knew he was there because she saw his mauve cloak billowing in the breeze from the corner of her eye.

How long had she been gone? How had she not heard anything? As Marai rounded the curve in the riverbank, she expected to see Ruenen sitting on a log, plucking at his lute. She hoped this was a stupid joke by Nosficio.

It was eerily quiet as she approached the campsite. The hair on her arms rose, skin tingling in warning. No crackling sound of a fire. No sound of movement. She slowed her steps, careful where she tread, making sure to avoid stepping on twigs or brittle leaves. Inching forward, she got her first glimpse of the empty camp.

Her clothes were where she'd hung them, but everything else was strewn about. The contents of her and Ruenen's bags had been dumped, rooted through. Someone had taken all their money again. Ruenen's lute had been left on the ground, but his sword was missing.

As was Ruenen, himself.

Marai dropped the fish and slithered into the camp, her feet not making a sound. She knelt at the log and spotted long scuffs in the dirt.

Signs of a struggle.

"I told you," came Nosficio's voice from behind her. Marai leapt around and pointed her sword at the vampire, rage bubbling up inside. He merely shook his head. "Why do you doubt me? If I wanted you and your friend dead, I wouldn't have told you. I would've just snapped both your necks while you were busy *flirting*."

Marai shoved down her anger. Now wasn't the time.

She noticed the large circle of footprints around the camp. Heavy boots. Many of them, two dozen or so. Their prints led them through the trees back towards the road, skid marks following, as if they had dragged Ruenen with them. Marai doubted these were mere bandits. There would have been no reason for thieves to kidnap Ruenen after taking their money and supplies. No, it was clearly the work of soldiers.

"Which side?" she asked the vampire. He'd moved to the shadiest spot of their campsite and studied Marai intently.

"Tacorn."

Fuck.

"He barely put up a fight."

Marai quickly stuffed their belongings back in their packs, grabbed her dry clothes and Ruenen's lute.

"You've warned me," she said to Nosficio, "now go."

"A thank you would be polite," he said, narrowing his eyes. He made no move to leave or follow. Marai had no more patience for him. Yes, he'd warned her, but that didn't mean she trusted him an iota. He was a murderous vampire. A true creature of nightmares. This was most likely all part of a game for him.

"Thank you," she bit back.

Nosficio's expression softened.

Marai tracked the footprints through thick dead leaves on the forest floor, every once in a while catching a spot of blood. Ruenen wasn't severely wounded, but the soldiers had injured him in some minor fashion. Before stepping onto the road, Marai surveyed the darkening path. She listened, closing her eyes, honing in on the sounds of the forest. A woodpecker drummed into the bark of a tree.

The road was quiet.

Marai looked back. If Nosficio still followed her, he clearly wanted to watch, not actively participate in the hunt. Fine. She didn't fear him.

Marai held out her palm and a small flame appeared. She knelt to the ground, and traced her other hand over the prints in the dirt. There was a set of hoof prints. One of the captors had a horse, but the others remained on foot. Marai closed her palm, extinguishing the flame, and set out on her way.

The soldiers had at most a half hour head start. She was alone, and she could move faster than a small unit with a prisoner in tow. Every so often, Marai froze at the sound of a twig snapping or scuffling in the distance. Probably an animal, possibly even Nosficio, but Marai took no chances. Her hand never left the hilt of her sword.

I never should have left him alone, she thought, cursing herself. She'd been so distracted by Ruenen at the river that she'd dropped her guard. She'd been foolish and sloppy. She'd known how close they were to the soldiers they'd killed, knew others would come looking for the perpetrators.

She wanted to roar into the night. She wanted to tear at her hair. She was smarter than this. Marai had to find Ruenen before he was killed or worse—brought to the stronghold of Tacorn.

Minutes passed as she crept along the road. She came to a halt when it branched off in three directions, but she didn't need to read the signs to know where the paths headed. Tacorn territory was to her left. Nevandia to her right. Straight ahead took her down the middle of both. She assumed the soldiers had taken Ruenen further into Tacorn, but there was always a possibility that they were bringing him somewhere else . . .

Did she dare risk using magic to see which direction the tracks took? She didn't want the soldiers to see her coming. Marai glanced around, listened, eyes frantically searching. She had to try.

She lit the little flame in her palm again, and hunted in the dirt for signs of the footprints. Those heavy boots tramped off to the left, the long scuffs mixed in amongst the prints.

Confirming her suspicions, Ruenen was headed to the double-walled fortress at Tacorn in the capital city of Dul Tanen on the highland moor. They must have suspected him of murdering the other soldiers, which was, unfortunately, the truth. Marai knew what Tacorn did to criminals.

But if they recognized him, realized who he was. . . . Ruenen would be taken directly to King Rayghast, who'd undoubtedly make a spectacle of his execution for all of Tacorn and Nevandia to witness. It would be a bloody, horrific message of supreme power. And Nevandia would crumble, as Chiojan had in that brutal massacre. And Rayghast would win.

Marai hardened, every muscle in her tensing, focusing, thinking of all the ways she would rip those soldiers apart.

They were several days' travel from the castle fortress at Dul Tanen. Ruenen was unquestionably still alive, but the window of time for his rescue was narrowing.

The cover of darkness was always her friend. She welcomed it with open arms as she raised her scarf and hood.

Marai became the shadows in the night. A phantom moving effortlessly. Noiselessly. The assassin, cloaked in the deepest black. She became nothing and no one. Just darkness.

She followed them for hours, all night long, until the unit stopped at the side of the road. Marai watched the scene unfold from the dark safety of the trees.

The commander, Boone, wore a smug smile, and halted his retinue with a fist.

"Take an hour to rest. I'll ride ahead to alert the King of our guest," he said, tone oozing with triumph. "Be at Dul Tanen in five days. Don't let him out of your sight. Someone must hold him at all times." He clopped off down the darkened road.

The other Tacorn soldiers took their time on this break. They tied Ruenen up to the trunk of a tree, his head covered in a burlap bag. He didn't move, but he was conscious. His chest heaved in frantic breaths.

One group of Tacorn sentries was not too far away. The soldiers had no fear in lingering for a few moments within their own territory. They bit into tough strips of jerky, swallowed a few sips of alcohol or water. Someone said a lewd joke. A few laughed. Another soldier started humming the tune of "The Lady Butcher" softly under his breath as he poured liquor onto Ruenen's body, for sport and retaliation.

"Shut it," said the next commanding officer to the soldier.

"Worthless piece of trash." The soldier struck the side of Ruenen's head with the liquor bottle and sniggered. Ruenen grunted, but didn't react otherwise. "Don't look much like royalty now, do you?"

All their torches extinguished into wisps of smoke, plunging their resting spot into darkness.

The soldiers fell silent. They stared into the night. The gust of wind was gone, and now the night was still, stalled in time with baited breath.

A piercing scream and a soldier fell to the ground, throat sliced open. The others unsheathed their weapons.

Another shriek punctured the silence. Another soldier dead. The others began swinging frantically at anything, scattering amongst the trees like roaches. They heard nothing. They saw nothing but black. Another scream. Another dead.

"*There*," shouted a young, burly soldier, and pointed to the tree nearest him.

An apparition, a specter, *Marai,* stood there, black cloak waving in the breeze that was now stirring. But the breeze felt wrong. It wasn't natural. It pulsated with something.

Magic. The air was thick with it, heavy and stifling. The soldiers struggled to breathe. It was deadly. Lightning crackling, air spinning, whirring, engulfing.

Marai moved, slashing and stabbing, man after man fell. Their yells of agony echoed in the dark, still night. A handful escaped before Marai could gut them. They'd soon call for aid from the sentries, the picket lines, and the patrol units. Tacorn forces patrolled the Red Lands voraciously at all hours, but they would be too late to help the remaining Tacorn soldiers.

When the last man fell, the magic receded.

Lowering her hood, Marai cut the bonds on Ruenen's wrists and the rope tying him to the tree. She ripped off the burlap bag and his eyes widened in recognition and relief. His right eye was heavily swollen. He also had a gash on his forehead that dripped blood down his cheeks. Ruenen removed his own gag as Marai helped him to his feet.

"You came," he said.

Armor clanged, and feet trampled through the darkness.

"No time to talk," Marai said as soldiers reappeared, having found reinforcements at a nearby sentry post. Thirty or more soldiers, Marai estimated. She didn't have a plan for all of them. Slash through? Too many bodies. Run away? Surrounded. She could handle ten to fifteen alone when she had the element of surprise. But thirty . . .

The soldiers attacked. Ruenen grabbed a sword from a dead soldier and went to battle.

Soldiers barreled in through the trees from all sides, encircling the area.

Where was Nosficio? *Damn that vampire!* He'd have been useful in this situation.

Marai backed up, right into Ruenen, their swords raised. She felt the moment he resigned himself to their fate; his shoulders slumped against her back.

She wouldn't let the soldiers take either of them.

She felt her magic at her gloved fingertips, but knew it wasn't strong enough to make a difference. *Dig deeper.* The air thrummed again with a strange power.

Ruenen's warm hand gripped hers.

Cold dread rushed through her as she stared at the hungry, vicious faces of the soldiers. Tacorn soldiers had brutal reputations. She would be raped. Beaten and then raped again. Marai might not make it to the castle. The soldiers might do away with her here and now, and make Ruenen watch.

Hands all over her flesh. Massive, filthy, wretched hands—hands that would also ferociously flay Ruenen's body. They'd strip the skin from his bones, desecrating the soul within, before Ruenen would beg for death. And they would not give it to him. Such horrendous things awaited him in the fortress.

Ruenen's hand was strong in her own, like he could feel the icy fear consuming her. He squeezed her hand tighter.

She focused on that feeling. That physical touch. That potent connection.

A hand in hers. Not ripping, not taking . . . strong, but . . . secure. The touch of a friend. No one had held her hand since she was a child. She could feel its warmth through the leather of her glove.

She cared about this man, and she refused to let this be the end.

We will make it to Andara. We will not die here.

Something ignited in her. Marai's mind went feral, animalistic, as her magic flared.

She dug deep inside, lower and lower, to the well of power within. It was taking over . . . she could feel the magic swarm her, engulfing her in a power she didn't recognize. It was hers, but felt different. Instead of the usual warm sensation, the magic ripped through her, wild and untamed, like streaking naked in the woods on a full moon.

You have a power inside you, Marai.

In her fear, she yielded to it. The power Keshel had spoken of. The power he'd known all along was inside her. Because he'd *seen* it. He'd felt it, and so had Nosficio. Ruenen must've felt it, too, because he ducked to the ground as she erupted.

White light, flashing, cracking burst forth from her hands. The whole forest lit up. Too bright. Too bright for Marai's eyes. Lightning burst into the night. Lightning that didn't come from stormy skies. It was an unpredictable, lethal power.

It only lasted a mere moment. Marai found herself on all fours, panting into the dirt. The ringing in her ears slowly dissipated. Her vision came back into focus. She blinked away the blurriness. Marai lifted her head to survey the damage.

Not a single soldier was left standing. Every soldier had been incinerated; they were just piles of ash on the ground. Dying torches lay in the dirt, as if they'd been dropped there. The closest trees had been splintered into fallen flaming pieces, and ones further away burned with red-hot scars etched into their bark. The edges of Marai's own cloak were singed and smoking. Everything within a wide radius of her had been electrocuted.

I did this.

She whipped around to see Ruenen huddled directly behind her, arms shielding his head. He slowly met her gaze, both of them now pale, wide-eyed, and shaking.

She skid away from him. "Stay away. Don't come closer. I don't want to hurt you."

"What . . . what was that?" Ruenen asked, ignoring her and crawling to her side.

"I don't know," said Marai, her voice raspy and ravaged, like she'd been screaming. She looked at her trembling hands. She felt no power in them now. In fact, a tremendous exhaustion washed over her. Every ounce of magic within her had been used. "I've never done that before . . . faeries don't have this kind of power. Not anymore."

Keshel had seen this in her. In the strange, magical way he'd always seen things. Marai had often felt a flicker every time her temper flared. Every time she started losing control, that power slinked under her skin, but she'd been afraid to use it. Always so adamant against using magic.

"See? I told you," Nosficio said from the dark. He appeared from behind a burning tree, looking fairly amused.

"*You,*" Ruenen snarled, getting roughly to his feet, holding up a sword protectively in front of Marai.

"Why didn't you help us?" Marai asked the vampire.

"This isn't my fight," he replied. "Tacorn isn't after *me*. Besides, I wanted you to release those pent-up powers. All you needed was a little push."

"We could've died," Marai continued, fists clenched.

"I think there's a lot more you have left to discover about your magic, Butcher. Lightning was only the beginning."

The vampire's eyes burned bright in the darkness, full of fascination. Suddenly, he perked up and tensed.

"You should leave," he said, going motionless. "It won't be long before soldiers grow curious about the light. I'll kill a few for you to grant you time."

"Thank you," she said, and meant it.

With a slick smile, Nosficio said, "I hope we meet again someday, Butcher." He then disappeared in a blur.

Ruenen watched Marai carefully, but not out of fear. No, never fearful of her. It was worry etched into his face as he looked her over, surveying the wicked tiredness that had overcome her.

She handed over his pack and lute, and they scurried back towards the central middle road. It was the fastest way out of the Red Lands.

Ruenen wasn't as light on his feet as she was, and he kept wincing at the pain in his head. Marai pressed them faster, harder, running through the dark woods, moonlight their only guide. They stumbled over roots and logs, slipped in muddy puddles. She could hear his labored breathing behind her. She ignored her own fatigued body. When Ruenen started to lag, she grabbed his arm and pulled. Marai didn't let go. She continued to drag him along, as Ruenen's strength began to fade.

Get to the road.

Finally, the woods cleared, revealing the vast highlands, sloping heather-strewn hills. The dirt road that cleaved the land in half would lead them straight through, Tacorn on one side, Nevandia on the other. The road was the space between them, demarcating their territories, but the valley was entirely open without much shelter or protection, save for the Nydian River.

Marai and Ruenen dashed across the pitched, open lands on Tacorn's side. They had the cover of darkness, and the crescent moon above didn't provide adequate light to see the two figures from the sentry posts on either side of the valley. Tacorn's were empty, but their signal fires burned brightly against the black sky.

Ruenen stopped, wheezing, clutching his side. Marai yanked his arm again.

"We cannot stop here," she hissed at him. Ruenen didn't look up at her. He bent over like he might collapse. Marai took his face in her gloved hands and made him look at her. Those brown eyes pained and fearful, searching her own. "Please, Ruen. We must keep running."

He blinked, hearing the plea in her voice. He then stood up and took a deep, centering breath. Then he was off again.

They reached the road, the gravel crunching beneath their feet. It was no use trying to stay quiet; that was a luxury one only had when there was time. Instead, they careened down that road, and Marai checked over her shoulder every minute.

Ruenen finally collapsed as the sun began rising over the craggy cliffs, crimson and ominous, a sign of the blood spilt that previous evening. The hilly peaks were wreathed in mist. Marai dragged Ruenen off the path to a large jagged boulder. She leaned up against it, and shoved her canteen into his hand. He took a long, desperate gulp of water, gasping for air.

There were no soldiers on the horizon, so Marai took a moment to address the wound on Ruenen's head. It had clotted, but the wound would get infected. She removed her gloves and ripped a piece of cloth from the hem of her cloak. She poured water on the gash to rinse it. Ruenen winced, hissing, but didn't move a muscle. Marai assumed it was because he didn't have the energy. His face was caked with blood, and the water washed some of it away.

With gentle hands, Marai dabbed away the blood, feeling his gaze upon her the entire time. She tied another ribbon of cloth from her cloak around his head as a bandage.

"Do you feel dizzy?" she asked.

"I mean, *yes*, but that might be because I haven't breathed for four hours," Ruenen said with a bite. "But no, I don't think it's that bad."

There was nothing Marai could do for his swollen eye that was beginning to change color. A hefty dark bruise now formed around it. The eye that wasn't swollen was wary and full of exhaustion, but she could also see the warm glow of appreciation. With light fingers on his jaw, she tilted his head left and right, examining him. At last, her eyes flickered to his.

Something curled in her stomach, a heavy, hot feeling. Marai let her fingers oh so gently stroke his jaw slowly before she removed them. He needed to shave; his coarse beard tickled the pads of her fingers. The intimacy of that act would've caused a younger, more innocent Marai to blush, but she was too tired to feel embarrassed. Marai became suddenly aware of the feel of his leg touching hers and inched over.

She divvied up dried venison, bread, and a handful of squashed berries Marai took from her pocket. Ruenen gratefully accepted it all and stuffed the food into his mouth. Marai plopped down next to him, leaning against the rock, letting her leg lightly nudge his. She tried not to draw attention to her own aching body. Her muscles were tensing, tightening. Only pure adrenalin had kept her going, and they still had so far to go before Marai dared to consider them safe.

"You found me pretty quickly," said Ruenen, mouth full of bread. "And why was Nosficio there?"

"He told me you'd been captured," Marai said. "He's been tracking us since Iniquity."

"Did he attack you?" Ruenen asked, face darkening.

"No. I don't understand his motives, but I have to be appreciative for his help."

Ruenen nodded slowly, gazing out across the highlands, possibly searching for signs of Nosficio. Marai also searched the horizon, thinking about Nosficio's *other* warning—the creatures in the shadows. What were they? What was going on in the Middle Kingdoms? On the Nevandian side of the road, the grasses were brown and brittle. The heather was dead. A sense of decay and death lingered, but on the Tacorn side, the valley was flush with color and growth, even this early into spring. Something foul was afoot, but Marai was too tired to guess.

"The commander recognized me," Ruenen eventually uttered, rubbing his left wrist. Marai stiffened as she remembered the strange birthmark there. "He knew about my mark. He went on ahead to tell Rayghast. He's going to be *really* disappointed when he returns to find me gone."

All the more reason for them to keep moving. But given Ruenen's labored breathing, the sweat dripping off his brow, Marai could pause a few more minutes.

"So . . . should we discuss what happened back there?" Ruenen looked at her intently. "Don't get me wrong—it was extraordinary and impressive, but also absolutely terrifying. I thought I'd be incinerated like those soldiers."

Marai's brows furrowed, trying to recall the moments before, what she'd felt, how that magic had manifested.

"I was frightened," she admitted, "and I was angry. I felt the magic surging in me, trying to get out . . . I couldn't contain it. The magic fed off my emotions. And I didn't care what it did. I let it go."

She didn't mention their hand-holding. She knew that was part of it, that connection to him, but couldn't bear to tell him.

Ruenen took a long swig of water, gazing off across the grass and purple heather; the sun a red beacon above the hills. "You said that's never happened to you before."

"It's not a power I've ever used or seen, even from other fae. But fae magic has been diminishing for decades, and those of us who are not pure fae . . . we don't typically have much to begin with."

Some fae had been gifted more unique magic, such as healing capabilities or future-seeing, like Thora and Keshel. Magic affected each faerie differently. But never, in all her life, had Marai heard of powers like the ones she'd just used. Creating lightning from thin air? It was *true* magic. She supposed it was conceivable that the fae of old, the ones who roamed the world before humans destroyed them, had this type of power. They had been far stronger, far more connected to the elements. Nosficio had hinted at that.

And for some reason, it worried Marai.

She wasn't supposed to have those abilities. That power couldn't belong to her. She was only half-fae. Her father had only basic magic. Her mother, a human, had none. She couldn't feel that clawing magic at her fingers anymore. It didn't rage through her blood. But she knew it was there; a fanged creature curled up deep inside.

Is this what Keshel had meant that fateful day?

Marai had been fighting with him. He'd scolded her for wandering off alone. She was ten, hardly able to defend herself if she ever ran into humans.

"This place is like a cage," she'd yelled, pacing around the cavern like a trapped wildcat. Always trapped. Stuck here in that cave with Keshel and Thora telling her what to do. With Leif and Aresti poking at her, pushing her, mocking her every word.

"Hiding keeps us all alive," Keshel had said.

"This is not a life. I can be more than this, if you would let me," she'd snapped at him, her voice echoing off the stone walls.

Keshel had reached out and took hold of her skinny arm. His dark eyes had gotten that clouded look, as they always did when he was seeing. Marai had watched as he came back; his eyes found hers, once again clear.

"You have a power inside you, Marai." He'd let go of her, like he'd been shocked.

Marai returned from the memory. She stared at her hands.

"What *is* magic?" she posed to the universe softly.

What had Keshel truly seen in that vision? She had never asked him to elaborate. She'd never wanted to know more. He'd been waiting for her to come to him . . .

Marai's mind began to spiral. Who were her ancestors? Was she tapping into *their* powers or was this something entirely new? So much of faerie history was lost. After the massacre of her people, that knowledge was destroyed, forgotten forever. She'd been too young when her father died. He never had the time to tell her anything of real importance about his people. The other part-fae children . . . they'd all been too young to know these answers.

Marai glanced up at Ruenen to see him open his mouth, then close it again.

"I don't know," he said, shaking his head. "Although, I will say, that was pretty amazing... what you did." His eye warmed, the other was still rather swollen, a smile tugged at his mouth. "I don't care where the magic came from. I'm grateful that you came for me."

Marai stared at him. Really, truly let her eyes take him in.

The tangerine sunlight brought out the reddish highlights in his chestnut hair. It was longer now than it had been when they first met, falling in subtle waves past his ears. At the moment, it was all tangled and matted with dried blood. Those damned dimples in his cheeks when he smiled. Such an easy, natural smile, it made her want to grin back because it was that earnest. High cheek-bones and perfectly arched eyebrows. A fuller lower lip.

He *did* look like his mother, Queen Larissa.

In that moment, with the morning sun beaming down on him, dirty, bloody, and swollen, Ruenen was possibly the most handsome human male Marai had ever seen. Because he didn't look at her like she was a monster. Because he never feared her. He gazed at her like she was worthy.

"You hired me to protect you," she said gruffly, ignoring the way her body wanted to lean into his. That heat crawled up her neck again, and lower, lower beyond her stomach. This wasn't her magic stirring.

Snap out of it, she growled to herself.

The magic had drained her. That was it—lowered her defenses. Her body and mind had been pushed to the brink.

Ruenen must have noticed the heat radiating off her, the stiffness in her posture. "Marai, I won't be able to move at all if you don't stop looking at me like that." His voice was deeper, a sensual caress across her skin. Her heart skipped a beat. She quickly scooted away and looked out at the highlands. Ruenen nudged her playfully with his shoulder, closing the distance she'd just created. "You must be tired of having to defend your weak little human prince."

Marai sniggered. "You are literally a full-time job."

Ruenen chuckled, a warm, affectionate sound. "I don't know what I'd do without you."

Marai's breathing hitched. Her heart pounded. Not because of his words, necessarily. But because he *meant* it. Because his face was open and honest and looked at her with such admiration that she thought she might faint from the shock. No one had ever looked at her that way. Certainly not Captain Slate Hemming from *The Nightmare*...

They were so close, sitting there shoulder to shoulder. She could have leaned in and gently swept her lips across his. Marai could almost feel his lips on her neck, his ragged breath in her ear, his hands in her hair...

But it wasn't Ruenen's hands she thought of then.

Marai leapt to her feet. She stepped away, putting distance between them again.

"We have to go," she snapped, grabbing her pack and throwing it over her shoulder. Ruenen stood with a deep, long groan of pain. He ran a hand through his tangled locks, frowning.

They pressed on, hour after hour, running and running because their lives depended on it, only stopping to rest in brief intervals.

Yet all the while, Marai's head was foggy. Her thoughts wrestled between Ruenen, her reaction to him, the almost loss of him, and what that would do to her.

Think about something else, she demanded.

More important than the matters of her heart, her mind returned to magic. The lightning.

It left Marai wondering—why her? Why now?

CHAPTER 14
Rayghast

Rayghast supped in his suite, a tray of decadent food before him in the plush armchair. He was alone, as he preferred. The evening was quiet, thick with something Rayghast almost thought was anticipation. Something was amiss. He felt it in his gut.

He knew it wasn't Nevandia. He no longer had anything to fear from their weakened state. Earlier that day in the throne room, his council had made that clear.

"Nevandia's lands continue to squalor, Your Grace," Wattling had said. "Our lands thrive. Merely glance out the window and you can see the green of Tacorn, even in winter. It's as if Lirr herself blesses us. She supports our cause against Nevandia."

"A good omen, indeed," said Cronhold with a nod. He was ancient, every year more skeletal than before, hardly able to move on his own. A young page stood behind his chair, ready to usher him around. "We shall soon regain the glory of our forefather's lands. Back before that traitor Tarken left to build his own kingdom."

The council murmured their approvals.

"A false kingdom!"

"The gods want us to take back what is rightfully ours."

Wattling quieted them all, raised his hands as if giving a sermon. "Two hundred and fifty appalling years Nevandia has been its own 'kingdom.'"

He sneered that last word. "When King Feist of Tacorn's right hand, Lord Tarken, rebelled and ran off into the night like a thief. The traitor took half of our people with them, slashed our lands down the middle and called himself *King*. King Feist vowed to take back what was his. We now stand upon the precipice of seeing the kingdoms reunited, with our glorious King Rayghast as the sole leader of the Middle Kingdom!"

The council raised their wine goblets in the air. "Hail, King Rayghast!"

"Laimoen will see to it that this bloody, forty-year war will finally end," Wattling continued after taking a long drink from his goblet. "Hail, Tacorn!"

Rayghast merely watched them.

The gods had nothing to do with what was happening. Laimoen would not stop this war. It wasn't Lirr and her blessing that made Tacorn's lands prosper. It was Rayghast. This land was bound to him, it fed off his desires. He simply touched the earth, felt the darkness pulse beneath his hands, said the words, and he sucked away the mere life from Nevandia, then gave it back to Tacorn tenfold. As he'd done since the day he became a man.

But the magic had stirred in him long before that.

Like the curse on his seed, this was another secret Rayghast would take to his grave. The *real* reason Nevandia's first King, Tarken, turned traitor on Feist.

Now, eating the fat pheasant and succulent greens before him, Rayghast could feel the magic in every bite. He savored it. A bite of pepper on his tongue. It tasted of power. Complete and utter control. Rayghast was close to unleashing his forces upon the weakening kingdom to his east. Finally, it was time to take back what was rightfully his. He could give his father peace in death at last.

"My King," came Boone's voice from the doorway. Boone hadn't been at the castle in weeks; he'd been out surveying the army, training soldiers, preparing them for their final assault against Nevandia. Soon, so soon. Rayghast had waited long enough.

Boone's beetle-black eyes glistened, wide and excited. Rayghast thought he saw an actual smile on the man's lips. "I believe I have him."

Rayghast never thought much of his heart, but right then, it skipped a beat. Slowly, he turned to face Boone, who puffed out his chest and lifted his chin. Boone hadn't appeared this confident since he first took the post as commander.

"Fetch the council," Rayghast told the guard at his door. The guard disappeared and Boone waited patiently, that smirk growing every minute they waited for the council. They all came, many in their bedtime robes. Cronhold hobbled in last, using his page as a crutch.

"You have the boy?" Wattling asked, skeptical, once Boone repeated himself.

They'd come close to this moment before, when they'd sacked the city of Chiojan in Varana. The boy had been there, but he'd slipped through Boone's fingers again. The soldiers had been far too caught up in raping and arson and lost sight of their mission. Rayghast had punished them all afterwards with fifty lashings apiece, by his own hand. The anger and bloodlust he felt in that moment—his magic called for him to take the whip. Every bloody lash against a soldier's back fed the corrupted magic in his body.

But the soldiers' ferocity in Chiojan had given him something valuable. Rayghast now had sway over Varana. The proud empire had fallen to its knees at Rayghast's strength. A new tool in his arsenal.

"He's in the woods. *Our* woods, with my men," Boone explained, speaking only to Rayghast, who hadn't moved a muscle from his arm chair.

"And how do you, uh, know it's him?" posed Cronhold, raising an eyebrow. "Did he admit that he's the lost prince?"

"How did you catch him?" asked Councilman Dobbs at the same time.

"A unit of my men were attacked on the road. A few survived and said they'd been attacked by a young man and woman. They said the strangers had tremendous skill with a sword. Well, Your Grace, any attack of Tacorn soldiers on our soil is a treasonous crime, so I hunted them down." Boone took a breath, as if readying to reveal the best part of his story. "We came upon the young man at the banks of the Nydian. At first, he seemed ordinary, a mere bard. That's what he's been pretending to be. But upon further inspection, I noticed he looked remarkably similar to Queen Larissa."

Larissa. Rayghast didn't care for beauty, it was a meaningless quality, but he could admit she had been an attractive woman. It was hard for anyone to forget her face. Pity she had to die.

It had been a glorious day when word of the Queen's death spread. And Vanguarden Avsharian, so overcome at the loss of his wife, had challenged Rayghast to a fight to the death. Rayghast had also kidnapped a Nevandian courtier, a cousin of Vanguarden, earlier the same day. Adding insult to injury, he took her as his third wife. The girl had fought against him, cut up his face with her fingernails. Rayghast had worn the scratches, fresh and raw, as another message to Vanguarden. He knew the sight had affected the handsome King. Another reminder of his weakness.

Rayghast had faced the King of Nevandia on the Red Lands, stared into his red, puffy eyes. The man had loved his wife, and that love had weakened him, made him impulsive. He fought hard, but distractedly. Rayghast beheaded him after only a few minutes.

A glorious day, indeed.

But Nevandia wasn't finished yet.

Vanguarden's cousin had died in childbirth. Not a surprise. She hadn't lasted long. Rayghast had already remarried again, his fourth wife a gift from Varana as allies. He might never have his heir, but he would have his kingdom reborn.

"They have the same eyes, same nose, although his hair is lighter," Boone continued on. "He appears to be the same age as the child would be, around twenty and two. Most importantly, he has the mark of the sunburst on his left wrist. He was sweating with fear, but I'll let His Grace make the final verification."

"So where is he now?" Cronhold asked more forcefully. Boone finally glanced at him, a sneer coming to his face.

"He's with my men in the woods, about three or four days' walk from here. Once he arrives, he will be chained in the dungeon." Boone then looked at Rayghast squarely. "Ready for your judgment, Your Grace."

"Well, this is quite a turn of events," Wattling said, nodding his head. "Our coffers will double . . . *triple* thanks to Nevandia's land and our alliance with Varana. We may become the wealthiest kingdom on the continent."

"Why did you not stay with the boy?" Rayghast asked, standing in one fluid move. He stepped closer to Boone. The commander shifted on his feet.

"I wanted to give you the news personally, Your Grace, so you could prepare for his arrival."

"That boy has escaped my clutches for twenty-two years," said Rayghast in his menacingly calm tone. "Did you think it prudent to leave him alone with just *anyone?*"

Boone did not balk. "They are highly trained soldiers, Your Grace, I'm sure they will bring him safely to us here."

Movement to Rayghast's right caught his attention. His fourth wife, Princess Rhia of Varana, now Queen of Tacorn, stood in the doorway of their conjoined chambers. She'd been gifted to him by her father, the Emperor of Varana, as a token of good faith. She was eighteen, but stood with the poise of a woman twice her age. Her long black hair was styled tightly onto her head where a silver tiara sat. She was flanked by her entourage of wide-eyed ladies-in-waiting.

Rayghast never allowed his wives near the council. It wasn't their place, but this was his bedroom, and a turning point within Tacorn. He would allow her to listen.

Cronhold raised a shaky finger. "What of the young woman you said he was with?"

Boone addressed the council, ignoring Rhia in the doorway. "We didn't see her. There was evidence a girl was with him, but she wasn't at the campsite when we took the prince."

"Any idea who this girl could be?"

"He claimed she was his mistress, but I believe it was all an act," Boone explained. "Based on the soldiers' accounts from the first attack, this girl fits the description of the Lady Butcher. And the prince mentioned he'd written a song about her."

"The Lady Butcher?" scoffed Dobbs. "She's not real."

Boone snapped his head in Dobbs' direction. "Not real? You haven't been out there, Dobbs. You don't leave the comforts of your estate or this castle. I can assure you, the Lady Butcher exists. And judging by the skill used to take down my men near Havenfiord, I'd say there's a decent possibility that she may be the young prince's companion."

Rayghast cared not if the prince traveled with the Lady Butcher or a common whore. She was unimportant.

"A woman assassin?" came Rhia's quiet voice. All heads snapped her way. She stepped further into the room, the flames in the hearth highlighting the planes of her cold, pale face. Her expression betrayed nothing, as it always did whenever she was in Rayghast's presence.

"Not only that, Your Grace, but the survivors claimed they saw her use magic."

"Magic? *Poppycock*," Wattling gasped. "We killed all the faeries. No one has magic anymore."

No one except Rayghast . . . but if *he* existed, then it was possible. This Lady Butcher was a faerie who'd evaded detection, and if she survived the purging . . . there could be others. Rayghast couldn't abide it. No faerie could be allowed to live. If Rayghast wanted to conquer Astye, no one, human or fae, could be powerful enough to stand in his way.

"Capture her and hold her responsible for the deaths of our soldiers. Either way, this girl has committed treason," Rayghast told Boone. He then faced the rest of his council. "When he approaches Dul Tanen in three days, only then will you tell the people of Tacorn that the Prince of Nevandia has been captured. I want them filling the streets when the prince is ushered through our gates. I want them to see our victory firsthand, to shout it in his ears. Prepare the dungeon. Prepare the guards."

The council nodded, a fire in their eyes, a pep in their step unlike anything Rayghast had ever seen from them. He turned his back on the old men; the scuffing, clomping and shuffling told him they'd all exited his chambers.

Rhia came to his side, head bowed demurely as always. She had sent her ladies away with the council. "What a felicitous day, my King." He barely glanced at her as he returned to his dinner. "I'm sorry that I disrupted the council. It was not my intention, but I saw a bright light to the North from my window, and I grew concerned. I heard you speaking with the council, and I thought it was about that."

"A bright light?"

"Way off in the distance, from the woods. So bright it lit up the sky like a lightning storm."

Rayghast went to his window and looked out past the city and its two encompassing stone walls, across the moors and hills to the forests beyond. Nothing. No sign of any light. He looked back at her.

Rhia read his skepticism. "Perhaps my eyes were playing tricks on me. My apologies, Your Grace." She bowed her head as Rayghast returned to his seat.

She sat in the chair next to him; the long bell sleeves of her robe-like dress sweeping the floor. Her back so straight and stiff Rayghast knew she wasn't sitting for comfort. "You will be a powerful ruler. Great and noble." Her tone remained level. Not oozing flattery like most. She was a guarded woman, and knew how to play the game.

Rayghast looked up from his supper. Rhia rested her delicate hands on her stomach. "And soon, my King and husband, you shall have a son. No one will ever be able to take that power from you."

Her eyes remained respectfully at the floor as Rayghast stared at her. She'd never bear him a son. She would die like the others. But she was his favorite of them all, if he could feel such a thing. The others were weak creatures. But Rhia . . . she was made of ice and stone. She'd make a great Queen of Tacorn.

"My father had died hoping this moment would one day come," he said to her slowly.

"You will finally succeed in wrangling back the kingdom that seceded," Rhia said, not raising her bowed head. But Rayghast saw the corners of her eyes tighten. "My father in Varana will provide whatever forces you require."

She stood, bending low in a deep, regal curtsy. His young wife then returned to her own chambers and shut the door softly.

His thoughts returned to the prince as he stared into the raging fire. Waiting in the woods. Three days away. Magic thrummed in his veins and clouded his brain, like black swirling smoke.

Soon, it whispered.

His blackened fingers twitched at the thought of holding the leather whip. Of striking it across the prince's flesh. He would take out every year of frustration, every failure, on the prince's weak body. Two hundred and fifty of them.

And then, once the young Nevandian prince was battered and barely breathing, Rayghast would sever his pretty head from his body and display it for all of Tacorn and Nevandia to see. He'd send it in a decorative box to the Steward.

Rayghast was the True King. He, alone, ruled the Middle Kingdom, and he'd use Rhia of Varana to help him conquer the other seven.

CHAPTER 15
MARAI

They kept running.

Through the valleys, past thawing crystal lochs and the Nydian River. Over ancient craggy hills, from the time of magic, before humans ruled. They ran parallel to the Nydian, which weaved through the valley like a cerulean serpent. Marai didn't know how much longer she could last. Her half-fae body was more durable than Ruenen's, but she was reaching the end of her endurance. Every time she looked back over her shoulder, Ruenen was further away, hardly able to move his legs. His skin turned pallid from exhaustion and dehydration.

Just a little farther, she pleaded. They were somewhere between the capital cities of Dul Tanen and Kellesar. The ruggedly beautiful highlands would come to an end soon. The danger would recede once they reached the forest on the other side, then they could continue onwards through the neighboring kingdoms of Ain and Syoto.

But then Marai heard a grunt and something fall behind her. She turned to see Ruenen lying face down on the road.

Cursing, Marai skidded to his side, turning him over onto his back. His lips were cracked and white. She gave him the rest of her water, but it wasn't enough.

"We need to keep going," she urged him as she poured water down his throat. He sputtered as water dribbled down his chin. He didn't have the strength to move his arm to hold the canteen himself.

"I can't," he murmured. His uninjured eye couldn't open.

Marai tugged on his arms, groaning in frustration when he didn't budge. She didn't have the strength to carry him. Her legs throbbed and her muscles rebelled against every single move she made.

Ruenen suddenly started laughing.

"I don't see what's so funny," she said.

"You and I . . . we always run, don't we?"

This wasn't the time for this conversation. *He must be delirious.* "What do you mean?"

Ruenen's face turned solemn, his laughter erased. "From our pasts. From the demons that chase us."

A shadow crossed his face, and Marai felt that shadow shroud her heart. Her eyes began to burn and she blinked away the fire in them. "I run from nothing." She straightened and put her canteen away.

"Oh?" Ruenen's good eye widened. "Never letting anyone get close to you? Always traveling alone, place to place?"

Marai's anger briefly flared, but it was impossible to get mad at the injured, exhausted man at her feet. "And what else do you run from, Ruen?"

A smile tugged at his pale lips. "Responsibility."

Ruenen closed his eye, content to remain on the ground. If he took up the throne, he wouldn't have to run from Rayghast anymore. Ruenen would rather hide forever than wear the crown. Marai couldn't understand why. It was his destiny to rule Nevandia, and there was a chance, however slim, that he could win against Tacorn on the battlefield. But how could Marai judge Ruenen when he was so right about her. Running from demons, indeed.

Then Marai heard a sound that made her heart stop.

Hooves. Pounding against the earth. Many.

She looked left—not from the Tacorn side of the valley.

She whirled around. There, in the distance, galloping down from a sloping hill, came the gleaming, golden figures of a Nevandian mounted patrol.

No matter her opinions on Ruenen becoming King, it wasn't her place to make that choice for him. Marai pulled and tugged with all her might on Ruenen, trying to get him to his feet.

"We need to move *now*," she growled, straining her body as she linked her arms underneath Ruenen's and tried to lift him from behind.

"*I can't*," he hollered in fury and fatigue. Marai fell backwards onto her rear, snarling out a curse.

The riders were nearly upon them. There was no running from this situation, so Marai stood, wielding her sword with the little strength she had left. Her father's blade gleamed in the sunlight. Dimtoir, the Protector. She'd never once wielded it to defend anyone before. Marai invoked the soul of her father, the defender. She stood her ground, Ruenen lying behind her. And she was willing to protect.

The Nevandian patrol halted within feet of her, their heads covered by golden helmets. Soldiers nocked their arrows in their bows, taking aim.

"What's going on here?" asked the deep voice of the commanding officer; a green plume on his helmet signified his rank. An emerald and gold sunburst emblem pinned his matching green cape to the shoulders of his armor.

"We were captured by Tacorn," Marai said, eyes shifting between each soldier, making mental notes of their positions, their weapons, the weaknesses in their armor. "Please, we're trying to get to safety. We're exhausted. My companion here can no longer move . . ."

"Captured by Tacorn?" repeated the commander, his tone incredulous. "For what reason?"

Marai glared at him. She hoped he could feel her anger through his helmet visor. "A misunderstanding."

"Are you Tacornian citizens? I see you wear no emblems."

"No, we're traveling tradesmen—"

"Sir," said one of the other mounted soldiers in warning. "Tacorn soldiers approach."

Marai's blood went cold. On the ground, Ruenen didn't move or make any indication that he was conscious, and Marai assumed he'd fainted. She risked a glance over her shoulder at the small unit of black-armored soldiers heading their way, crossing through a shallow part of the Nydian. One man carried a Tacorn flag high into the air. Even from a distance, they exhibited a commanding, fearsome presence.

"Please," she begged the captain. She knew her tone was forceful, edged, not at all the sweet, emotional, pleading tone she knew he wanted to hear. She was vulnerable, but she would not show him her fear. "They'll kill us."

The captain considered her for a moment. He knew what happened in the Tacorn dungeons.

"Even if we let you go," the captain said, "you won't get far. Not in his condition."

The Nevandians raised their weapons as they waited patiently for Tacorn to arrive at their edge of the road. Marai positioned herself closer to Ruenen with a better view of both units, Dimtoir raised in defense. The Tacorn leader, Boone, was the first to reach the road.

"These are our prisoners," he proclaimed, but his eyes focused solely on Ruenen's body. Out of the corner of her eye, Marai saw Ruenen recoil. So he was awake . . . unable to do more than listen. "We'll be taking them with us."

A few Tacorn soldiers moved to dismount their horses, when the Nevandian commander raised a hand. His own soldiers aimed at those who'd tried to move towards Marai and Ruenen.

"You seem quite eager to get them back," the Nevandian captain drawled. "Perhaps they are of some significant value."

"That is no concern of yours," spat Boone. "They're our prisoners, responsible for the deaths of several soldiers. You *will* back off, Nevandian scum." There was something else in his voice, a slight tremor.

Concern. And Marai assumed it was not due to the Nevandians... but what awaited him back in the capital of Dul Tanen if he returned without Ruenen a second time.

The Nevandian captain did not take kindly to the insult. His spine stiffened. He'd heard the worry in the Tacorn commander's voice, as well. He wasn't dumb, he knew there was a very good reason why Rayghast wanted these prisoners. Whoever Marai and Ruenen were, Tacorn was willing to fight for them. They were valuable.

When Nevandia did not lower their weapons, refusing to yield, Boone said icily, "very well, then."

And arrows flew.

Marai heard the *thunk* of arrow meeting flesh, the drop of a body onto the ground, the whizzing of other arrows all around her. She leapt onto Ruenen's body, covering him and her own head.

"*Don't hit him,*" shouted Boone to his own men, words laced with panic. "Rayghast needs him alive."

The soldiers dismounted, swords raised, as they clashed across the road. Marai and Ruenen were surrounded. Any arrow could hit them. And Nevandia would rather see them dead than in the hands of their enemy.

Once again, Marai tried to raise Ruenen to his feet. His face was so white, Marai wasn't sure it was from the dehydration anymore. It was the dread and understanding of their situation. That there was no escaping it. Torture and death awaited them from either side.

Ruenen took Marai's hand. It was nothing more than a touch; he didn't have the strength to hold her. "Leave me, Marai."

She glowered at him as her heart stuttered. "No."

"You can still run," he said. "Now, while they're distracted."

Two soldiers from opposing sides stepped nearer, a fierce battle between them as their blades collided. The Tacornian was far larger, brawnier than the Nevandian knight. They almost crashed into Marai and Ruenen, but she shot to her feet, entering the fray. Marai sliced the Tacorn soldier across his exposed thigh in one swift movement. She'd severed his femoral artery. As he crumpled into a heap, the Nevandian knight looked at her.

"Thanks," he said, his voice youthful.

Marai nodded once, then immediately returned to Ruenen's side.

"I cannot leave you here," she said. "I swore I'd get you to Andara. I never, ever fail a job."

Ruenen huffed out a pathetic laugh. He saw it for the lie it was. Marai wasn't staying because of the commission. It hadn't been about that for a while. She didn't *want* to leave him, to run away like a coward.

No, she wouldn't run this time.

"In that case, I release you from our bargain," he said with a tired smile. An arrow whizzed, lodging in the dirt by his head. His eye widened, but he squeezed Marai's hand harder, bringing her attention back to him. "You've done more for me than you know. Please. Save yourself. Go to Andara without me."

She shook her head, a furious roar bursting from her throat. She *refused* to leave him. She wouldn't let him be taken and tortured. Perhaps both sides would defeat each other. If she jumped into the scrimmage, replicated the lightning back in those woods, she could ensure all the soldiers died. That would give them a window of time to escape before reinforcements came. But they wouldn't get far before the others would track them, not in Ruenen's condition.

Marai stared at the crimson-soaked ground. There was a reason why they called this area the Red Lands . . . so much blood spilt here, so many dead from hundreds of skirmishes. Their blood would coat the valley, too. She and Ruenen would be two more bodies added to the tally. Vanguarden had been beheaded by Rayghast not far from this exact spot. This journey had been a fool's errand.

Someone grabbed Marai from behind, pulling her away from Ruenen, pinning her arms to her sides.

"*No,*" she bellowed, her voice breaking. Marai reached for her magic, but felt no spark. She tried again, but the well was bone dry. The bucket came up empty. She was too tired to summon magic.

She thrashed and snarled like a wild cat as the Tacorn commander approached Ruenen. Ruenen tried to stand; the muscles in his forearms and legs strained, his whole body shaking with the effort. Boone kicked Ruenen in the stomach. Marai swore she heard a rib crack. Boone shoved Ruenen back to the ground. He left his foot there on Ruenen's back, a posture of conquest.

More Tacorn soldiers appeared across the river. The Nevandians started to fall back, retreating to their side of the valley.

A soldier tied ropes around Ruenen and shoved a burlap sack over his head. But he wasn't fighting. He couldn't, or wouldn't, protest.

A second pair of hands grabbed Marai's arms. Before she could swing her sword, someone knocked her upside the head with the blunt edge of a weapon. Her vision went black as her body hit the ground.

She awoke in the dark with a splitting headache and a tinny ringing in her ears. It took a moment to orient herself due to the stifling burlap covering her head. Its strong scent made Marai's head swim. Pain shot across the back of her skull where the soldier had struck her.

Judging by the steady jostling beneath her, she'd been tossed across the back of a horse. Every part of her was bound, gagged, and confined. She could barely move her ribcage to take a breath.

She listened to the sound of a drawbridge lowering, a metal gate rising, hooves clopping across cobblestones, the shouts of a crowd.

They must have arrived at Tacorn's capital city of Dul Tanen, a several days' ride from where they'd been on the moor. Marai had avoided Dul Tanen during her travels. Its reputation for brutality was well-known, and Rayghast operated the city with an iron fist, granting his soldiers leave to do as they pleased. They'd prowl through the streets, bullying, abusing citizens on a whim. Tacornian women fared the worst, suffering abuse by anyone's hand. Soldiers could do whatever they wanted to a woman at any time, even if she was married, and bore no consequences.

The crowd seemed to be aware who the prisoners were. Unsurprising. Rayghast would want this public, for his people to know his victory. Something hit her. A rock. Sharp pain exploded across her back. Another struck her in the face. Curses were thrown her way, as well, from male voices. "Bitch" and "whore" were the tamer ones. But most of the ire was spewed at Ruenen.

"You're dead, Prince!"

"Fucking coward!"

"Nevandian filth!"

If Marai had use of her arms, she would have ripped out their tongues.

But she couldn't blame them. These people had been fed Rayghast's hatred of Nevandia for years. The war had gone on so long, it was all many of them knew. And Ruenen was their chance of ending it. This parade through town was a celebration for the citizens of Dul Tanen. A symbol that no more of their sons and husbands and brothers would die.

Marai's horse stopped and someone removed her from its back. Now standing, she swayed on her feet, feeling sluggish and groggy. Once again, she reached for her magic, but when she did, her head pounded and stomach twisted. Nausea roiled over her. She recognized the signs of a mild concussion.

She was then dragged between two sets of strong bodies, down an echoing stairwell, each sound reverberating loudly off the walls. She stopped feeling the pain, nausea, and exhaustion. All she felt was the searing cold of fear. She knew where they were taking her. Judging from the sound of other dragging boots across stone, Ruenen was still with her. The soldiers weren't separating them yet.

A cell door screeched open and Marai was pulled inside. The door swung shut behind her. Her arms and legs were then unbound. The rope around her wrists remained, and was pulled up into the air. They hooked that rope to something dangling from the ceiling. Marai could barely reach it; the tips of her boots grazed the floor. Her shoulders and upper back screamed at the strain and pull on them. A soldier ripped the burlap sack from her head. Her eyes adjusted to the large dark cell, lit only by candlelight and one small window close to the ceiling. She counted five soldiers filling in the space. To her left, seven feet away, Ruenen had also been strung up, dangling as she was by a hook from the ceiling.

Boone was there, without his helmet. His eyes blazed in triumph as he assessed Ruenen. The man reminded Marai of a hawk with his aquiline nose and alert eyes. He seemed disappointed with what he saw in the prince. Boone grabbed Ruenen's face and forced his eyes open.

"You'll pay dearly for the humiliations you've made me suffer."

Marai swung out a leg, barely scraping the commander's pants. She let out a vicious roar that bounced off the walls. The sound and effort made Marai's head spin.

"Take your hands off him!"

Boone let go of Ruenen and came to Marai's front.

"You're the Lady Butcher, I presume," he said, looking her up and down, unimpressed. "You're not at all what I expected." He punched her in the face. Pain erupted across her jaw and cheek, straight into the nerves of her teeth. "That's for all my men you killed."

Marai spat back in his face and sneered, despite her splitting headache. "It was my pleasure."

Boone struck her again, this time low in the gut. Marai grunted, pain filling her, and Ruenen twisted against his bindings. At least his feet could touch the floor. He had better leverage than Marai, but he was weakened from their fleeing.

"Stop! She's innocent," he stammered to the commander. "It was me . . . I killed all your men. Let her go."

Marai's heart clenched at his words. She met Ruenen's good eye and shook her head. She would not leave him here alone. Boone grinned knowingly. Marai would never be released, even if she had been truly innocent. She'd be used as a form of torture for Ruenen. They would break her first just to hear him beg.

And she knew he would. Ruenen would beg for her life. She didn't deserve it.

"You're not here because of my men. We've been *searching* for you, Prince," Boone told Ruenen. "The King will be down shortly. He's busy with preparations, but I know he's looking forward to meeting you." He then strutted out of the cell, head held high.

Marai looked frantically up at the hook. It was attached to a thick chain nailed into the stone ceiling. She pulled downwards with all her sluggish strength, and the rope cut deep into her wrists as she twisted and flailed.

Somehow, she'd find a way to get them free. There had to be a way. The guards watched her, entertained, pointing and laughing as she gagged from the effort.

She snarled at them all. "*Fuck you.*" It only made them louder. The sound assaulted her ears, causing her head to hammer against her skull.

Now that Boone was no longer touching her, Ruenen hung limply. All the fight had gone from his face.

"Don't you *dare* give up," Marai commanded him. "Fight, Ruen. You must!"

He didn't acknowledge he heard her at all. The guards laughed again at her desperation and at Ruenen's submission.

They quieted at the sound of footsteps in the hallway.

The steps were unhurried. Languorous. As if their owner knew he could take his time. Because his prisoners were never leaving alive.

Rayghast entered the cell and Ruenen's body went as taut as a bow string. The whole cell took a collective breath and held it. The air shifted, became heavier. Ruenen's eye darted up and finally came face to face with his hunter.

Rayghast's dark eyes, as empty as infinite voids, drank in the sight of the lost prince dangling in his dungeon. With a sweep of his hand, the guards left to stand outside the cell, closing it.

"Prince," Rayghast said with a slight bow of his head to Ruenen. "You do look like your mother."

Ruenen paled. Taller and broader than Ruenen, the physique of a true warrior, Rayghast looked over his prey hungrily. His bald head reflected the flickering light, casting a shadow upon his sharp face. Ruenen's eye darted away, not meeting the King's. His head flopped down in defeat.

Marai noticed the strange coal-color of the skin on Rayghast's arms. No one's skin was pure black in that way. She knew he painted himself when going into battle. Was that was what he'd done here? Dipped his arms in paint, or had it tattooed permanently past his elbows.

"How long I've waited for this day." Rayghast didn't sound excited. Or relieved. His tone was almost . . . dull. No emotions whatsoever.

Rayghast turned his attention towards a table. Upon it sat all manner of devices Marai cringed to look at: pliers, knives, hammers. Her own weapons also lay there, now belongings of the Tacorn dungeon. Ruenen's lute was propped up next to the table, toying with him. Rayghast grabbed the handle of a long leather whip and brought it to his chest reverently.

"Two hundred and fifty lashes. For all the years your traitorous ancestors pretended to govern a kingdom."

Two hundred and fifty lashes. A wave of nausea and icy panic rushed through her at the thought of that whip striking Ruenen's bare back.

Marai twisted again, yanking down hard on the chain. *"Touch him and you die."*

Rayghast's head snapped to her. Marai met and held that intense stare. He stepped closer to her. Then so fast, his finger appeared on her cheek. He dragged his fingernail down her skin. It didn't hurt, but it was predatory. Controlling. His silent way of telling Marai that she was powerless against him. She would not flinch away. She would not give him that satisfaction.

"You are brave," he said. It was strange to hear the compliment from the King's lips. He cupped her cheek with his hand.

And then she felt something at his touch.

A spark. A tingle of magic.

A dark, smoky tendril caressed her mind in greeting. *Hello, faerie girl.* The voice in her head wasn't Rayghast's. It was both ancient and young, soft yet threatening, and it seemed spine-chillingly delighted to meet her.

Marai's world reeled.

Rayghast had *magic*.

But Tacorn *hated* magic. It'd been Rayghast, himself, who had ordered that final attack on the fae camps that killed her parents. Humans couldn't use magic. Rayghast couldn't have fae blood. That tingle didn't feel at all familiar to elemental magic. It felt *other*. Rayghast was human, Marai could tell from his touch, but the tingle across her skin, the bite of pepper at the back of her throat, the scent of sulfur in her nostrils... was the same strange sensation Marai had felt ever since she stepped into the Middle Kingdoms. This magic, whatever it was, dark and deadly, was under Rayghast's command.

The King had faerie blood. There was no other explanation. Even if it was just a tiny drop, Rayghast used it to wield this new, dark magic.

Marai's head spun, but not from the concussion.

It was a secret. It had to be. No one in this kingdom knew that Rayghast had magic. If anyone did, he would surely have been dethroned and killed already. That was how much Tacorn despised and feared magic.

Marai's own magic sparked to life in defense beneath his touch. The tendrils across her mind slunk back, disappearing, as if her power burned it away.

Rayghast showed no emotion on his face. No relish. No thrill. His face was as empty as his soulless eyes. He must have gotten used to hiding his magic, as well as his emotions, so that no one would ever know the true King of Tacorn.

"Curious," he said, lowering his hand, looking at his stained fingers. Was that flare of magic against her skin supposed to do something? Had her own power protected her?

As Rayghast turned back to Ruenen, Marai fought against her bindings. Now that she was attuned to his magic, she could sense it hovering in the dungeon air like a dark nimbostratus cloud. Tacorn's lands bloomed with magic. As if in response, Marai felt her own power, a trickle of glowing, bubbling water, begin to slowly replenish the well. Her magic was returning, feeding off of Rayghast's. But she needed more time . . .

Rayghast trailed the whip lightly down Ruenen's chest. "I can't wait to watch you bleed, Prince."

Marai nearly wretched. He was more demented, sicker than she ever imagined. He would delight in every drop of blood spilt, in every anguished cry.

Rayghast then set the whip down again on the table. "Later. Before the people."

A public whipping.

Now instead, his fingers wrapped around the handle of Marai's dagger. Rayghast grabbed Ruenen by the hair and yanked his head up. Ruenen's good eye widened as that blade pressed right below it, a drop of blood welled at the site. "This eye first."

Ruenen didn't make a sound, but Marai could see him trembling.

"He can go," she blurted, desperately grasping, stalling. "Ruenen can leave these shores and never return. You can put him on a ship, yourself. Send him far away to Andara. Then no one will ever know that there was a lost prince of Nevandia. You can have the territory. Let him go."

Marai had never once pleaded before, but she'd beg on her hands and knees for Ruenen's life.

Rayghast met her gaze again. "I never thought the Lady Butcher cared for anyone, but the prince has swayed your heart, it seems. How interesting."

He let go of Ruenen, whose head flopped down like a rag-doll's. The King set the dagger back onto the table.

He snapped his fingers and two guards entered the cell.

"The unit whose soldiers were killed . . . they're outside, correct?" he asked the guards.

"Yes, Your Grace," one replied. "Right by this cell window, as instructed."

Rayghast didn't blink as he stared at Marai. "Take the girl there. Let them have their way with her."

The two guards nodded. Rayghast looked once more at Ruenen, who lifted his head to Marai. The fight returned, and Ruenen finally struggled against his bindings. He muttered the word "no" repeatedly. Rayghast turned to face his guards.

"I'll be back later. Tell the men to take their time. And bring her close to the window." Rayghast faced Ruenen, eyes flickering to the small window. "I want the prince to be able to hear her screams." He watched with something akin to satisfaction as Ruenen's face blanched. The king then calmly walked out of the cell.

Once Rayghast was out of view, the two guards approached Marai.

"No, *please*," Ruenen begged, his voice cracking. "I will do whatever you wish. I did it—I killed them all. Please, let her go free!"

Marai's heart shattered into a million pieces. He'd given up on himself. Ruenen accepted his own fate, but he was willing to fight for *her*. Tears stung Marai's eyes. She wouldn't accept it. Not one fucking bit.

Once the guards unhooked her wrists, they began dragging her from the cell. Marai roared and snarled, trying to ignore the hammering pain in her head, the nausea in her stomach. She bit the hand of one of the guards. As he yelped, she kicked the other in the groin. A third guard entered and tried to help restrain her.

She shouted his name, over and over, the words ripping from her throat. Ruenen staggered as close as the chains would allow him, which wasn't far at all.

"*Please*," he cried to the soldiers as they hauled her into the hallway. "Marai!"

The sound of his pained, pleading voice lit fury in her stomach. "Ruen!"

That familiar sensation tickled at the ends of her fingers as she pushed aside her physical pain, tucking it away inside.

She reached deep within towards the core of energy. The newly discovered well brimmed with dangerous power. The putrid air in the dungeon came alive with magic. She could feel it charged in her, waiting to be unleashed. But she was too far from Ruenen . . . if she used that power again, she may not be able to control who it struck.

But she had to try . . .

Marai planted her feet and with a mighty twist, wrenched herself free of the guards' grasps. She raised her bound arms, reaching out before her, fingers like claws.

For a moment, the guards stared at her. Shocked at her determination and maneuvering.

Then the ropes that bound her wrists burned away.

What was it Nosficio had said? The fae of old could create *doors* . . .

Marai unleashed the magic within her.

Please, she begged the heavens and to any gods who would listen, *let me find the strength to save us!*

There was a bright light, a tremor through the castle, and something opened wide in front of Marai. It wasn't lightning that appeared this time.

It was a hole.

A rip.

It flickered and pulsed with power and shining colorful light. Through the hole, Marai saw blues and tans, she could almost feel *heat.*

The soldiers backed away, faces aghast. They didn't try to touch her again.

A door. To somewhere else.

Marai didn't hesitate as she lurched forward and grabbed the sword at the belt of one of the guards. She cut him down. Then a second, before the third ran off up the stairs, calling for reinforcements.

She swayed and skidded back into the cell. She grabbed Dimtoir and her dagger from the table and slashed at Ruenen's bindings. He crumpled to the floor with a grunt. Marai hauled Ruenen to his feet as sensation returned to her body. She and Ruenen stumbled towards the magical door, though not before he grabbed his lute.

The thunderous noise of clanking armor and heavy footsteps sounded on the stairs.

There was no time to contemplate the door's safety and where it would lead them. They had to take the chance.

So Marai, with Ruenen's full weight leaning against her, staggered into the opening. She could feel it pulsating around her, the threads of magic flicking across her skin, tasting her, knowing her. She closed her eyes against the bright multi-colored glow, as vivid as her father's stained-glass wings. Marai sensed Ruenen tense beside her, but they kept walking. The hard stone disappeared beneath her feet. Marai didn't open her eyes again until she felt a warm breeze caress her skin.

Her eyes adjusted to the light reflecting off golden sand and azure waters.

The ocean. The door, the portal . . . had led them to the ocean.

Ruenen collapsed onto the sand as Marai turned. The portal remained open and the soldiers on the other side staggered forward. They stared astonished at the strange magical occurrence in the hallway of the dungeon. Commander Boone appeared in the stairwell and charged forward.

"Get them. *Go through*," he shouted and the soldiers rushed towards the hole. Behind them all, Marai spotted Rayghast, his jaw clenched so tightly he could crack his teeth, his face a portrait of wrath.

So he *did* have actual emotions.

Marai lifted her arms, concentrated, and closed the portal, melding it back together. The dungeon and Rayghast were gone. The last thing she heard was a bellow of fury from the King. Blood would be spilt in that dungeon, but it wouldn't be hers. Marai crept closer to where the portal had been, reaching out her hands to see if she could feel it.

Nothing. No trace of magic, except for that strange bubbly, rich, clean scent in the air. The scent of her magic. It was as if the window had never existed.

A wave of exhaustion and nausea took over. She vomited right there in the sand, falling to her knees. Her body was so parched that hardly anything came up. Head swimming, Marai keeled over to the side, letting the warmth of the Southern sun envelope her. The door had transported them across the continent.

A seagull flew overhead, cawing, circling, wondering where the hell those two people on the beach had come from.

"Marai . . ." came Ruenen's tentative voice. The sand rustled as he turned his body towards hers, breathing heavily. "How did we get here?"

She opened her burning eyes. He looked at her with worry and wonder etched into the planes of his face. He seemed a little more alert now that they'd escaped, but Marai's brain was too foggy. She didn't know how it was possible for her to create *a door* out of thin air.

"We'll roast if we stay out here," she moaned, flipping over to survey the beach. There was a cluster of palms a little ways away. Their collective boughs created a pool of shadow below them. Marai helped Ruenen to his feet and they trudged over, dropping the lute and weapons as they collapsed.

Marai felt sleep take her as the waves crashed against the beach, a calming lullaby for her hectic mind.

CHAPTER 16
Rayghast

Faerie blood in a mortal body can twist the mind.

He wasn't meant to have magic.

One drop of blood. One desperate cry, as his father beat him day after day, was enough for Rayghast to call up the dark power from beneath the earth.

It was his behavior as a child that led King Hershen to recognize that his son wasn't normal. As a boy, Rayghast plucked the wings off butterflies. He struck his own tutors if they displeased him. He sat for hours in the dungeons to learn how to properly torture someone. Just to hear their screams.

And when he touched things . . . they died.

The magic only worked with a physical connection. His hands had to touch something in order for the magic to flow. Even then, Rayghast had to *ask* for it. He'd call upon the magic, as if in a trance, and could feel *something else* take over. He was a vessel for the dark powers of the universe.

Rayghast was an abomination, something that shouldn't exist, a daily reminder from Hershen. His father had tried to hide it from the world. Somewhere along the family tree, a faerie sowed its wild oats, perhaps in the hope of prolonging the inevitable mass extinction of its people from the continent. Hershen had no magic of his own, the mutated blood had skipped him, but Rayghast was the prince, next in line to the throne. King

Hershen had told his son to snuff out his powers, to never use that mighty gift from their wicked ancestor. Most people had forgotten that faeries once ruled the Middle Kingdoms. And who could blame them? The fae had been gone for years. No one cared about their history.

Rayghast was taught that his powers were disgraceful. Dangerous. But the young prince practiced in secret. He couldn't tamp it down, as his father demanded. It was impossible to control. The magic wanted to be used, like a living thing with a mind of its own. Every time Hershen struck Rayghast in anger, the magic flared inside him. Once Hershen died and Rayghast ascended, there was no one to tell him what to do anymore. So instead of hiding this power, he used it.

He called upon the dark magic. "Suck the life from Nevandian lands. Bequeath it to my own. Make me stronger."

And the magic *did*.

Rayghast stood in the dungeon. Boone dangled from the ceiling, his eyes already plucked out by tweezers, blood dribbled down his face. Rayghast placed his hands on Boone's cheeks. The commander jerked back and gasped.

"You will never disappoint me again," Rayghast said in a low voice.

For a mere day, the princeling had been captured. Twenty-two years he'd waited. The seemingly intangible victory had suddenly become reality. That anticipation had been potent, filling Rayghast with actual satisfaction. Something akin to excitement and ecstasy, but the King of Tacorn did not have those emotions. The magic and twisted faerie blood had sucked those away, too.

He'd thought it was all over then. Finally, this long war with Nevandia would end. He could put his father's legacy to bed. The old king's soul might finally be proud of his fae-blooded son. Rayghast had seen the prince's face, his resigned eyes. Rayghast had touched him, held his fate in his grasp. Shed a drop of his blood. The prince was weak. A coward.

He hadn't the balls to meet Rayghast's eyes. He didn't deserve the title of "King." The boy was not fit to rule his own kingdom.

Rayghast had had it all planned out, as if one might plan a ball: he would hang the prince's body off the barbican. He and his massive army would ride over to Nevandia's capital city of Kellesar, and demand the Steward for his surrender. Steward Holfast would have no choice; his own paltry army would be vastly outnumbered by the forces of both Tacorn and Varana. The hope of his people would be easily broken, as thin and fragile as a cobweb.

Once King of both Tacorn and Nevandia, Rayghast would settle into Kellesar's much larger, more modern castle. His men would raid the villages for signs of rebels, forcing the Nevandians to become his subjects or die. He would give back the magic he'd stolen so the lands would once again be fertile. The people would view it as a sign from Lirr that Rayghast was the *true K*ing. Tacorn and Nevandia would become one. The way it had been years ago. The way his father had dreamed.

But that hadn't come to pass.

Heqtur Boone, the Hero of Pevear, had failed him for the last time.

"Please, Sire, I have served you faithfully," whined Boone through ragged breaths. "I only care for your victory."

Come to me, Rayghast thought into the darkness.

Writhing black smoke traveled up from the tips of Rayghast's blackened toe to his fingers. Boone screamed as his flesh seared at the magic's touch. Skin charred as dark magic drained the life from within. Boone's ashy skin flaked off. Such torture fed the twisted magic in Rayghast's body, urging him for *more, more, more.*

Boone's body went limp. The man's heart stopped beating. Rayghast stepped away as the darkness receded.

Rayghast left the cell and walked back upstairs into the main hall. Five guards stood at attention.

"Hang the commander from the barbican."

An hour later, Boone's body dangled from the castle walls for all to see. Three dungeon guards swayed next to him, ropes around their necks, a sign that failure would not be tolerated. Rayghast stared up at them from the courtyard, the quiet gasps of citizens behind him. The torture had been satisfying. It quelled the bloodlust, but it was also disappointing. Rayghast would now have to find a new commander. He'd had such high hopes for the Hero of Pevear. There were so few others of value and mettle.

Rayghast was exactly where he'd been days before. No prince. No Nevandia. Rumors would spread of the lost prince, from town to town. Nevandia would hear of it, eventually, if they hadn't already.

"Call a council meeting," Rayghast ordered to a passing guard.

His council and several generals assembled quickly. Rhia had asked to join in on this meeting, as well. She stood next to his throne, the picture of a submissive queen, and wore Tacorn's colors of black and burgundy, but in a traditional Eastern robe. Her ladies-in-waiting stood in a cluster behind her, eyes downcast. Normally, he would have denied her request—women were not welcome in rooms of power. But none of Rayghast's other wives showed any interest in his work. He was curious to see why Rhia bothered herself with things a woman would never understand. So he let her in.

"I want to be heard plainly," he began to the silent room. "I will not tolerate any further mistakes, or death will come to all of you. I will replace this entire council if I must."

Rayghast watched his wizened council shift in their seats, their throats bob, their faces pale. Oh, if only they knew how truly frightened they should be. Black flames flickered in Rayghast's veins. If they knew about his powers . . . the secret in his bloodline . . . The greatest lie of all was what had split Tacorn and Nevandia to begin with. Two hundred and fifty years ago, Lord Tarken discovered King Feist of Tacorn had magic, too. Disgusted, Tarken refused to be led by a king with faerie blood. Nevandia was not the place of warmth they claimed it to be.

Rayghast's own soldiers and council couldn't get the job done, so he brought in those who worked in the shadows. He'd hired three dozen trackers, hunters, and assassins. Men like that Lady Butcher. The girl had more fight in her than the princeling. She was ferocious, a paragon of her namesake. Rayghast's heart had flared at the delight in breaking her. He should've guessed that the tingle across her skin meant she hid magic, as well. When he'd called upon the dark magic, her skin did not flake away like the others. The dark power would not obey his command. Her magic was different—wilder, brighter, less controlled. She wasn't inhibited by touch the way Rayghast was.

And in that way, she had, more so than Prince Ruenen, become Rayghast's greatest threat. She had the power to stop him.

He addressed the hunters and soldiers scattered about the room. "The prince *will* be found. He *will* be brought to me, and he *will* be alive, preferably in no shape to escape. His death belongs to me alone."

"It shall be done, Your Grace," one of the hunters said. The others nodded.

"That girl with him, the Lady Butcher, she has *faerie blood*. She used magic within my dungeon. She will be killed on sight. She cannot be free to rescue the prince again. She created some kind of doorway, something magical she formed in midair. Take heed of her powers. She is dangerous, but not unstoppable. Head South with all haste."

"South, My King?" asked Dobbs.

"There was a beach on the other side of that doorway she created. Those palms only grow in the South. That's where you will look for them. The prince may already be onboard a ship. If that's the case, go after him."

Rayghast turned his back on them all. He heard the shuffle of their feet as everyone vacated the throne room. Finally, he heard the last steps leave, Cronhold's feeble trundle, and the heavy doors close. Rayghast lowered himself onto his throne, dark magic prowling under his skin like a caged beast. He needed to expend it before he lashed out at someone and exposed himself.

"My King, how can such a thing be possible? How can someone create a door?" Rhia asked him, lowering her head and bending her knees slightly. She was *so skilled* at playing docile.

"Magic allows for many possibilities, but it's not infinite. Even the Butcher has limits to her magic. We must kill her before we find out what else she can do."

"But I thought faeries were annihilated decades ago." Rhia's voice turned cold.

Rayghast wondered the same. "It appears we were not as thorough as we thought we were."

"If she lives, there may be others . . ."

"Then we will hunt them down and kill them."

Rhia did not flinch. Instead, she shifted topics. "Do you think the prince is headed to the harbors?"

Rayghast sat on his throne and trilled his blackened fingers against the armrest. "He'll catch a ship abroad. If he's already sailed away, I will not stop hunting him. As long as the prince lives, he's a threat. He could return at any year and claim his birthright. He could rekindle the war, even if I succeed in overtaking Nevandia in the prince's absence, especially with the Lady Butcher's help."

Rayghast would need to follow him. To the edge of the unchartered world. As many men as it took. As many ships. As many years. Whatever the cost, Rayghast would have what he wanted. He would have his kingdom. And his father . . . the late king's mission would finally be complete: one kingdom, whole and dominant, one strong enough to take on the North and massive kingdom of Grelta. And eventually the powerful Eastern kingdom of Syoto.

Varana was already his ally; what was to stop him from gaining more?

Rayghast pushed aside the thought of the prince, and sifted through the other tools in his arsenal. There were many ways to forge alliances between kingdoms.

"Your sister is of marrying age, is she not?"

Rhia stilled. "Eriu? She's . . . she's eleven. Not but a child."

That cold exterior melted into fear. Color drained from her face. Her eyes widened, pupils dilating. Rayghast noticed her held breath.

"I shall arrange a match for her. One that benefits both Tacorn and Varana."

Her nostrils flared, but after a moment, Rhia's face returned to its impassive state. She bowed her head again, and clasped her hands together.

"What do you want, My King?" her quiet, distant voice questioned.

Rayghast snapped two blackened fingers and Rhia's face lifted. She had lovely eyes, angular, chocolate brown, and so cold. "I will unite the kingdoms of Astye under one banner. I'll make a unified country with myself at the helm. For generations to come, I'll be remembered as the one true king of the continent. The Father. The supreme ruler. I will be limitless."

If that frightened the young queen, she did not show it. Instead, she looked down demurely, as always.

"Then so it shall be, my King."

With a wave of his hand, she was dismissed. He watched Rhia leave, her slippers barely making a sound on the stone, as if she were a ghost. But Rayghast was not fooled—his wife was stronger, smarter than she let on. He almost respected Rhia for it. She would make an excellent queen, by his side in the future as he conquered, as long as she remained obedient.

All that stood in his way was one slippery prince and that fae abomination.

CHAPTER 17
Marai

She refused to move or flutter her eyes open. That salty, fresh, humid scent had woken her. Marai let the ocean breeze kiss her skin, enjoying the peace. She'd always loved being on the Southern beaches of Henig. It was completely different from the rest of The Nine Kingdoms. Nowhere else on Astye did palm trees grow large brown coconuts and bright crimson flora. She'd spent plenty of time on the beaches, on the water, before she became the Lady Butcher . . . there was a part of this world that always called to her.

Marai was covered in sand. She felt its grit all over her—inside her shirt, down her pants, in her hair. Her stomach roiled, head throbbed, but she didn't care.

They'd made it to safety. They'd made it to the sea. She'd kept her promise to Ruenen, who was fast asleep at her side.

She turned to watch him breathing. His chest rose evenly up and down. Color had returned to his face. She wouldn't wake him yet, though Marai knew they both needed water. His face, covered in a myriad of bruises, was so innocent when he slept. Marai had never thought to look before. He seemed serene, as if they hadn't just escaped from being tortured. The thought of those dungeons, what had nearly occurred, made her volatile stomach clench.

She sat up, the sand hissing down her back. Her head pounded and her body rebelled against all movement, but she got herself standing. Marai's next mission: find drinkable water.

Leaving Ruenen behind to rest, Marai headed off towards the familiar port and town. Her feet sunk into the sand, the sun strong against her face and neck. She rolled up the sleeves of her shirt; sweat already dripped down her brow. By the time she passed the circular huts on the outskirts of the port, she felt ready to collapse again. Her mouth was as dry as the sand. It was always warm in the south. Temperatures never truly dipped in the winter months, and summers were humid and rainy.

Off in the distance to her right, she caught sight of ships. The harbor. She'd thought to bring them somewhere safe and the portal had brought them here. Exactly where they needed to be.

Except . . . there was nothing safe about the harbor in Cleaving Tides for Marai.

She hadn't been here in four years, but the town hadn't changed much since her last visit. The village of huts outside of town were built from wooden poles with roofs of woven straw and palm leaves. Umber-skinned children kicked a ball back and forth, weaving around the huts as women washed clothing and wove baskets.

Once inside the main town, the hilly, cobblestone streets were shaded by tall palms. Rope, vine, and wood bridges connected lookout towers, hovering far above the shorter buildings for the best viewpoints out to sea.

This place was as familiar to Marai as the grains of sand on the beach. As an adolescent, she'd wandered the port, its shops, and the elegant estates above in the hills. She'd made regular rounds by the butcher, the baker, the exotic tea vendor, the rope maker's establishment further up the road, apothecary . . . only to look in their windows, since she'd had no money. The dress shop had been her favorite. Marai hadn't worn a dress in ages, but the colorful, fine fabric always captured her fancy.

Cleaving Tides was the busiest port city on the continent due to the fact that it was the southernmost point of the land. Marai now scanned the harbor, then the bustling streets. No one she recognized. Marai let out a breath.

The Tides housed a diverse population, a mixture of people from many different countries and areas of The Nine Kingdoms. Languages as varied as the people were uttered freely on the streets, although everyone knew the common Continental tongue. Fashions from all over could be seen and purchased. Colorful, fragrant spices from distant lands wafted from a merchant's cart.

A nearby fish merchant took one look at her and said, "you've been through hell."

"Water," she gasped, then added, "please."

The fishmonger eyed her, but went to a large barrel behind him and poured her a glass. She drank it greedily in one gulp. Marai handed him back the cup and he kindly refilled it.

"Thank you," she said as he returned the cup to her hand.

The merchant observed her blood-stained clothes and face, her wild hair. He reached under his table and pulled out a flask. He downed its contents, then filled it full with water and passed it to Marai.

"Thank you," she uttered again and felt her eyes burn a twinge.

"Are you okay, lass?" he asked her, his accent from another country. Casamere, perhaps. "Need any lodgings? The inn over there is decent."

Marai shook her head. "I don't have any money. I was robbed. I'll be fine on the beach."

"Gets cold at night," said the merchant, eyeing her. She was aware of the colder temperatures; she'd slept on the Cleaving Tides beaches many times. "What about a healer?"

"No, thank you. This water is all I need."

Marai pocketed the canteen and her eyes grazed the busy harbor again. Dozens of boats, varied in size, with flags of all colors, waited at the docks.

Muscular sailors loaded heavy barrels and crates on and off them. People mingled around, drinking, laughing, discussing business.

"You sure look like you could use some help," said a man behind the fish merchant. He'd been standing there, leaning against the wall of the building. Marai hadn't given him a second glance, but he was looking over *her* with mild interest.

Marai stiffened as the man walked to her side. He was tall and lean and smelled of jasmine.

"As I said, I'll be fine."

The stranger's grey eyes twinkled, so light compared to the rich mahogany of his skin. Something seemed off about those eyes. "You're tough for a woman."

Marai scowled. "Is that supposed to be a compliment?"

"You said you'd been robbed. I don't know many women who'd be out and about after such a harrowing experience," the man said, crossing his arms. His face was sharp and beautifully unique. Dark silky locks framed his jaw from underneath a knit cap. It was rather hot out to wear something so warm, especially since the rest of his lightweight linen attire fit in with the weather. "You must be hungry."

He turned to the fishmonger and assessed the fresh fish at the table and surrounding baskets. Marai's stomach had been growling incessantly since the highlands, but she had been forced to ignore the pangs. Her mouth watered at the sight of the crabs and shrimp. Now that she was hydrated, however, she could return to Ruenen and fish for their dinner.

"Can I have a handful of shrimp and one carp for the lady, please?" asked the stranger to the merchant. Marai had to stop her jaw from dropping.

"That isn't necessary," she said, but the man ignored her remark.

While the merchant chopped off the head and tail, and wrapped the fish in brown paper, the stranger turned back to Marai. "What brings you to the Tides?"

"Traveling," she explained quickly.

"Ah, a sailor? Where are you going?"

Marai stiffened. "Casamere." She hoped the fishmonger would hurry up.

The stranger scoffed. "There's nothing interesting in Casamere. Dull place. If you're *really* looking for an adventure, you should come to Andara."

Marai froze. The man's silver eyes twinkled at her reaction. *Andara.* Was this the captain Ruenen had booked passage with? It seemed like too much of a coincidence, but without Ruenen present, Marai refused to trust anyone.

"I'm not looking for an adventure," Marai said. "I have family in Casamere."

The merchant handed the wrapped fish to the stranger. The man passed over payment and turned to face Marai, smiling broadly.

"Pity," he said, and handed the fish to Marai. As their fingers touched, Marai felt a spark skitter up her skin. She almost dropped the fish on the ground. The man's grin widened, showing all his perfect teeth, aware that she'd felt the magical pulse he sent. "Although, you could bring your *whole family.* They'd be very welcome in Andara."

This was the second person in mere hours that Marai had met who had magic. Unlike Rayghast, this stranger's magic was elemental. Was he working for Rayghast? Or maybe he was like her . . . a fighter-for-hire? Or a pirate? A dozen questions wanted to pour out of her, but Marai reigned herself in. It was unsafe to discuss magic in public with anyone, never mind a stranger. Her other hand carefully reached for Dimtoir's handle.

"Thank you . . . for the fish," she stumbled out, unsure how she put the words together in a sentence.

The man waved a hand, like it was nothing. "Always happy to help those in need." He began to walk away, then stopped to speak over his shoulder. "If you're curious about life off this continent, come to Andara. We have *all manner* of interesting folk there."

He lifted his hand and pushed back one side of his cap, revealing a long, pointed ear. Marai's breath caught as she watched him scratch his earlobe, nonchalant, then pull the cap back over. He flashed Marai a toothy grin again and sauntered into the crowded street, whistling a jaunty tune.

He was fae. The urge to run after him was overwhelming. She'd never met another faerie before, aside from her own people. And he'd confirmed what Ruenen had said . . . there *were* faeries in Andara. Could that exotic, unexplored land hold the key to understanding Marai's magic? Could her people, Keshel, Thora, and the others, finally find safety there?

Marai struggled to catch a breath. Her mind spun. Whenever she felt herself getting her feet, the rug was ripped out from under her again. So much of what she'd come to know had been altered. Rayghast, the King of Tacorn, a human, had fae blood and magic. A stranger, another faerie, had found Marai and affirmed the rumors about Andara, a place where she might find answers, where she might finally be safe. The weight of all this new information began crushing her. She took a quick swig of water, closed her eyes, and focused on her breathing.

Go back to Ruenen first.

Once her breathing steadied, Marai opened her eyes. She would think about all that tomorrow. Today, she needed to eat. With fish and water in hand, Marai tromped back to the palms on the beach. Ruenen was awake and leaning against the trunk of the middle palm. His clothing and hair were damp; he must've bathed in the water while she was gone. There was no trace of blood on him anymore, other than the wound on his brow. His eye was still swollen, however, rimmed in mauve and black.

She didn't want to trouble him about her encounter with the fae male. Not yet. Tomorrow, when she brought Ruenen to the port, he'd confirm if the stranger was indeed the captain of the ship Ruenen bought passage on.

"I got nervous . . . I wasn't sure where you'd gone to," he said weakly, voice cracking.

Marai tossed him the flask and he drank and drank until he couldn't anymore.

"I went into town, and I got us dinner."

Ruenen nearly melted. "Thank the gods."

Marai collected branches and palm fronds to make a fire. Ruenen set about sharpening two small sticks. Marai snapped her fingers, attempting to ignite the fronds, but nothing happened. She tried again. The portal had taken more power than she was used to . . . that well inside her felt depleted. She concentrated hard, sinking deep down to the bottom of her power. On the third try, the fronds ignited, and they had their fish and shrimp roasting over the flames.

Ruenen's stomach gave a loud, desperate howl.

"I don't know how to dissect what happened," he said.

"We don't have to speak of it," Marai said, mimicking his quiet volume. Neither of them had been broken. They were alive. They weren't gravely injured. It was a miracle, and Marai didn't want to question it for fear it would all turn sour again.

Ruenen closed his eyes and took a breath. "Not that. Not him." She knew he meant Rayghast and the dungeon. Ruenen's pleading voice echoed in her ears. She didn't want to remember what happened in that dungeon. How they almost died. How they almost lost each other . . .

Ruenen opened his eyes. The haunted look was gone, but his jaw was tight. "Can we talk about how you *did* that?" He kept his tone and face casual. He wiped away the sand from his arms, trying to look at ease, but- Marai wasn't fooled. There was nothing simple about what had occurred.

There was so much more they needed to address, so many unspoken things about the past few days. But maybe talking about magic was a simpler thing. A bridge between the hard realizations that neither of them wanted to cross yet.

"I don't know," she stated. "I felt trapped in a corner, desperate, and the magic sensed that and just . . . happened. Like the last time."

"But what was that thing we travelled through?" Ruenen asked, eye shining with wonder. "I may not have been totally with it, but I remember *that*."

Marai hesitated. Not because she didn't want to tell him, but because she frankly didn't know how to explain. "Some kind of portal. A door between two places."

"How did it know to bring us here?" Another good question.

"I thought about it . . . our bargain, as you said," began Marai slowly, trying to remember the details of that frenzied moment. "I thought about how I was going to fail you. I wasn't going to get you to Andara. And maybe because I was thinking about this place so much, how we needed to get to safety . . . the magic knew."

Ruenen ran a hand through his hair, sprinkling sand in his lap. He leaned back up against the tree and huffed.

"Magic is mysterious," he said with a laugh.

Marai felt herself smiling, too. "Yes, it truly is."

"Makes me wish I could do magic." His eye met hers. "But . . . why you? Why now?"

Marai shrugged, turning their makeshift spits over the fire, letting the fish skin get crispy. "I think I've had this in me all along. Keshel, one of my people, he always told me I had this power, but because I never wanted to practice, the magic's only now surfacing. All I know is that it's helped us out of two tricky situations, so I'm not going to question it. In case the magic doesn't work the next time . . ."

Ruenen's smile faltered. "Well, let's hope there isn't a next time. We're here now. We made it in time. Tomorrow, I'll find my ship and set sail off this damn continent."

Step one of their journey was now complete. She'd successfully protected the lost prince, rescued him from the dungeon, and brought him to the port where he'd sail away, far away from Rayghast, to Andara.

How many times had Ruenen evaded Rayghast's capture now? The King must be so utterly filled with rage. He'd do whatever it took to get Ruenen back. Marai remembered what Ruenen had said a few nights prior . . . Rayghast would follow him to the ends of the earth. Even if he left these lands for Andara, Ruenen would always be hunted, until Rayghast was defeated. There was a bit of destiny to this situation. Ruenen would never be free so long as Rayghast lived. The only logical outcome was for Ruenen to kill him. There was no other way out. It was Ruenen's life or Rayghast's, and Marai filled with such loathing at the thought of Rayghast taking control of Nevandia after Ruenen's death. Not after all the prince had suffered and lost.

And now she, too, was a target. Rayghast would blame her for Ruenen's escape. He knew she was fae. If she survived the massacres, Rayghast would hunt for others. Keshel, Thora, and the others were once again in danger because of her. But Marai didn't regret it. Not one single bit. She'd do it all over again, so she could meet him . . .

Marai blinked, unaware she'd been staring at Ruenen. A blush came to his cheeks under her gaze.

"Your fish is burning," he said.

Marai quickly turned the spit. The fish was cooked anyways. She placed the fish and bright pink shrimp on green fronds and they ate in silence, watching the sun set across the water. Marai always forgot how majestic the ocean was until she was before it. How wonderful it was to be out on the water, feeling so small and insignificant, but not wary of it. She was one of the millions of stars in the night sky. Open spaces had always signified freedom to her. A life away from the confined cage of that cave where she grew up.

She took a deep breath of the briny air. The temperature started to drop, so Marai wrapped herself tightly in her cloak. Ruenen picked up his lute and smirked.

"Since this is my last night on the continent, allow me to serenade you with some of your favorites," he crooned with a wink of his good eye. Marai rolled hers. It was hard to imagine that a few hours ago Ruenen had been begging for her life. They both acted like nothing significant had happened between them.

"What will you call yourself in Andara? I hope Ard the Bard has officially been retired."

"Ah, yes, don't worry, Ard is no more," Ruenen teased, strumming quickly on the lute, back and forth. "Not sure yet. I suppose I have the long journey ahead of me to contemplate. Let's hope I survive the trip and those rough waters."

He began playing "The Lady Butcher", much to Marai's chagrin, and he kept giving her simpering looks. She listened, finished her dinner, and watched the tangerine sun set behind the water, disappearing into a far-off world, just beyond the horizon, the line where sea met sky.

Next, Ruenen plucked the melody for his latest song, the ballad that he still didn't have lyrics to. He hummed along, though. It was pretty, and it made Marai think of moments like this . . . watching the sun set on a quiet beach. Of a sky with a million stars. Of endless beauty. Of caring. It filled her with longing and hope and other wistful things. One day, when he'd put lyrics to it, Marai knew the song would be well-received.

"You could've left me," he said once he'd finished the song. "On the moor. I'd released you from our bargain."

Marai didn't look at him, couldn't in that moment. She gazed out at the ocean as the sun's final rays ebbed away and the glorious moon shone above. "Do you honestly think I could have left you there to be tortured?"

Ruenen set his lute in the sand. She *was* the Lady Butcher. The mercenary of the shadows, the harbinger of death who'd never missed her mark. But Marai sat there in the sand, hair blowing in the breeze, feet bare. She didn't feel so menacing in that moment.

"I hired you. I'd already paid you in full. Any other mercenary would have gone." Ruenen swallowed. Marai avoided his gaze. She didn't want him to see the truth in her eyes. "But you didn't. You stayed. You protected me with your life. You got me out."

She remembered the moment when she'd shielded him with her own body. As the arrows flew, Marai hadn't thought about it for a second in that valley. It'd been her natural impulse. She'd wanted to protect him, and in the dungeon, she would've clawed out the eyes of any man who tried to hurt him. Marai would have fought with all her strength, every second, until someone had taken a blade to her throat.

They both knew it had nothing to do with the money. Nothing to do with Andara.

Marai finally risked a glance at him once she'd made her face impassive. "Of course I stayed. I'm not heartless."

Ruenen's eye shimmered in the moonlight's reflection on the water. "No, you're not." His throat bobbed again. Even in the night, Marai could see that endearing blush come to his cheeks. "Thank you for staying. Thank you for fighting for me."

His gaze was too intense, too heartfelt, and Marai squirmed under it.

"You're welcome . . . for saving you," she said. "Thrice."

Ruenen laughed, shaking his head. Marai tried to keep neutral, but it was impossible with that merry sound, the ease of him next to her.

"I actually think it's more than that. I've lost count," he said, holding that dimpled smile in place. It made him look so young, not at all like someone who had been hunted and nearly killed. "I'm going to miss that . . ."

"Miss what?"

"Your smirks. Your eye rolls. Your glowers." Ruenen paused, his smile fading. "The times when you speak, and the times when you're silent and make me wonder a thousand questions. And I'm going to remember your face. For the rest of my life, I'm going to remember your face, Marai."

That brown fawn eye grazed every inch of her, like he was memorizing every detail. Marai didn't move. She didn't breathe. His gaze was dazzling starlight, an ocean mist, and warm honey. She felt it all over her skin. Gods, she truly felt it. Something deep stirred in her, a heaviness, a flush, tightly knotted coil down near her hips.

"You've never told me if you decided . . . to come with me to Andara," he whispered, his upper body leaning towards her. No, she hadn't told him. She hadn't wanted him to know how badly she'd hoped Andara would be the answer to all her problems. That she could have a future. "Rayghast will hunt you down, too, if you stay." His eye darted to her mouth, that beautiful blush mixing with the bruises on his face. "We'll start over. Together."

Together.

Any other girl would lean over, close that distance between them, and kiss him. A normal girl would've said something kind and affectionate, proclaimed her feelings for him. That girl would tell Ruenen that yes, she would give up everything and go with him. That she'd be happy to spend her life with him, go on this adventure, discover a whole new world of magic and wonder. Ruenen deserved that girl. Gods, he deserved so much more than the cards he'd been dealt in life. Whatever sick game Lirr and Laimoen had created for him . . .

But Marai wasn't that girl. She couldn't be. It wasn't in Marai's soul to be her . . . a girl worthy of him. She had been tainted with too much blood on her hands. Before she became the Butcher, she had been tarnished and ruined. For anyone, but especially someone as good as Ruenen. For a bard. For a prince. All she could give him was a lifetime of sad songs.

Her people were now in danger because of her. It would be selfish and wrong to leave them, to run away to Andara while Rayghast hunted them down and killed them. She couldn't let that happen.

So Marai made her decision. She looked away, wrapped her arms tightly around herself and said, "I can't."

She lay on her side, back to him, and tried not to feel the heartbreaking disappointment emanating from him. "Goodnight, Ruen."

His silence was heavy as he eventually accepted and lay down to sleep.

She was up at dawn. The sun was already bright and hot reflecting off the sand and glistening ocean. Marai went down to the water, letting the cool tide stroke her feet, in and out. Alone, as she should be. She sunk slowly into the wet sand with the ebb of the tide. Wispy clouds dappled the pale blue sky as small sand crabs scuttled across the surf. Pure white seashells littered the beach. It was a small thing, to stand here. She could let the tide wash away the thoughts of the dungeon. Of mysterious shadow creatures and strange faeries. Of last night.

Marai dove into the water, and rinsed her hair and body. As she climbed back to the beach, Ruenen was awake, lute in hand.

"We should get to town," he called to Marai, tone clipped. "I don't want to miss my ship."

She walked back to camp and grabbed her weapons and canteen. Ruenen stood waiting, arms crossed, frowning deeply. He refused to look at her.

Marai let out her breath. This was good. He *should* be upset with her. He *should* know that Marai wasn't someone to feel affection towards. To care for. He needed to get on that ship and never come back. That was best for both of them. Then Marai could return to the cave in Ehle, hope Keshel forgave her, and she could protect them. She'd deal with Rayghast's retribution whenever it came, and it was coming. The cruel king wouldn't allow any magic but his own to survive.

They set off towards Cleaving Tides. Ruenen and his chilly silence trudged next to her. When they reached the Tides, Ruenen's demeanor shifted. His eye opened wide, taking in every sound and sight, craning his neck, gaping at the bridges overhead. He brazenly studied a group of surly sailors making a shady deal with brusque handshakes. They gave him a threatening look and Ruenen lowered his head and kept walking.

Marai hung back, leaning against the bait-and-tackle shop wall as Ruenen asked around the docks, looking for his captain. Eventually, a man in a wide-brimmed hat approached Ruenen and shook his hand. Marai couldn't see his face, but she noticed the rugged cutlass sword at his hip. Ruenen and the sailor exchanged words. The man nodded tersely, then gestured to a small rowboat tethered to the dock. His ship must have been out in the open waters.

Ruenen came to Marai's side with an enthusiastic smile. A second sailor joined the man and packed a few small crates onto the skiff, getting ready to leave.

"Got here just in time," he told her. "They were going to leave without me if I didn't show."

Marai nodded, and tried to pretend she didn't feel the rush of sadness that sliced through her heart like a blade.

"I guess this is goodbye, then," she said briskly, trying to keep her face barren of emotion.

Ruenen stared at her for a long moment, as if waiting to see if her mask would crack. Then he slowly held out his hand. "Goodbye, Marai."

She took his hand and gave it a quick shake, feeling the calluses on his fingers from his lute and sword. He squeezed and Marai could feel every ounce of sentiment Ruenen conveyed in that one touch. She tried not to feel anything. She tried to stuff it all down, lock it up inside.

Walls up. Shields up.

"Try not to fall overboard," she joked as she dropped his hand. A ghost of a smile appeared on his lips.

"I can't promise anything." Ruenen started to turn back to the rowboat, but didn't take a step. "I hope you find the answers, Marai . . . to your magic. I hope you find what you're looking for."

Marai didn't know how to respond. She pursed her lips and glanced away. She wished Ruenen didn't know her so well. She wished he hadn't been paying attention these past few weeks. She wished he didn't care.

Ruenen put a hand on her arm and leaned closer to her ear.

"Who knows, maybe Andara really *is* a land full of magic. If I learn anything, I'll send you a letter."

"Your letter will never reach me," Marai said in a hushed, intimate tone.

His lips were so close to her ear, she could feel his breath, as gentle as the sea breeze. She risked a glance up at him and saw that sad brown eye. The flecks of gold. The other eye was a little less swollen today. He nodded in understanding and stepped away.

Ruenen walked down the wooden boards on the dock, lute slung over his shoulder. He turned back once he reached the rowboat and took a deep breath.

In that moment, she struggled to find any words to say. How could she ever go back to the way her life was before? He'd changed her. That fast, he'd brought down those walls and forever altered who she was. What could she say to him? The words choked up inside her throat.

But he was waiting, standing there waiting for her to say or do something. She forced herself to speak.

"Take care and be well, Ruenen," she called up to him, forcing her face to betray nothing of the void she felt inside, and the implications of the truth.

He hadn't just been a commission, and he hadn't been a companion, either. Whatever there was between them, it had left its mark on Marai, and she could feel the emptiness returning, that emptiness she felt before they met. Before Ruenen had wormed and pushed his way into her heart and brought down those walls.

No, she was wrong. He hadn't wormed at all . . . he'd been kind. He'd been brightness and joy and laughter. He'd been fresh air and music. He'd always been himself. And it had been the most natural thing in the world.

Ruenen deflated at the words she said . . . they weren't the ones he'd been hoping to hear. But no matter what Marai felt for him, no matter how much her heart ached at his departure, she reminded herself again that she wasn't that girl.

She wasn't the girl who got the happy ending.

Ruenen smiled halfheartedly and waved goodbye, but there was little joy in the gesture. He stepped into the bobbing boat. She knew she'd always remember that final smile, the sun beaming down on him with all its goodness and warmth, an obvious reminder of what she'd be losing. Being alone had been easier before she'd met Ruenen . . .

Marai decided to wait there on the dock. She'd sit and wait until the rowboat pulled out. She'd sit there and watch Ruenen disappear beyond the horizon, off on his next great adventure.

Maybe I can bring them there. The thought eased the tightness in her chest. She needed to retrieve her people in Ehle before Rayghast got to them. *Maybe we can all restart in Andara. Together. Maybe this doesn't have to be goodbye . . .*

Before she could tear her eyes away from Ruenen's skiff, someone grabbed her from behind. Someone with enormous, muscular, hairy arms.

Foul mead-smelling breath was hot against her ear, as a gravelly voice said, "I'll be damned."

Marai's body turned to ice. That voice. For a moment, she froze, unable to move or think.

She knew her captor. She knew the crew he hailed from, whose ship must be nearby. Her eyes raked across the water to see it . . .

Indeed, there it was: *The Nightmare.* A black ship anchored not too far from port. She'd been so distracted by Ruenen that she hadn't spotted the ship, its menacing obsidian flags whipping in the winds.

"Never thought we'd see you again," growled the voice, though it seemed pleased, eager. Marai heard the snigger of several others behind her as the man, affectionately known amongst the people of the Tides as the Ox, dragged her backwards across the wooden dock.

Shoving her panic aside, Marai came to her senses. She snarled and yelled, thrashing the best she could under the strength of his near strangle-hold. No one nearby came to her aid. No one dared upset the Ox. They all averted their eyes and walked the other direction, including the fishmonger from yesterday. She reached for Dimtoir, but a hand was already there. Another man, Jesup, removed her weapons, even the knife she had hidden in her boot.

They'd know where to look for her concealed weapons, because they had been the ones to teach her.

"He's going to be so happy to see you," Ox said, the smell of his breath so potent Marai gagged. She continued to shout and fight, managing to get a good kick into Ox's shin, but he was used to holding people down. He knew all the right places to grab to quell someone else's strength.

"Is that any way to treat a lady, fellas?" came a voice that made Marai immediately still.

Ruenen stood on the dock, arms crossed, face serious and sharp.

"Piss off," the Ox snapped at him.

Ruenen took a sturdy step towards them and the other pirates stepped forward. "The lady doesn't want to go with you."

"This doesn't concern you, whelp. Get lost or you'll regret it."

The pirates raised their rugged cutlass sabers. Marai sent a beseeching look at Ruenen, one she hoped he'd read and would cause him to stop, turn around, and get back on the rowboat. But Ruenen took another step, eyes blazing, even the swollen one.

"I'm afraid I can't do that," he said with conviction and authority. The ferocity in his face was the same as in Iniquity; his back straight, head held high. Like a king.

"Are you his toy?" Ox asked in her ear. His tone was threatening.

"No," breathed Marai, "I hardly know him. We just . . . traveled to the Tides together, that's all." She hated the begging in her voice, the pathetic sound of it, but she wouldn't let Ox's men harm him. "He's nobody."

If those words upset Ruenen, he didn't show it. Or rather, he didn't believe it. Ruenen kept glancing at her face, reading the desperate plea Marai tried to show him.

"Let her go. Now." There was an edge to his voice that Marai had never heard. He looked . . . dangerous. It sent a shiver through her.

"Not sure he knows he's a nobody to you," sniggered a pirate to her left. Fishlegs was smaller than Ox, a little gangly, but his eyes were wild, and the way he held his knife was proof he knew how to use it well. One word from Ox would send that knife flying at Ruenen's heart.

Ox tightened his arm around Marai's neck, and she gasped for air as it constricted her windpipe.

"*Take your hands off her*," Ruenen shouted, launching himself at the Ox. He never made contact before the other pirates were on him. The sailor with the wide-brimmed hat appeared and tackled Ruenen to the ground. Marai recognized his face now, another one of the pirates from *The Nightmare*. Jesup smashed Ruenen's lute upon the dock, the neck snapped in two, held together by one sad string.

Ruenen threw a punch. Fishlegs knocked him out with one strike, an uppercut to the jaw. Ruenen's head lolled lifelessly to the side as Jesup and the man with wide-brimmed hat lifted him up.

Marai kept fighting. They wouldn't take her back to that ship. She swore that she'd never again set foot on its deck. Marai made such a racket, screaming and growling like a rabid dog, that the Ox grew tired of her.

He put pressure on just the right spot, on the same spot of her skull where she'd been hit before. Her head exploded in pain. Her mind went blank and body limp, falling instantly into unconsciousness.

CHAPTER 18
Ruenen

The stench woke him. A strong scent of stale ale, vomit, urine, and musty decaying wood brought him back to consciousness. Disorientated, Ruenen's eyes adjusted to his dark surroundings. The back of his head throbbed, and Ruenen put a hand there to feel crusted blood in his hair. He remembered the seedy looking men on the dock. Marai's frightened face. His tussle with the gangly man. Ruenen had a black eye, a gash on his forehead, and now this bleeding lump.

Not the best week...

He looked to his right and saw Marai lying lifelessly on the damp, wooden floor beside him. His heart tightened, a panic rushing through him, as he scrambled over to her side. Ruenen placed his hand on her cheek as he checked the pulse at her wrist. She was still warm; her chest moved up and down, heart beat evenly—alive.

He croaked out her name, stroking wet hair from her face, but she didn't stir. Ruenen looked around, hoping to find a less damp place to lay her. He deflated when he saw the iron bars on three surrounding sides, enclosing them within a small jail cell. From one prison straight into another. Although there were no windows, Ruenen heard the crash of the waves, caws of seagulls. The slight rocking and creaking beneath him could only mean one thing—they were on a moving ship.

Was this the ship to Andara? If so, why were they imprisoned? The sailor with the wide-brimmed hat who was supposed to take Ruenen to the ship had attacked him, too, had known the pirates hurting Marai.

Lirr's Bones...

How long had they been unconscious? How far from shore were they? Ruenen leapt to his feet, stumbling a little as the ship shifted in the water. He clasped onto the large iron lock on the cell door. He yanked and pulled as hard as he could, but it wasn't going to budge. Growling, Ruenen kicked the bars, but only succeeded in hurting his foot. He collapsed to the ground, cursing himself.

Yet, it never once crossed his mind to regret his choice.

He'd heard her yelling and there were no second thoughts as he abandoned the rowboat. The horror of seeing Marai's small body in the headlock of that massive brute hadn't vanished from his mind. Nothing else had mattered in those moments. He would've done whatever it took to save her, as she'd done for him in Tacorn. He could never repay her for rescuing him, but he'd tried on that dock. Tried to be as brave as she had been.

Not that his intervention had helped in any way... now they were *both* locked in a cell onboard what he could only assume was a pirate ship, and not one going to Andara.

All those people on the docks had looked the other way. Everyone ignored what was happening right in front of them. A young woman had been kidnapped in broad daylight by several large men, and no one turned their heads. Whoever these pirates were, they were feared and respected, allowed to run amuck however they pleased.

Ruenen took Marai's pale hand in his own. He wasn't a hero. He'd only made matters worse. Now they were trapped on this ship. Andara felt even farther away than before, and he had little hope that they could escape this new predicament. His thumb gently stroked the smooth skin on the top of her hand, noticing the calluses on her palms. Ruenen leaned back against the wall, closed his eyes, and resigned himself to imprisonment. At least until Marai woke up . . .

The ship lurched and Ruenen's eyes jolted open. Marai stirred. Her eyes fluttered open.

"Marai," he whispered as she sat up with a wince, taking in her new surroundings. Marai's face plummeted as realization hit her. Ruenen watched her shrink away from him, huddle in the corner of the cell, and wrap her arms around her knees.

"Are you okay?" he asked.

She didn't acknowledge him at all. Her eyes stared distantly at the floor.

"Did they hurt you?"

She was white as a sheet. Damp clothes clung to her body. She squinted her eyes, as if trying to quell a pain in her head. "I have a concussion."

Ruenen thought she'd been walking sluggishly ever since the Tacorn dungeons. The giant brute on the docks had made the injury worse.

The pirates had taken their weapons, but they weren't bound. Optimism stirred in his chest. Together they could come up with a way to break out. There was always Marai's magic. Ruenen bet Marai could probably find a way to open the lock, then they'd steal a skiff and row back to shore.

"Do you know what ship we're on?"

A small nod.

"Is it to Andara?"

Eyes narrowing, she shook her head.

"Do you know these bastards?" Ruenen asked, pointing to the ceiling. She'd mentioned before that she spent time on a pirate ship, and that they'd taught her how to use a sword.

Hunched and small, Marai's posture was closed off. Scared. It made him apprehensive. Marai was often silent, but never tried to make herself so diminutive, invisible. Those violet eyes had a glassy, haunted look. He reached for her and she winced, quickly removing her hand from his touch.

"Marai," he urged gently. She finally glanced up at him. Gods, she looked so young, so frail.

"I know them," she said, then looked away, ducking her head between her knees. It didn't surprise him that Marai knew the pirates. She was the Lady Butcher, after all. She'd worked in the underworld of society for years; she was bound to make enemies with the likes of them. "I'm sorry, Ruen."

"What do you have to be sorry for?" he asked, taken aback by the shame in her tone.

"You came to help me," she said, not lifting her head, "and you missed your boat. And your lute . . ."

Ruenen's heart clenched then, remembering the moment when his beloved possession had shattered on the ground. He could hear the cacophonous, distorted sound of those strings snapping, neck breaking. The only thing of sentimental value he'd ever owned, and now it lay on the dock of a backwater port town, if it hadn't already been thrown out to sea like garbage.

"That wasn't your fault. You didn't force me to help you. I heard you . . . and no one else was helping. I couldn't walk away."

Marai lifted her head and looked at him, her face full of disgust. "It's my fault. I should have been more careful. I *knew* they often made port at the Tides. It was a foolish, amateur mistake. If I'd seen them earlier, I wouldn't have stayed to see you off."

She ground her teeth, seething. Their situation was unfortunate, but Ruenen didn't think it was as bad as being in the Tacorn dungeon. Nothing on earth would've made him blame Marai for any of it. Actually, there was very little Marai could ever do to make him dislike her, to hate her, to blame her. All he wanted in that moment was to hold her, but the way she'd flinched at his hand earlier, he knew she wouldn't accept that.

Marai barreled on. "You needed to get away from Astye. You needed to be safe. Now I've taken you from one dangerous situation into another. I'm so sorry, Ruenen. You're here because of *my* inanity."

Her eyes shimmered, and Ruenen's heart broke. He couldn't help himself. He crawled to her and wrapped his arms around her, showering her with his forgiveness. He could feel her trembling, but she didn't recoil. He was struck once again by how small she was, how bird-like her bones were, how delicate she seemed underneath all the cloaks and intimidation. Ruenen placed his cheek on top of her head and pulled her closer. Her fingers latched onto his shirt and didn't let go. Together, they breathed, they warmed, they comforted. There wasn't much more he could do, but Ruenen hoped this one thing would center her again; that she'd find that strength inside because she could feel his forgiveness pulsing through his skin.

Footsteps sounded from further down the hull and Marai stiffened. Ruenen dropped his arms and she got to her feet unsteadily. She steeled herself, setting her face into the mask of the Butcher. She grabbed hold of the bars, and Ruenen watched her push aside fear and sorrow as she stared down the three pirates stalking towards their cell.

The one in the lead was the massive oaf from the dock. Ruenen's lips wanted to pull back into a lion-like snarl from the sight of him. The other two men were small in comparison, but broader and taller than Ruenen. One of them carried a lantern, granting Ruenen a chance to see a little more of their prison.

The hull of the ship had no windows or doors, just a rickety set of stairs that led up to the deck and cabins. All around lay crates and barrels of gods knew what. Most likely stolen goods. They were in the darkest, deepest part of the ship, their only company a quartet of rats scurrying around, searching for food.

"Welcome back to *The Nightmare*, Marai," the giant, bearded thug said. He had a large metal hoop through his left ear. His nose looked like it had been broken at least twice. "Never thought you'd be stupid enough to come sniffing around the Tides again."

"It wasn't my intention, I assure you, Ox," Marai snapped at him, and the men all sniggered. Her bravado was back, and Ruenen was relieved to hear that edge to her voice again. Marai was adept at putting on that mask, even when he knew she was trying to hide her dread.

"After what you did, you shoulda known you'd signed your death warrant." Ox looked her up and down, apathetic. "Still a skinny faerie bitch, I see. I thought you'd have grown better accessories by this point."

More laughter from the other men as Marai shot a nasty curse their way, complete with a strong middle finger, and a vicious glare.

"You always loved to show off those alley cat claws," said Ox with amusement. Marai's grip on the iron bars tightened, her whole body going taut, as she glowered at them. It was all Ruenen could do not to reach through the bars and punch them as they continued their jeering.

"How far from shore are we?" Marai asked.

"You weren't out long. A couple hours." That was better news than Ruenen could have hoped for. If they escaped shortly, they could probably get to shore by nightfall, maybe even catch the right vessel before it sailed away. He could see Marai's brain working that out, as well. "But you know there's no way you're getting off this ship. We know *all* your little secrets, Marai, don't forget. Not worth trying."

Marai was tense, eyes wild, but Ruenen could see the resignation as her shoulders sagged. They knew she was half-fae, which also meant they knew about her magic.

Another set of footsteps approached from the stairs. Ruenen watched Marai's face shift again as she recognized their owner.

"The captain's coming," said the shortest, pockmarked pirate.

Marai stepped away from the bars, putting her back against the wall, still as the dead. If at all possible, more color drained from her face. She'd stood bravely against Rayghast, Boone and the Tacorn soldiers, so impossibly outmatched and outnumbered. She'd been strung up in the infamous Tacorn dungeon. She'd fought her way to escape. Now, in this cell, the thud of boots treading closer, Ruenen didn't recognize the woman standing next to him.

The captain. How frightening was this man to make Marai back away, to stand so paralyzed? Ruenen's heart galloped in his chest as each casual footstep rebounded throughout the hull of the ship. The pirates parted, sickening sneers plastered onto their faces, as they watched Marai.

Finally, a man stepped into the lantern light. Ruenen had imagined the captain would be more brutish than Ox, larger, scarier. An eye-patch and missing teeth. A face so wrought with battle scars that he wouldn't be recognizable by his own mother.

No, this man standing at their cell was nothing like what Ruenen imagined.

What was worse, Ruenen *knew* this man.

The captain was striking, if Ruenen was being honest with himself. He'd thought so when he'd first met him. Thick, wavy golden hair effortlessly fell to his shoulders. The captain's eyes, even in the lantern light, were bright blue, and locked onto Marai huddled against the wall. He had full, pouty lips, high cheekbones, a straight, elegant nose. Colorful tattoos of blue and green and black snaked up his neck and down the muscled length of his arms, the rest hidden underneath his shirt. The captain was shorter than Ruenen, but far more built. He moved with an air of predatory grace as he leaned forward against the bars and smiled devastatingly.

This was the captain whom Ruenen had met in that tavern. This was the man who was supposed to take him to Andara: Captain Slate Hemming.

"Welcome home, Marai, my love," the captain purred like a seductive, nighttime promise. Ruenen might vomit right there all over the captain's face. Honestly, he wished he could. Might make the captain look less attractive... Ruenen felt something like jealousy rise in him, along with the queasiness, at the man's familiarity with Marai.

Marai merely looked at Captain Hemming, ferocity returning to her face. His smile never faltered.

"I'd say you look well, but I think we both know that's a lie," he said lightly. The pirates snickered behind him again. "Smell pretty awful, too, although I am aware that's probably our doing. We'll get you a bucket." More laughter. Ruenen wanted to punch every one of their teeth in. "Despite appearances, I'm tremendously happy to see you, Marai. It's been *far* too long. How many years?"

Marai took a small step away from the wall and tilted up her chin. "Four years, and yet you're still sailing the same, rotting ship. Can't afford a better rig? You hoard enough money and jewels from your crew, Slate, that you could've probably bought two more ships by now."

The other pirates went silent, but the captain widened his feral grin. "I missed you." He finally turned his attention to Ruenen, looking almost bored. "You again. What a surprise. Do you two know each other?"

Marai glared at him. "No. He was just someone in the wrong place at the wrong time."

"That's a fib, Marai. Come now, look at him," Hemming said, gesturing offhandedly to Ruenen. "He can't stop staring at you, and he looks like he'd love nothing more than to murder me."

"Shall we try and see?" Ruenen grabbed the bars near the captain's face with a snarl. The man's blue eyes flickered with pleasure, but he didn't balk.

"Cute," the captain drawled.

Ruenen's blood pulsed in his ears. "You promised to take me to Andara. I paid you for my passage. Release us both, and we'll put all this behind us, so long as we get to Andara."

Marai glanced between him and Hemming. "*He's* the captain you hired?" She shook her head in disappointment, and sighed through her nose. "Of course he is."

Captain Hemming cocked an eyebrow. "I was never going to take you to Andara. A year ago, I was approached at a port in Ain by some bounty hunters hired by King Rayghast of Tacorn. They told me the King was searching for a young man with brown hair and eyes, and a sunburst mark on his left wrist." Ruenen went cold as Hemming grinned. Everything came crashing down. A landslide of rocks tumbled into his stomach. All the hope Ruenen had built up in his heart, burst into flames at the captain's admission. "I knew who you were the moment we met at that tavern. That mark on your wrist is incredibly unique. I only agreed to help you because Rayghast is offering a rather large bounty for your capture. I was traveling alone at the time, and couldn't possibly get you to Tacorn on my own. You were so deliciously hopeful and naïve, believing Andara held your salvation. We're sailing back to that port in Ain, where I'll deposit you with Tacorn soldiers and collect my substantial earnings."

Shame heated Ruenen's neck. He'd played right into Hemming's game. *I should have known better than to trust a charismatic snake.*

"You can't take him there, Slate," Marai barked, stepping closer. "Rayghast will kill him."

Hemming's full attention turned to Marai. "You think I care? He's only alive right now because of that bounty. *You* are the one I care about. We have important business to attend to. I hope the reason you finally returned to Cleaving Tides is because your conscience got the better of you. I'm speaking, of course, of the item you stole from me. Here to make amends by returning it, my love?"

Marai crossed her arms. "I don't know what you're talking about."

The captain's smile faltered for a moment. "Oh, yes, you do." He straightened up. "I want it back. You made a grave error when you stole it from me. Then wounding me on top of that?" He placed a hand to his chest. "I'm seeking payback now."

Marai took another step towards him, looking more like the woman Ruenen had come to know. "Has it ever occurred to you that one of your *trusted* crew members stole it? Or you foolishly misplaced it? As I said before, you do have *oh so many* rarities in your cabin that it would not surprise me if you lost track of certain items."

Her eyes flashed to the Ox and the other pirates. Ruenen noticed them shift uncomfortably, pondering that statement, wondering if their captain was truly holding out on them.

Hemming chuckled, low and sensual, as if he wasn't at all concerned. "You were always so clever."

"If you must know, I've been avoiding the Tides all these years because I couldn't stand the thought of seeing your hideous face and limp cock again. You're not as irresistible as you think you are," Marai hissed confidently.

A couple of the pirates, even Ruenen, sucked in air. Hemming's face tightened and his eyes darkened.

"That's not what you said to me when I fucked you, Marai," he cooed in a voice like silk. Dangerous, powerful silk.

Ruenen felt his entire body go numb. The thought of her having *sex* with that man . . . of his hands on her body. . . Rage unlike he'd ever known built inside him. Marai's fists clenched at her sides.

Hemming's sneer was both alluring and perilous. "Join me tonight for dinner. We'll discuss the item when we're in *private*." His eyes flashed at Ruenen. "Sorry, mate. Three's a crowd."

Blood boiling, Ruenen shot him the finger. "Bastard."

"Eat dinner alone. I'd rather stay down here with the rats," Marai scoffed.

Hemming turned his back to the cell, golden hair glistening in the lantern light, hands in his pockets. His pirate flunkies followed at his heels, but the captain managed to toss out one last remark.

"I usually pay my whores, Marai, but you were so awful that I didn't think you were worth the money. No one could enjoy trash like you."

With that, the pirates left.

Ruenen felt more than sick. He'd never felt so disgusted, so infuriated, so full of hate for another person. As horrible as Rayghast was, the king had never slept with Marai, had never spoken to her in such a demeaning way, had never lied to and tricked Ruenen. He was certain that he could never loathe anyone as much as the captain in that moment. Ruenen got so fleetingly lost in that wrath that he failed to notice Marai sway, then slide down the wall of the cell, hands shaking.

"Ignore him," he managed to say through clenched teeth, "he was trying to rile you up."

But Marai didn't look angry. She looked defeated, so utterly lost. Eyes wide, but seeing nothing. Ruenen felt that familiar pain in his heart to see her in such a way. He knew how it felt when a demon of the past reared its ugly head.

"Captain Slate Hemming," she murmured, "and this ship, *The Nightmare,* were my family. My home. For three years." Her throat bobbed.

"You don't have to tell me, Marai," Ruenen said, watching as her face contorted into a grimace. "You don't need to explain anything."

Marai shook her head and winced in pain. "It was him . . . all this time, while we thought we were heading to Andara, we were really heading here to *him*. Ironic, isn't it? That the one person who could grant you freedom was the one who'd stolen mine?"

Ruenen was suddenly very aware of his hands and how they awkwardly reached out to her. He quickly stuffed them into his pockets, cursing his body's impulsivity.

"You can tell me anything," he said, although he wasn't sure he wanted to hear about her relationship with the captain, but he'd listen, and avoid the temptation to punch something.

Marai took a deep breath and began. "I told you my parents had given me to an older child during the massacre: Keshel. He'd been designated to raise a hoard of part-fae children. We all grew up together, moving from place to place, hiding, slowly getting picked off one by one as humans discovered who we were. It wasn't a life. I hated every second of it. I didn't feel . . . in control. All I wanted was to have a choice, to take care of myself, to *do* something, *be* someone else. So I left the others and went out into the world on my own. I was twelve."

Her violet eyes met Ruenen's. She knew he, of all people, would understand. Marai's horrifying childhood reminded him of his own. It wasn't pity he felt for her. No, a kinship surged through him. A respect for having survived this long, for going out on her own, despite the odds.

A rough, hateful laugh came from her throat. "I was so utterly unprepared for what I experienced. I was a child, and thought I knew everything, but things were far more dangerous and lonelier than I ever imagined. I tried to hide who I was, but at the time, I wasn't good at it. I was chased out of so many towns, barely escaping with my life. No one wanted a beggar child in their midst. No one wanted to hire me for anything . . . until I traveled South.

"I found my way to Cleaving Tides, and the first time I saw the ocean, Ruen, I wept." She closed her eyes, as if visualizing that first view of the water. "I thought, 'this is where I'm supposed to be.' Something about the vastness of the ocean, the openness, how I couldn't see the end. I was the only person in the world, and I was standing on the edge of something powerful. Freedom called to me there. It made me feel safe for the first time in my life."

Ruenen had known what that was like, finally feeling secure after a tortuous life. Master Chongan and his kind family had done that for him. They'd given him a home and a purpose. They'd made him feel like he belonged. They'd given him hope for a future. Ruenen also knew too well how that feeling can slip through your grasp in an instant. His memories flashed to Monks Amsco and Nori, to the strangers on the road who'd helped him. So many innocent people, other places he'd called home, destroyed because of him.

The corners of Marai's eyes tightened, a crease formed between her eyebrows as that haunted look returned. As if she mourned the girl who had stared at that ocean and hoped and wept.

She almost snarled the next words. "And then I met a dashing young captain, and he hired me to be his thief. He taught me how to kill, and I thought myself in love with him. But I was too young to understand what kind of man he was, and too naïve to understand love. He took something vital from me... my innocence. My freedom. My body. I continued to kill and steal for him, every day losing another piece of myself, until I finally gathered the courage to leave."

Marai glanced up at Ruenen; those violet eyes so bright in the darkness of the hull, like flickering flames of amethyst fire. "I wanted to hurt him. I wanted to *take* something from him, so I did. I took something I knew would infuriate him. You see, Slate doesn't just deal in pirated goods. No, Slate Hemming is obsessed with *magic*."

CHAPTER 19
Marai

"Magic?" Ruenen repeated, eyes going wide. "Does he have fae blood?"

Marai's stomach knotted, bile rose in her throat, she couldn't catch her breath. Telling Ruenen the truth had sucked away the rest of her strength, and she now felt sick and exposed.

"No, he's as human as they come," she said, "but Slate is a collector and dealer of magical objects, manuscripts, and histories. Secrets. So I stole something precious from him, a bloodstone ring that called out for me. I took it and ran. And I never looked back."

After four years, those memories brought bleak feelings to the surface. Marai couldn't face them. She didn't know how to push those thoughts and memories aside and move on. Now that she was back onboard *The Nightmare* and had seen Slate again, she felt like not a day had passed. She could feel his hands holding down her body, raking over her . . .

It was better not to feel anything at all, to become a void, than to let all those feelings of shame overtake her. It was easy to put the cloak on, to melt into the shadows, and . . . exist.

But Marai forced herself to lift her gaze to Ruenen, and what she saw in his face was like looking into a mirror.

Ruenen stared at the space where Slate had been standing, his face contorted in horror and disgust, in rage. His fists balled up so firmly his knuckles went white. The muscles in his neck were taut.

"That's why you became the Lady Butcher," he finally said, his voice strained and quiet. It wasn't a question. He understood. Gods, somehow, he understood. Marai could have wept in relief, but she wouldn't. No, she had so much bottled up inside that tears were nearly impossible now.

Marai nodded. "I had nowhere to go. I was too ashamed to return to the other fae. After all I'd done, I couldn't face their rejection. I'd become a tool of violence and shadow. Those skills are only useful in the darkness."

"You aren't a tool," Ruenen said, those soft fawn-like eyes so ferocious in that moment. Marai had never seen him this upset before. She'd seen him frightened, but never truly angry. He'd been beaten and pushed to the brink of exhaustion, but had never appeared so ready to rip someone to shreds. That was how Marai had felt every single day since leaving Slate years ago. It was odd to see that rage paralleled in someone else. Someone who didn't seem to judge her, who didn't see her as the villain in her own story. He didn't think she was a monster. He'd listened, accepted and *felt* for her.

Marai hung her head and stared at her calloused, thin fingers as if they were to blame for everything. "I thought perhaps Andara might be the solution, to unshackle me from my past, but I realized yesterday . . . it was merely an escape. An excuse. I would just be running someplace farther, not actually confronting the fractured pieces of me. I don't know where else I can belong but on my own."

She glanced back up at him. The corners of Ruenen's eyes softened, as did the lines of his brow. "I've never belonged anywhere, either."

"I made a vow after I left Slate, and I've upheld that vow all these years," she said, her voice hollow and aching. "I am in control. Every commission I've ever taken was one *I* made the choice to take. I never let another person lay a hand on me. No man has touched me, or even come close enough to try."

Until you...

She'd let him in. She'd let him touch her. And she hadn't minded. In fact, Ruenen's touch grounded her. It connected her to those missing parts, the pieces she'd locked away. Perhaps that's why her magic was suddenly surging, because she'd finally opened the box keeping the emotions and memories at bay.

But that increase in magic came at a price. She'd broken her vow and everything she swore to be. The one stable thing in her life since leaving *The Nightmare*.

Marai's heartbeat quickened. Her chest tightened.

Sensing her rising panic, Ruenen changed the subject. "I suppose you have the ring since you asked about it in Iniquity."

Her breathing slowed as her mind shifted back to less stressful conversation. She closed the lid on that box of emotions again. She felt the corners of her mouth twitch as the mask slid back into place. "Maybe."

"What is it exactly?"

"I wish I knew," Marai said. "In my travels around the continent, I asked other merchants and dealers about a magical bloodstone ring. But most knew nothing about it, or if they did, it was only hearsay. From what I've pieced together, the bloodstone ring once belonged to one of the original faerie queens."

"You mean, one of the old fae you mentioned before?"

Marai nodded. "I don't know why the ring is magical, nor do I know what kind of power it contains. Slate coveted it because of who the ring belonged to. Never, in all my years of owning it, has it displayed any kind of magic. Other than that day the ring called to me, it's been merely a token."

"Perhaps the ring's been biding its time for the right moment," mused Ruenen, raising his eyebrows. That fury that had overtaken him had receded by now. He looked at Marai with his usual softness and a spark of playfulness. "Or all it really wanted was to get far away from Hemming's slimy grasp."

"I truly don't care what the ring is or does. All I know is that Slate wants it," Marai stated with a sneer, "and I will do whatever it takes to make sure he never gets his hands on it again. He doesn't get to have *everything.*"

Not any part of her. Not ever again.

"Where's the ring now?"

Marai bared that sneer into a wicked smile, voice dipping lower. "If I tell you, I'd have to kill you."

It was impossible to tell the time from down in that cell, but Marai assumed it was evening when Ox and Fishlegs returned with their lanterns. Time for her fated rendezvous with Slate.

"You," Ox spat with a nod towards Ruenen, "back against the wall."

Ruenen did as he was told, but glowered the entire time. Marai wondered what horrible thoughts were going through his head. She wondered if Ruenen was dark enough to think of the gruesome things Marai wished she could do to the pirates. He was probably far too good for those thoughts.

Ox lifted up heavy, iron shackles as Fishlegs unlocked the cell door with rusted keys. Marai held out her hands in reluctance, and Ox clamped those heavy chains down upon her. The weight of them pulled her down, ripping at her wrists and shoulders. The pain in her head throbbed at the movement.

"Marai," came Ruenen's voice from behind her. She looked back over her shoulder to see him watching, pained and anxious. "Please be careful."

She wished she could reassure him, but when it came to Slate, Marai seemed to lack all common sense. She wasn't sure what she was capable of doing around him, and her magic wasn't responding. She let Ox drag her from the cell and up the creaking stairs, heard that cell door clink shut, the keys locking it once again with Ruenen inside.

Ox guided her past the familiar swinging hammocks where members of the scorbutic crew lounged, playing cards, drinking, and smoking. They leered at her, growling threats and insults as she passed.

"Faerie bitch."

"I hope the captain cuts your throat."

"Can't believe we let that *thing* onto our ship."

They hadn't forgotten her, the fae girl who'd nearly killed their captain and shamed them all. She held her head high, blocking out the nasty, hissing swears. Then she was taken up another set of stairs to the main hallway of the ship. She knew the door they came upon—the captain's quarters. A place she'd visited many times. A bed that was all too memorable.

Ox knocked and opened the door, revealing that same rectangle table, large enough for four. At the moment, the table was set for one. And he was currently seated, drinking a glass of wine, a full plate of food before him. She tried to ignore the sudden hunger pang in her stomach at the sight and smell of food.

"Glad you could join me," Slate said with that charming, false smile. "I'd ask you to sit, but it seems there's only room for one."

"I'm not hungry anyways," she said, "at least not for that slop."

Marai's stomach gave an unfortunately loud growl at that moment, causing Slate's mouth to twist into a wider, depraved grin.

"Of course. I'm curious—what've you been up to since our last meeting? I heard there was a hellion of an assassin called the Lady Butcher who's been all the gossip recently." He eyed her pointedly.

"Never heard of her."

Slate chuckled deeply, shaking his head. "Funny. You would make a *perfect* mercenary. In fact, I'd hire you myself to track you down." That sinful glimmer in his eyes flashed for just a moment. "Let's get down to business, shall we? Where is my ring?"

"I told you. I don't have it."

Slate's smirk disappeared. He was now deadly serious. "I'm tired of this game, Marai. Give it to me now or I will have Fishlegs search you... in all those *private* places."

"I sold it."

"Liar." He gestured to Fishlegs, who sauntered over gaily. He twiddled his fingers in Marai's face before those hands started patting her down.

"It was obviously something of value, for you to keep it squirreled away like that... away from your crew," Marai said. She tried not to feel Fishlegs' forceful hands on her torso, shifting her clothing. He wasn't at all subtle when he ran a hand across her breasts, shooting her a toothy grin.

She reached for her magic on instinct, dropping a bucket into that well, but it came up empty. Her magic hadn't recovered enough from creating that doorway. The emptiness left her feeling entirely powerless.

Marai hadn't taken a breath since he started. She was still as a statue. Marai glanced at Ox beside her. "Since you didn't bother to share the ring and the dozens of *other items* you keep locked away in that secret room, I guessed the ring would fetch a high price."

Ox looked momentarily dumbfounded, and Fishlegs' hands froze on her hips inside her pockets. It was the second time Marai had mentioned the items, and the second time Slate didn't deny it. Both pirates shifted awkwardly on their feet. Their eyes darted around the room for signs of the secret door, but she knew where it was. She had half a mind to point it out. Marai briefly pondered if Slate would soon have a mutiny on his hands.

He set down his wine glass with a hard clink. "I can hardly imagine that the item you went through all the trouble of stealing from me for revenge ... you would flippantly sell."

"Then you don't know what it's like to be a young, starving girl, alone on the streets, fighting for survival. You don't understand the heartbreak and anger I felt," Marai replied, sharing that shard of icy truth.

"I do know what it means to be hungry," Slate snapped at her. "I was orphaned after a terrible hurricane killed my parents, destroyed my village. I *do* understand anger and heartbreak, Marai. Before I became a captain, I even knew how to love."

Marai bit out a harsh laugh. She didn't believe that for a second. This man had no heart. No compassion.

Fishlegs' fingers had begun to explore again, grabbed her rear, and trailed down her inner thigh. The disgusting creature enjoyed every second of this violation. Again, Marai tried to remain calm and call upon her magic. It fizzled and snuffed out. She was entirely defenseless, but still had her iniquitous tongue.

"I got rid of that ring as soon as I found a buyer. All it did was remind me of you, and I never wanted to think of you again."

"You strive to make me your enemy," Slate said, "but you knew who I was and still loved me. You accepted all the darkness in me."

"I never accepted, Slate," she said through gritted teeth. "I was forced to bear it."

Fishlegs finally finished his pat down, and rose to his feet. He met Slate's eyes and shook his head, then returned his gaze back to Marai. He made a show of licking his lips before returning to her side.

"Where did you sell it?"

"Ruenen goes free."

Slate's eyes narrowed. "You're in no position to make demands."

"I'll tell you what you want to know if you swear on your life and your ship that Ruenen will be set free. You'll give him a rowboat so he can get back to shore."

Slate pursed his lips, considering. "Fine. The ring in exchange for Rayghast's prize."

"Swear it."

Slate put a hand to his heart. "I swear on my life and on my glorious *Nightmare,* most feared vessel on the open sea." Every word dripped with falsity. Marai knew never to trust him, but she had to at least try to barter for Ruenen's freedom.

"Did you ever even go to Andara? Or was that another lie you told Ruenen, as well?" she asked.

"Oh, I sailed there, right after your betrayal," he said casually. "Everything I told your friend about Andara was true. I'd heard rumors of its magic, and wanted to see it for myself."

So he could steal more magical objects and secrets. Marai wasn't surprised. It made sense that Slate would brave the perilous waters to Andara if it was rumored to have magic and faeries.

"Your turn," Slate said with a polite gesture.

"I sold the ring in Fensmuir. A simple jewelry merchant gave me a decent price for it. The coin fed me for months," Marai said, nonchalant. The lie came so easily to her tongue. Fensmuir was a bustling town in the Southwest, within the kingdom of Ain. It was known for its busy markets with merchants from all the nearby islands. Close enough to port cities to attract multitudes of merchants and buyers. Cleaving Tides was in the neighboring kingdom of Henig. It made sense that Marai, fresh off *The Nightmare* with a valuable ring, would go to Fensmuir to sell it.

"You must care a great deal for that whelp if you're willing to protect him," said Slate, eyeing her, searching for the lie.

"Why does that ring matter to you so much? What's so important about it?"

"Other than the fact that you stole it from me?" For a moment, Slate considered her. Then he picked up his knife and fork and cut into the braised snapper on his plate. "I was told it once belonged to the great Faerie Queen, Meallán."

Marai had heard of Meallán before, in passing, by both her father and Keshel. She was one of the original ancient fae. Slate may have been human, but he always did his research on the magical pieces he plundered, obsessed with their origins.

"The ring is old, as you might expect, harkening back to when fae ruled this land and humans were nothing but slaves to them." Slate had never shown any type of malice towards fae and other magical folk, unlike most humans. He was never disgusted or afraid of Marai's magic, her strange eyes, or fae blood. He'd *encouraged* her to use her magic. That was one of his rare positive traits; he didn't care about a person's background, he only cared how he could use them to his own benefit.

"Eventually, the humans became angry and revolted against Queen Meallán and her people. They burned down those great kingdoms, and brought the Faerie Queen to her knees. As they ripped the clothes from her body, bound her arms and legs, and held a sword to her neck, she conjured her final spell."

Slate chewed his fish and roasted potatoes. Marai watched him ravenously, both for the food and the end of his tale. She'd never heard this one before. "Meallán cursed them all. She proclaimed that any faerie who wore the bloodstone ring upon her finger would bring about the downfall of the human race. The bearer of the ring would wield tremendous power and become the rightful heir to her faerie throne."

A shiver went down Marai's spine. She didn't entirely believe in curses. She'd never seen one successfully come to fruition.

"Do you believe that story?" she asked.

"I believe anything can have power if you will it," Slate said, his gaze upon her unblinking, weighted in arrogance. "Did you ever put the ring on?"

"No," she said truthfully. There had been times when she'd been tempted, but the ring reminded her of Slate. She'd always kept it hidden on her person.

But a part of her wondered . . . if she ever *had* put the ring on . . . but Marai didn't wish for the downfall of the human race, no matter how repugnantly she'd been treated by them. Despite how they had slaughtered her people. She didn't wish to reign over any kingdom, never mind take up a lost faerie throne. But now she understood Slate's interest in the ring: the cursed, magical possession of one of the original Queen of the Fae. An object of immense, dark power.

"Will you wear the ring now and wield it to gain that power? To exact your revenge upon the humans? Upon me?"

"I already told you that I sold it. Whoever has the ring now is probably keeping it on a satin pillow in their own hidden room," Marai said. "Seeing as how there are very few of fae blood left in this world . . . the odds of someone actually wielding it are quite slim."

The captain stared at her again, those slate blue eyes so alluring, yet shadowed with the appetite for power. Whether he believed her lie or not, he took a long drink from his glass.

"You've changed, Marai," he said. "There's a coldness in you that wasn't there before. You were never made of sunshine, but you at least knew how to smile." He pushed back his chair and stood before her. "I always admired your determination, though. When you wanted something, you'd find a way to get it."

"I learned from the best," Marai jeered as his face neared her own. Every muscle in her body tightened. Her lungs couldn't contract. Slate's finger gently traced the outline of her lips, then down her neck to rest on the hollow between her clavicles. She wouldn't let herself flinch. She couldn't show him how much his touch harmed her. As Marai stared into those dazzling blue eyes, she found herself wondering how she ever loved this man. How had she not seen his slime, his arrogance, his darkness? Nothing remained of that childish love. She looked at him now and felt nothing but hatred.

He must have read this on her face. "So cold," he said. He did not remove his hand.

"How long did it take you to heal?" Marai asked him savagely. The v-neck of his billowing shirt was so low that Marai could see the ragged, red scar across his chest. She tugged on the cruelty lessons she'd learned from him, those things she was now used to saying as the Lady Butcher. "It appears that in my haste, I missed my mark. I meant for the strike to be fatal. Better to be alive and ugly than dead and beautiful, I suppose."

The captain's eyes snapped open in vehemence. His fingers turned to claws against her chest, then he struck her hard on the face with the back of his hand. She'd seen the blow coming, but could do nothing to avoid it, since she was held by Ox and Fishlegs. The blow caused her legs to weaken, and she nearly stumbled over. Marai tasted blood.

"You may have changed in some ways, but you'll always be a weak, pathetic little girl," Slate said. "I knew you'd one day crawl back here to my ship. No one in this world could ever love a mess like you."

Something snapped in her then. The game of cat and mouse was over. Everything she never said to him . . . it all surged to the surface.

"*You took advantage of a child*," she shouted. "You manipulated and lied and stole my innocence. You used me and my body for your own demented pleasure."

"I don't recall you ever once saying no."

"It doesn't excuse what you did. I was young, I didn't know how to stop you, but you, as an adult, should have."

She spat in the captain's face. Slate grabbed her neck with both hands, squeezing hard on her windpipe, as her bloody spit dripped down his cheek. Though her lungs were on fire, Marai held firm, never dropping his gaze.

"You were nothing when I found you. I did everything for you, gave you a home on my ship, taught you, paid you, but that was never enough. You greedy girl, now look where you are. You're *still* nothing. Pathetic." He let go of her, then gestured roughly to Ox and Fishlegs. "Let's see if you're more willing to cooperate after I give your friend to Rayghast."

His first and second mate dragged Marai from the room, where she gasped and coughed from the near strangulation. They brought her back down past the pirates in their hammocks. They all seemed delighted by her injured appearance.

One of them heckled, "serves the bitch right," as she was dragged past. Someone threw a shoe at her. A bottle crashed at her feet.

"You're dead now, faerie scum."

Ox and Fishlegs tossed her unceremoniously back into the cell. She hit the floor with a pitiable thump. Ruenen was immediately at her side, taking in her red, swelling cheek and the indigo bruises sprouting up on her pale throat. He looked murderous and also incredibly sad. Those brown eyes widened, glistening with emotion, so different from the heartless pair of blue eyes Marai had just looked into.

"What did he do to you?" Ruenen asked, gently angling her face to get a better look at her while Ox and Fishlegs had the lanterns close. Marai said nothing, and would not until the pirates left. Ruenen leapt at the cell bars. "You and your captain will pay for this."

Ox and Fishlegs regarded him with little interest. They turned their backs, hanging one lantern from a hook on the wall, leaving Ruenen and Marai alone in almost darkness. She could see the outline of Ruenen as he returned to her side. His gentle fingers found hers; touched them, nothing more. The gesture was small, but nearly broke Marai in half from the tenderness.

"I know this is probably a foolish question, but are you okay?" he asked, the candlelight flickering across his face.

Marai nodded once. His concerned expression didn't change.

"Did he try to get the ring from you?"

"I told him I sold it."

"Did he believe you?"

"Doubtful."

"Did he search you?" A stricken look crossed Ruenen's face. He'd probably seen her untucked shirt. She knew he was imagining the ways Slate could have touched her.

"No, but Fishlegs did."

Anger flashed across Ruenen's face. His hands balled into fists. He closed his eyes and let out a long breath. When he opened them again, he appeared less murderous. His fingers traced the chains at her wrists.

"I'm fine," Marai assured him, but not heartily. "Slate will dispose of us both regardless of if he gets the ring back." She unlaced her right boot. The chains bore into her flesh, making it difficult to maneuver. Marai then rolled down her thick sock and chucked it to the side. There, in between her toes, was the bloodstone ring. In the lantern light, the red splotches glowed magnificently. "If I'm going to be killed soon, I might as well wear it this once."

Marai hesitated . . . it could be a disastrous idea. But she slid the ring onto her left ring finger.

A spark. The ring trembled. Magic, like boiling water, bubbled at the bottom of her well. A kind of rightness floated through her. Perhaps it was the prospect of proudly displaying the ring she had hidden for so long. She was able to finally look upon it without heartbreak. Maybe the ring's power was simply in its symbolism, but she felt her magic stirring again, whirring inside her, rallying to the ring's call.

Marai held up her hand, showing off the stone to Ruenen, who regarded it with cautious skepticism. At Marai's neutral expression, he asked, "Well? Do you feel anything?"

A newfound strength and determination flooded through her. "There may be magic in this stone after all."

Ruenen's eyes widened. "Why do you say that?"

"I no longer fear Slate."

No, now she wanted to destroy them all.

CHAPTER 20
Ruenen

Time started to bleed, each minute into the next, in one continuous loop. Hour after hour of endless darkness. The candle in the lantern had burned out, pitching them into the black again.

No one came.

The thirst in Ruenen's throat was unbearable; the hollow ache in his stomach just as bad. It had been several days since he'd last eaten that fish on the beach. Oh, how he should have savored it. If he closed his eyes, he could imagine the salty taste, the delicate texture . . . a different kind of torture from the one he would soon be experiencing in the Tacorn dungeon.

He and Marai both faded in and out of restless sleep. Sometimes, the pangs in his abdomen jerked him awake. Long hours passed. Marai's nightmares returned. He could hear her breathing turn labored, and he watched horrified as her body twitched involuntarily. He could only imagine what sort of terror she experienced when she closed her eyes.

Ruenen leaned his back against the wall of the ship. While the lantern's candle had flickered with light, he had watched Marai mindlessly fiddle with the ring on her finger. He wondered if she was aware she was doing it; her mind was clearly elsewhere.

When he'd seen the marks on her cheek and neck, it'd nearly sent him into a vengeful daze. Ruenen had never felt so enraged in his life, which was surprising considering how much brutality he'd witnessed. He wanted to clobber the captain for what he'd done to her, for making her eyes so haunted, for devaluing her so horrendously. The shock of the intensity of his anger concerned Ruenen. He was usually a level-headed person. He sought lightness, had always tried to keep himself above those kinds of primal reactions, but seeing those ugly bruises take form on her delicate skin made him tremble with suppressed rage. Every time she moved, the sound of those heavy shackles on her wrists grated against his ears and heart.

"Can you use your magic to get them off?" he asked her, but she shook her head. If she felt as weak as he did, Ruenen could understand why she was unable to summon her magic. She didn't have the strength to create the little flame on her fingers.

Ruenen was furious with Captain Hemming, but he was also upset with himself. There was nothing, absolutely nothing, Ruenen could do to help her. He didn't know how to get off the ship. He didn't know how to stop Hemming from taking the ring and hurting her again. He didn't know how to take away her pain, to comfort her.

Marai had always been so closed off and now he finally understood why. Ruenen's touch, his attempt at comforting, was the last thing Marai wanted. She didn't need another man's hands to touch her ever again. His hands would remind her of Hemming's. Of Fishlegs violating her upstairs. And Ruenen hated that.

Ruenen was not Captain Hemming. He'd never hurt Marai in any way. He couldn't bear to. All he wanted to do was hold her, make her see that there were good men in the world. His fingers ached to touch her. It took everything he had to keep his hands in his lap and not reach across that invisible line.

He was falling for her.

It was clear to him now. He'd had plenty of time in silence to come to this conclusion.

All those days on the road, all those hours together . . . he'd been a goner from the moment he'd first seen her face, when her hood had fallen back. He'd wondered then if some kind of magic was making his heart thunder so. Now he knew what he felt for her was not magic. It wasn't fanciful and romantic. It was complicated and messy. It was fear and confusion. Ruenen had never felt this way before. No woman had made him feel such strong emotions. It was as if he'd sprained his heart. Marai wasn't perfect. She was moody and acerbic. She closed herself off from intimacy, from relationships. She ran from them. Marai was unattainable.

But none of that mattered. All he knew was that the woman in the cell with him, his companion, his unlikely friend, had become the most precious thing in his life.

He could feel himself slipping, into the darkness that he also tried to run from. He wouldn't let his mind travel to the monastery, to Chiojan, to the Tacorn dungeon, to his imminent death by Rayghast's hand . . . Ruenen had to keep both himself and Marai from falling into despair. So he did the only thing he could.

Ruenen sang.

He sang and sang, even though his throat and mouth were parched and dry. Even though his voice cracked and ached for water.

The singing kept him from that dark pit. It lifted him from sorrow. He internalized and visualized the lyrics he sang; the measures and notes splayed out before him. Five black lines of ink stretched into the darkness, cut into sections of bars and measures, creating a musical staff. Every note and word hit him deeply. He sang every song he knew, and when he ran out of tunes, he hummed new ones he created on the spot.

Marai sat in silence. If he couldn't physically comfort her, this was the next best thing. He sang like his voice was an embrace, wrapping strong arms around Marai, holding her close. He sang like every note caressed her, easing away her pain. Ruenen hoped she felt it.

He didn't know how long they sat in that cell. Days. But he'd continue singing for as long as breath remained in his lungs, until he was physically wrenched away from her.

Ruenen heard the sound of footsteps, saw more flames approaching. He glanced to Marai, hardly able to see her at all. She was merely an outline in the dark.

"I'm here," he whispered to her, hoping that would bring her solace.

The pirates, Ox, Jesup, Fishlegs, and a few others, were back, swords at their hips.

"The captain wants to talk to you both," said Fishlegs with a sinister grin. "We've reached the port in Ain."

"If you behave, faerie, we'll take the shackles off," Ox told her. "Might want to spend the last minutes of your life unchained."

Dread pooled in the crater that was Ruenen's empty stomach. This was it—the final confrontation. If the captain didn't get this ring back, he'd take it by force, and then stuff Ruenen in the rowboat to take him ashore.

"We'll behave," came Marai's voice, odd and monotone.

Fishlegs unlocked the cell door and Marai walked up first. She was too weak to lift the chains herself. Ox grabbed her arms roughly and unlocked the metal from her wrists. They dropped to the floor with a thud. Marai looked at her ruined wrists, flesh red, raw, and bleeding. She rubbed the blood between her fingers, almost in a daze. She then touched those fingers to the bars as she passed through. Ruenen followed her, legs as stiff as metal rods.

Ox led the way through the hull and up the stairs, the other pirates filing in behind them. They were so close that Ruenen could smell the reek of their unwashed bodies. He knew he probably smelled no better these days. Marai's fingers gently trailed up the stair railings. As they reached the second level, the ship brightened with natural sunlight, blinding Ruenen. Through squinted eyes, he could fully see Marai.

Both of her arms stretched out wide, like a scarecrow in a cornfield. Her fingers touched everything she passed with an eerie gentleness. Was she taking in her surroundings? Trying to remember every bit of this ship that would become her tomb?

A small seed of optimism started to grow inside Ruenen—or did she have a plan?

As hopeful as he was becoming, Ruenen watched her ominously: the strange hunch of her shoulders, the downward tilt of her head, evenness of her breathing. He'd studied her movements throughout their weeks together. She'd never done anything like this before.

That's when he noticed the ring remained on her left hand. The dark jasper bloodstone reflected the sunlight as they passed a window before climbing the next set of stairs. Looking closely, Ruenen saw a hazy white aura around Marai, or maybe it was a trick of the light.

No, there was the subtle spark of magic at her fingertips.

"You're unusually quiet, Marai," said Ox with a snigger. "Did you go mad in that cell?" He shook his head and made a "loony" face at Jesup when Marai said nothing.

Ruenen could sense an *oddness* in the air, right to the marrow in his bones. The walls crept in. Something hid behind every corner. The pirates were none-the-wiser.

At the top of the stairs, they turned into a hallway, allowing Ruenen a chance to glimpse Marai's face. That red mark bloomed on her cheek, but those violet eyes were cold, calculating, narrowed. His unease grew as he saw that slight smirk gracing her mouth. It was the Butcher's face. Unfeeling.

There was nothing broken about this woman.

The pirates led them to a door; Marai's ten fingers stroked the wooden walls of the cramped hallway. Ox knocked, a voice inside answered, and they all entered Hemming's quarters. Marai and Ruenen were shoved between the pirates, whose hands sat on the hilt of their swords, imposing.

The captain sat at his large desk in front of three bay windows. It was a beautiful day on the ocean, with crystal blue water, clear skies, gulls swooping past. Maps, charts, and books covered the desk; Hemming sat on a battered and torn chair, a pirate king on his throne, examining a weathered compass. Ruenen spotted Marai's sword and knives against the wall in the corner. The captain's lavish bed was pressed against the opposite wall. Ruenen glared at the furniture that had once been Marai's torture device.

"We've now reached the climax of your story, Marai," Hemming said, raising his eyes from the compass. "Are you ready to be compliant?"

Marai said nothing. Ruenen glanced to his right to see her stare at Hemming with that same odd smirk on her face. Hemming didn't like it. He'd expected her to fracture in that dark cell, not grow stronger. The captain stood, expression falling into a scowl. His eyes flashed towards Ruenen.

"Perhaps you'll be more willing to answer once I give him over to the Tacorn spies waiting for us on the dock. After all, he's no one, right?"

Hemming stepped around the desk and walked to the corner. He took hold of Marai's fae sword. Jesup thrust him forward, and Ruenen's knees slammed painfully into the desk. Jesup yanked Ruenen's hands onto the wooden top, as Hemming placed the blade to Ruenen's wrists.

"You can't kill him," Marai said dryly.

"Oh, I'm not going to kill him. Rayghast wants the boy alive, but no one ever mentioned if the King also meant *unharmed.*" Hemming's eyes never left Marai. He wanted her to grovel. Ruenen knew she wouldn't.

"Give me the ring or I take his hands, here and now," snarled Hemming, the cold metal sharp against Ruenen's skin.

Ropes of regret tightened around Ruenen's heart. So much regret, so many words left unsaid, songs unsung. He'd never play music again. He'd never trace Marai's body with the pads of his calloused fingers, all her sharp edges. He'd never see her again. But a thought burned brighter within him—he was proud of her. There she stood, facing her nightmare, and it was an honor to be by her side.

Marai stepped forward. She held up her left hand, showing off the smooth jasper ring, juxtaposing her bloody wrist.

"You want this?" she asked the captain. His eyes blazed at the sight of the stone. "You'll have to pry it from my cold, dead finger."

Baring his teeth, Hemming pulled back the blade and swung.

Marai leapt at the captain's feet like a mountain lion, knocking him backwards to the floor. She stood quickly, kicking Dimtoir from his hand. She scrambled to the corner, grabbed her own knife, and chucked it at Jesup standing behind Ruenen. He heard a grunt, then a gurgling sound. Jesup collapsed next to him, knife stuck in the pirate's throat.

Ruenen grabbed Jesup's cutlass as Marai took hold of Dimtoir. Hemming was back on his feet, sword in hand, as Marai charged him, metal meeting metal. Ruenen had no time to watch them battle—other pirates were stepping in. He had to leap backwards to avoid the slash of Fishlegs' cutlass. In an instant, he was fighting three men, as Marai battled Hemming and Ox.

The cabin was too small for such a brawl. Ruenen kicked Fishlegs backwards over a chair as he sliced through the leg of a burlier pirate. The other two men swung at him. Ruenen blocked every attack. He barely had time to glance over to see how Marai was faring. He had to hand it to Hemming. Never before had Ruenen seen anyone challenge Marai in sword skills. He shouldn't have been so surprised... Hemming had taught Marai everything she knew.

Ruenen managed to cut down the injured pirate. He stabbed him in the gut, now doubly wounded and bleeding out onto the rug. Ruenen smacked the scrawny pirate across the face with the butt of his sword. A few of Fishlegs' teeth spewed across the room.

It was a dance. Ruenen placed his feet accordingly, weaving in and out between Marai and the pirates, slicing and parrying as he went.

At one point, the only way to dodge was to roll across Hemming's bed. Fishlegs' sword thrust into the mattress, narrowly avoiding Ruenen's back.

The door opened to reveal a long-haired, heavily tattooed pirate. For a moment, he gaped at the scene before him, then gave a war cry and jumped into the fray on Ruenen's side of the room.

Marai kicked Ox with all her might, using the desk as leverage, and the enormous man stumbled backwards into Ruenen's path onto the bed. Ruenen's sword plunged into Ox's stomach. Ox leaned over, gasping at the wound, and Marai leapt cat-like across his back. Hemming went to strike, but accidentally cut Ox down the length of his spine. The large, intimidating pirate let out a strangled howl, then collapsed onto the bed, a pool of red staining the white sheets.

Marai jumped onto the desk, and Hemming followed her. There, they swung and slashed with such speed and ferocity Ruenen could barely follow their movements. They fought in a symphony of movements, back and forth. Clash and clang. A duet of opposing instruments, similar in song, competing for volume.

Dimtoir's blade began to glow with a fierce white light, as if Marai's power was being channeled into it. The ancient fae engravings burned gold, shimmering, as lightning snapped, snaking around her hand and sword.

Fishlegs threw a knife at Ruenen, who ducked. It missed his head, but grazed his shoulder. Warm blood dripped down his arm. Ruenen shoved a chair at him in response. The long-haired pirate grabbed Ruenen from behind. Fishlegs sauntered over, a triumphant look on his face, sword at the ready. Ruenen flipped his captor over his shoulder and down to the ground, then swung to meet Fishlegs' blade. He sliced across his torso, then upwards from stomach to neck. The pirate was dead before he hit the floor.

Marai fought Hemming with all her focus and strength, her magic seeping out. She was surrounded by strands of lightning, crackling in the air. If

Hemming was frightened by her power, he didn't show it. If anything, he stared wide-eyed, amazed at the sight.

After several more moves, Ruenen cut down the long-haired pirate. He watched Marai reach out her hand, magic bursting forth.

Lightning snaked through the cabin, stronger, faster, and brighter than before. Dimtoir and the bloodstone ring glowed. *Marai* glowed with white light. Ruenen dove under the bed to avoid it as the bolts engulfed Hemming. The captain fell flat onto his back, muscles seizing uncontrollably in blinding light. It was a mighty, dark thing to witness. Such power . . . Ruenen shivered, scenting charred hair.

Marai's radiant sword pressed against the captain's throat as her magic receded back inside her. Hemming stilled. Thin red lines appeared across his face and neck, branching out across his skin like the limbs of a tree, residual scars of the lightning passing through his body. His hair and clothing had been badly singed.

Hemming's eyes widened, teeth grinding together as he lay on his back in submission.

"What are you going to do?" he huffed through gasping breaths. Marai was breathing heavily, too, her face a mask of calm, but rippling below the surface, Ruenen could sense her fury like that magic in the air. "Will you kill me? Your first love?" His tone was mocking.

Marai held her arm steady. "I'm not surprised that you would view love as a weakness. However, my fleeting love for you has only made me stronger."

Using tremendous restraint, Marai swiftly cut Hemming across the cheek. She could have easily beheaded him, slashed his throat. The captain let out an agonized cry as blood gushed from the wound.

"You fucking *bitch!*" Hemming clutched his face, red dripping through his fingers and onto his maps. It was a deep cut, the edges of the wound gaping open to reveal the inside of his mouth.

Marai once again put the blade tip to his throat. A final warning.

"I'm showing you mercy," she growled at him, eyes flaring at the horrified look on Hemming's face. "Not because I'm weak, but because I want you to be reminded of me every time you look in the mirror. I want my face, right here in this moment, to be burned forever into your mind. You hold no power over me anymore. Remember, Slate . . . I'm not who you tried to make me."

She leapt off the desk and sprinted out the cabin door. Ruenen followed her down the hallway, and burst into the open air and bright sun. The pirates on the deck rushed towards them, swords drawn. Marai and Ruenen cut down the few closest to them before Marai grabbed his arm. She dragged him up onto the thick, wooden railing of the rickety ship.

"Do you trust me?" she asked, stabbing a pirate in the gut.

"Always," Ruenen said. Marai dropped her hold on his arm and turned to face the water.

"Cover me."

Marai raised both hands, face wrought with concentration. Buying time until she was ready, Ruenen swung at a few pirates, killing two in one move. But more were coming, climbing down from their positions on the masts and rigging. He nearly fell overboard as the ship tilted in the water.

"Any chance you could speed things along?" he shouted over his shoulder.

Marai lowered her arms and Ruenen turned. A large shimmering, horizontal hole appeared over the water. Ruenen could clearly see a beach on the other side of the portal Marai had opened. He didn't have time to be astounded; Marai grabbed his hand and together they leapt off the railing, careening towards that open portal. If they didn't aim properly, they would plunge into the water. Ruenen closed his eyes and prayed to Lirr's mercy.

His feet touched the ground, but couldn't support the force of his landing. He and Marai crashed to their knees in the surf. A wave splashed over their heads. Ruenen took large, sputtering breaths as he turned to look behind them.

Marai had portaled them to the nearest beach. *The Nightmare* was miles away in the distance. She was already on her feet, dripping from head to toe as she staggered onto the dry sand.

Ruenen crawled through the sand, laughing deliriously as he went. He collapsed onto his back. They were alive! He chuckled again as he sat up and thrust a rude gesture in the direction of *The Nightmare* and Captain Hemming.

He yelled across the water, "Fuck you, bastards!" Freedom had never felt so good.

Fingers snapped and suddenly, *The Nightmare* burst into flames. Ruenen stopped laughing.

He looked up at Marai, whose fingers lingered in the air. She watched the flames engulf the vessel with a strange look of victory. Her body heaved, as if every movement were torturous.

"I thought you said you'd show mercy . . ." Ruenen said.

Marai took off the ring and lowered her arm. "I did. I gave them plenty of time to evacuate the ship."

She pocketed the bloodstone ring, and took a seat next to Ruenen to watch *The Nightmare* burn.

CHAPTER 21
Marai

Marai's magic had been fully drained from their exploits on the ship. The ring had granted her a momentary spurt of power, but now she had nothing left. Her body moved slowly, and her limbs hung limply around her. Her concussion was no better, either. She wasn't strong enough to portal them away from the beach. In fact, she couldn't summon any magic at all. She could barely stand for more than a moment. They made a campfire the old-fashioned way. In better shape than her, Ruenen managed to scrounge up a couple sand crabs for them to roast over the fire.

They took shifts that night on pirate patrol. Ruenen took the first shift, sensing Marai was close to collapse. No one disturbed them, though. No pirate had made it to shore.

Marai was already awake from her patrol shift when Ruenen stirred at dawn. She stood in the waves, looking out to where *The Nightmare* had once been afloat, the ring on her finger once more.

"My magic has recovered enough," she said after Ruenen had washed off the blood and sand. Her fingers flexed, sensing the magic trickling back. "I think I can portal us to the Tides, with help from the ring, but then I'll probably be empty again for another day."

"Back to the Tides? Why?"

Marai gave him a long look. "I thought you'd want to be on your way once more."

Ruenen frowned. In all the drama, he must have forgotten the other villain who so desperately sought them. His shoulders slumped at the reminder that they'd escaped one mad murderer, only to return to the grasp of another.

"Yes, I suppose you're right," he said. "Although, I doubt any other captain would be willing to sail to Andara. Think you and your ring have the power to open a door and plop me straight there?"

"I don't know how far my portal can travel. We know very little about this kind of magic, and I don't have much strength right now. I don't want anything to go wrong..."

Ruenen smiled, as bright as the sun. "That's all right. Don't want to push our luck any further, do we?"

The ring pulsed and glimmered on her finger, drawing on her power. Marai created a portal for the third time. It didn't come effortlessly to her; it took a moment for her to gather the energy, center it, to create the door, nut then it was there, quivering with magic and multi-colored light, like an aurora borealis.

Ruenen stared at the portal in wonder. "Do you think your new powers have something to do with the ring?"

Marai shrugged and threw a hasty look out at the water. "How about we ask questions after we are farther away from the wreckage?"

They walked through the portal and appeared on the familiar pristine beach right outside of Cleaving Tides and its port; the cluster of palm trees they'd slept under a few nights before directly in front of them.

Marai felt a prickle of that old worry when she stepped back onto the dock. It was habit. Although she knew Slate was gone, or at the very least indisposed, she assumed that lingering sense of unease in this place would never leave her.

For so long, her existence had felt like a held breath. Now she could finally release. Her head felt clear, a fog had been lifted. Her body lighter. The crushing weight gone. She'd said the words. She'd watched that wretched ship go up in flames. It didn't matter if Slate remained alive. He knew *she* was responsible for his downfall. The pirate captain would never come after Marai again.

As she and Ruenen walked down the faded planks towards the harbor master, the rest of Cleaving Tides was in the middle of its usual afternoon bustle. The citizens acted as if two people hadn't been recently abducted by pirates on its premises. She knew she shouldn't care, but Marai found herself glaring at people she passed who gave her shocked looks of recognition. They'd ignored her calls for help. They'd let Slate Hemming's crew drag two unconscious bodies away. Marai knew Slate had been highly feared. He got away with everything. She couldn't entirely blame them for not wanting to be taken, as well. Would she have stepped forward to protect a stranger? Marai knew in her heart . . . she wouldn't.

They'd lost such precious time during their imprisonment onboard *The Nightmare*. How many days had they been jailed there? Marai guessed three or four, but she couldn't be certain. It'd been impossible to tell time correctly in the hull. Assuming she was correct, it'd been about five days since they'd been in Tacorn. Five days gave Rayghast sufficient time to send out messenger pigeons to his search parties across Astye. If someone rode hard enough . . .

Marai was so, so tired. Her magic was weak, and her body ached and throbbed. She sat on the edge of the dock while she waited for Ruenen to finish his discussion with the harbor master. She took off her tall boots and socks. Her nose crinkled at their atrocious smell. She rolled up her pant legs and dangled her feet into the cool water.

She'd always love the sea. Marai was always going to look out at the water and sigh, breathing in its fresh saltiness, its crispness. That was something Slate could never take away from her. The ocean was freedom, but it was also a past life. The sea foam dissolved; an echo of the girl she once was. The ocean crashed and broke upon the shore, but also soothed. Sitting there, letting the water lap against her shins, Marai felt a piece of her snap into place again; a puzzle trying to put itself together.

As if in response to her sudden calm, the bloodstone ring pulsed within the fabric of her pants. A warning that it, too, was a puzzle piece, a part of her. For good or malice. By putting it on, it had claimed her in some way, and she it.

Ruenen joined her at the dockside, sticking his feet in with a satisfied exhale. For a while, they sat in silence and watched the gulls swoop down to the water and snatch fish. Marai loved to hear their noisy caws as they glided overhead.

"What did the harbor master say?" she asked.

"No one else is stupid enough to sail to Andara." Marai was surprised not to hear any disappointment in his tone. "There's a boat to Casamere leaving tomorrow . . ."

"You should beg for passage on that ship. Get off Astye, and buy yourself some time," she said. Ruenen twisted his mouth into a thoughtful frown. Marai glanced at his shoulder. "How's your arm?"

Ruenen looked down at the cut and shrugged. "Eh, not bad. Bleeding stopped once we got to shore. It's not deep. My shirt is ruined, though." Despite washing, his cream tunic was forever tinged brown and red, and was torn in several places. "How are *you* feeling?" Marai pursed her lips and looked the other direction. "Please, I need to know that you're okay."

Marai forced herself to look at him. Concern shown on every plane of his face. "I'm adjusting."

Ruenen nudged her playfully with his foot and said, "Tell me about the ring."

Marai took a breath and thought. "When I put it on initially, my magic stared to rebuild and heal. The longer I wore it, the more my own power surged and gathered, wanting to be used. I think the bloodstone bolsters it. Makes me stronger."

"How did you know that trailing your blood around the ship would cause it to catch fire?"

"There was this little voice in my head," she said, remembering the echo in her brain. "I felt this *urge*, this prodding, to kill everyone onboard. The ring sensed my anger, my hatred, and adapted. The power was mine. I was in control, but I think the bloodstone was guiding me, showing me that I could dig deeper within myself." Marai met Ruenen's gaze. "That I had the strength to tear everyone on that ship apart."

You have a power inside you, Marai.

What else had Keshel seen in his visions?

Ruenen smiled softly. "You've always had that strength, Marai, but you never realized it."

Marai searched his eyes, saw the tenderness and longing in them. His words were weightier than he'd realized. She felt bare, *seen*. Would Ruenen ever stop surprising her with his goodness? How could he look at her that way, *say* those things to a woman who'd spent her entire life killing and running?

"I hope that Queen Meallán's vengeance won't be pointed at *me*," he said.

"Why you?"

"Because my relatives were the ones who slaughtered your people . . . the last of the fae . . ." Ruenen's face darkened, his brow furrowed, as shame crept in over him. "My grandfather was the one who initiated the massacres."

"I've never blamed you for what happened," Marai said, squaring her shoulders to face him. "You're not responsible for the decisions of your ancestors. As I'm not responsible for the fae's enslavement of humans centuries ago. If the ring ever pressed me to harm you, I would toss it away in that barrel of fish innards over there."

Ruenen laughed, a pure, honest, joyous sound. He always laughed so easily. Marai wondered how it was possible for him to laugh after all he'd been through.

"It was awesome, you know," he said lightly, kicking his feet in the cool water like a small child. "You. Your power. Frightening, for sure, but . . . I wasn't afraid of you. I never have been." He met her stare. "You're a fucking goddess."

Once again, he sucked the breath right from her lungs. His eyes went to her mouth, then flitted to her cheek and bruised neck. She must have looked ghastly. He certainly appeared worse for wear, but he didn't seem to mind. Ruenen cocked his head, sizing her up, as his brown eyes returned to hers. She saw the pain in them, pain for her, what had been done to her.

"A goddess?" she repeated breathily.

"I believe I said *fucking* goddess," Ruenen said, smiling.

He leaned in, the slightest bit, and Marai, like a tide, was pulled towards Ruenen's moon. Their noses touched, the slightest contact, and it sent her reeling.

Is this too soon? Should I . . . want him like this?

Marai pulled back, feeling the nerves jump around inside her stomach.

Ruenen bit his lower lip, eyes downcast, and oh gods did Marai suddenly want to suck on that lip. That intensity rose up her whole body, igniting her like a fire, so she hastily put on her boots, then stuffed the bloodstone ring back into her sock for safekeeping.

"We should go," she declared a little too forcefully, getting to her feet. "We'll come back tomorrow to put you on the ship to Casamere, but we should avoid public places until then."

Ruenen followed and she could feel him radiating disappointment. But he was kind, he understood . . . he wouldn't push her. He respected her boundaries.

Gods, no matter hard she could try, she would never be good enough for him. Unworthy in every way.

"We'll go back to the beach and camp there," Marai continued, trying not to let that thought choke her up. A good man. He was a *good* man. She had to repeat that fact to remind herself that not all men behaved like Slate.

"Maybe I shouldn't go," he said, halting Marai mid-step. "To Casamere. Or anywhere else."

"What do you mean?"

Ruenen's back straightened, his face set in determination. It was a regal look that sent a shiver up Marai's spine. "Maybe I'm tired of running. Maybe it's time to stand my ground and fight back, not abscond to some remote corner of the world."

Vines of worry curled around Marai's heart. "Rayghast will kill you if you stay."

"Perhaps . . . but maybe with you, we could defeat him together." His gold-flecked eyes pinned Marai in place. What he was asking . . . What he wanted to do . . . Her stomached churned with hummingbird wings.

Marai opened her mouth, unsure of how to respond, what she could possibly say to such heavy words—

A prickle sparked on the back of Marai's neck. A warning.

She spun around, scanning the shops and alleyways. Something didn't feel right. She sensed *eyes*.

A hunter knows when she's being hunted.

"What's wrong?" asked Ruenen, voice low, suddenly tense.

Marai didn't answer. She took his hand and dashed into a dead-end alleyway. She unsheathed her sword. If people were following them, the alley created a bottleneck. Marai would have an easier time defending that way.

They waited in tense silence. Marai heard no disturbances on the dock. People strolled by the alley entrance without glancing their way.

No one came. Was she being paranoid? Had Ruenen's revelation sent her into a foolish panic?

She sheathed Dimtoir again. That's when she noticed that she hadn't yet let go of Ruenen's hand.

He'd moved so much closer, positioning himself slightly in front of her, protectively. He'd been willing to fight with just his bare hands.

Ruenen was a mere breath away, and Marai made the mistake of looking up at him. Her body turned molten as she saw his eyes darken, a flush come to his cheeks, his chestnut hair falling in waves, framing his angular face. A soothing hush fell over the alleyway.

Ruenen inched closer, and this time, Marai didn't pull away. She was tired of resisting. Tired of denying that she wanted him.

She let his lips softly meet hers. A whisper of a kiss. He inched back, eyes scanning her for any sign of discomfort.

Marai raised onto her tiptoes and pressed her lips to his. This time, it wasn't soft. This time, she had accepted. She hadn't a thought in her brain except *want. Need. More.* Marai got lost in it. Her hands grasped the fabric of his shirt. She wanted to rip it off, lay him down in the dirt, and let him consume her.

Ruenen's hands enveloped her. One wrapped around her waist, the other cupped the base of her skull, fingers entwined in the strands of her hair. All she could feel was his heat mixed with hers, his mouth on hers. And his *tongue,* oh gods, she couldn't think as it slid in, caressing her own.

No one had ever touched her in this way.

Then her back hit the shop wall. He'd closed all the distance left between them; she was caged in by his arms and the wall at her back.

Something switched in her. The snap of a mouse trap, cold and slicing.

Hands.

A man's hands.

Slate's hands.

Slate had never touched her like Ruenen was, with so much yearning, forceful, yet gentle. But it didn't matter—all she could feel were strong hands raking over her body. The memories of Slate crashed down upon her, the feelings of weakness and shame, of being trapped. How he'd held her wrists, forced her legs apart. Hands were a trigger, an emotional recall, and Marai couldn't control it.

She shouldn't have let this happen. She wasn't ready for this. She realized then that while she'd slew her demon, the scar he'd left behind would always remain. Marai spiraled downward, panic rising, into a place she didn't recognize. She didn't know how to crawl back up from this dark, terrible place in her mind, in her soul.

She'd made a *vow*. A vow to that young girl who had been taken and ruined. Marai wasn't going to let another man have her. She belonged to no one. No one would ever have that power over her again. No one would ever make her feel weak and inconsequential. She wouldn't be discarded and abused.

Marai shoved Ruenen off her with such might that he stumbled backwards. He looked as if she'd slapped him, horrified, shocked, confused. She stepped farther away from him towards the alley entrance, barely able to comprehend the words he was saying to her. His mouth was moving, but she couldn't hear. Shaking. Couldn't catch her breath. The ringing in her ears muted all sound.

The bloodstone ring thrummed once more within her sock, causing Marai to glance up.

A shadow. A man. In a dark cloak hovering at the mouth of the alley, sword unsheathed. Two other hooded figures rounded the corner.

More men. More hands. Those raking, awful, taking hands. Marai trembled and stepped backwards into the alley past Ruenen.

Bounty hunters. Men like me.

The hunters had arrived quickly, just as Marai had feared. They'd been sent after Ruenen by Rayghast, that much was certain. Slate would never be able to send someone after her so fast.

She should have known that Rayghast would send the men here first. He'd seen the white sand and palm trees through the portal. She shouldn't have come here. She shouldn't have *kissed* Ruenen.

Get away. Now.

She backed up, Ruenen shaking his head, eyes wide in fear, wondering what he'd done wrong.

Everything. Everything was wrong. Her back hit the dead-end wall. There was nowhere to go. Marai's vision darkened, blacking out completely in her panic.

Ruenen called her name. She could hear the hunters swarm him, Ruenen's grunts and growls reaching her ringing ears.

She had to get away. She clawed at the wood and plaster wall for support. She couldn't stand hearing her name, from his lips, reverberating off the walls.

She'd been ruined, tainted, at a young age, by massacres and manipulation. The only thing she was good for was being the hand that dealt you death. Ruenen was buttery sunlight on a winter's morn. He was a cool breeze in the humidity. Tart fruit on your tongue. The smell of summer rain and the vibrancy of a hibiscus bloom. She could never be his. She was as untamable, as harsh and cruel as the sea in a storm. She'd always be a monster. Heartless. A cloud shrouding Ruenen's light.

What a terrible, disgusting creature she was. Standing and listening to him get captured. She ran from him, as she would always run from any man, any form of intimacy. No matter how hard she'd try, Marai would never be good enough for Ruenen. Never.

"Get the faerie," ordered a gruff voice. Heavy boots approached her.

She reached for her magic, but it merely flickered, protesting against further use. She tried to tug essence from nothing. Marai was a husk; sucked dry. Partly from her overuse of magic, but mostly from her stupid rushed plea for intimacy.

She reached into her pocket, but the ring wasn't there. It was unreachable in this frantic moment, tucked into her sock.

Magic. She needed magic.

Her name rang through the air, a pleading she would never forget, as she raised her hands.

She pulled and begged. *Help me,* she implored into nothing.

Then her vision cleared, like the magic had ripped open the curtains in a dark room. Magic fed off her panic. It ate up all her chaos. It was something dark then, the magic. It didn't come from nature. It didn't come from her body or the ring. It came from *somewhere else.* It tasted different on her tongue, like dusk and danger, that scrape of pepper in her throat. As if she were borrowing magic from someplace she shouldn't be.

The portal appeared before her. Marai didn't care where it came from. She didn't care where it took her—as far from that alley, that harbor, that dark place as possible.

Marai stepped through the portal; her feet touched unforgiving, cracked red dirt. Heat whipped around her. Familiar.

Her mind slowly crawled out of that dark place. That fear receded. Whatever had overtaken her, it rolled away like the tumbleweed passing her by.

Marai's body stilled. She remembered how to fill her lungs with air. The magic, that dark power was gone. None of her own remained, but none of the borrowed magic did, either.

Realization swept over Marai. She spun around in time to see Ruenen's appalled, frantic expression in the distance as he stared at her through the open portal. He was held now by four hunters who wrapped his limbs in rope. He thrashed with all he had.

They'd take him back to Tacorn. To Rayghast and that cell. From prison to prison to prison again. They'd take him back, and Rayghast would kill him.

Marai came to her senses. She lurched towards the portal, but it shrunk instantly, closing her there in the Western desert, Ruenen lost on the other side.

"*No*," she shrieked, trying to form another one, but the magic would not come. Again. Again, and again, she tried. Empty. Her arms twitched and ached from being held in the air. She looked at her hands and started.

The tips of her fingers had turned black. Not decrepit, but they'd been stained, as Rayghast's arms had been.

Marai collapsed to her knees, the full weight of what had occurred roiling in her stomach like rough ocean waves. She had to get back. She tried and tried to form the portal, but her arms only shook in spent magic, as devoid as the desert was of water. She reached into her sock and pulled out the ring, shoving it onto her blackened finger. It did nothing. She was too weak, too frantic to use it.

She called his name through the dead space of her new surroundings. Tears flowed down her face.

She'd left him.

Marai had run away from Ruenen and let him be captured. She'd doomed him to hours or days of torture by Rayghast.

That final image of his face, the betrayal he must have felt. Gods, Marai hated herself.

His hands . . . he wasn't Slate. Slate was gone, but it hadn't mattered. She'd been transported to the place of darkness her mind had always gone to as a girl when she'd lain in Slate's bed. And now Ruenen was paying the price for all her past failures. For her weakness.

She'd condemned him to death.

Marai knelt there for hours. The hot sun beat down upon her, roasting her skin, turning it a vibrant lobster red. She didn't notice. She stared at that empty space where the portal had been, where she had last seen him. Her hands sat on her lap, palms up, fingertips black, perhaps permanently so. A punishment? A cost for reaching out to a magic that wasn't hers? She couldn't bring herself to move.

She knew where she was. The Badlands. Like the ocean, it, too, was vast and empty, but nothing about this place felt like freedom. Somehow, her heart had called for this desert when she'd opened the portal. Marai hadn't known she'd thought about it. But the portal had dropped her here. The portal knew her, even when she didn't know herself. She wanted to be safe, but mostly, she was tired, so tired.

There was nothing she could do for Ruenen. It'd been hours. He was most likely tied to the back of a wagon on his way to Tacorn now. And Marai had no magic left in her to save him.

She got unsteadily to her feet and turned to the canyon behind her. It was majestic. A thing of natural beauty. Layers and shades of russet shale rock. But she didn't truly see it at all. Her eyes passed over the red dirt and marbled rocks. She spotted the large boulder that hung over the edge of the cliff. The rope tied to it there, for ones like her who knew the way. The only clue of life in this wasteland.

Like a black smudge in a sea of copper, Marai walked towards the boulder. Hoping her body didn't give out, she clung to the rope and slowly descended into the canyon. The river below was the only source of water for miles. It was the perfect hiding spot for a group of banished, unwanted individuals.

The scratchy rope gnawed at her palms until her feet hit the ground. At least this part was shaded from the blazing sun. Marai stumbled towards the entrance of a small stone dwelling, built under the overhanging cliff, right into the canyon itself.

She heard the tightening cord of a bow. She raised her hands in submission, not fear.

A shadow towered over her, the arrow at her back. But the shadow lowered its weapon and a strong hand twirled her around.

"It's you," said the male's voice in disbelief. He was handsome in that ethereal fae way. His long sandy blond hair was pulled back in a tight bun, save for the one curl in the front. Familiar green eyes looked at Marai in wonder and concern as he took in the sunburned sight of her.

Marai understood why the portal had brought her here. In her panic, she'd reached out for someplace good. Someplace she could be cared for. It wasn't some fantastical, mythical place like Andara, where she could hide and never be found. No, she'd come here to heal the broken shards of herself. To put the puzzle back together. To re-erect the walls. She couldn't save Ruenen. What use was she to anyone, including herself, if her past could overtake her in such an all-encompassing way?

She had to heal, and this desert, so devoid of life and compassion, was the only safe place she could think of. Because it wasn't the place she came to . . . it was her people.

Her eyes raked up to the pointed ears of the half-fae male before her.

"Take me back, Raife," Marai said and collapsed.

The story continues in . . .
Red Lands and Black Flames
Dark Magic Series Book 2
Available Now

Never miss a release day, cover reveal, or giveaway–sign up for J. E. Harter's monthly mailing list on her website:
https://jeharterauthor.wixsite.com/j--e--harter-author

GLOSSARY

AIN -   Kingdom in the Southwest on the coast of Astye

ANDARA -   Far away, mysterious country

ASTYE -   The largest continent, home to The Nine Kingdoms

BAUREAN SEA -   Body of water in the South

BENIEL -   Kingdom in the Northwest of Astye

CASAMERE -   Large country off the continent

CHIOJAN -   Capital city of the Kingdom of Varana

CLEAVING TIDES - Prosperous port city in Henig, the Southernmost point of Astye, wealthy area above in the hills called High Tides, harbor and beaches called Low Tides

CLIFFS OF UNMYN - On the Northern Coastline, part of the White Ridge Mountains

DUL TANEN -   Capital city of the Kingdom of Tacorn

DWALINGULF -   Large logging town in the lower North

EHLE -   Kingdom in the Southwest of Astye, known for its deserts and canyons of red dirt

FENSMUIR -   City in the Kingdom of Ain

GAINESBURY -   Small village in the Northern White Ridge Mountains

GELANON - Holiest day in the entire year, a winter holiday known for fasting, throwing minerals into fire to show colors for gods to see for blessings

GRELTA -   The Northernmost and largest kingdom on Astye, cold and snowy most of the year

HAVENFIORD -   Large town on the border of Grelta and Tacorn

HENIG -   Kingdom in the Southeast, busy harbors and port cities

INIQUITY -   Town of criminals, also known as the Den, the Nest, Vice, etc.

KELLESAR - Capital city of the Kingdom of Nevandia

LIRR - Goddess of Creation and All Living Things & Fertility

LIRRSTRASS – Capital city of the Kingdom of Grelta

LAIMOEN - God of Destruction and War, Lirr's partner

LISTAN -   Small, sandy country off the continent

MIDDLE KINGDOMS - Name for the two middle countries on Astye–Tacorn and Nevandia

NEVANDIA - Kingdom in the middle of Astye, in a bitter forty-year war with Tacorn

NYDIAN RIVER -   River that stretches East to South on Astye

PEVEAR -   Town on the outskirts of Tacorn, once the site of a bloody battle

RED LANDS - Nickname for the Middle Kingdoms–a land so covered in blood

SILKEHAVEN -   Small town in the Northern White Ridge Mountains

SYOTO -   Empire in the Southeast of Astye

TACORN -   Kingdom in the middle of Astye, in a bitter forty-year war with Nevandia

UKRA -   Country off the continent

VARANA -   Empire in the Northeast of Astye

WHITE RIDGE MOUNTAINS - Large Northern mountain range made of obsidian rock

YEHZIG -   Small, tropical isle off the continent

ACKNOWLEDGEMENTS

I'm sure every debut author says the same thing, but publishing this book was a JOURNEY. And a huge learning experience full of unexpected twists, just like in "B&B," but a little less dark. I started writing this book in March 2022, because this was a story that I honestly needed to get out of me. It had been simmering in my brain for months, and I finally decided to just do it. I honestly loved every second of creating these characters and this world. I think, deep down, I always knew I'd be here someday, I just never imagined it would be *now*, or that it would feel so incredibly freeing.

Let me start, first and foremost, with my amazing editor Erin Young. Thank you for your detailed notes, suggestions, advice, and genuine care for my book. I'm lucky to have someone so knowledgeable and excited by this story and characters.

Thank you, Miblart, for my incredibly awesome cover design. You perfectly captured the mood of "B&B."

Alec McK for the world map of Astye, and somehow making sense of all my world-building notes.

Kate–thank you for over a decade of friendship, and for your guidance, endless support, and general silliness. You were the first person to know anything about this book, and you immediately gave me the confidence to pursue publishing this. Thanks for keeping me sane with the endless hours of phone conversations. Even though you're across the country, you were part of this book every step of the way.

Molly–you've been my adventure buddy and support system throughout the past year as I traversed this new world, and basically restarted my life. I wrote and edited 75% of "B&B" in your kitchen in Summer of 2022 while you were abroad and I watered your plants. Thanks for lending me your kitchen table, your basement, your ear, and your open arms.

Extra special heartfelt shoutout to my critique partner Addison, who not only read this book first, but read it *twice,* and provided the most detailed, helpful, supportive feedback. Thank you for believing in my story. Honestly, "B&B" would not be what it is without you!

My other beta readers, who read very different drafts of "B&B" and helped it progress. Thank you all for your time and care with my book baby.

To my indie author friends and ladies at BWWG–I love these groups of fellow-author-cheerleaders! Thanks for providing me with your good vibes, support, and advice. While we all write in different genres and styles, I am so happy to have found pockets of talented and kind female authors. I'm so proud of us all for pursuing our dreams!

To my parents, who didn't once say I was crazy for doing this (or at least, didn't say so within my proximity). You listened to all of my complaints, wins and losses, and shockingly seemed to believe I had the potential to publish "B&B." Thank you for everything you've done for me, in my whole life, of course, but specifically within the past year. No parents are more supportive and loving, and I thank the universe every day that I have you in my corner.

To my sister, who I think knows I wrote this book, but I never told her anything about it. But thanks for being the weird older sister who taught me that being nerdy is cool. I'm writing today because you read "The Hobbit" to me dressed in cloaks (blankets) in your bedroom when I was five. This is all your fault.

To my nephew–you are small, but full of stories already. Use that big brain of yours to create worlds and characters of your own. I can't wait to see what amazing things you're going to do!

And thanks to you, dear reader, for picking up this book and stepping into my brain for a minute. It's a crazy place to be, but I'm so glad you're here with me!

BONUS MATERIAL

Read on for bonus prequel chapters of
Marai and Ruenen

Marai

Keshel had always told her to be smart.

Thora had said to be good.

Even Raife had told her not to be so brash; to cool that hot head of hers. To blend in.

Marai wanted none of that. Adventure and life had called to her across the open sea. She'd been sitting on the edge of one of the bridges in Cleaving Tides when she caught a glimpse of blond hair at the dock. A man she'd never seen before.

His stance was informal and relaxed, as if he didn't care about the conversation he was having with the harbor master, but judging by his clean appearance, brushed hair, tailored clothing, he *did* care. He was exquisite. Marai's eyes raked him up and down from underneath the wide brim of her hat. She blinked a few times, thinking the sun was playing tricks on her.

No, his hair truly was golden. Glistening. Radiant.

He laughed at something the harbor master said and clapped him on the shoulder. The charming man then passed over several coins and said farewell, walking off towards one of the docks where two women approached him. The women smiled and giggled, batted their eyelashes. One of them stroked a finger down the man's chest. A sly, crooked grin appeared on his face, as if he knew how easy it was to attract this kind of notice.

Once the women left, Marai climbed down from the canopy of bridges above, following the stranger from a distance. She didn't know what drove her to follow him, but she felt utterly compelled. She perched herself behind a large barrel that was going to be loaded onto a nearby ship. The man sauntered over to a black vessel, and greeted the crew, shouting directions at them. The name on the ship's bow said *The Nightmare*. The paint was faded and dull. The figurehead was a fearsome creature with claws and teeth; its black and red paint chipping away. The ship was old, a grandparent in these waters, with deep cracks splintering the sides, and chunks missing from the wooden railings. Hard to believe it was still floating.

The beautiful stranger climbed aboard the deck and continued giving orders as grimy, sinister looking men hauled goods off. The rest of that day, Marai watched the captain from a safe distance. She couldn't take her eyes off him. He commanded with ease, like he was born to do it. His men listened, efficiently working, loading and unloading, swabbing the deck. Marai couldn't help but be impressed by the way he moved; shoulders back, head held high. He had power. He had control.

After the moon had risen high above the water, Marai silently crept after the captain as he entered the busy, raucous tavern. She slid in through the door and found a dark corner to melt into. The tavern was humid and sticky. Sweat dripped down her back. The whole place smelled of unwashed bodies and smoke. She'd never come into the tavern before. There'd never been a reason until that night. She didn't drink, and hated crowded, tight spaces. They provided more opportunities for people to discover what she was.

Why am I here? she kept asking herself. It made no sense to risk her safety this way. He was just a man. And she was a girl. A faerie girl. There was no reason to be so drawn to him. Not only that, he was a sailor. He was bound to leave town soon and be gone for months, at least.

Keshel and Thora's warnings reverberated in her ears: *leave now. This isn't wise.*

Marai considered walking out the door when she looked up and saw the captain staring at her. She stiffened, feeling that unfamiliar blush staining her cheeks. She cursed herself again. Leif and Aresti would tease her something dreadful if they saw her flush so. She wasn't some delicate flower who blushed at a male's gaze, but something about this captain made her legs go wobbly, her heart thunder in her breast.

The captain waved a sun-blessed hand for her to join him at his table. Several crew members sat with him, drinking and commiserating with the local women. Marai cautiously approached his table, removing her taupe hat, swiping loose strands of hair from her sweaty face.

"Hello, there," the captain drawled, raising an eyebrow at her. Marai somehow stuttered out a greeting. "You've been watching me all day. Is there a reason?"

Marai nearly toppled from embarrassment. She picked at her fingernails, but never once dropped his gaze. Seeing him up close was better.

"No reason, other than I was intrigued by your business dealings," she shot at him, causing the table to go silent.

"My business dealings?" repeated the captain, raising his other eyebrow now to match. "What exactly have you seen?"

Marai's mouth went arid, but she didn't back down. "I've seen you exchange a large amount of coin with the harbor master and guards to look the other way. Whatever you're dealing in, it's not something you want known. Although, everyone seems to know who you are here, so you're not being very secretive about it. People seem to respect you and what you do. Or fear you. Anyone with eyes can see."

For a moment, no one moved or spoke. Marai wondered if she had overstepped with her bravado. Would that enormous man sitting next to the captain take that blade to her throat?

Instead, the captain smiled coyly, evidently impressed.

"I'm not the only captain in these waters who prefers discretion. My business is my own." The captain leaned back in his chair, giving Marai a better glimpse of the intricate tattoos on his arms and neck. They were depictions of the mythical water dragons. Marai had seen a sketch of them in a book once before. They were one of many fictional, superstitious tales sailors were prone to tell. The ones snaking up the captain's arms were detailed with vicious looking faces, mouths full of teeth, and long talons on their hands. She was mesmerized by the tattoos' details and colors.

"What's your name, girl?" the captain asked with a hint of amusement. He clearly didn't mind her staring.

"Marai," she said as he looked her over.

"I'm Captain Slate Hemming." He reached out a hand. Marai tentatively shook it, feeling the strength of his fingers. She felt that foolish blush on her face again. "What are you, Marai?"

For a moment, Marai forgot to breathe. She considered bolting for the door, but she didn't think she'd make it far. When someone wanted a faerie dead, they always caught up to it in the end, and these men, she could tell, were trained killers.

"My apologies, that was a terribly rude thing for me to ask," Captain Hemming said with a shake of his head. "I can tell that you're not an ordinary girl, Marai. I've been sailing my whole life, and I've met my fair share of interesting people and creatures. I can tell when someone is hiding something."

Marai nervously picked at her cuticles again. The crew members watched her suspiciously. Captain Hemming merely waited, looking up at her with those blue eyes. She couldn't resist.

"I'm half-fae," she practically whispered. The captain's eyes opened wider, but there was no expression of revulsion or fury. No one grabbed her. No one threw her to the ground or brandished a weapon.

"Well, that seems like a gift from the gods," he proclaimed. Marai felt a weight lift from her shoulders. "I imagine you're quite stealthy and quick, aren't you?" Marai nodded. "Can you do any magic?" Marai nodded once again, but with a vague shrug. "Do you have a family? A home?"

Her heart clenched a little as she thought of Keshel, Thora, Raife, and that cave.

"No, I only arrived here a month ago. I am . . . alone . . ." she said, hating how pathetic that sounded.

Captain Hemming leaned forward across the table. "How'd you like to join our crew?"

Marai nearly fell down. "Sorry?"

Although they didn't move, the scowls on the men at the table deepened.

"Captain," began the biggest one, "we can't take one of *them* onto our ship."

"I've been looking for someone with your set of skills, and I think we could both benefit from this partnership. You'd have room and board on the ship, and my protection. But you'd be working for me, following my orders and my rules. I don't take kindly to disobedience."

Slate's eyes flashed, a warning sign Marai should have heeded. In that one second, his expression seemed . . . sinister, possessive. But then he was holding out his hand, a sly smile on his lips, and Marai barely noticed her hand taking his again. A quick jerky handshake and the deal was made.

"I look forward to having you on the crew, Marai."

When she boarded *The Nightmare* to set sail to distant lands, Marai was filled with excitement. She could hardly believe she was leaving behind the land that hated her, that had killed her family. She was getting her wish to go out to sea. More than that, she'd been welcomed with open arms by a compassionate captain. He saw her for who she was, and he didn't fear her. She felt so utterly grateful for his acceptance that she didn't care at all what he asked her to do.

At first, Marai just completed basic chores, the same duties as the other sailors. She did everything to perfection, hoping to make a good impression on Captain Hemming. He'd taken a risk bringing a girl onto his ship. Marai was aware the crew was less than fond of her being there. They hardly said a word to her, and gave her constant looks of disdain. She also knew Ox, Jesup, and Fishlegs gave her the worst of the chores to complete. She wasn't insulted, though. She probably would've felt the same way if some nobody had joined her crew. It was all the more reason to try her best. And Marai wasn't unhappy. She didn't mind their treatment of her, the hard labor, the terrible food, or smelly, uncomfortable hammocks. For now, she had a place to call home.

One afternoon, weeks into their voyage, after swabbing the deck for hours, Marai felt the captain's eyes on her. She looked up from her mop and found him gazing at her from the railing on the upper deck. He sauntered down towards her. Marai wiped her wet hands on her pants.

"Why don't you ever use your magic?" he asked, eyes sparkling. "You could do your chores much faster if you did."

"I don't use magic," she said quickly, making Captain Hemming frown.

"That's ridiculous. If I had magical talents I'd use them all the time."

Marai crossed her arms. "Not if your entire species was slaughtered because of it."

The captained considered her, the shimmer gone from his eyes. "That sword you have . . . why don't you wear it on your belt like the rest of the crew?"

Marai shrugged. "I didn't think it was necessary."

"You must always keep your sword with you. A good swordsman is never left unprotected. You never know when someone may surprise you." So fast, he unsheathed his own sword and held the blade to her throat. Marai froze as the crew snickered. "See? You need to be smarter than that. Go get it."

Marai did as she was told, feeling stupid and so much like a child. When she returned from below deck with her father's sword, Slate looked it over approvingly.

"That's a nicely made piece."

"It was my father's," she explained. "Faerie-made."

There was a glint of envy in the captain's face, but it was gone in an instant. He began instructing her on how to hold it properly, how to balance its weight, where to place her feet. He slowly swiped his sword and commanded her to block it. When she did, he shook his head and corrected her movements.

"Why are you teaching me all this?" she asked. Marai had never properly learned before. She had always swung and hoped her aim was true. She hadn't had much use for the sword while she was in hiding with the other fae.

"I won't have you be a burden on my crew," Slate said, all business. "No one can be spared to watch over you in a fight. Especially if you won't use magic."

Over the next several months, Slate taught her sword fighting. It became a routine. Every afternoon, once morning chores were finished, Marai was forced to spar with various members of the crew. Each challenger was more skilled than the next.

"Try again," Slate would command. "*Again.*"

Slate wasn't patient with her, always finding something wrong with her movements, making her restart.

Marai defeated every member of the crew. All she yearned for was Slate's approval, which he never truly gave, but she knew she was one of the best fighters on the ship.

"Girl's damn faerie blood gives her an advantage," whined Jesup.

"Fucking magic," said Fishlegs.

But she hadn't ever used magic in a duel with them. That was cheating. She'd bested them all with her own natural skill, and she was proud of that.

"What about you, captain?" she challenged, sounding bolder than she felt. She pointed Dimtoir at him. "You should never turn your back on someone with a weapon."

Slate turned, his eyes flashing in amusement and something predatory. Captain Hemming attacked viciously. Marai barely had time to block. He was highly skilled; the most skilled swordsman Marai had ever seen. In a mere moment, she was on her back again, aching from head to toe.

The captain sheathed his sword. "Keep training." He turned and went to dinner, leaving Marai on the ground, feeling more determined than ever to become the best.

Every time she went up against the captain, she wasn't sure if she should win . . . Slate clearly never lost. So Marai held back a little in those sparring matches with Slate, because she knew that if she did ever win . . . she may not live to tell anyone.

They made landfall off the coast of an exotic island. Ukra, Slate told her. Ukra's dark-skinned inhabitants wore fine, gauzy silks and golden bangles. Slate called Marai into his private quarters. He was dressed stylishly in a blue silk tunic that matched his eyes. He'd pulled his hair back with a ribbon, and looked so dashing Marai could scarcely stop staring.

"I need your assistance tonight, Marai," he said. "I've been invited to a lord's estate for dinner. It's been some time since they've had any traders from Astye docked here. They seem excited to discuss business."

"Why do you need me?"

Slate was perfectly capable of conducting his own business.

"While I'm dining, you will sneak into the estate. The lord keeps certain . . . valuable items up in his chamber. I want you to procure them for me."

For a moment, Marai's heart stopped.

Slate wanted her to steal from someone who wanted to do business with him? It made no sense. It had to be a joke.

"What items?"

"You'll know when you see them," Slate said, nonchalant. "Use those fae skills of yours. Be quick. Be silent. And bring the items to the ship before dinner is over." He stepped towards the door, but stopped when Marai didn't budge. "Is something wrong?" Those blue eyes bored into hers. "May I remind you of our bargain? You follow my orders. All of them."

Marai swallowed, and Slate moved swiftly before her. His hand raised and Marai cringed, thinking he would strike her, but instead, he cupped her cheek gently. Her breathing hitched as his thumb stroked softly along her cheek bone.

"You're the only one I trust for this mission. You're special. Please, do this for me."

Foolish young Marai melted. She had no power against him.

She became his thief that night.

She climbed stealthily up the estate lattice, in through the large window to the bedroom. It was a grand, white and gold space with a large bed and armoire. A space fit for a wealthy merchant lord. She snuck to a dresser where she spotted several elegantly carved wooden boxes. She lifted the lid off one to reveal exquisite golden jewelry, most inlaid with glittering diamonds. Each piece would have fed her for months back on Astye.

She grabbed a bracelet and a recognizable spark ran up her fingers.

Magic.

The sound of laughter from the hallway jolted her from the confusion. Marai quickly grabbed one box, filled it with the oldest, most unique pieces. Many of them gave her that same subtle, magical spark. She left the way she came and no one, not a single one of the guards, had been aware of her presence.

Slate had been more than pleased when he'd returned from dinner. His eyes lit up when he touched one of the bracelets. A smug look of awe and possession dawned on his face.

Does he know it's magic?

In front of the whole crew, he announced, "Marai did excellent work for us tonight. She retrieved some highly valuable items. Because of her, we'll all be able to eat."

Perhaps his words were for show, but Marai locked them inside her heart.

"Those bangles are magic," she said to Slate once away from the others, following him to his cabin door. Slate's hand froze on the doorknob. "That's why you had me steal them, am I right?"

"Don't ask questions. Just do as you're told," he replied.

When they made landfall again at another island, she became his thief once more, without him hardly needing to ask. She knew Slate didn't just deal in money and jewels, but in secrets and magic.

It was always, "Marai, I have an errand for you," said with a look of hunger.

Sometimes, the items looked insignificant, such as a boring dented chalice from the isle of Yehzig, or an aged silver locket that wouldn't open from the small, sandy country of Listan. Once she was even instructed to pilfer a piece of old parchment.

They all felt the same. The items hummed or sparked when she touched them. She tasted the bubbly, rich aftereffects of magic on her tongue.

Several times, Slate handed over one of those special items in a secretive business deal. In return, he'd receive a chest of coins or jewels.

The rest of the crew never get to see any of those earnings, she thought after adding up her own coins from a recent mission.

Upon reading the misgivings on her face, Slate had come by with a heart-fluttering smile. "For being my special little thief." He plopped two more coins into her hands, paying her for her silence. She didn't mind, as long as he kept smiling at her that way.

Then he asked her to kill.

She'd felt terribly guilty taking that first life. She'd tried to subdue the man she'd stolen from with magic, but she was untrained, unfocused, and he broke through her weak barrier easily. In that moment, she wished she'd practiced her magic more.

"*Disgusting faerie bitch*," the man shouted, spittle flying.

Marai slit his throat.

"Don't fret over humans like them," Slate had said. "They slaughtered your people. They'd all do the same to you in an instant."

She hadn't felt as guilty after that, and soon, she became numb to it. Marai stopped counting how much she had stolen, how many people she'd killed. All for Slate.

The pirate life suited her. Her crew mates were like her: men who had no choices, were rejected by society, and sought an escape. And she loved Slate from afar, savoring any scrap of attention he tossed her way.

Until one night, two years later, when that grew into something more.

The crew were all drunk. They'd ravaged another ship from the King of Casamere's fleet. The goods and wine they'd taken would catch a hefty price. Slate seemed rather inebriated. He almost never drank more than a glass at a time. He never liked to slip that control.

Perhaps it never would've happened if he'd been sober.

He came up to Marai, who'd been laughing with the others as Fishlegs told a vulgar story. Slate looked her over appraisingly, like she was one of the glittering jewels she stole for him.

"I know we're a bunch of brutes on this vessel, Marai, but you . . . you are unique," he said, taking a lock of her hair in his fingers. "A treasure."

Marai's fragile, girlish heart leapt at his nearness. He inched closer and licked her jaw line, sending a shudder down her entire body. She arched as his hand grabbed her waist, pulling her to his hard, sculpted chest.

"Sometimes I forget that there's a woman onboard," Slate whispered hot against her ear. Marai gasped. She loved him, yes, but she wasn't sure she was ready for this.

Dragging her by the wrist, Slate brought her into his cabin. He slammed the door behind her and shoved her up against it.

Slate's lips were on hers. He was ravenous. It didn't feel right. None of this felt right. He hadn't asked her if she wanted this. She wasn't ready for this kind of intimacy.

Marai tried to pull away. "Captain, please–"

Slate's large, strong hands gripped her arms, then her hips, traveling up her shirt and to her breasts. Marai gasped and tried to wriggle free, but he shoved her from the door to his bed.

The world spiraled around her. She couldn't breathe. As much as she'd wanted his love, she hadn't expected this–this animalistic claiming of her body. She didn't know how to stop it.

Slate ripped off her shirt and commanded her to take off her pants. Marai did so with trembling fingers. Then she was utterly naked before him, and he before her. Her eyes widened at the sight of his strong male body. She'd always wondered what he would look like. She had wanted to touch those muscular arms, but this wasn't how she envisioned it. She didn't want those powerful arms holding her down.

She shoved against him as hard as she could. "Please—"

"You would deny me? After everything I've done for you? All I've sacrificed for you?"

Marai's defenses crumbled. He had sacrificed a lot for her. Letting a faerie girl onto his ship? Teaching her? Trusting her?

"Don't you think I deserve a little in return?" he asked, kissing up her neck.

Was that what love was . . . sacrifice?

The captain shoved her onto the bed. Marai saw stars. White light. And then all she saw was his beautiful face, sweating, teeth bared in a familiar, smug smirk. It wasn't a look of love.

She felt pain. And she thought the pain would leave eventually, but it didn't. He didn't listen to her whimpers or shouts. He ignored her flinching and struggling. He kept going.

In desperation, she reached for her magic, but she couldn't focus. She couldn't draw on it. The magic flickered and crackled in her veins, but she didn't know how to use it.

He must've seen or felt it, because he hovered over her ear. "Shh, darling. My Marai. Tell me you love me. I know you want to." Words caught in her throat. "Say it. Say you love me."

"I . . . I love you," she stammered through gasps.

"Yes. Again."

"I love you," she said louder, more clearly.

A short while later, Slate said nothing to Marai as he sat down at his desk, naked, and looked at the large map splayed across it.

Marai quickly put her clothing back on and exited the cabin.

Was this what love was? What two people did? As she curled into her hammock for the night, listening to the snores of the drunk pirates, she didn't want to do it again.

After that night, Marai was officially his. He never asked her to come to his room. He demanded it.

"You are my everything," he'd say to soothe her whenever she squirmed. "You and your gifts . . . you're very important to me."

He never left her alone in his room, and she was never allowed to sleep next to him, no matter how worn out she was after he'd had his fun. By the end of each encounter, Slate ignored her and returned to his maps and charts. Marai would dress quietly, always ashamed, and leave the cabin.

She was a child and knew nothing of love. Sacrificing pieces to satisfy the other? Perhaps that was simply how the world worked. It didn't feel right, but she took whatever kernels of affection he gave and held onto them. They were all she had.

After over three years at sea, *The Nightmare* finally returned to Cleaving Tides. Marai was glad to see the familiar faded gray planks of wood across the harbor, the weathered shops and stalls, the looming, magnificent estates above in the High Tides. But Marai felt differently towards the continent and its inhabitants now that she'd had time away from it. The ocean no longer sparkled with the same magnificence. The shops and streets were dull and uninteresting.

She was sixteen. A woman. She'd seen more of the world than most of them ever would. She no longer viewed people as good or bad; everyone had become the same to her. They were all shades of gray. She no longer felt fear or resentment towards them.

On a midnight stroll around the harbor, Marai caught the sound of a woman's flirtatious giggles. She spotted the woman up against the wall of the inn, arms wrapped around a man who was currently head-first in her ample bosom. The giggling woman seemed to be . . . enjoying the encounter. Marai never made those noises or expressions when she was with Slate.

Was something wrong with Marai that she didn't find sex pleasing? That it hurt her and she was loathe to do it? She loved Slate, but . . . she often believed his actions were not of a man who returned those feelings. Every night she was called to his bed, she left with feelings of shame and emptiness.

The woman shrieked with pleasure. It was when her male companion lifted his head that Marai could see him clearly.

Slate smirked and licked his lips, then clamped those lips down on the woman's neck. She squealed and arched into him.

Marai's heart clenched and ached. Was it all for nothing? All the sacrifice, indignity and pain not for love at all? She'd suffered through his advances because she thought he loved her. But he'd never once said those words. Slate had made her say them plenty, but he'd never actually said it himself. He threw out compliments, leading her on, earning her trust.

Marai didn't dare stay any longer. She ducked around to the front of the inn, chest heaving in pain. She could still hear the woman laughing, Slate moaning . . .

"Did I hear a rumor that you've been sleeping with that little vile creature you have onboard?" the woman asked through gasps.

Marai heard Slate groan in pleasure, not annoyance. "She's just exotic entertainment. A warm body to stave off the need." The woman gasped again, louder this time, and Slate growled and grunted. Marai felt tears stinging her eyes. "She's nothing."

Marai took a step back and collided with an enormous, broad chest. She turned to see Ox regarding her like she was some kind of pest.

"Do you honestly think he cares about you?" the first-mate asked her. "He only keeps you around because you serve his needs. You're an *object*, girl. One of his trinkets."

Marai stumbled down the dock, out towards the solitary beach, leaving the sounds of Slate and the woman behind. She collapsed to her knees, wrapping her skinny arms around her middle, and wailed up at the crescent moon.

When the first blazing rays of the sun appeared on the horizon, Marai stood. She dashed into the woods, pressing further away from Slate and *The Nightmare*. Betrayal. Loss. Anger. Tremendous sorrow. Marai let them take her. She let those feelings engulf her as she ran away from the life she had built.

But it had been a false life. All of it had been manipulation and fabrication. Marai had been taken in by his face and pretty words, blinded by a girl's foolish love for a man she did not fully comprehend. He'd used her, over and over again. All she was left with now was nothing.

This pain wasn't merely about Slate, though. No matter where she went, nothing ever felt right. Nothing felt good.

She came to a clearing. She gave herself a moment to breathe. Marai looked down. Her father's sword was there in her hands . . . she held it tightly, shaking.

"Why? Why would you make me this way?" she shouted up to the sky. She hoped her voice reached Empyra, that magical world in the clouds where the gods lived in peace, toying with their creations below. "Why give me life just to let me suffer?"

I could end this, she thought. She could simply end this burning humiliation, this hatred at herself and at him. *All it would take is a slice of the blade to my throat or wrists . . .*

The sun climbed above the treetops. Marai paused as a bright ray shone down upon her face.

Was it Lirr? Was the goddess giving her a sign? Marai let that beam warm her face. The hand of the goddess stroked her cheek.

Taking her own life wasn't going to make anything better. She had to be stronger than this. Slate had taken her virginity. He had taken her heart, but she wouldn't let Slate take her life.

Marai stabbed Dimtoir into the dirt and knelt before it.

"I vow here, before this sword, to never, ever, let love blind me. I vow to never again give another person control over me. From now on, I am my own master, and no man shall ever hurt me, touch me, or claim me. Or they shall perish by this sword."

She felt the magic in the air then. Her words hung heavily amidst the crisp smell and bubbly rich taste. The vow was now more than words. It was engraved into her heart, in the very earth beneath her feet.

Marai waited until night fell before she quietly rowed back to *The Nightmare*, wrapped in a cloak of ebony.

Using those unique fae-skills Slate valued so highly, Marai climbed aboard the ship; a specter, tiptoeing across the deck, until she reached Slate's cabin. Most of the crew remained at the Tides, drinking and gambling. She had to be quick; it wouldn't not be long before one of the crew standing guard would see her rowboat in the water.

She knocked on the wooden walls of the cabin, searching. Those items she'd stolen for him had to be in his room somewhere, hidden in a secret location. Eventually, she heard that empty, echoing sound and pushed.

The wall gave way and clattered to the ground. Marai winced and hastened her task. Inside the hidden chamber were all the relics and papers of Slate's stash. Items hummed or pulsed as Marai passed.

The only things Slate truly cared about were the items in this room. But which one would hurt him the most? She could only carry one with her, but that was all she needed to exact her vengeance.

Something thrummed on the corner table and caught her eye. It almost . . . sang to her. Marai turned and saw the bloodstone ring perched upon a satin pillow. The stone was beautiful, opaque green jasper with spots of red, and set in a simple silver band. She didn't recognize it. It was an item Slate had procured before she joined his crew. Marai found herself drawn to it. She reached out and took the ring gently from its pillow. It pulsated against her hand, acknowledging her, as she stuffed it into her pocket. She quickly climbed back through the hidden door, only to find herself face to face with Slate.

The blood had completely drained from his face. His beautiful face contorted with rage, looking so much like the water dragons in his tattoos.

"Give it back," he snarled, holding out his hand. "Whatever you took, give it here. Now."

Marai threw him her haughtiest glare. "Who says I took anything? I was just looking."

Slate cursed vehemently and stepped towards her. "If you don't hand it over, I'll slit your throat."

Marai stepped closer to him, angling her neck for his easy access. "Go ahead. You can do no more harm to me than what you've already done."

"What are you speaking of?" he snapped, hand tightening on the hilt of his sword.

"I was just a warm body to you. Exotic entertainment."

Slate's eyes flashed. "You shouldn't have been nosing around."

"You taught me to do that," Marai sniped right back. "You forced me into your bed every night."

"Oh, you enjoyed it, you slut. You *love* me."

Marai spat in his face.

"What did you take?" Slate ordered once again, wiping off the saliva.

"I took nothing. And I want nothing from you. Ever again."

Slate bared his teeth at her. "You'll not leave this ship alive."

Marai was prepared for this. He might be able to overpower her in a swordfight. He'd taught her, after all. But there was something she had that he could never possess, something Slate only wished for.

Marai had *magic*.

This time, she wouldn't pretend to be anything but what she was.

With a snap of her fingers, a small flame erupted. She tossed the fire onto his clothing. In the moment he was distracted, ripping his shirt from his body to douse the flame, Marai had leapt onto the windowsill and pushed one of the large bay windows wide open.

Slate dove forward and grabbed onto her ankle. His fingers dug in, grip so strong that Marai couldn't shake him loose, so she sliced Slate across his bare chest. Marai had cut through several of his complex tattoos, ruining the artwork. Slate screamed in pain and fury as Marai plummeted into the sea, leaving him yelling down at her from the window.

She swam and swam until she reached the shore further from the Tides.

Marai said her farewells to the pirate captain, there on the sandy shore, and to the crew, the ship, and life she'd come to know. But more than anything, she bid farewell to the girl who had given her heart and body to a man who hadn't deserved her. To the girl who only desired love and a home.

That girl was gone.

The young woman standing on the beach pulled the black hood over her face, secured the sword at her belt, and stalked off into the night, becoming nothing more than a shadow and a name.

RUENEN

His earliest memory was the smell of incense. Of standing in the open hall of the monastery. The pale stones were cold beneath his small feet. He used to pad around shoeless, running from the monks who chased him. A group of pious men who'd sworn off marriage and children, now forced to raise a boy. And not just any boy. A boy with a secret. A dangerous one.

Monks Amsco and Nori called him Leander. For a long time, he thought that was his name. It wasn't until he turned four that they told him his true name was Ruenen. That was the same day they told him he was a prince. That his parents were a great king and queen. But those were foreign words to a boy who'd been raised in a world of gods and goddesses, of prayers and hallowed halls.

"You mustn't tell anyone who you are," said Nori, in his mother-henning tone. He was always the worrier of the two head monks. The one who looked out the window every day, searching beyond the horizon for *something*. His long orange robe hid his fragile body, his bald head shaved like all the other acolytes of the Goddess Lirr. His dark, soft hands trembled. Any loud sound made him jump. Maybe he had always been that way. Or it was because of the child they sheltered.

Amsco told Ruenen he was special, and that when he grew up, he would have "responsibilities" and "duties." Ruenen was too young to understand what those entailed. All he knew was that he hated his lessons. They were boring. Long hours spent sitting down when his young body only wanted to run and play.

"A prince must sit still," Amsco would scold at him in his quiet, stern way. He never yelled, but had the ability to make you listen. He was old. His face was covered in wrinkles, but he was always the one to catch Ruenen when he ran amok. The old monk was spry for his age.

There was never anyone to play with. The other monks shook their heads and tutted as Ruenen passed. He suffered through the tedious lessons on manners and royal customs, on geography, on politics, reading and arithmetic. It was all so terribly dull, but he listened because it was what he was born to do.

Ruenen's small universe consisted only of the arched and pillared hallways, the cloisters, library, refectory, infirmary, and dormitories. His room was the size of a broom closet, but as a boy with no possessions to call his own, he took up no space. He was meant to appear an insignificant waif of some passing peasant. His clothing was that of an urchin. Unsuspecting in every way.

What he did know was that someday he would be old enough to take the throne and preside over this kingdom called Nevandia. When he was king, Amsco told him he could make his own rules and tell people what to do. But for now, he had to listen. He had to learn.

Nori wanted him to be a good king. He said that a lot. "Be kind. Be merciful." Ruenen didn't know why he *wouldn't* be kind. But he listened. He learned. He grew.

Until he stopped feeling like a kid. Until he began to understand what "responsibilities" and "duties" fully entailed. The weight began to press down upon his shoulders, heavy as the crown he would someday wear. He stopped running and playing.

And then one day, the horses came. He sat outside in the gardens, slate tablet on his lap, carefully drawing his letters with chalk. Such a loud sound disturbed him from his writing practice. He heard the horses galloping down the road and lifted his head to look. Amsco and Nori tore from the building. Ruenen had never seen them move so fast. A peasant woman and her daughter stood with them. Only when the monks walked closer did Ruenen notice their panicked faces.

"Leander," they called. Ruenen was used to seeing Nori worry, but Amsco never worried. Amsco was always calm. That was what made Ruenen approach. If Amsco was scared, something was wrong.

Nori knelt before him. "You must go now," he told the boy. "Quick, before they see you."

"Go where?" Ruenen asked as a burlap pack was thrust into his small hands.

"Stay with this good woman. If anyone asks, she is your mother. You are her son. And this is your sister," Amsco instructed, gesturing to the two females. Ruenen had so rarely seen females before. They were as unfamiliar as those approaching armored soldiers on horseback. He shrunk away from her, stepping closer to Nori.

"But why?" asked Ruenen. He was having trouble tearing his eyes away from the black cloud approaching on the road. A boy with a thousand questions, Amsco often called him.

"You must stay silent," Amsco said, yanking Ruenen's face towards his own. The boy met Amsco's clear blue eyes. "You cannot speak of this place. Don't tell anyone your name. Who you are. Anything. Do you understand, child?"

Ruenen shook him off. "No, I don't. Why do I have to go?"

Nori brushed Ruenen's hair from his eyes, a fatherly gesture Ruenen so rarely received.

Ruenen then nodded in resignation. "I understand."

"Don't look back," Amsco said, with a pained look. "Whatever you hear, keep running, Leander." Then he and Nori turned away, their ginger robes so bright against the pale stone and green grass. They walked inside the monastery. Ruenen never saw them again.

The peasant woman grabbed Ruenen's hand and dragged him across the meadow. Ruenen turned back just once when they were far enough away. He saw the thick dark smoke. The flash of silver metal. He thought he heard a scream, but the woman yanked on his arm and pressed him to go faster. His little legs could barely keep up.

Once they got to the road, they kept running. They didn't stop. The daughter complained, but her mother only shushed her. Ruenen didn't say a word. The woman barely looked his way. That night, they slept in the woods. Ruenen curled up on a bed of leaves and moss. He had dreams, but he couldn't remember any of them.

The first town they reached, the woman found someone else to take him. She had done her duty, she said. She'd gotten him this far. She told the farmer that Ruenen was her sister's unwanted bastard child.

Ruenen would always remember her telling the man, "the boy must be protected. At all costs. The boy must live."

The farmer must have understood the gravity of her words, because he plopped Ruenen into his wagon, covered him with hay, and brought him to another town further south. There, he passed Ruenen to someone else. Each time the boy was exchanged, the same words were spoken.

As it was for two years. Ruenen eventually became aware that he was always in peril, and that he was a danger to everyone he traveled with. He never knew the names of his saviors. Many were begrudging. Some were gentle. But all were kind, because they protected him. Even if they said not a word to him, they still opened up their hearts and let a boy travel with them.

Ruenen saw much of the continent that way. North, South, East, West . . . it took two years for him to get to Chiojan. He was ten by then. Ten and fatigued and old before his time. He was tired of running away from something he didn't understand.

When the silk merchant came across Tomas Chongan, Ruenen expected much of the same. The blacksmith happened to be at the market that day and had overheard the merchant trying to pass the boy off to an old farmer and his wife. The old farmer hadn't wanted him. Chongan volunteered to take the boy, instead.

"Would it be possible to get a meal before we leave?" Ruenen had asked the burly stranger who now held his fate.

The blacksmith raised an eyebrow. "We're not leavin' anywhere. I live here."

He brought Ruenen to a row of cottages. One of them had a workshop attached to it. The blacksmith had a forge and a wife and children. Before entering the house, Tomas Chongan shaved Ruenen's head, put him in a heavy leather apron, and covered his face in soot and ash.

"You'll have to earn your keep here. You'll be my apprentice," Master Chongan said, then brought Ruenen into his home.

"What's this?" his wife asked, waving a wooden spoon in her hand. She was a strong woman. Ruenen could see both her fierceness and kindness written plainly across her face. The three round-faced children behind her gaped at the skinny urchin boy with their father.

"New apprentice—Hiro. Parents are dead. No other family," Master Chongan had gruffly explained. His wife questioned him no further and passed Ruenen a bowl of nettles, rice, and dumplings. He sat around a kitchen table with a family for the first time in his life. He was so quiet. He didn't ask a thousand questions. He didn't even ask one.

Chongan was a large man, which was unusual in the East. Ruenen remembered his thick arms and how his hands were always dirty. No matter how much he scrubbed, dirt eternally lived under his fingernails and in the ridges of his knuckles. Mistress Chongan, the only way Ruenen would ever address her, would put her hands on her hips and watch Master wash his hands. She never believed he truly tried to clean. It used to make Master laugh. His deep joyous cackle reverberated in Ruenen's chest and warmed him. It was the sound of happiness. The sound of ease. Of family. Of a life that Ruenen had never known before. Unlike the hallowed silence of the monastery, Master Chongan's home and forge were loud. If someone wasn't chatting or laughing or the kids weren't arguing, you could hear the pounding of a hammer on steel. The hiss of hot metal in oil. The crackling of the forge.

Ruenen loved his life with the Chongans. They treated him like a member of their own family. They never asked him a thing about himself. He never offered them a glimpse into his past.

He enjoyed blade-smithing. He loved the feel of a sword in his hand. How it could be both a thing of beauty and of violence. A tool and ornamentation. Master was an excellent instructor, and Ruenen soon grew strong as every day he hammered away at steel, and worked the two immense bellows to stoke the fire. He also loved Chiojan. He enjoyed the busy city and Eastern customs, the pavilions and pagodas, the smells of spice and jasmine, the people who came to the forge.

Whispers and rumors brewed on the street that Tacorn was searching for someone. As safe as he felt with the Chongans, Ruenen knew there was still a price on his head. He'd learned about King Rayghast and the feud between Tacorn and Nevandia. He began to comprehend that the reason the war in the Middle Kingdoms continued to drag on was because of him. Because he hadn't declared himself King, or been caught by Rayghast. But Ruenen wasn't ready to be a king. He wanted to stay with Master Chongan.

In his early teens, Ruenen finally began to discover himself. The things he liked. The things he wanted. He heard music for the first time; music that wasn't religious chanting. His lute, a gift from a passing bard, was almost always by his side. During lulls in the day, he'd experiment, letting his fingers learn the strings and chords. Music and sword fighting were two passions that he was determined to practice daily. Neither came naturally, but Ruenen was a diligent student, better than he ever was with Monks Amsco and Nori. He tried not to think about them.

There was also Master Chongan's daughter.

Yuki was a year older than Ruenen and she always smelled like lavender. She was soft and lush and warm. She was the one to approach him in the forge alone one night. She kissed him by the fire and allowed him to put his dirty hands on her delicate skin. He and Yuki had many a-frolic in the hay. He didn't love her, but he certainly liked her a lot. She didn't expect anything from him except for consensual intimacy. He kissed other girls in Chiojan, but Yuki was always there, a steady feminine presence that he'd never had before.

"I like your eyes, Hiro," she told him once.

"My eyes?" No one had ever complimented his appearance before.

"They sparkle in the light." Yuki smiled. "And you have a lovely mouth."

Ruenen had shown her then just how lovely his mouth was.

He remembered when the news of King Vanguarden's passing reached his ears. He heard it from a man in the shop, purchasing a dagger. Ruenen's gut wrenched. He knew his time with the Chongans was limited. Without a king on the throne, Ruenen was next in line. He was duty-bound to take up his father's place.

The day Tacorn came to Chiojan, Ruenen was with Yuki out back by the chicken coop. His hands were up her dress. The backdoor banged open, fowls flapped out of his way. Ruenen and Yuki leapt apart as Master stomped towards them.

"Get inside," he said. Ruenen expected to see anger on his Master's face, or disappointment, but certainly not fear. Yuki and Ruenen disentangled, then sat down at the kitchen table with the rest of the family. Master paced around, raking his sooty hands through his thinning hair.

"Will you tell us what's going on?" Mistress Chongan asked.

"Tacorn is here," Master announced. Mistress and the children didn't seem concerned, but Ruenen felt a stab of panic in his heart.

"Tacorn? What do they want in Chiojan?" the oldest Chongan son asked, three years Ruenen's junior.

"That lunatic Rayghast—always stepping into someone else's territory," Mistress Chongan said with a shake of her head.

"They're burning down houses, searching for someone they believe is being harbored here."

"Well, we're safe inside the house. We're harboring no one," said Mistress Chongan, taking hold of her children's hands. Yuki bit her lip. Master Chongan looked at Ruenen. He looked at him long and hard. The blacksmith might have guessed then it was Ruenen Tacorn was after, but he never said a word.

Master went to the forge to grab weapons. He wanted everyone inside the house to be armed. Ruenen grabbed a knife and snuck out the back. He ran. He ran as far as he could from the Chongan's house. He couldn't put them at risk. Once the soldiers left the city, he'd go back and explain everything to them. Until then, he would keep his distance.

He hid in an alleyway and listened to the screaming and shouting and smelled the smoke.

It reminded him of the monastery, but a hundred times worse.

Ruenen curled into a ball, and covered his head with his arms.

People ran through the streets as buildings burst into flames around them. The tangy scent of blood wafted through the air, thick, pungent. The city smelled of death.

Ruenen saw the Tacorn soldiers drag several boys his age past the alley entrance. Boys with brown hair who didn't look Varanese. They were rounding them all up for interrogation. A soldier spotted Ruenen in the alley and came for him. Ruenen fought for his life; the fear was palpable in his veins. Everything he'd learned in his lessons, he utilized. Somehow, he stabbed the man in the gap of his armor between neck and shoulder. A lucky strike. The soldier crumpled at Ruenen's feet. Ruenen stared at his bloody, shaking hands. It was the first life he'd ever taken. It wouldn't be the last.

This was all because of him. People were dying because of *him*. All he had to do to end the carnage was to give himself up, to step into the street and declare himself the prince. He could save the other boys they'd rounded up, thinking they were him.

Hours and hours Ruenen hid in that alley. He didn't come out. His hands didn't fall from his ears. Those boys didn't return home.

And when the soldiers departed, leaving the city stripped, burning, and raw, Ruenen staggered back to Master Chongan's house.

Everything on the street was ablaze. The house and forge. The chicken coop. Soldiers had pillaged the blades in the shop. He saw the ground, bloodied trails of drag marks in the dirt. Bodies had been taken away. Ruenen dashed through the streets, calling out their names. No one looked his way. He came to the nearby square.

Ruenen fell to his knees.

The tears poured down his face.

His heart splintered into a million tiny shards.

The Chongans' mutilated bodies hung from the city's central government hub. Yuki's clothing had been ripped from her body. Master's eyes plucked out. Ruenen couldn't bear to look.

The soldiers had known he was there. Somehow, they'd tracked him down to the forge.

Their deaths were on his hands. What had he done while they slaughtered this innocent family? Ruenen had balled himself up and hid. A cowardly child. A waste of a sacrifice.

A well had opened inside him and the sobs wouldn't stop.

Ruenen didn't know how long he lay there at their feet, begging for their forgiveness. He pleaded to the gods to take his life instead. He remembered the chants of the monks at the monastery. He intoned the words he'd long forgotten. The songs welled up inside him.

The city quieted. The flames were doused. Streets were cleaned. The bodies were buried or burned. And a seventeen-year-old boy pulled himself up from the ground and staggered from the square. Master always kept a stash of money hidden away for emergencies. Ruenen lifted the floorboards underneath the bed and pulled out the large sack of coins. Without arming himself, Ruenen left Chiojan through the broken city gates. He walked and walked until he couldn't anymore. For a while, he didn't feel anything except basic human needs like hunger, thirst, exhaustion. Ruenen wasn't aware where his feet were taking him. He numbly followed a path.

Slowly, over the months, feeling returned to his body. After a year, his heart let go of the Chongans. And Monks Amsco and Nori. He let them all go. Their deaths would amount to nothing if he didn't survive. If he didn't live.

He briefly considered going to Nevandia and declaring himself, but that thought brought forth crippling anxiety. Ruenen didn't want power. He didn't want control. He'd already proved himself a coward. Who wanted a spineless king? He didn't know how to lead. He'd just make things worse.

That was when Ruenen lifted the lute into his lap and began to play again. He became Ard the Bard. He put his past aside and began planning for his future. He'd become a traveling bard, never staying put, never endangering anyone again.

But he could always feel the heat of Tacorn breathing down his neck, a fang-toothed serpent that never slept. Rayghast still hunted him, and he would never stop. Ruenen felt resigned to leave the continent behind.

Then he came across a tavern during a Northern blizzard, and he saw a mysterious cloaked woman at the bar and he knew. Ruenen knew this was his one ticket to freedom.

About the Author

J. E. Harter is a lover of music, theatre, beaches, cats, and books (obviously). "The Butcher and the Bard" is her debut novel. She lives in NYC with two fluffy children Simon Catfunkel and Ziggy Starcat. When not authoring, she is (hopefully) inspiring young performers as a youth theatre director. Visit her website to sign up for her monthly newsletter:

https://jeharterauthor.wixsite.com/j--e--harter-author
Instagram: @j.e.harter
TikTok: @j.e.harterauthor
Facebook: J. E. Harter Fantasy Author

Printed in Great Britain
by Amazon